..to **find** his gold had sprouted hundreds of shoots

Uncle Jack's Rainbow, a Prologue

This is a prologue that is not. It should have been written before or, perhaps, when I wrote the book of five short stories "Uncle Jack's Rainbow" but somehow I got immersed in publishing and proofreading and forgot. So here is the missing prologue (or is it an appendix?) that provides some explanation to each story's origins. I suppose I should explain that the way stories are born and develop fascinates me and, therefore, I assume others will be similarly interested.

Featherfoot

Of the five stories this is the one whose origins of which I am the least certain. The wallpaper in my daughter's bedroom had something to do with it since it showed a wildflower and the fairy associated with it. Where the rest came from was while walking and two or three separate ideas got strung together as I told myself the story. I do know, however, that there is an element of early childhood experience in the story but it is not necessarily obvious. There is also a certain theme that is common to varying degrees with the other stories. What that is I will leave to the reader. The idea of silent walking is, I believe, a feature of Native American tales.

The Golden Finger

Again a lot is owed to a walk and some to distress. But the story was originally inspired by an old Polish tale with different characters and outcome. There is also a Midas element as well as an unanswered question that I intend to address in a future story.

Prologue

The Unrequited Garden

Walking again, this time on the Malverns. Just the sight of a certain hill provoked the story from the subconscious but where the narrative and characters came from I know not except that as I unfolded the story they popped out. Some of the themes, however, are fairly obvious. When I later visited the hill that inspired the story it had a wall with no doors – presumably a coincidence?

Uncle Jack's Rainbow

Running around allotments in Birmingham in my early childhood provided all the mental scenery for this story but where the story itself came from and the characters is a mystery. Again the tale told itself.

The Picture

A friend of mine told me a Japanese story, concerning a picture that had a certain form. Two or three months later out popped this story when a notice on a certain well-to-do house in Sutton sparked a rebellious narrative. I will have to drop off a copy to the owner of the midwife property.

Chris is an accomplished storyteller and has been telling stories professionally for over twenty years.
He started at junior school, becoming an instant success with pupils and teachers!
His Birmingham background brings colour and life to his tales which originate from all over the globe.

Uncle Jacks Rainbow

and other short stories

BY CHRIS LOWE

Featherfoot and the Fairies

Featherfoot and the Fairies

There were three remarkable things about Featherfoot or Thomas Reeves, for that was his name when this story begins. Other than these three facts, which I will come to presently, Thomas was a very ordinary, less than bright boy whose looks were verging on the ungainly.

The first remarkable thing was that Thomas was born on New Year's Day over a century ago. In the village he grew up in he lived a pleasant enough childhood though he was occasionally teased for his lack of wit and his less than beautiful features. At school he was on the slow side and physically he was solidly average so on sports days he was usually among the "also rans". The second remarkable thing was that Thomas, from the day he could put two thoughts together, knew when he was going to die. Not just the year, not just the month, but the actual day. He carried this knowledge without wearying.

As he grew to be a young man his contemporaries began to talk of how they would earn their living. Some, who could write well, planned to become clerks and book-keepers, even schoolteachers. Some, mainly the girls, planned to go into service. The strapping lads looked forward to jobs on the local farms. Thomas possessed no great reading and writing skills; he would not grace a large house's staff with his physical appearance; and he was on the weedy side when it came to stature. As the day to leave school approached he became more and more concerned. He possessed only one skill and this was the third remarkable thing about him.

He could walk COMPLETELY silently
  and I mean COMPLETELY.

Nothing could be heard when Thomas chose to walk in this fashion.
He could walk on gravel and not make a sound.
He could walk on dried leaves and they would not crackle. It was even said that Thomas could walk on fresh snow and leave no footprint! For this reason by the time he was ten Thomas had become known as Featherfoot and was called so by all who knew him. Indeed most people in the village had difficulty remembering his "real name".

But what use is walking silently when you need to earn your living? And he certainly would need to do this for his parents were not well off. Featherfoot thought and thought and worried over what he might do. He envisaged himself at the Mop Fair standing alone after everyone else had been hired. To help him to think he did what he always did ….. he walked and he walked. The more serious his thoughts became, the more silently he walked.

The last day of school was less than a week away when Featherfoot walked deeper into the woods than he had ever done before.
Featherfoot saw more than you or me as he walked, even when he was distracted in deep thought. His coming was not announced by the pad or thud of footprints even if he chose to run. Animals and birds of all kinds were taken by surprise when he appeared suddenly like a whisper from among the bushes or round a bend in the path.
And so it was that on this day Featherfoot caught his first fairy.
Less than ten inches high, she was standing by the side of the path among St John's Wort, or Hypericum as fancy folk call it. You and I have seen the same but we did not know it.

We have **all seen fairies**
and did not **know it.**

Featherfoot and the Fairies

..Featherfoot began to earn a good living

For when fairies hear you or me coming they appear to turn into flowers and we pass them by as one more bluebell, dog rose or buttercup.   But a fairy who does not hear someone coming is not able to disguise themselves in such "clothing".
So it was with Featherfoot and his fairy on this day. She was unable to escape then and forever.   For once a fairy has been seen by a person they can never evade them again whether they hear them or no.
This truth was imparted by the frightened fairy to Featherfoot though she had little cause to be scared of Featherfoot other than that he was a human and, therefore, a danger whether he meant to be or not.

Featherfoot thought hard about his encounter and what he had learnt. Soon he began leading others into the wood. He would ask them to stay still while he walked on – then, when he came upon one of the little folk, he would call to his patron (for so they were) to come quickly and see their first fairy. In this way Featherfoot began to earn a good living. Many fairies became "captive" to people who, once they had seen them, could re-visit the woods anytime they wished and, provided they were prepared to walk long enough discover their very own member of the small folk.

But fairies are the breath of nature and tender as meadow flowers. They, like meadow flowers, cannot stand to be walked on, or in their case seen, for if they are then they will eventually fade and die.
Thus Featherfoot endangered all in the realm of Fairie. By the end of the year Featherfoot was not short of shillings and come the following spring he was anxious to get out into the woods again and earn lots more money.

Featherfoot and the Fairies

So it was on a fine spring day that he discovered a fairy ring. The fairies danced lightly like zephyrs, laughing as they flittered around and Featherfoot, in his eagerness, stepped into the ring. Something you or I should refrain from doing unless you wish to sleep for a hundred years. For that is what happens to those who venture into a ring of dancing small folk and so Featherfoot immediately fell fast asleep.

When he awoke, however, it was only a few hours later. He found he was in a large cave with tree roots forming a vaulted roof and the sides of a great hall or cave. At the end of the cave on a throne of silver and glistening flowers was the fairy king.

His face was not that of an **angel** or that of a **devil.**

It was something between fearful and commanding. He beckoned to Featherfoot to follow and led him into a small antechamber at the rear of the throne. No one knows what the king said but Featherfoot took no one else into the woods and from that day onwards Featherfoot lived in a small cottage in the middle of the wood. And he wanted for nothing.

Each day he would walk in the wood learning more about the wood and its inhabitants, be they fairies, animals, birds or bees. He became famous for his knowledge of nature and of all living creatures and plants. Though still "uneducated" he was visited by the great and wise alike. Professors and princes would seek him out to ask his advice or learn more about nature and the woods.

So it was until Featherfoot grew into a much respected and beloved old man. One winter's day he visited the churchyard, as was his custom from time to time, but on this occasion unlike others he went into the church and spoke to the priest. As they emerged and walked down the churchyard path, the snow crunching under the priest's feet, they shook hands and Featherfoot, supported by his staff, which was now his constant companion, walked slowly and deliberately back to his cottage. One week later on New Year's Eve Featherfoot died.

On New Year's Day the priest and six men arrived at the cottage with a bier. They went inside. A few minutes later they appeared at the door carrying the coffin of Featherfoot towards the bier. As they did so the priest stopped suddenly. He looked round. There in the snow all the way up the cottage garden path and out into the wood the path was lined with flowers on each side. There were primroses, snowdrops, daisies, daffodils, dog roses, bluebells; flowers of all kinds as far as the eye could see. They walked on with the bier. The flowers continued along the lane, down the road to the lych gate, along the churchyard path and all the way to the grave.

The next day
the flowers were **gone.**

The Golden Finger

The Golden Finger

In a land far away there lived a king. He was a wise king and a good king. He had a beautiful and loving wife. His kingdom was strong. Where necessary he had fought his enemies, defeated them and then offered them their kingdoms back. With others he had negotiated peace and trade. By such means the kingdom's borders became secure and the people prospered. So safe was his country that no invading armies ever threatened and the king was able to set his palace in the middle of the great wood. It towered out of the trees and was made of the finest oaks, elms and pines. Its sheer size dwarfed the trees round about it. The kingdom was happy and content and so would the king have been if only he had an heir. But his loving marriage was childless and he and his queen were now too old to bear children.

The king worried constantly about what would happen to the land after his death because his only successor was his nephew. He had done his best to train him in kingly matters and wise counsels but the boy remained a selfish and vain fool. His obsessions were power, status and gold. As the years past the king grew frailer. His beloved queen died and he could only confide his fears to his nephew's old nurse, who, having brought up the child, knew full well his shortcomings and foolishness.

"If the time comes, nurse, and my nephew has need of your brother, you must send for him."
"Ah yes, my poor brother! Be assured if he is needed I will send for him, your majesty," replied the nurse.

Not many months after this the king died and his nephew succeeded to the throne. He wasted no time in indulging his lust for gold...
A wooden palace, even with all its magnificent carvings and it pagoda like towers, was much too humble for him. He began **HIS GREAT WORK!**

He was **determined** to cover the palace in **gold!**

It did not matter that the palace was nearly a mile round. He had soon emptied the coffers. He began to sell the palace's many treasures including its furniture and livestock. His palace of gold would rise glimmering among the trees.

After nearly a year his work was still unfinished and he needed more money for more gold. He sat in the throne room, his advisors round about, demanding they find the means to get his precious gold.
But they could not see any way of getting more gold. Everything that could be sold had been. They were advising his majesty that the palace was a bare shell when in came a serving boy with the king's drink.
The king grasped the boy crying: "Yes! Yes!"

The boy's mother was distraught when she heard he was to be sold into slavery and other boys and girls were to follow. The nurse knew it was time. She hurried to his majesty and whispered in his ear about her brother.

"Bring him to me!" yelled the king. "Bring him to me!" Word was sent to bring the brother urgently to court.

The Golden Finger

"Give me the finger!"

Everyone was gathered in the throne room. The king's desire was almost palpable. Beads of sweat glistened on his brow. His eyes stared. He was consumed with desire. A silence fell as steps were heard coming up the stone stairway to the throne room. The door was pushed open. In walked a tall figure dressed totally in black, a huge cloak flying after him. The king began to shout, partly standing as he did so.

"Show me! **Show me!**" he screamed.

The man stopped in the centre of the room and began very slowly to pull a gloved right hand out of a deep pocket. He carefully slid the glove off and held his hand aloft. The index finger glistened gold. A gasp rippled round the room. For a second or two he stood there. The king yelled, sweated, lusted. Suddenly a mouse scampered out from underneath the crowd closely pursued by a cat. He stooped as it passed and touched it. It turned to gold. As the crowd gasped, the cat was also transformed with a mere touch. The man returned his gloved hand to his pocket. The king walked slowly forward, mouth agape, eyes staring, swaying slightly from side to side. Sweat now drenched all his kingly robes.

The following day the king accompanied the man around the castle ordering him to turn to gold what few sticks of furniture were left. When they were gold he had all the palace servants brought before the man. Moments later a line of gold statues was all that was left.
On the second day the king and the man with the golden finger were seen in the surrounding woods, the king rushing from tree to tree with the stranger. As they moved, they left a forest of gold behind them.

The Golden Finger

When darkness fell the man insisted they stop, and carefully replaced his hand back in the deep pocket.

The next morning the king was more agitated than ever.
"We must be able to go faster today. Much faster!" he cried.
The stranger looked darkly at him.
"We can, your majesty. We can."

He took the king to the top of a small hillock in a clearing. A pine tree stood at the top. He took hold of a branch with his left hand and pulled it down, his hand travelling along the branch and stripping off the needles into it. He held up the hand and a breeze began to blow. As he opened his hand the needles danced into the air. He took out his right hand and touched the flying needles. As each touched each other and then the surrounding trees the hillock became surrounded by gold. With salivating lips the king rasped:

"Faster! **Faster!**"

The king was led to the top of the tallest hill in the forest. It overlooked all the great wood. The king looked about. Tree upon tree surrounded him. He turned to the tall figure who was watching carefully and said:

"Give me the finger! I want the finger!"
"You want the finger!"
"Yes! Yes! Give me it!" screamed the king, his eyes burning with desire.

The stranger took out a silver dagger and laid his right hand, fingers extended, on a nearby tree stump. The king screamed again.

"Give me... **the finger!**"

The stranger sliced the finger off and stood there trying to staunch his bleeding hand. The king put his hand out to grab the finger.
His first finger touched it and immediately his finger turned to gold and the stranger's finger returned to flesh. Excitedly the king rushed to one of the trees on the hill and grasped a branch with his left hand. As he stripped the branch of needles the stranger reached towards the tree stump and in an instant his hand was whole again.
He turned to the king and said:

"Do you really wish to turn all the great wood to gold? This is the third day. If you do this, all the people, all the trees you have transformed will forever remain as gold."

"Yes! Yes!" he bellowed, his brain totally fevered with gold.
"Take care then, you must be sure which way the wind blows.
Check its direction"

The king stood with his left hand held high. He looked frantic in his greed.
"How do I check that?" He roared in his fever.

"I know! I know!"
he bawled
and he **wetted** his right index finger...

The Unrequited Garden

The Unrequited Garden

Some say it is Bredon Hill, which lies to the south of Worcester and south-east of Malvern; others say it is May Hill near Ross, where the inn at Glasshouse bears resemblance to that in the tale. But with those that say it is this or that hill you can be sure they never live on or near the hill they name. For my part I would caution all those who dwell on or near a pleasant hill to take care if it lies anywhere near the line of Offa's Dyke because those who know which hill it is will not reveal the secret for fear of the wizard's wrath and so the wizard's garden lies hidden to most to this very day.

In the time before present history began and before the present magic had begun there was an older deeper time and a stronger magic. The magic and its practitioners lie long buried but not dead. For the old magic lies only dormant. It is still robust. Do not stir it. In this time on a hill, which I cannot name, lived a king, a wizard king. His power was unchallenged and has never been surpassed. People for miles round about came and asked him to put right all manner of things and cause all manner of things to happen. If he saw fit, he made happen what they wished. Those that scoffed at the supplicants did not do so within earshot of the wizard or his servants. For if they did they never again had a mouth to mock but starved like the nymph or dragonfly that only lives for a day. Centuries in those times passed like days do now and the wizard ruled for years - commanding and ordering his part of the then young earth. But all times and magic fade and the wizard knew his time must pass and his powers must sleep. He was weary of pleading and of being asked for this or that or indeed everything and anything. No man or woman had ever asked him what he had wanted. They knew his power was without limit so what could he want? On the eventide of his age the wizard sat in the garden of his palace looking out over the purple blue fields and forests that glimmered in summer night's fading heat. As he gazed he placed a curse on his beautiful garden and with little more than a flick of his staff raised his palace to a pile of rocks. He buried his treasure in the centre of the garden and left the garden, taking only his staff and his cloak. Where or how he went no one knew and his age faded. All in his garden perished except for the high wall that surrounded it. The wall had no door - wizards do not need doors.

The innkeeper served **yet another tankard,**

"They could drink," he thought but he preferred not to think where they might have got their money from. His two customers were the roughest and meanest he had seen in many a moon. Their clothing was dirty, their voices cracked and their skin pockmarked. Why young Jack wanted to listen to their tales was a mystery to Garth. For some reason the youth was much impressed with their so-called adventures but then youths are sometimes easily impressed by the most unlikely characters. Seth's excited and bumbling explanation of where he had just been, therefore, was an annoyance to the revellers and their audience of one, an annoyance that is until Seth mentioned "garden" and "looking over its wall". The roguish strangers and even Garth paused and listened as close as they could to the young shepherd's ramblings. Seth being "simple" was capable of little except goodwill to all he met. Young Jack had understood more than most of the company in the inn that day and so our two verbose and well drunk travellers asked him to go with them and Seth. That way Seth might better show them his find of a walled garden.

The Unrequited Garden

..taking only his staff and his cloak

Seth almost ran up the hill and into the middle of the trees and the thickets at its centre. As the thicket became almost impenetrable, Seth grew more agitated, almost shouting that the wall was just through these last few thorn bushes. A wiser man would not have pushed so hard into such cruel spikes but Seth, protected to some degree by his buckskin shirt and trousers, barged straight in, breaking twigs and even branches off as he went. The two travellers went after him telling Jack to wait while they saw if it was "safe".

Jack waited for nearly an hour worrying about Seth and the strangers. One returned briefly and with greed glinting in eyes asked Jack to get a cart. When he returned as directed, no one came. Cries were heard that sounded like Seth, and Jack pushed hard and frantically through the bushes. From here on in young Jack's report of events is mixed up to say the least. It seems he found Seth's young body, blood matting his hair but of the strangers Jack would only yell,

"Wizened dust, Wizened dust!"

What possessed Jack to bury Seth's broken body in that place no one knows, but it caused him to stay a while in the walled and dead garden.

When Young Jack returned, his hair was white and he complained of how dark the inn was to Garth as he wept hysterically. Garth managed to retrace the party's steps and recovered the handcart. He even found and looked over the wall but something or someone prevented his entry and not only would he not go back up the hill and point out the thicket, he would not talk of the garden to any except

The Unrequited Garden

his daughter Lucy, and then only to forbid her to venture up the hill. Many strangers and adventurers followed asking about the garden and listening to Young Jack's incoherent ramblings as if they were the wisdom of the ages. But when they asked Garth what he knew, his eyes turned to steel. He looked through them and asked if they wanted more ale or if they had drunk enough because he wished to close the inn for that day. If they persisted, he pointed to the blind and white-haired figure in the corner settle and asked them to guess Young Jack's age. They looked at the old man to whose ramblings they had been listening; observed his creased face, the sunken unseeing eyes and the grizzled hands and just as they were about to venture a guess the innkeeper would say he was not yet twenty one and he was but sixteen when he first returned from the garden.

Most fell silent and left.

Of those that persisted and went up the hill and into its thickets the majority left frustrated after a few days. Some were never seen again though their horses or ponies returned to the inn.

As the years passed, Young Jack's ramblings carried less currency. Those that showed interest initially began to scoff at the "old " fool when he could not answer their questions sensibly and Garth's relation of his true age only brought derisive laughter. Only Lucy listened to Jack with any concern and when her father was not listening promised him she would one day bury the remains of his two other companions of all those years ago. Though how she was to keep her promise was not clear even to her. Her promises calmed Jack down, as the thought of their remains lying untended in that terrible place seemed to perturb him more and more.

Garth found it easier to let the priest assume he had buried an old man than explain that Jack had not reached thirty when he was found dead on the hillside, a shovel gripped tightly in one hand and a bunch of crushed flowers in the other. There was only Lucy to weep at the grave, for only Garth and his daughter attended the brief funeral. A few weeks later, Garth was weeping with anger and fear as he discovered that not only was his daughter missing but so was the shovel from the inn stable. Tears streamed down his face and sickness filled his stomach as he spurred his horse up the hill. A blind panic had taken hold as he galloped along the forest track and sheer amazement mixed with relief followed as his daughter came whistling and singing down the path cuddling a huge garland of forest flowers and berries in her arms. As he knelt looking up at his daughter, tears of relief washed his cheeks and the girl of not yet twelve explained that she had been to "her" garden again to put some flowers on the graves.

Had she not been afraid to enter that place? her father asked, but the young girl explained she had only been afraid of what he might say. She was truly sorry to have upset her father but she had made Jack a promise and when he had been found on the hillside near a thicket she had some clue of where the garden lay. When she had entered the day after the funeral it looked as if it had been blasted by some violent wind, old trees and bushes were ripped apart and dust lay everywhere. Everything was so cracked and shrivelled in the garden it looked like the very life had been sucked out of anything that had once lived and as if no rain had touched the earth for centuries. Yes, she had been frightened but she kept seeing Jack's dulled but tear-filled eyes. She had almost run away from the garden when she kicked what she thought was a round stone nearly buried among some old wizened twigs.

The Unrequited Garden

She saw that it had eye sockets and there were remains of teeth and a jawbone nearby.

But she remembered her promise to Jack and kept it, burying the remains and those of its companion she found nearby. She even planted the seeds she had brought on each of the shallow graves. As soon as she had done so, rain had begun to fall and she realized that the birds she heard singing had broken the silence of the garden. A silence she had not recognised until it had disappeared. From then on she had returned each day to the garden taking new seeds and plants each time, determined to give something to that dusty earth. She took her father's hand and led him up the hill. When he saw the garden for a second time there was no foreboding, for it was not the same garden. This one was full of colour, full of life and full of thankfulness. Gifts had been brought and nourishment given.

Lucy tended the garden every day after this and shortly after a house was built amidst the thickets. Garth's daughter and grandchildren prospered in that house, which stands to this day. It is said that when the house changes hands each new owner is cautioned by the old one to look after the garden and plant something new from time to time. So if you own a house on a hill in Worcestershire, Herefordshire, Shropshire or the like be sure you follow any such instructions.

Uncle Jacks Rainbow

Uncle Jacks Rainbow

Thinking about it I suppose it was the war that put such people together but when I was there I never thought about it. Only now has it occurred to me. Oh, and which war? Showing my age again - the Second World War. It defined everything in our lives at the time. "Dig for victory" and ration books applied to all. So rich, not so well off and poor, we could all be found on the local allotments, especially at the weekends, with whole families beavering away at small plots of land hoping to fill them and their own bellies with vegetables and fruit.

Thus it was that the Broughs (or scruffs as some called them) and the Knight-Camptons (K.C's) were cheek by jowl on adjacent plots. Horticultural neighbours who would never by choice cross each other's paths in their working or home lives. Abigail Knight-Campton or AbiKC as she was widely called spent her days languidly avoiding as much toil as possible. She would also bunk off to the sparse areas of undergrowth near the railway line or she could be found supervising, or rather criticising, Billy Brough. An easy thing to do, as young Billy had been taught to be deferential to his "betters" and he did not possess the wit for a smart retort. Besides his mellow and considerate nature meant he was not disposed to aggression - verbal or otherwise. AbiKC was in her element. She had a natural victim to prey upon and lauded her superiority over the wretched boy - practice for life really. Her siblings, Hubert and Fiona, were also able to join in the sport, laughing and poking fun at Billy's dull wit and his clumsy ways when they played games together.

Only when he was helping Uncle Jack with his plants did Billy come to life. Even then they laughed at what appeared to be intense concentration, so intense he actually breathed heavier! Billy was, in fact, enthralled. Once he was planting, weeding, hoeing or watering Uncle Jack's fruit or veg his fascination drew him into a world of his own. Uncle Jack's title was purely honorary. As far as his fellow plot-holders knew he had no family and he did not seem to possess a past, but over the years he "fostered" a succession of junior gardeners by a mixture of gentle tuition and engaging stories. Billy listened to these with almost as much attention as he gave to the plants. For this he paid too. AbiKC, Hubert and Fiona guffawed as he related tales of magic and myth as if they were true.

 "All stories are true," protested Billy, "Uncle Jack said.Providing the teller is sincere and bears no malice. Stories are like seeds - some spring up immediately and you can eat their fruit; others take time to grow and you have to wait for the harvest."

"And you believe that ignorant, smelly, ugly old man," AbiKC sneered. Billy nodded shyly and as he looked down at his scuffed "Daily Mail" boots he thought of Uncle Jack's stocky squat frame, his rough stumbled chin and his horny calloused hands and thought, "He isn't ugly or smelly. Well, only of Digger Flake. He's just comfortable and, and wise ..yea ..wise."

It was Midsummer's Eve when Uncle Jack told THE story of the rainbow. He had often told stories about rainbows and always pointed them out to Billy with his own childlike delight at their spangled colours that seem to glisten in every raindrop that lay on the leaves, the flowers and the felt roof of the shed. Billy had the widest smile when AbiKC and followers asked him,

Uncle Jacks Rainbow

..and wandered off towards Railway Hollow

"What's the stupid old man been saying now?"

"He's told me about the pot of gold at the end of the rainbow and I'm going to look for it! See over there!" Billy pointed excitedly towards a rainbow that had appeared almost as he spoke. It seemed to disappear into Railway Hollow, a bush-filled dip near the railway line. AbiKC and company seemed to have saved up their cruellest sneering laughter for this occasion.

"You stupid ignorant boy," pontificated AbiKC. "Haven't they taught you about light refraction and spectrums at school?"

"No," said Billy, who did not understand a word of what she said, and wandered off towards Railway Hollow. Damning laughter followed him but Billy was oblivious.
Hours later he struggled out of the hollow and back up the hill still clutching the long- handled spade Uncle Jack had lent him.

"Well, did you find the pot of gold?"
"Yes, Abi," replied a weary Billy.
"Come on! Where is it then?"
"The little man told me to bury it and showed me where."
"You're lying, you nincompoop!"
"No, I'm not, he said I would be better off I did so – honestly."
"Well, if you really have re-buried a pot of gold, you must be the thickest stupidest person ever!"

"I did. It was full of tiny little pieces of gold and..." But Billy's explanation was drowned out completely by the laughter and hooting

Uncle Jacks Rainbow

of AbiKC's clack. Billy's bestial nature was now confirmed. What could such people ever hope to achieve?

"Factory fodder, **factory fodder**,"

yelled AbiKC, repeating what her father said from time to time when he encountered what he considered to be an ignoramus.

Not long after, the KC children went back to boarding school and Billy was forgotten completely as they mixed and met with more and more people who mattered.
For some reason which AbiKC could not understand, however, Mr & Mrs Knight-Campton kept on the allotment even when ration books were consigned to the backs of cupboards. The reason was simple. What had started as a bit of bore but a necessity had become a love. They now produced some of the best vegetables in the city leisure department's "pleasure gardens" and Mrs KC's preserves were eagerly sort after at produce shows. So it was that on a sunny afternoon in September the now grown-up KC children were all assembled in the allotment pavilion waiting assuredly but bored to see their now aging parents pick up several first prizes. The show had picked up considerable renown over the years and this year a celebrity was to present the prizes. Who? The KC children did not care. He or she was bound to be some jumped-up local councillor type who could hardly string together a grammatical construction.

AbiKC's interest picked up rapidly, however, when a powder blue Bentley Continental glided in through the iron gates of the allotment site. A large-frame man was driving, smiling and waving all at the same time. AbiKC, Hubert and Fiona squinted at him, looked at each other and gasped:

BILLY!

For the next half hour Billy had their complete attention and without a single sneer he told them of how he had gone back on Midsummer's Day to find his gold had sprouted hundreds of shoots. How he had later tended and harvested all kinds of flowers, grains and vegetables. Then founded his own seed company and prospered almost without effort as his seeds produced up to ten-fold more than his competitors without the use of artificial fertilisers and herbicides. How rich was he? AbiKC had rudely but excitedly asked. In truth Billy was not quite sure - not through stupidity but he had lost interest in the exact figures. He was doing what he loved, growing plants and tending the land. He was still breathing heavier as he judged the prize produce in the show - still fascinated.

The time came to present the prizes and Billy beamed especially widely when he presented Uncle Jack with the prize for the best sweet peas and a few other winning entries. After the presentation Billy hurried off to Uncle Jack's plot and they sat on the brick and plank bench in front of the shed while Billy told Uncle Jack about the pot of gold and his good fortune. They talked till dusk when Billy stood up shook Uncle Jack's hand and hugged him before saying good bye and leaving Uncle Jack to his tidying up as he called it. waving and smiling as he did so. He then turned, carried his tools into his shed, mooched about a bit inside and emerged with an old sack. As the sun set Uncle Jack walked into Railway Hollow swinging another pot in the sack, his spade over his shoulder.

Uncle Jacks Rainbow

The Picture

The Picture

"One Trip Thomas" was the name given to him by townspeople. It started as a bad joke, turned slowly into a bitter comment and ended as a curse. He started his shipping business from an impressive house by the quay. A young man envied by his peers. He had speculated in the capital's financial markets and won a small fortune; bought Quayside House and an aging clipper. Risking everything, he had sent her out on a six month voyage and she had brought him back a bigger fortune. But admiration turned to fear and then hate as townsfolk lost husbands and sons on what seemed liked successive voyages. He had the knack of making voyages pay both outward and homeward bound. But the homeward's profit came too regularly from the insurance company's coffers. Somehow, no one knew how, he always had insurance to cover his losses, while wives and children in the town and thereabouts could only cover their loss with tears. Soon no one local would sign aboard his ships.

But he amassed a great fortune and the symbols of wealth as rapaciously as the sea devours a sandbank. His houses became bigger and grander as he moved up the hill that overlooked the small port. The gables of his final edifice broke the smooth silhouette of the hilltop and his kingdom sat astride the town. He greedily acquired every bauble of wealth and status. Nothing evaded his grasp as his power and reputation spread. Nothing that is except Her. She was also feared by the townsfolk. People would call her "a weird one" and cross the street rather than say "Good day ". Her scrutiny was feared: large piercing blue eyes shot a glance of icicle steel. "Don't cross her" was the advice shopkeepers gave to customers as if they had learned the hard way that honest trading was essential to welfare when dealing with "The Picture Woman" as she came to be known.

No one knew her real name and no one cared to ask. She painted her pictures, uninterrupted, on the quay, the beach or the hill. Only children would dare get close enough to watch the outlines form.

"She uses the sand in her pictures when on the beach and mixes her paints with a touch of seawater. The juices of berry or grass are somehow squeezed into her paintings of the hills."

This was news the children brought back. "She's Fey stay away," was all their parents would say. But her painting drew the little ones and they watched in silence. Very little was known about her. She seemed to have come to the town many years ago. No husband, living that is, but there was a son separated from her by an argument. No one knew more, though some said he had sailed for Australia or Tasmania after the rift. One Trip Thomas had pursued her for years and with growing urgency as her pictures became ever more fashionable in genteel circles of London, BUT she would not sell to him. The last item of his desire evaded him.

When the slump came and the markets collapsed, Thomas was sure he would acquire a picture but tantalizingly no one would sell.
Their owners clung on to the pictures and "She" would not even parley with him or any agent he sent to bargain. But the townsfolk, hit by financial adversity, did again seek work aboard his latest vessel, bound for the Cape of Good Hope and beyond, so it was said. In desperation and fear menfolk signed up despite their misgivings. Their wives either begged them not to venture or remained sullenly silent when told the news. Nearly a score signed and hoped for fair seas.
The clipper reached Cape Town, where New South Wales was added to

The Picture

"She's going to sell" and the crowd swayed angrily towards her

her destinations. News came months later that she had reached there and loaded a fine cargo for the return trip. There was some toasting in the inns that night but as the weeks passed brooding eyes looked more often into empty glasses and brooding wives looked more intensely at empty chairs. When the news came that the Lloyd's Bell had tolled and the ship's name had been posted, the curse was uttered: "One Trip Thomas, No Return Trip!"

When new gold and black wrought iron gates went up at the start of the drive to Thomas' mansion, the drinking and talking in the inns turned to mutters, whispers and then shouts. The mob moved up the hill, flaming torches in hand and mouths that snarled a vengeance. They reached the gates, broke the locks and circled the house. Lights flickered inside as they shouted, "One Trip! One Rope! One Trip Thomas! One Rope Thomas!"

The Picture Woman sat at her kitchen table and pored over the Exeter broadsheet. A facsimile of One Trip's Australian Vessel was at the top of the page and a list of names hung underneath. She took a quill, dipped it into ink and circled the
twenty-fourth name in the list. Folding the paper, she tied a black ribbon around it and placed it and a picture from the hearth into the dresser drawer.

The cries were getting harsher and quicker. A stone smashed the stained glass window in the main gable. The house waited for the flame of a torch but silence fell instead. All heads were turned. A figure was coming up the hill, a spark of light in its left hand. As The Picture Woman reached the edge of mob, it parted as a silent message went by

The Picture

"There was no storm last night, just an angry mob and a broken window"

look to look. Eyes fixed on the canvas-wrapped parcel held under her right arm. "She's going to sell" and the crowd swayed angrily toward her. "She's giving in to One Trip." But as cudgels started to move upwards she stopped and looked the nearest "would-be attacker" in the face. With those eyes sweeping passed, his and the others' courage failed. She walked on. Pulled the bell handle and waited. A hundred eyes and silence waited with her. When the door opened, she was ushered into the house. Fifteen minutes later she stepped out empty-handed and the crowd moaned and rushed towards her. She threw the lamp on the floor and a line of flame sprang up between her and them. They stopped and as they stared silently into her eyes, she walked through the dying flames and the parting crowd. At the far edge of the crowd she stopped and turned to one of the women, thrusting a jangling bag into her hands before disappearing into the darkness.

As soon as day broke Mr Thomas' butler arose. His wife, the cook, said he should see what damage the storm had caused as well as the mob. "What storm, wife? There was no storm last night, just an angry mob and a broken window." His wife protested he must he deaf - she had been kept up most of the night listening to the wind and sea.
The butler shrugged, put his master's breakfast tray together and ascended the stairs. As he mounted the last few stairs to the first landing he saw the new picture of his master's unfortunate vessel in pride of place. But as he turned to cross the landing One Trip's body lay opposite.

The body being found sodden with water, a post mortem was hurriedly carried out and drowning was listed as the cause of death:

drowning
in salt **water.**

T⬛
A⬛

Fifth Edition

Penina Coopersmith
Photography by Vincenzo Pietropaolo

FORMAC PUBLISHING COMPANY LIMITED

Contents

Maps — 4
Overview Map — 4
Neighbourhoods Map — 6
Hotels Map — 8
Restaurants Map — 9

About This Guide — 10
Contributors — 11
Exploring Toronto — 12
A Brief History — 15

Toronto's Top Attractions — 19
Toronto's Best — 20
Museums and Galleries — 41
Independent Galleries — 57
Theatre and Dance — 60
Symphony, Chamber Music and Opera — 66
Glenn Gould — 72
Nightlife — 74
Dining — 80
Shopping — 87
Sports — 94

Copyright © 2006 by Formac Publishing Company Limited.

All rights reserved. No part of this book may be reproduced or transmitted in any form or by any means, electronic or mechanical, including photocopying, or by any information storage or retrieval system, without permission in writing from the publisher.

Formac Publishing Company Limited recognizes the support of the Province of Nova Scotia through the Department of Tourism, Culture and Heritage. We acknowledge the financial support of the Government of Canada through the Book Publishing Industry Development Program (BPIDP) for our publishing activities.

For Cataloguing in Publication Data and photo credits, please see page **232**.

CONTENTS

Toronto Parks and Recreation Trails	99
Annual Events	109
Day Trips	115
Gay Toronto	125

NEIGHBOURHOODS AND DISTRICTS 131

St. Lawrence Neighbourhood	132
Financial and Theatre District	140
Queen Street West	150
Chinatown and Kensington Market	158
Queen's Park and the University of Toronto	164
Yorkville and Bloor Street	170
Yonge Street	176
Cabbagetown	182
Little Italy and Greektown on the Danforth	187

LISTINGS 193
INDEX 223

Formac Publishing Company Limited
5502 Atlantic Street
Halifax, Nova Scotia, B3H 1G4
www.formac.ca

Distributed in the United States by:
Casemate
2114 Darby Road, 2nd Floor
Havertown, PA, USA, 19083

Distributed in the United Kingdom by:
Portfolio Books Limited
Unit 5, Perivale Industrial Park
Horseden Lane South
Greenford, UK
UB6 7RL

Printed and bound in China

▲ OVERVIEW MAP

Overview Map

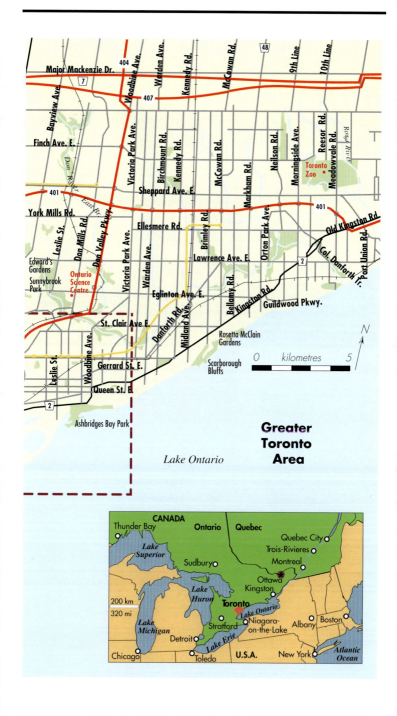

▲ Neighbourhoods Map

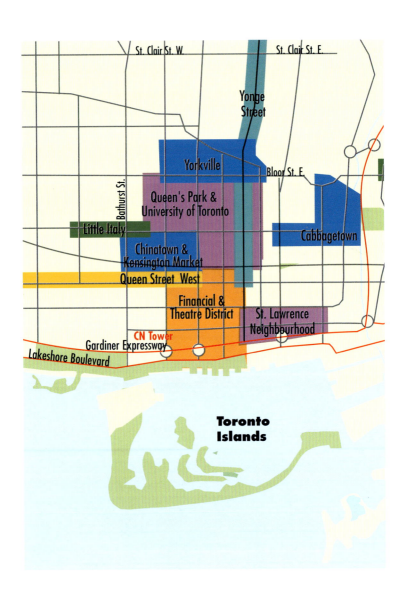

Neighbourhoods Map

▲ Central Toronto Hotels Map

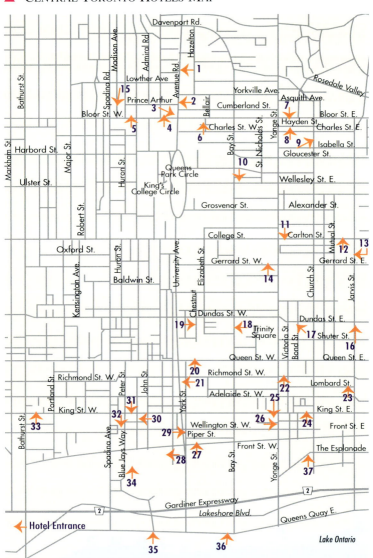

1. Howard Johnson Inn Yorkville
2. Four Seasons Hotel
3. Park Hyatt Hotel
4. Hotel Inter-Continental
5. Holiday Inn Toronto Midtown
6. Windsor Arms
7. Toronto Marriott Bloor Yorkville
8. Comfort Hotel Downtown
9. Town Inn
10. Sutton Place
11. Days Inn
12. Best Western Primrose Hotel
13. Ramada Hotel & Suites Downtn.
14. Delta Chelsea Inn
15. Madison Manor
16. Grand Hotel & Suites
17. Bond Place
18. Marriott Eaton Centre
19. Metropolitan Hotel
20. Sheraton Centre
21. Hilton Toronto
22. Cambridge Suites
23. Holiday Inn Express Downtown
24. Le Royal Meridien King Edward Hotel
25. The Suites
26. Hotel Victoria
27. Royal York Hotel
28. Intercontinental Toronto Centre
29. Strathcona Hotel
30. Hotel Le Germain
31. Holiday Inn on King
32. SoHo Metropolitan
33. Travelodge Toronto
34. Renaissance Toronto Hotel at Roger's Centre
35. Radisson Plaza Hotel Admiral
36. Westin Harbour Castle
37. Novotel Toronto Centre

CENTRAL TORONTO RESTAURANTS MAP

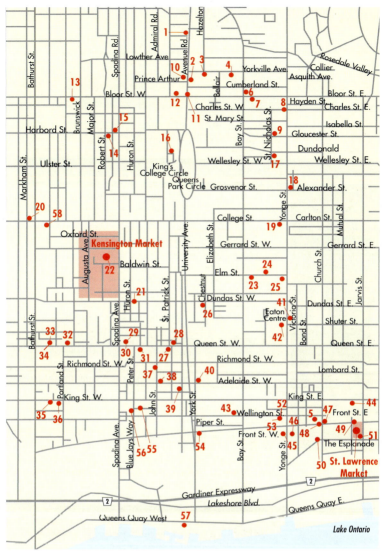

Restaurants with very similar locations are shown with a single dot and locator number.

1. Trattoria Sotto Sotto
2. Studio
2. Truffles at the Four Seasons in Yorkville
2. Avenue Lounge
3. Bellini
4. Zerosun
5. Sultan's Tent
6. Pangaea
7. Scaccia
8. Green Mango
9. Le Matignon
10. The Host
11. Roof Restaurant
11. Prego Della Piazza
12. Signatures
13. New Generation Sushi
14. Messis
15. Splendido
16. Gallery Grill
17. Segovia
18. Carman's
19. Fran's Restaurant
19. Gamelle
20. Pony
21. Asian Legend
22. Jumbo Empanadas
22. Perola's Supermarket
22. Supermarket
23. Oro
24. Bangkok Garden
25. Barberian's
26. Hemispheres at the Metropolitan Hotel
26. Lai Wah Heen at the Metropolitan Hotel
27. Tiger Lily's
28. Queen Mother Café
29. Le Select Bistro
30. Rivoli
31. Peter Pan
32. Tequila Bookworm
33. Shanghai Cowgirl
34. Gandhi Cuisine
35. Thuet Cuisine
36. Susur
37. Luce
38. Avalon
39. Monsoon
40. The Keg Steakhouse
41. Superior
42. Baton Rouge
43. Canoe
44. Biagio
45. Acqua
46. Biff's
47. Jamie Kennedy Wine Bar
48. Le Papillon
49. Mustachio's
50. Esplanade Bier Markt
51. Churrasco of St. Lawrence
52. Jump
53. Richtree Market Restaurant
53. Masquerade Caffe and Bar
54. Epic at Royal York
55. Rain
56. Wayne Gretzky's
57. Pearl Harbourfront Chinese Cuisine
58. Aunties and Uncles

▲ About This Guide

Welcome to this guide to Toronto!

The *Toronto Colourguide* will help you get the most out of your stay in Toronto. The introductory chapters, Exploring Toronto and A Brief History, provide an overview of the city.

The maps in the introductory section give you a general view of the city, and offer a guide to the organization of this book. The Overview Map shows routes into the city and main highways and streets. Its legend applies to all the maps in the book, so it is worth taking the time to orient yourself with its help.

The book is divided into three main sections. The first, Toronto's Top Attractions, contains articles that will guide you to the famous as well as the less-familiar sites and attractions in the city.

The second section, Neighbourhoods and Districts, contains nine chapters that provide walking tours of the city's most interesting communities.

Finally, section three contains select listings, with practical information on everything you'll want to do or find in Toronto: accommodations, dining, nightlife, attractions, festivals and events, theatres, shopping, galleries, sports and outdoor recreation — as well as information on special travel services and tips. Information on attractions and sites described in the first or second sections is also included in the listings.

This book is an independent guide. Its contributors have made their recommendations and suggestions based solely on what they believe to be the best, most interesting and most appealing sites and attractions. No payments of any kind are solicited or accepted by the creators or the publishers of the guide.

In a city as lively as Toronto, things change quickly. The safest thing to do about information you're relying on in this book is to confirm it with a brief phone call.

If your experience doesn't match what you read here — or if you think we've missed one of Toronto's best features — please let us know. Write us at the address on the contents page (page 3).

Several chapters have been contributed by authors who are local experts in their fields:

DENISE BALKISOON (Nightlife) is Toronto born and bred. Currently a freelancer, she has worked with publications including *Toronto Life*, *Shift*, *Azure* and *Report on Business*.

CHRISTINE BEEVIS (Parks and Trails) has been hiking, running and skiing through Toronto's many parks and rec trails for the last 30 years (and has paddled the Don River twice). Her writing has been published in magazines such as *ON Nature*, *Pathways* and *UnderCurrents*.

CHRISTINE BOOCOCK (Dining) is a Toronto-based writer and editor. She has written for *Restaurant, the British Dining Magazine*, and currently contributes restaurant reviews to *Toronto Life*, among others.

ALEX BOZIKOVIC (Distillery District) is an editor at the *Globe and Mail*. He lives in Toronto and writes about the city, architecture and the arts for local and national magazines.

CONTRIBUTORS

DEREK CHEZZI (Sports) is the Online Editor at *Maclean's* magazine. He has written for a variety of newspapers and magazines including the *Globe and Mail*, *Toronto Life* and *Eye Weekly*.

PENINA COOPERSMITH is a longtime Toronto resident who works as a writer, lecturer, broadcaster and editor.

SKY GILBERT (Gay Toronto), writer, director, and drag queen extraordinaire, is one of Canada's most controversial artistic forces. Mr. Gilbert is also an award-winning playwright whose work has been performed in many major cities including New York, London and Toronto, where he is also the founder of Buddies in Bad Times Theatre. He is currently turning his protean energies to writing novels and teaching.

JOYCE GUNHOUSE and JUDY CORNISH (Shopping) met at Ryerson Polytechnic University, where both were studying Fashion Design. With a sense of humour and style, they have been creating their collection, Comrags, since 1983. Many awards, international distribution and a flagship store have made Comrags one of Canada's best-known designer labels.

CHRISTOPHER HUME (Art) has been the art and architecture critic at the *Toronto Star* since the early 1980s. He has written for major publications in Canada and the U.S. and appears regularly on radio and television. He lives in Toronto.

ADRIAN HO (researcher) quit the financial world in a fit of self-loathing, never wanting to hear an alarm clock again. He sleeps and writes in Toronto.

JON KAPLAN (Symphony, Chamber Music and Opera) has been senior theatre editor at *NOW* magazine for 25 years, reviewing stage productions, opera and classical CDs. He has been theatre editor at CJRT-FM and is the Toronto correspondent for the London-based *Plays International* and the New York-based *Back Stage*.

VINCENZO PIETROPAOLO has been photographing Toronto for over 25 years. His photojournalism and landscape, portrait and architecture photography has been widely published.

VIT WAGNER (Theatre and Dance) writes about culture for the *Toronto Star*. During his more than a dozen years at the paper, he has covered the theatre scene in Toronto, from the big commercial musicals to the smaller avant-garde productions. He has also reported on the Stratford and Shaw festivals.

NANCY WON is a freelance writer and editor based in Toronto. She has worked with major Canadian publications including *Toronto Life*, *Azure*, *Canadian Gardening*, *Food & Drink* and the *Globe and Mail*.

BETTY ZYVATKAUSKAS (Day Trips) is a contributing editor to *Toronto Life* magazine's annual *Getaways and Day Trips* guide. She is the author of *Great Getaways: the Best Day Trips in Southern Ontario* and *Naturally Ontario: Exploring the Wealth of Ontario's Wild Places*.

— The Publishers

EXPLORING TORONTO

Toronto's past and present make it a great place to visit: a clean, safe, modern city that is easy to get around and offers lots to see and do. Detailed information about climate, travel arrangements, currency, customs, accommodation, emergency care and other vital data can be found in the listings at the back of this guide. In-depth descriptions of Toronto's top attractions and activities, and walking tours of Toronto's many pleasant downtown and midtown neighbourhoods, follow. First, though, we offer a quick introduction to finding your way around.

Before you come, you might want to contact Ontario Travel, the Ontario government's tourist hotline (1-800-668-2746), or Tourism Toronto (1-800-499-2554 from outside the city, or 416 203-2500 from within), both of which will happily send you free pamphlets and answer questions about accommodation, special events and the like.

TORONTO ISLANDS FERRY

EXPLORING TORONTO ▲

CN TOWER AT DUSK

The quickest way downtown for those arriving at Lester B. Pearson International Airport is by limousine or taxi. Only slightly less convenient are the buses that run every half-hour or so to the subway stations closest to the airport and straight downtown to the major hotels. The price of the bus is about one-third that of a taxi. If you are coming in by train, you will arrive at Union Station, right downtown and opposite the Royal York Hotel. Those arriving by car, or planning to rent one at the airport, should ask about parking when booking their accommodation.

In truth, however, most visitors will find they hardly need or want a car, except perhaps to visit the Toronto Zoo or other attractions located at the city's edges. Within town, you will quickly learn that while driving is not a problem, parking is. Fortunately, Toronto's transit system is excellent. Its buses, subways and streetcars traverse 1,412 km (877 miles) of streets and will get you just about anywhere you want to go within the city. For fares, schedule and route information, call the Toronto Transit Commission (TTC), (416) 393-4636. Of course, you can always hail a cab. But one of the joys of Toronto is that it is an easy city to walk in, which is why part of this guide has been structured around neighbourhood tours to take on foot.

DINERS AT SCARAMOUCHE

Once you're settled, but before plunging into attractions or neighbourhoods, there are a few activities that will help you get acquainted with Toronto. Several companies provide guided tours that will give you a sense of the city's scale and layout while introducing you to major attractions like City Hall, Harbourfront, the Rogers Centre and the CN Tower. Toronto Hippo Tours (416 703-4476), for instance, employs amphibious vehicles that plop into the lake after touring the downtown for an up-close view of the harbour.

In the summer, low-cost walking tours are run by groups such as Heritage Toronto. Information about these and other city-organized tours — as well as special events — can also be obtained from Access Toronto (416 338-0338). The Royal Ontario Museum's ROMwalks (416 586-8097) are also excellent.

Smaller operators offer a variety of interesting tours, usually on foot. In the past, outfits that designed custom tours usually catered only to large groups. Now, however, a growing number of companies will work with family-sized units or even individuals. Among these is Lost World Tours (416 947-0778), which promises to make you a "Torontonian for a day."

For a view of the city from its harbour, nothing beats the ferry boat rides to Toronto's islands (see p. 94), but for a guided tour, you might prefer a one-hour trip on the ships of Toronto Harbour Tours (416 203-0178).

To help you plan your days and evenings back on earth, pick up a free copy of *NOW* or *eye*, weekly newspapers published Thursdays, both of which have complete listings for theatre, music, dance, films, the club and restaurant scene and special events. *Toronto Life*, a monthly magazine, also provides listings, as well as the latest Toronto gossip.

KRISTINE BENDUL AND DAVID GOMEZ IN MIRVISH PRODUCTIONS' *MOVIN OUT*

A Brief History

Like other great cities, Toronto owes its size and character to a combination of factors including its setting, the values and aspirations of its residents and the events that have befallen it.

QUEEN'S QUAY, HARBOURFRONT CONDOS

EARLY EUROPEAN SETTLEMENT

For thousands of years before European explorers came to the area, the native trade routes between Lake Ontario, Lake Huron and Georgian Bay converged on settlements at Toronto, which is said to mean "a place of meeting." In 1615, Etienne Brûlé, a companion of explorer Samuel de Champlain, was shown the site when he came to invite the Andaste nation to join in a campaign against the Iroquois.

Later, after the Dutch had settled what is now New York, they struggled with the French for control of the fur trade and the Toronto portage became a route for war parties. The rivalry made the surrounding region a no-man's land. At last, in 1649, the Huron and their French allies won a decisive victory.

POLE ART ALONG SPADINA

Seventy-one years later, French colonists established a fort at Toronto, one of a network spread throughout the lower Great Lakes region and the Midwest. The Toronto fort was strategically located to allow the French to tap the rich fur trade between Lake Ontario and Georgian Bay and to fend off the British, who had established their own posts in upstate New York.

SOLDIERS AT FORT YORK

The first French post was abandoned in

15

▲ A Brief History

SPADINA QUAY

1730. A subsequent structure, Fort Rouillé, was destroyed in 1759 by the French themselves to prevent it from falling into the hands of the British during the Seven Years' War. Less than twenty years later, the British, having won control of the region, investigated the abandoned site and decided the region would suit an English settlement. For the grand sum of £1,700, 149 barrels of flour and such other goods as blankets and axes, they purchased approximately 400 square miles from the Mississauga people, an acquisition known as the "Toronto Purchase."

In 1793, Colonel John Simcoe, a veteran of the American Revolution and the first lieutenant-governor of Upper Canada (now Ontario), chose Toronto as his seat of operations because of the vantage point it offered for naval defence from the Americans. In addition to building a garrison, Fort York, he laid out a ten-block plan for the town, thereby establishing the north-south, east-west grid pattern the city retains today. He also changed its name from Toronto to York.

The only significant test of York's military strength came on April 27, 1813, when several hundred British, Aboriginal and Canadian soldiers resisted 1,700 Americans and the guns of two dozen warships for over five hours. The British blew up their gunpowder magazine and retreated, leaving so many American casualties behind that the embittered victors looted and burned much of the town. The British retaliated the following summer by taking and subsequently burning much of the slightly larger, and politically far more important, settlement of Washington.

By then, Simcoe was long gone from York. Little remains of what was there in his day, save some of the street names, among them Yonge Street, which Simcoe had the Queen's Rangers lay out in a straight, thirty-mile path north through the wilderness to the limits of the Toronto Purchase.

SPADINA LRT LINE

A Brief History

Resolution of the British-American conflict proved a major impetus to the town's growth. Now able to think of Upper Canada as a secure British outpost in the wilderness, English settlers began to arrive in larger numbers.

The second major impetus to the community's growth was the opening in 1824 of the Welland Canal. The canal, which linked Lake Erie and Lake Ontario, made the town an important trade centre along the Montreal-Chicago shipping axis. From a small outpost of some 600 souls in 1813, the settlement had expanded to a burgeoning metropolis of more than 10,000 when in 1834 it was returned to its original name.

Growing City

Within thirty years of its 1834 incorporation, Toronto's population had grown by 30,000. Many immigrants came as a result of the potato crop failures in Ireland, but there were also thousands of escaped American slaves. Many, but not all, of the ex-slaves returned to the United States after the Civil War. A mixture of northern Europeans, mostly Germans, Dutch and Belgians, also came to farm in the surrounding regions or to open businesses serving their compatriots in the agricultural community.

By the 1880s and 1890s the population — now approaching the 200,000 mark — was becoming ever more diverse. The first Asian immigrants came with the building of Canada's railroads. The discovery of fabulous nickel, silver and uranium deposits in northern Ontario in the first three decades of the twentieth century set the stage for Toronto's post-World War II emergence as Canada's financial capital. The minerals drew skilled miners from Poland, the Balkans, Silesia and Hungary. As well, industrialization sparked a large-scale internal migration, drawing a flood of rural youth to the big city. By 1910,

HARBOURFRONT

LIBERTY VILLAGE BUILDING

Toronto had clearly become the pre-eminent centre of industry, trade and commerce in English Canada. By that time, too, commercial activity in the city had moved north and west to the areas that are now the modern, largely high-rise core of the city, and roads and rails stretched along the harbour, giving the central city the layout and something of the look it retains to this day.

After the Second World War, Toronto and its environs took off, quadrupling in size, from just over 1 million in 1945 to over 2 million in 1971 to 4.1 million by 1995 (Greater Toronto Area). Skilled labourers, craftspeople and refugees flocked here from Italy, Greece and central Europe. Students and skilled and unskilled workers came from all over the British Commonwealth, the Caribbean and the Indian subcontinent. After various international upheavals, large blocks of new immigrants contributed something of their culture and cuisine along with their numbers: Hungarians in 1956, Czechs in 1968, Chileans, Argentinians and Vietnamese in the 1970s. The bigger it got, the more Toronto attracted new investment. Money and people poured in from Hong Kong and from Europe throughout the 1990s.

SPADINA POLE ART AT KENSINGTON MARKET

Today's Toronto has a population of 2.5 million (Amalgamated City of Toronto), making it the fourth-largest city in North America. As it struggles to reorganize itself, the long term effects of amalgamation remain to be seen. What is clear, however, is that with a population comprised of people from over 75 different cultures — the largest of which accounts for less than one-fifth of the population, and more than a dozen of which have more than 100,000 members — there is no longer a single majority culture.

Toronto's Top Attractions

TORONTO'S BEST

Toronto is replete with attractions and destinations that merit anywhere from a half-day visit (Casa Loma, Spadina House and the Ontario Science Centre) to at least three-quarters of a day (Black Creek Pioneer Village), a full day (the Toronto Zoo), and then some (Ontario Place, the Canadian National Exhibition in season, and Harbourfront).

CN Tower

The CN Tower is the city's most popular attraction. When the weather is clear, the view from the top is spectacular. To the north you can see Lake Simcoe. To the southwest, it's possible to make out the mist rising from Niagara Falls. It is an ideal way to get an overview of Toronto — even on days when it is not clear enough to see great distances. All sorts of interesting things present themselves: roofs that have gardens or jogging tracks; the weird cubes almost directly below, atop the Canadian Broadcasting Corporation (CBC) building (these cubes are actually studios); the roar of the crowd when a game is on at the Rogers Centre. But most interesting of all (unless it's winter), is to see how green Toronto is. Except for the financial district, there seem to be trees everywhere. There are the parks and the Toronto Islands, of course. There are the Don and Humber Valleys and the many ravines that carry the rivers' tributaries. And then there are the backyards and the streets, all but a few of which are lined with trees. So from atop the CN Tower, a fair portion of Toronto vanishes.

Every year, some two million visitors ride the six elevators 114 storeys (346 metres) to the seven-storey LookOut Levels that comprise the fat white donut slung two-thirds of the way up the tower. Access to these

THE CN TOWER'S SKYPOD

Toronto at night

observation decks is priced between $10.99 and $15.99. For an additional $7.50, visitors can continue thirty-three storeys higher, to the SkyPod, 447 metres above the ground. When the wind is not too strong, the "shorter" ride takes only fifty-eight seconds. When it is windy, the tower sways and a slightly slower elevator system is used. Much of the "donut" is filled with the microwave broadcasting equipment that is the $57-million tower's *raison d'être*, but there is plenty of room for visitors and lots to do. There are indoor and outdoor observation decks and a glass floor that you can walk on, if you dare. There is a futuristic laser-tag game called Q-Zar, and a variety of virtual sports at the Edge Arcade. There is also a café called Horizons and a surprisingly good revolving restaurant, 360, for which reservations are strongly recommended. Be forewarned that there is almost always a long wait at the elevators, both up and down.

ROGERS CENTRE

The home of the Toronto Blue Jays and Argonauts is right next door to the CN Tower. When the stadium opened in 1989, the hype surrounding the SkyDome, as it was then known, was deafening: "the world's first multipurpose stadium with a retractable roof," "the Jumbotron, at nine storeys, the largest video display board in the world," and so on.

But whether or not you are a sports fan, the great white clamshell remains an impressive feat of engineering. Its 11,000-ton roof spans 205 metres and reaches a height of 86 metres (31 storeys), making it a highly visible landmark. The roof consists of four panels, two of which

Rogers Centre

▲ Toronto's Top Attractions

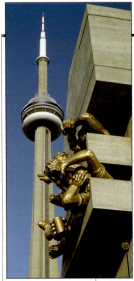

MICHAEL SNOW'S "AUDIENCE" SCULPTURE AT THE ROGERS CENTRE

slide into one another then rotate 180 degrees, with a third one to fit into the fourth. The panels move at a rate of twenty-two metres per minute, allowing the roof to close or open in a mere twenty minutes. The field itself also changes shape mechanically, allowing a change from baseball to football mode in ten hours. Up to 50,600 people can be accommodated at baseball games, 53,000 at football events, and as many as 67,000 at concerts. Tickets for Jays and Argos games may be purchased in person at the Rogers Centre, online or by phone, using the information provided at www.rogerscentre.com.

When there is no scheduled event, there are one-hour tours that provide a behind-the-scenes view that visitors to the Rogers Centre would not otherwise experience. These tours include a museum, memorabilia from past events, and the chance to walk on the artificial FieldTurf field. You may also visit one of the private suites, which cost between $1 million and $2 million for ten years of use, not including game tickets or refreshments. You also get a look at some of the more than 1,400 artifacts that were uncovered during the archaeological dig that took place prior to construction, as the site was part of the early settlement of the city.

If you are taking in a game accompanied by young children, there is an indoor playground on the first level near Section 115, should they grow restless. Another way to see a game is to stay in one of the Renaissance Hotel's seventy rooms that overlook the field. Or you can grab a burger at the Hard Rock Cafe, located beside Gate 1. During events, the rock music is turned off, and for a price you can get window seats overlooking the field. Nearby, for hardcore devotees of The Great One, is Wayne Gretzky's restaurant (99 Blue Jays Way).

HARBOURFRONT CENTRE

HARBOURFRONT

Harbourfront is an amazing four-hectare complex of theatres, galleries, shops, studios, and restaurants located next to the lake and ten minutes from downtown. Harbourfront is the place for those who like theatre, dance, music, art, film, crafts, literature, shopping, antiques, ethnic festivals, ice skating or sailing. In fact, an entire

TORONTO'S BEST

MUSIC GARDEN

vacation could easily be spent here, much of it at little or no cost. Only in the cuisine department might Harbourfront be said to fall a bit short. It's not that there aren't a lot of places to eat: eateries range from low-end, independent fast-food restaurants like Lakeside Eats and the café at York Quay Centre to the pricier Captain John's, and even the haute Chinese of the Pearl (at Queen's Quay). It's just that Harbourfront's choices in dining pale in comparison to the choices it offers in most other areas.

Harbourfront stretches along what once was Toronto's main port. The opening of the St. Lawrence Seaway and the switch from manually handled shipping crates to large, uniform, machine-manoeuvred containers began moving the port eastward starting in the 1950s. By the early 1970s, only the large grain silos remained busy. There were few port activities left here, other than the island ferries and the police and fire boats, and very little industry. In the last days before the 1972 federal election, in a bid for Toronto's affections, the governing Liberals promised to purchase the entire area and make it all into parkland.

What happened next was fortunate. Torontonians were happy about having more trees, trying to reconnect the city to the lake, and so on but, they said, why would people come here when so much of the lakeshore is already green and the islands, which are already largely parkland, are so close at hand? Why don't we add a bit of spice? Something unique. And so the programming aspect of

HARBOURFRONT

THE ORIOLE AT HARBOURFRONT

Harbourfront was born. Since the mid-1970s, Harbourfront has constantly added new events — there are more than 4,000 every year — and new sites in which to hold them.

Theatrical presentations range from new Canadian works to pieces linked to the many cultural festivals, and are held at the Harbourfront Centre Theatre or in the York Quay Centre. Dance has long been celebrated at the Premiere Dance Theatre, inside the large Queen's Quay Terminal, and now the National Ballet has a new production facility in the Carsen Centre at King's Landing.

Music is everywhere — in various spots in the York Quay Centre and at free concerts for everyone on Sundays at the Harbourfront theatre; throughout the warmer months at the outdoor Molson Place; and often just out on the lawns. It is embedded in the landscape, courtesy of Yo-Yo Ma and designer Julie Moir Messervy, whose six-part garden celebrating Bach's First Suite for Unaccompanied Cello is the site of concerts in the summer and a relaxing place for a stroll year-round. Also on the gardening front are some 24 artists' gardens, ranging from the sublime to the ridiculous, scattered throughout the area. Some are new, and others date back to 1990 when the program first began. A self-guided tour sheet can be obtained at York Quay.

TORONTO'S BEST

THE POWER PLANT

There is an art gallery in the Power Plant, a building that once provided the juice for chilling the huge terminal warehouse, itself once the world's largest refrigerator. Artisans and their wares are on display at the Craft Studio. You can buy the glass, metal, ceramic, and other works you see in production next door at Bounty. Both are also located in the York Quay Centre.

Harbourfront has also helped rekindle an interest in reading. Authors from around the world give readings here almost every Tuesday evening, but the highlight of the year is the autumn International Festival of Authors. Now in its early thirties, it attracts just about anyone who is anyone in the literary world. Other major festivals are held throughout the year, but perhaps the best known is the annual mid-May Milk International Children's Festival,

QUEEN'S QUAY TERMINAL

which, for a very nominal sum (about $9-$15 for a weekend pass), allows access to dozens of performances by musicians, dancers, acrobats, actors, storytellers, magicians and others.

The main retail centre for Harbourfront is in

▲ Toronto's Top Attractions

the Queen's Quay Terminal. Its more than 100 stores are mainly of the upscale variety and feature beautiful clothes and jewellery, fine crafts and household furnishings. Flea, craft and international markets are also held, often in conjunction with festivals, usually in Ann Tindal Park.

Harbourfront also takes advantage of its proximity to Lake Ontario, hosting marine-related events and offering sailing and boating courses and boat, canoe and skate rentals for use on Canada's largest artificial rink.

ONTARIO PLACE

Ontario Place might be described as an intellectual's theme park: an upscale thirty-nine hectare futuristic urban playground. But what, you might well ask, is its theme? Allegedly something to do with "exploiting advanced technology to shape the society of tomorrow." It matters not if this objective is not immediately evident. What makes Ontario Place unique is that it offers most of the activities available at traditional theme parks — and adds a few of its own — while eschewing much of the attendant honky-tonk and commercialism. The setting doesn't hurt, either. Built on a series of islands and pods that sit on giant stilts above the water, there are lots of trees, fine views of the city and the lake, cool breezes on even the hottest days, and enough space to enable you to step back from the crowds. As well, there is music at the Molson Amphitheatre and at other locations on site.

The roughly $25 admission price to Ontario Place includes a "Play All Day Pass," good for all attractions except for Molson Amphitheatre concerts. These include the Children's Village, the Children's Festival Stage, the

TORONTO'S BEST

CNE BUILDING

Lego Pod and the Nintendo Power Pod. The village offers some of the most imaginative playground toys ever created, while on the stage there are concerts, puppet and magic shows, storytelling and other performances throughout the day, no reservations required. The Pods are located in the weird white steel-and-glass pavilions that stand eleven metres above the water, making them good places to head to, especially if it's raining.

On nice days, there is the Soak City water park, which features water toys and slides for kids of all ages; the Wilderness Adventure Ride, which takes you through the forests and canyons of northern Ontario; water-based rides like the Hydrofuge and Rush River, each of which has three slides; pedal boats and bumper boats, and even canoes; the MegaMaze, actually seven different mazes in which to get lost; and a miniature golf course. The IMAX theatre and Omnimax Theatre are open year-round. There are about a dozen fast-food outlets (only one of which is operated by a major chain) and about a half-dozen full-service restaurants, of average price and quality, to choose from.

PRINCES' GATES

THE CANADIAN NATIONAL EXHIBITION (CNE)

The Ex, as it is commonly known, has its roots in the great agricultural and industrial fairs of the nineteenth century. Thousands flocked to inspect and enjoy the produce, livestock and other hallmarks of rural culture like fiddling, quilting and floral displays. It was here, too, that electric streetlights and streetcars were first shown off, where cinema made its Toronto debut, and where the proof of human progress was proudly displayed. Through the years, air shows, stomach-wrenching rides on the midway and cotton candy have

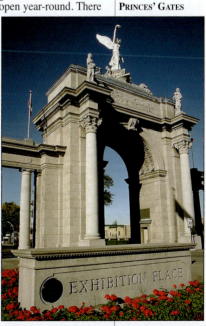

▲ Toronto's Top Attractions

perhaps overshadowed, if not quite replaced, the rural origins of the fair, to say nothing of the faith once placed in progress.

Today, there are many permanent buildings with year-round uses on the site. The grounds are home now to not only the Ex, the large annual fair, but to events like the Royal Agricultural Winter Fair, the Home Show, the Boat Show, major craft fairs and other exhibitions. Canada's Sports Hall of Fame, opened in 1955, operates year-round and is free (except during the Ex, when admission to the grounds is charged). The former Arts, Crafts and Hobbies Building is now home to Medieval Times, a dinner theatre in which the play features knights in shining armour jousting on horseback.

In the early 1990s, local politicians flirted briefly with replacing some of the CNE's buildings with more profitable ventures, as befits such a valuable site. Fortunately, they were largely unsuccessful. Torontonians made it clear they did not want to lose the fire hall and police station, the Music Building (originally the Railways Building), the Ontario Government Building and the Automotive Building, all built before 1930, or even the more recent 1950s-style Shell Tower. As a result, many of the buildings have been designated heritage sites. These monuments of an earlier time, along with such favourites as the Princes' Gates — opened in 1927 by His Royal Highness Edward, Prince of Wales, and his brother, Prince George — will remain.

**DUFFERIN GATE (BELOW);
NATIONAL TRADE CENTRE (BOTTOM)**

TORONTO'S BEST

The National Trade Centre (NTC) is a relative newcomer to the CNE grounds, and is the largest tradeshow facility in Canada. Part of its vast exterior mirrors the Automotive Building opposite, while the rest dazzles the eye with round towers punctuating a glass facade. The NTC is a fine example of how new construction can both pay homage to existing structures and make a unique architectural statement. Also on the site, but only coincidentally, is the Officers' Quarters of Stanley Barracks, a fine stone structure built in 1841 as part of the fort that replaced the original Fort York.

ONTARIO SCIENCE CENTRE

"It must be fun!" wrote the centre's architect, Raymond Moriyama, back in 1964 during the planning phase of this Ontario centennial project. And fun it is! One of the city's most-visited attractions, the Ontario Science Centre succeeds admirably in providing people of all ages with some of the sense of wonder and pleasure that motivates professional scientists. Prices range from $8 for children to $14 for adults. Special exhibits and IMAX films are extra. Parking is $7.

Its more than 800 exhibits invite you to twirl knobs, push buttons, fiddle with instruments and test your skills using gizmos related to astronomy, biology, chemistry, communications, ecology and physics. Favourites include the real rainforest in the Living Earth area and the pitching cage at the Sport exhibit. Demonstrations at various locations throughout the day include the popular laser show, the electricity demonstration and the changing programs in the mini-planetarium, Starlab. Special exhibitions range widely from explorations of human nature to travels through Siberia. These are often augmented by lectures that bring to mind the days before radio and TV, when public talks were the main way of conveying the latest in scientific discoveries to the masses.

ONTARIO SCIENCE CENTRE

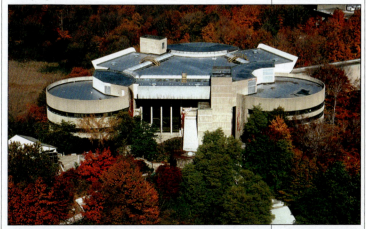

▲ Toronto's Top Attractions

THE SCIENCE CENTRE

The Centre's shop, an outlet for the small chain called Mastermind, offers a wide selection of books, software, educational toys and science kits.

The Centre is vast: five levels cascade down the Don Valley, providing low-tech views that contrast comfortably with the exhibits and the building itself, and more than enough opportunity for walking. The Timescape exhibit, installed along one of the longest parts of your trek, unearths the mysteries of time by presenting materials (stones, fossils and the like) from millions of years ago to the present. If there are any drawbacks to the Centre, it's that its success is overwhelming. The only way to avoid the crowds is to arrive the moment the place opens (10 a.m.). Weekdays are no better than weekends; as many as 10,000 children a day come on school trips. Although even toddlers seem to have a good time, getting the most out of the exhibits requires at least a Grade 3 or 4 reading ability. The weakest link is in the food department: only vending machines and a fairly institutional-type cafeteria, with nowhere to eat nearby.

TORONTO ZOO

Have you always wanted to go to Africa but lacked the time? Then head to the African Pavilion at the Toronto Zoo to catch perennial favourites like gorillas and chimpanzees, as well as a host of lesser-known species. Along with the fauna, there is an array of indigenous flora, through which many of the animals appear able to wander at will, particularly the birds, who fly freely around the verdant enclosure. In the areas adjacent to the pavilion are ostriches, African elephants, white rhinos, cheetahs, a variety of antelopes, hyenas, big cats, giraffes and many more.

The Toronto Zoo, designed in the 1960s and completed in the early 1970s, was among the first in the world to group its collection of 5,000 animals according to their region of origin rather than by type. You will find monkeys, snakes, rodents, and so on, not only in the African Pavilion but, where appropriate, in each of the four other pavilions: the Americas, the Malayan Woods, Australasia, and the Marco Polo Trail (next to which you can test your camel-riding skills).

The zoo was also among the first to try to recreate natural habitats, rather than using small enclosures, for its collection. Thus, it sometimes appears as though you could reach out and touch the animals on display; although it also sometimes means you can't find the animal at all! In other words, this zoo was designed primarily for animals rather than for people. As well as showcasing its collection, it is

TORONTO'S BEST

also an international leader in research and species-survival projects.

The zoo is huge, spread over 287 hectares, making it impossible to cover it entirely in one visit. You will have to pick your priorities. Excellent maps and signage help enormously in this task, as does the posted schedule of feeding times and other events, such as meeting the keepers of various animals. There is an open-air tram, the Zoomobile, which takes you directly to some of the more distant pavilions.

You will want to pack a picnic unless fast food is your fare of choice, since that's the only food available to the

▲ Toronto's Top Attractions

Casa Loma (above and below)

human animals at the zoo. Throughout the summer, the zoo is pretty crowded, so be prepared to contend with the herd. If you can get there on a weekday or at any other time of year, you will have a much more enjoyable experience. Admission prices range from $11 to $19.

Casa Loma and Spadina House
You could be forgiven for wondering whether the Disney-esque castle perched on the escarpment above the Spadina-Dupont area is a set for some movie in progress. But it is not. It is the turreted fantasy of industrialist Sir Henry Pellatt made manifest. The $3.5-million, ninety-eight-room folly, built between 1910 and 1913, was both his home and, at least in part, his undoing. Within 10 years of its construction, Pellatt, a pioneer of electrification, a philanthropist, and a soldier, had lost two wives, his business and all of his belongings. By the time of his death in 1939, he lived alone in a single room in a grim industrial suburb.

The castle, designed by John Lennox, architect of Old City Hall, is now owned by the City of Toronto, and since 1937 has been operated by

TORONTO'S BEST ▲

CASA LOMA GARDENS

the Kiwanis Club of Casa Loma. Visitors are welcome to wander the castle, the huge stables and the grounds. In the late 1980s, the Toronto Garden Club restored the gardens, which are now magnificent. In the main, Casa Loma has been kept much as it was, although the original $1.5 million worth of real and pseudo-baronial furniture was sold to help pay Sir Henry's debts. During the Christmas season, visitors can take part in an array of entertainments — music, drama, puppetry, and more — designed mainly for children. Proceeds from visitors go to maintain the buildings (Sir Henry spent about $25,000 per year just on heating) and to the Kiwanis Club's many good causes. Throughout the year, there are special fundraising events, many of them open to the public. For instance, in mid-November, the National Ballet School runs its Sugar Plum Fair, featuring fine crafts to benefit its scholarship fund.

Just to the north and east of Casa Loma is Spadina House. The third house in the city to bear this name (which is supposed to be pronounced spa-DEE-na, but usually comes out as spa-DIE-na), it was built in 1866 by James Austin (hence Austin Terrace), one of the founders and the first president of the Dominion Bank, and remained in the family until the 1970s. Today, it is the grandest of several nineteenth-century homes owned and operated by Heritage Toronto and the only one to contain its original furnishings,

Toronto's Top Attractions

Spadina House

Spadina House Interior

fixtures and works of art. Except for the 2.4 hectares of grounds, which, like those at Casa Loma, are maintained in their Victorian and Edwardian splendour by the Toronto Garden Club, there is no idle wandering around here. Supervised tours are included with the price of admission.

TORONTO'S BEST

SPADINA HOUSE

CIVIC CENTRE: CITY HALLS NEW AND OLD AND OSGOODE HALL

No other building in Toronto captures the city's optimism as well as the "new" City Hall, so called to distinguish it from the Old City Hall (just across the street), which it replaced in 1965. As with two of the city's previous city halls, the design was the product of a competition, this one the work of the Finnish architect Viljo Revell. From the air, the domed council chamber and curved towers resemble an eye, a symbol in Finland for the tradition of democratic rule. From the ground, the complex is often described as a clamshell hugging a flying saucer.

The civic pride engendered by new City Hall's design is reflected inside by the constant parade of visitors. In the lobby is a large, detailed model of downtown Toronto, which is very useful for orienting yourself. Helpful, too, are the racks of pamphlets about sights and special

CITY HALL

35

▲ Toronto's Top Attractions

CITY HALL AT NIGHT

NATHAN PHILIPS SQUARE AND OLD CITY HALL

activities in and around Toronto, and City Shop, a bookstore that sells excellent guides, maps and souvenirs. Another favourite feature is *Metropolis*, one of several works by local artists, many with a local theme, that are displayed throughout the building. *Metropolis* is David Partridge's riveting three-dimensional wall sculpture made entirely of nails of different sizes and materials. The piece is meant to represent the way cities grow from dense cores to spread-out suburbs, but its major attraction seems to be that a coin inserted at the top can find its way down to the bottom.

Popular as the new City Hall is, it is the large outdoor square that it embraces — Nathan Phillips Square, named for the mayor responsible for the building's construction — that attracts crowds. Even on the coldest winter days, skaters flock to the ice rink, which is transformed into a cooling fountain in the summer. Throughout the warmer months there are concerts and other performances almost daily. There is a farmers' market every Wednesday, a weekend art show in midsummer and a host of other special

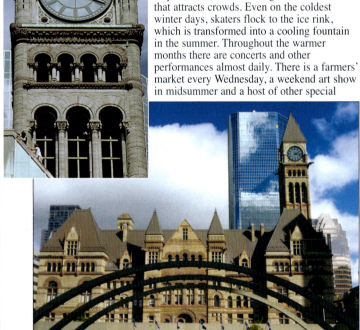

Toronto's Best

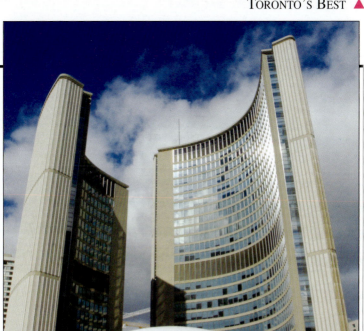

CITY HALL DURING THE DAY

activities for visitors of all ages. Also in the square is the Peace Garden, a small stone cube that has one corner broken away in remembrance of the destruction caused by war. The piece was built by the city in 1984, Toronto's sesquicentennial, to express the desire of all Torontonians for world peace. Perhaps the most famous work, however, is Henry Moore's *Three Way Piece No. 2*, commonly called "The Archer" by Torontonians. The piece was selected by architect Viljo Revell, who was a friend of the English sculptor, but despite a generous budget for artwork for the new building, council believed that an abstract piece would be unacceptable to taxpayers and decided not to purchase it. Following that decision, the mayor who succeeded Nathan Phillips, Phil Givens, led a successful campaign to raise the necessary funds by private subscription.

Just east of Nathan Phillips Square is Toronto's Old City Hall. The Toronto architect responsible for this building ensured he would be remembered by having "E.J. Lennox Architect A.D. 1889" carved under the eaves on all four sides of the building. He managed to incorporate not only the grimacing faces of the municipal politicians of the day, but also his own likeness in the carved stonework above the main entrance. In its heyday, the intricate stonework, generous proportions, stained glass, handsome council chamber, well-chosen furnishings and airy atmosphere engendered as much pride in Toronto's citizens as the new City Hall does today. The ninety-one metre-high clock tower, which appears from the south to cap Bay Street and is still prominently visible from many parts of downtown, was designed to be more than a landmark; it was an essential component of the building's advanced ventilating and heating system. Today, Old City Hall is used exclusively for its courtrooms and is visited primarily by those on court business.

▲ Toronto's Top Attractions

Osgoode Hall

West of Nathan Phillips Square is the grandly classical Osgoode Hall. Built originally as a sort of union hall for the Law Society of Upper Canada and named for the province's first chief justice, William Osgoode, it now houses the Ontario Court of Appeal and continues to serve its original purpose as well.

No fewer than three firms had a hand in its design prior to 1860, and another six have had a go at it since then — all of them extremely prominent, and therefore, one would think, somewhat egotistical. Yet their work has harmonized to create an exquisitely elegant, if somewhat forbidding-looking building, and its library (which is open to the public) is widely considered to be one of the most elegant rooms in Canada. In another of its elegant rooms is one of the best kept secrets in the city: The Restaurant at Osgoode Hall. Open from noon to 2 p.m. on weekdays, it serves up fine French fare and has an excellent wine list.

The fence surrounding Osgoode Hall and the gate on Queen Street were constructed not to intimidate the public, but to keep out wandering cows. Functionally and architecturally, these three buildings beautifully reflect the growth of the city from a straight-laced, austere provincial capital to a somewhat overstuffed, rapidly growing Victorian centre of trade and commerce, to a worldly but community-oriented modern city.

The Distillery District

A unique relic of Toronto's early history, this neighbourhood of Dickensian industrial buildings hosts a wonderfully diverse group of art galleries, shops, cafés and restaurants. Passing crowded patios on the Distillery's cobblestone streets, visitors will never guess that the area was dead empty just a few years ago. Indeed, when a group of local developers publicized "The Distillery Historic District" in 2003, many Torontonians were mystified. Few had ever visited the six-hectare site, a well-preserved collection of red-brick and limestone hulks that was once home to the Gooderham and Worts distilling empire.

To be sure, Gooderham and Worts has a prominent place in the city's history. It got its start in 1831, when James Worts, freshly arrived from Suffolk, England,

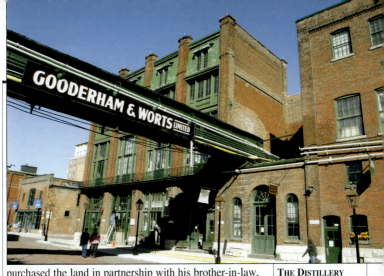

THE DISTILLERY DISTRICT

purchased the land in partnership with his brother-in-law, William Gooderham, and set about building a mill. The two families soon joined the city's ruling class and their distillery became the centre of Toronto's industrial district. (Their former head office, the so-called "flatiron building" on Wellington East, is an icon of the city).

After the last batch of alcohol was produced here in 1990, the plant was closed down and the area was mainly used as a movie set. It continues to host shoots for Hollywood productions like *Chicago*, *The Recruit*, and *Cinderella Man*, but remained a secret to everyone except local film crews and architectural historians.

Then the transformation began, in which a carefully selected mix of tenants began moving into the 44 buildings on site. Subsidized rents drew galleries, artists and craftspeople to the area, which has been kept franchise-free.

Past the parking and construction on Parliament Street lies the best way to enter the area: from the north, between the sturdy yet fanciful buildings of Trinity Street. At the far end on the right, the Stone Distillery Building holds the visitors' centre. It hosts guided walking tours focusing on the area's social history, industry and architecture. Helpful maps are available. Next door, the Monte Clark Gallery hosts some of Canada's best contemporary art. The white planes of the gallery fill only the bottom of the cavernous former distillery, whose tarnished steel and brick are as compelling as the art.

The plaza just to the east is the heart of the district. In warmer months, it's the venue for a Sunday farmers' market, which offers tastes of organic Ontario produce. Here, you'll also find Balzac's Café, serving fine lattes on vintage marble tables. The café is housed in a magnificent old structure — the former pump house — that has been left alone as much as possible. Photographers can have a field day.

39

BALZAC'S CAFÉ IN THE DISTILLERY DISTRICT

(Digital cameras are available for rent across the way at Pikto, which will also develop your shots at the end of the day).

It's also worth catching a glimpse of the Corkin Shopland Gallery, designed by husband-and-wife architects Shim Sutcliffe. The remarkable space is one of several galleries in the elaborate Pure Spirits building, just north of the old pump house. Corkin Shopland's unorthodox mix of photography and painting with antique ceramics finds a perfect complement in the large, labyrinthine interior. Smooth, subtle greys set off the bleached floors and patinated brick.

Next door, the Case Goods Warehouse offers some of Toronto's best shopping for crafts. The open studios let you visit with local artisans at work and leave with newly made ceramics, clothing or chocolate.

To the east, the brand-new Young Centre hosts a local theatre school and the internationally renowned Soulpepper company. In summer and fall, it's worth planning your visit around a show. But the building is worth a look at any time: designed by award-winning local firm KPMB, it bridges two ancient buildings that were once used to age alcohol, with a glassed-in atrium and stylish café. It's a blend of young and old in every sense.

Nearby, free tours of the Mill Street Brewery offer an interesting diversion, and the microbrewery's products are well worth a sip. The Tank House Ale, named after the building that houses the operation, is a pleasantly crisp red ale. The Coffee Porter serves more exotic tastes.

The Italian restaurant 1832 and the Pure Spirits Oyster House are fine options for meals. In summer, you can enjoy some barbecue outdoors here to the sounds of live jazz. At other times, the Distillery Canteen on Trinity Street offers reasonably priced, quality pub food. It's perfect fuel for a solid day of looking at Toronto's past and its cutting edge.

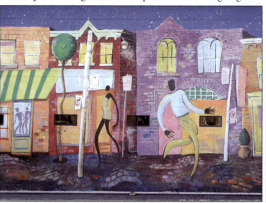

Museums and Galleries

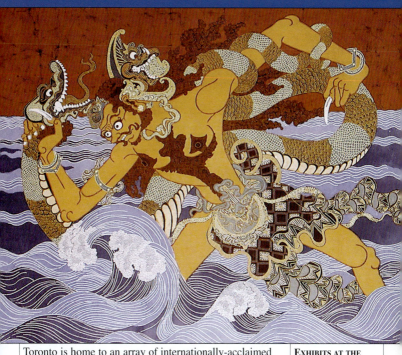

Toronto is home to an array of internationally-acclaimed public museums and galleries. There are the large and eclectic collections of institutions like the Royal Ontario Museum (ROM), which features natural, archaeological and social history, and the Art Gallery of Ontario (AGO), which houses fine art from diverse periods and cultures. Then there are the smaller and specialized offerings of the Bata Shoe Museum, the Gardiner Museum of Ceramic Art and the Textile Museum of Canada. Specialization is also the hallmark of a large number of quite small, lesser-known institutions that contain materials representing such things as police work and firefighting, hockey and other Canadian sports, cars, interior and industrial design, television, medicine and even contraception. Toronto's diverse cultures are displayed at several excellent small museums or institutes, while Toronto's own history is well-represented at Black Creek Pioneer Village, Fort York and numerous period homes throughout the city. Here we will cover the best of the well-known institutions, but be aware that in its quiet, non-assuming way, Toronto has been building a large collection of easily seen art all over town. Dozens of corporations have put paintings, sculpture and specially-commissioned work of all kinds in and around their buildings, and hundreds of pieces have been placed in libraries and other public buildings, at intersections, in

Exhibits at the Textile Museum of Canada

Toronto's Top Attractions

ROM ENTRANCE

parks, on streets and bridges, and in the changing display at the city's downtown, outdoor sculpture garden. So, while a visit to a gallery or museum will be well-rewarded, so too, will a thorough look at all you pass as you traverse the city.

Royal Ontario Museum (ROM)

The ROM has never aspired to modesty. Until 1955, it was actually five museums, each with its own entrance and director. They covered the subjects of archaeology, paleontology, mineralogy, zoology and geology. The original building, now best seen from the south, is an exuberant pre–World War I Romanesque concoction rich with a veritable tapestry of carved arches and stonework. The first major addition came in the 1930s, a flattened art deco-ish version of the Romanesque structure, which formed what is now the east wing facing Queen's Park, through which one enters today — though not for long as

still more changes are in the works. During the course of constructing that addition, the four mid-nineteenth-century "totem" or, more accurately, crest poles from British Columbia — three by the Nisga'a nation, one by the Haida — that now grace the main stairwell inside were lowered into place from above. The tallest one is a mere six inches (fifteen cm) from the ceiling! Subsequent additions over the past two decades have filled in the courtyards and made the

ROM one of the biggest museums in North America.

Since 2004, the ROM has been under renovation, and it is possible that what you read below will not be entirely accurate as the renovations continue. Sections of the gallery will remain open on a rotating basis throughout the renovations, which are scheduled to continue through 2006 up to early 2007. The changes will be major, including, for example, a complete reorientation that will see the museum's main entrance relocated to Bloor Street. Called "Renaissance ROM", the 40,000 square feet of additional or reallocated space will permit the ROM to finally display its fabulous collections of textiles and costumes. Its Canadiana galleries will be expanded and there will be a new First Nations gallery, as well as a new, direct connection to the subway system. The most obvious change will be the huge glass pavilion that will serve as the new entrance. The project is being designed by Daniel Libeskind, architect of Berlin's internationally-acclaimed Holocaust & Jewish Museum and a finalist for the work at New York's World Trade Center site.

Before you get to the five-million-odd objects in the over forty galleries that make up the ROM's collection, you pass beneath the impressive mosaic ceiling and floor of the entry rotunda. Look up and see, set in the coruscating gold and bronze of over a million Venetian glass mosaic tiles, images of other civilizations and cultures; at your feet, a marble sunburst heralds one's passage into the ROM proper. The ROM's collection is not easily defined by categories. Broadly speaking, it has a life and earth sciences component, a Canadiana component, and an ancient civilizations and European component. Within each, there are comprehensive exhibits of fairly narrowly defined aspects, and modest collections of broadly defined aspects.

To help you get an overview of the museum's collections, and to help you decide how much of the place to tackle, the Samuel Hall/Currelly Gallery provides a foretaste of the collections with cases displaying artifacts and

43

Toronto's Top Attractions

TOTEM POLE

BYZANTINE CROSS

DINOSAUR GALLERY

specimens keyed to the museum's floor levels. This space used to house the museums's collection of armour (now on the third level), as can be seen from artist Sylvia Hahn's large murals of medieval life. For the jousting scene, she gave the spectators the faces of museum staff members at the time (1943). The grey-haired gent, second from the right, is C.T. Currelly, first director of the Royal Ontario Museum of Archaeology. Briefly, the street level (main floor) contains the ROM's magnificent Chinese collections, its Korean collection — the largest in North America — and its deservedly popular mineral collection in the (S.R. Perren Gem and Gold Room).

The level somewhat confusingly called "1B" is the Canadian Heritage floor, which contains materials from Canada's indigenous peoples to contemporary art works, the latter in the Roloff Beny Gallery. But a huge stock of Canadiana, including everyday household items and fine antiques and paintings, is located off-site altogether, in the Sigmund Samuel Building just to the south of the ROM.

The museum's second floor is devoted to life sciences, and the third to various aspects of Mediterranean civilization. Several rooms throughout the building are used for special exhibits, sometimes blockbusters like "Egyptian Art in the Age of the Pyramids" or "Arts of the Sikh Kingdoms", or to show off parts of the vast collections normally held in storage for lack of exhibition space. For instance, the ROM's textile collection, which ranks fifth in the world and contains woven, dyed, printed and hand-worked pieces from near and far, is rarely seen. Nor is its wealth of hundreds of musical instruments.

Highlights of this profusion are found scattered throughout the building. One of the most popular parts of the Life Sciences collection (second level), for example, is the several rooms of reconstructed dinosaurs or their skeletons happily stationed amidst what seems to be their original habitat. Its thirteen full skeletons span the Jurassic and the Cretaceous periods, and there is much to be

MUSEUMS AND GALLERIES

gleaned from accompanying flora. Nearby are rooms filled with invertebrate fossils — from Australian bacteria that are 3.5 billion years old, to the assorted aquatic animals found in British Columbia's Burgess Shale that are a mere 535 to 515 million years old, to a glimpse of Toronto life as it would have been 440 million years ago. There is a gallery explaining evolution, and others filled with displays of mammals, birds, insects and reptiles, and a marvellous bat cave (with some 2,500 simulated bats!) that accurately replicates Jamaica's St. Clair cave. Throughout these displays, the emphasis is on explaining connections between and among living things, on providing a context in which to understand how and why different forms of life have flourished or declined.

In the significant Mediterranean World collection (third floor), you can see materials spanning Mesopotamia (Sumer, Babylon, Assyria and Elam) and ancient Iran, ancient Egypt, the Greek, Roman, Byzantine and Islamic worlds. The periods included range from 10,000 B.C. to

the 1800s. The ancient Egypt gallery contains one of the most dazzling mummy cases ever found — that of Djedmaatesankh, a court musician — which is so valuable in and of itself that it has never been opened. The Greek World and Imperial Rome also get their due: the former with a sculpture court of gods and athletes, the latter with busts of emperors and citizens. You can sail to Byzantium to take in the Joey and Toby Tanenbaum Gallery of Byzantine Art or stroll through a sampling of an entire — but small — Islamic city, including a mosque, shrine, house, garden and market. The Samuel European galleries fill in the picture north of the Mediterranean from the

▲ Toronto's Top Attractions

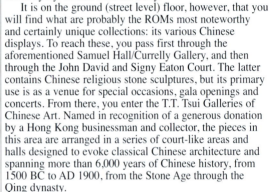

Middle Ages to the twentieth century. The arms and armour gallery that takes you from chain mail to machine guns is always a hit. Medieval Europe's religiosity is well represented by pieces depicting saints, and containers for holding saintly relics. The Judaica Gallery showcases Jewish ceremonial art from the 1500s onward. Nearby is a variety of reconstructed rooms, each filled with a veritable antiques road show of the furnishings and art of different periods of European history. Also on this level is a deluxe and extensive collection of Art Deco furniture donated to the ROM by Sylvia and Bernard Ostry.

It is on the ground (street level) floor, however, that you will find what are probably the ROMs most noteworthy and certainly unique collections: its various Chinese displays. To reach these, you pass first through the aforementioned Samuel Hall/Currelly Gallery, and then through the John David and Signy Eaton Court. The latter contains Chinese religious stone sculptures, but its primary use is as a venue for special occasions, gala openings and concerts. From there, you enter the T.T. Tsui Galleries of Chinese Art. Named in recognition of a generous donation by a Hong Kong businessman and collector, the pieces in this area are arranged in a series of court-like areas and halls designed to evoke classical Chinese architecture and spanning more than 6,000 years of Chinese history, from 1500 BC to AD 1900, from the Stone Age through the Qing dynasty.

There is a tale to this collection's existence. Many of the pieces were supplied by George Crofts, an Anglo-Irishman who worked as a fur trader from the turn of the century through China's major upheavals in the 1920s. Throughout this period, Crofts managed to acquire pieces ranging from the Imperial wardrobe to a massive Ming temple and accompanying tomb sculptures, complete with stone arches and, most amazingly of all, a procession of early sixth to late seventh century AD ceramic figures of

MUSEUMS AND GALLERIES ▲

soldiers, musicians, ox-drawn carts and assorted attendants that once lined the avenue leading to the burial plot, the Bodhisattvas. For all those years, Crofts' name was kept secret so that rival dealers would not discover his identity.

From the Tsui Galleries, you pass into the Chinese Tomb area. Popularly known as the Ming Tomb, the collection actually ranges from the Yuan dynasty (fourteenth century), to the Ming (fifteenth to sixteenth centuries), to the Qing (seventeenth to twentieth centuries). The pieces formerly were displayed outdoors, but at the conclusion of the ROM's most recent construction project, only shi shi, the ROM's Chinese stone lions, were left to face the elements. Dating from the 1600s, the lions are thought to have once guarded the main gateway to the Su Wang Fu, a magnificent palace in Beijing destroyed during the Boxer Rebellion of 1900. Today's nasty pollution requires that even these hearty beasts — who after 300 years of guard duty spent an entire year journeying to Canada — must be encased in plastic to protect them.

Finally, in the Bishop White Gallery of Chinese Temple Art (named for Bishop William Charles White, a Canadian Anglican bishop who was stationed in Henan province from 1901 until 1934, when he became the first curator of the ROM's Chinese collections), enormous thirteenth-century wall paintings of Buddhist and Taoist gods serve as a backdrop to towering Buddhist sculptures. On a smaller scale, the collection includes hundreds of intricate jade and

TORONTO'S TOP ATTRACTIONS

***THE MARCHESA CASATI* BY AUGUSTUS JOHN AT THE AGO**

HENRY MOORE SCULPTURE

ivory carvings, delicate perfume bottles, fine porcelain dating back almost 1,000 years and many other treasures. Taken together, these collections represent one of the largest and most important ensembles of Chinese artifacts outside China. The only drawback to this fabulous collection is that too little information is provided about many of the pieces.

In addition to its collections, the ROM is a major centre of research. Consequently, there are many public lectures and tours that more rigorously supplement the information in the galleries. Funding cutbacks over the past decade have inspired the ROM to recreate itself. From a purely erudite and somewhat stuffy shrine to the past, it has become a mecca for community and social events, a venue geared to all ages and filled not only with surprising artifacts, but with diverse activities. During the warmer months (May through September) the ROM offers walks, many of them free, through Toronto's diverse neighbourhoods. There are also special events for children, concerts in some of the

MUSEUMS AND GALLERIES

Study in Movement by Emily Carr at the AGO

acoustically fine courtyards and one- and two-week summer day camps. On the third Friday evening of every month, the ROM even caters specifically to singles! Also contained in the ROM is the Discovery Gallery, which enables anyone over age seven to handle objects from the collections and to view them using microscopes, magnifying glasses or other appropriate forms of technology. During some hours, museum staff take pieces from this gallery around on small carts, so that while viewing, say, the mammals, you

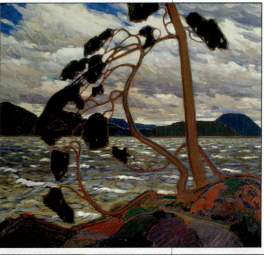

The West Wind by Tom Thompson (below); Henry Moore Sculpture Gallery (bottom)

L'Incendie du Quartier Saint-Jean vu vers l'ouest by Joseph Légaré at the AGO

might get to handle skins from different animals as well as obtaining additional information about the display. The museum has several shops: one devoted to relevant books and the ROM's own publications, another to replicas of works in the museum, a third to products for children, and the largest to an array of gift items. There are to be three restaurants when the current renovations are complete.

THE ART GALLERY OF ONTARIO (AGO)

From its modest beginnings around World War I as the Art Gallery of Toronto in the old house known as the Grange, which is connected to the south side of the modern museum, the AGO has grown gradually to a museum comprising fifty galleries with a collection of more than 24,000 pieces.

The AGO is another Toronto museum that is currently undergoing renovations. Toronto-born architect Frank Gehry is overseeing the new design, which features a

Blue Nude by Henri Matisse visits at the AGO

MUSEUMS AND GALLERIES

ELM TREE AT HORTON LANDING BY ALEX COLVILLE AT THE AGO

dramatically sweeping façade of glass and Douglas fir, as well as a major expansion of the interior gallery spaces. Rebuilding is scheduled to last through the spring of 2008.

During the construction, between 30-50 percent of the gallery's space will be closed. Other spaces will not be able to display works of art because of their proximity to the construction zone and have been adapted to present artist's projects, education programs and displays about the Transformation AGO project. On the bright side, general admission prices will be reduced to reflect the inconvenience.

The gallery is doing its best to keep as many of its major works on display during the period of change. These include an extensive collection of works by Henry Moore, excellent landscapes by Tom Thompson and the Group of Seven, and fine modernist works by the likes of Dali, Man Ray and Duchamp. Another highlight is Rubens' *Massacre of the Innocents*, recently purchased by media mogul Kenneth Thompson for $117 million dollars and donated to the museum.

THE GARDINER MUSEUM OF CERAMIC ART

A bijoux museum displaying North America's largest collection of European porcelain and other clay-based articles of the past five millennia, the Gardiner is located directly opposite the ROM. This museum, too, is undergoing extensive renovations, and will remain

HARLEQUIN AT THE GARDINER MUSEUM

Toronto's Top Attractions

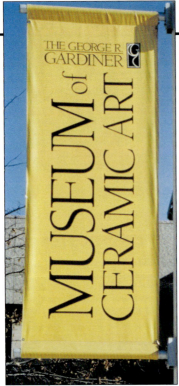

closed until the spring of 2006.

Both the building and much of its permanent collection were the gift of George R. Gardiner and his wife Helen. Pieces from virtually all the well-known ceramic centres of Europe — Sèvres, Saint-Cloud, Plymouth and Bristol, Vienna and Meissen among them — along with a sampling of blue and white Chinese porcelain are on display. You will also find seventeenth-century English Delftware and slipware, Italian Renaissance majolica and, remarkably, Picasso-esque tin-glazed earthenware intended for everyday use, soft-paste porcelain from Chelsea, and hard-paste porcelain from the Meissen factory and its rival, the Viennese Du Paquier factory. Of special interest are the tiny figurines depicting the stock characters of the Commedia dell'arte. Information on each piece, the factories that made them and the processes employed, is clear and thorough.

The Gardiner also boasts a fine collection of ancient American ceramics, some dating as far back as 3,000 BC, and its smaller selection of fifteenth- and sixteenth-century Italian majolica.

BATA SHOE MUSEUM

If you're like most people, your initial reaction to the very idea of a museum devoted to shoes will be a snort of derision: "What's this? A foot fetishist's wonderland?" But hold the snort. The odd little Bata Shoe Museum — the building is even shaped like a shoe — is actually a delight.

The All About Shoes exhibit gets you from the earliest sandals to the latest in haut monde in a room so well laid out that your feet don't even get tired. Adults will learn a lot wherever they tread and will no doubt get a charge from the footwear of the rich and famous: Elvis's blue suede shoes and Elton John's sneakers, for instance. Some visitors will enthuse over the workwear collection of boots specially designed for everything from mining to rice harvesting, while others are sure to delight in the Gentle Step, an

SHOE FROM VIVIENNE WESTWOOD'S 1993 ANGLOMANIA COLLECTION

MUSEUMS AND GALLERIES

BATA SHOE MUSEUM

overview of the changing role of nineteenth-century women and the variations in shoes (and costumes) that reflected these developments. Special exhibits are well-designed, informative and always pun-filled. Little Feats, for example, displays children's shoes from around the world, while One, Two Buckle My Shoe, draws on children's literature ranging from classic fairy tales to contemporary urban stories to depict the ever-present role of feet, footwear and shoemakers. Another, called Loose Tongues and Lost Soles, focuses entirely on humorous foot-related sculptures and works on paper, ranging from caricatures by Daumier to cartoons from the New Yorker.

TEXTILE MUSEUM OF CANADA

Perhaps because few would find it kinky to collect fabric, the Textile Museum generally lacks the humour of the Bata, although a recent show on modes of dress was called "Moral Fibre." Lacking also the financial backing of the shoe-wealthy Batas, it is housed in a non-descript building

AFGHANISTAN EXHIBIT AT THE TEXTILE MUSEUM

behind City Hall rather than in a Cinderella-inspired slipper. Apart from these distinctions, however, the Museum for Textiles competes very effectively as an internationally-known centre for the collection, display and documentation of its chosen subject. It contains over 10,000 pieces of ethnographic and historic textiles — including woven, knotted, hooked and tied, dyed and natural wools, silks, cottons and grasses, the well-stocked H.N. Pullen library (over 3,000 items), and a lovely gift shop filled with woven and reading materials from around the world. In addition to its own vast collection, only a small portion of which can be displayed at any one time in this 4,000 square foot facility, the museum hosts traveling exhibits. Recent visitors have included the hooked mats of the Grenfell Mission — a selection of the nearly forgotten, but once immensely popular work (it was carried by Eaton's) of women from Newfoundland and Labrador. Another was an amazing display of European lacework spanning several centuries.

HISTORY ON DISPLAY

Toronto displays its heritage at numerous sites throughout the city. There is, of course, its sizable collection of historically and architecturally noteworthy buildings — even whole neighbourhoods, such as Cabbagetown. There is Toronto's First Post Office and several restored nineteenth-century schools. For devotees of soldiering, there is Fort York, site of the garrison first established by the British in 1793. The fort is operated by Heritage Toronto, which gives tours several times a day through tiny barracks that once housed over 100 people. The highlight for many visitors occurs on July 1 (Canada Day), and August 1 (Simcoe Day), when cannons boom and mock soldiers are put through their paces. There is the Riverdale Farm in the Don Valley, which houses livestock representing heritage breeds, and the nearby Brickworks

MUSEUMS AND GALLERIES

and Todmorden Mills, both of which hark back to nineteenth-century industries. There are fine homes like Spadina House, Casa Loma and the Grange (currently closed for renovations) as well as more modest abodes like Colbourne Lodge and Mackenzie House. All these demonstrate life in the periods in which they were built. The granddaddy, though, of these living-museum type sites is the forty-year-old Black Creek Pioneer Village.

BLACK CREEK PIONEER VILLAGE

If you are not already a fan of the "living history" style of presenting life in earlier times, Black Creek may convert you. With the exception of some remnants of the Stong farm once located here (the piggery, the barn and two homes), most of the forty-odd buildings on the site were rescued from decay somewhere in southern Ontario; the rest, like Roblin's Mill, were built from scratch.

Visitors can get a good idea of how a variety of household and farm implements were made and used: the harness maker makes and repairs leather items, the blacksmith shoes the village horses, the cooper produces barrels and buckets, the seamstress sews the villagers' costumes, the broom maker makes brooms from corn grown behind the shop, the cabinet maker makes furniture and the tinsmith produces

THE FORT YORK GUARD

Toronto's Top Attractions

INTERPRETERS AT BLACK CREEK

various housewares. In addition to the horses, who haul around a hay wagon you can catch to cut down on walking (or just for fun), there are chickens in the coop, hogs in the piggery and cows in the pasture. You'll also find a printing press, a cider mill, a grain mill, a small school, a church, homes reflecting various degrees of wealth and even a Masonic Lodge.

The restaurant is not bad, and there are usually freshly baked pies and bread. There are several vegetable gardens, a garden devoted to dye plants used by the weaver, a well-researched medicinal herb garden, a kitchen and folk-remedy herb garden and a Pennsylvania German square garden. There are weekend and month-long special events, such as the Spring Fair, corn roasts, apple-baking contests, pumpkin parties, craft demonstrations and sales, theatrical and musical performances and, from mid-November until December 24th, special Christmas activities. Of course, it is true that no animals actually meet their demise in the slaughterhouse, and there is little to indicate that life in the times depicted was nasty, brutish and short, but despite these gaps, Black Creek does a good job of providing a highly enjoyable and informative outing for the whole family.

MILL AT BLACK CREEK

INDEPENDENT GALLERIES

CHRISTOPHER HUME

In the beginning, there was Yorkville. It was the 1960s and Toronto was just waking from its long provincial slumber. Though it soon would be gentrified beyond recognition, Yorkville suddenly found itself the front line in the War of Love. As the hippies arrived in the Victorian enclave near Bloor Street and Avenue Road, so did artists and art dealers.

ABOVE: *THE POWER PLANT* BY TIM HAWKINSON
BELOW: *MOUNTAIN VALLEY, SPRING #2* BY ANNE MEREDITH BARRY

YORKVILLE

Walter Moos was the first, setting up shop in Yorkville Avenue in 1959. He would later move further downtown, but his appearance was enough to start the ball rolling. And though the counterculture has long since disappeared from the scene, Yorkville still boasts more than a dozen art galleries. The dealers here tend to be high-end types, their stables filled with senior artists from Canada and the world.

The Mira Godard Gallery, at 22 Hazelton, is a Yorkville fixture. Godard represents some of the country's best-known artists: Christopher and Mary Pratt, Joe Fafard, and Edward Burtynsky. Although no hotbed of artistic ferment, this is where the visual arts establishment struts its stuff.

Open House by David Craven at the Sable-Castelli Gallery

Harbourfront and the Surrounding Area

Off the beaten track, the Power Plant, at the Harbourfront Centre, 231 Queen's Quay West, has emerged as the premier showcase of the most contemporary of contemporary art from Toronto, Denmark, Germany and New York. Dramatically housed in a former generating station, this noncollecting gallery finds itself looking sometimes down and dirty, sometimes very slick, but rarely dull. Before reaching the Power Plant, art lovers will have travelled through the gallery-rich district along Spadina Avenue and Richmond Street. Running the gamut from up-market to low-rent, this is home to the good, the bad and the ugly of the Toronto art scene.

The city's original artist-run gallery is A Space, at 401 Richmond Street West. Around for more than thirty years, it has become more a soapbox than a showcase. Post-feminist, pre-millennial, pan-sexual: the revolution is in full swing here. In the same building is a mix of nonprofits sharing floor space with commercial galleries like Wynick/Tuck Gallery, which carries some big names in the world of art: Kim Adams, Greg Curnoe and Lawrence Weiner.

Vault at Sandra Ainsley Gallery

West End

Further west at 788 King Street West is Art Metropole, a gallery, book and multiples shop. This is a great place to buy cool artist-made multiples, jacket crests by General Idea and felt postcards by Joseph Beuys.

A few doors down you'll find Toronto's, if not Canada's, most idiosyncratic gallery, the Ydessa Hendeles Art Foundation, at 778 King Street West. Hendeles has transformed a two-storey commercial building into a shrine for leading-edge work from Europe, the United States and Canada. One of the top art collectors in the world, Ydessa Hendeles is as likely to show film-based work by Douglas Gordon and sculptures by Maurizio Cattelan, as she is to display her own outstanding collection of over 1,800, individually framed teddy bear photographs. A word of warning: The Foundation is only open Saturdays, from noon to 5 p.m.

Corkin-Shopland Gallery

Deep in Toronto's west end, near College Street and Lansdowne Avenue, is the Morrow Avenue complex, a cluster of galleries gathered around a renovated industrial courtyard. The Olga Korper Gallery, at 17 Morrow, is dedicated to the conceptual and sculptural. It is stunning even at its most minimal. By contrast, the Christopher Cutts Gallery, at 21 Morrow Avenue, is given over to both abstract and figurative painting, and Peak Gallery, at 23 Morrow Avenue, to emerging local artists.

WEST QUEEN WEST

It's been said that artists are the first sign of a neighbourhood's gentrification. This has never been more true than along West Queen West. Once filled with film studios, fleabag hotels and greasy spoons, the area has quickly developed into the city's hippest district with juice bars and galleries among second-hand appliance stores.

From Bathurst Street onward there are at least twenty galleries that change regularly with each new crop of art grads. Among the fray is dealer Katharine Mulherin who operates two galleries along the strip, at 1080 and 1086 Queen Street West. Mulherin has dominated the neighbourhood since 1998 when she opened her first gallery and started showing work by people she knew. Her stable now includes top painters Dana Holst, Michael Harrington and Eliza Griffiths.

There are dozens more galleries in the vicinity, including the worthwhile but hard to find Paul Petro Contemporary Art at 980 Queen West (there is no sign out front — look for a baby blue doorway). DeLeon White Gallery, at 1096 Queen West, is the most chic on the strip. Specializing in environmental art, they have taken full advantage of the gallery's high ceilings and garage door entrance with massive installations by Doug Buis and Peter von Tiesenhausen.

EAST END

The latest art district to emerge is at the Gooderham and Worts distillery, a stunning 5.2-hectares of interconnected historic buildings located at 55 Mill Street on the edge of Lake Ontario. This site is being billed as the city's newest centre for arts and entertainment. High-end tenants occupy spacious galleries, including Canada's leading photography dealer Jane Corkin of the Corkin Shopland Gallery in Building 61. In Building 32 is the Sandra Ainsley Gallery, specialists in contemporary glass art. Fans of Dale Chihuly should not miss this one.

GARDEN LILIES BY MARY PAVEY AT GALLERY ONE

ARIA BY DORIS SUNG AT A SPACE

SANDRA AINSLEY GALLERY

THEATRE AND DANCE

VIT WAGNER AND JON KAPLAN

LES MISÉRABLES AT THE PRINCESS OF WALES THEATRE

THE PRINCESS OF WALES THEATRE

The live performing arts rank as Toronto's greatest cultural asset. From theatre and dance to classical music and opera, the city offers an incredible variety of choices for those who want to indulge their cultural interests. Check out what's currently playing in the listings of the weekly *NOW* or the Thursday What's On section of the *Toronto Star*.

MAJOR COMPANIES

In the past fifteen years, Toronto has grown to become the third-largest centre for live theatre in the English-speaking world, after New York and London. The commercial scene is dominated by Mirvish Productions, run by the father-and-son team of Ed and David Mirvish, who have mounted world premieres, such as a musical adaptation of *Jane Eyre*, but

Theatre and Dance ▲

Royal Alex

are mainly involved in bringing popular Broadway and West End shows, from *Les Misérables* to *The Lion King*, to Toronto. The mega-musicals are housed in the spacious and comfortable Princess Of Wales Theatre, while the more cozy and historic Royal Alexandra Theatre was home to the ABBA-inspired musical *Mamma Mia*! Recently, the Mirvishes have put the shows from their subscription season — including Broadway hit *The Producers* — in other restored landmark theatres such as the Canon and the Winter Garden. Audiences are eagerly awaiting the world premiere of a musical version of Tolkien's *The Lord of the Rings*, which the Mirvishes are co-presenting and staging in the Princess of Wales – complete with Hobbit-like tree-roots extending into the theatre.

The Canadian Stage Company, Toronto's largest not-for-profit producer, offers a full, September-to-May subscription season at the St. Lawrence Centre's Bluma Appel Theatre and its own venue on Berkeley Street, with programming that includes new Canadian work alongside revivals by well-known foreign writers such as Tom Stoppard and composer Stephen Sondheim. The company's annual Dream in High Park outdoor production, running during July and August in a grassy amphitheatre, is one of the calendar's most popular and populist events, with families gathering as early as two hours before show time to secure a clear view and enjoy a picnic dinner.

Soulpepper Theatre presents the finest of shows from the classical repertoire, ranging from Shakespeare and Molière to Chekhov and Beckett. Eight years old, the company – which features the work of some of Canada's finest actors and directors – is finally moving into its own home in the newly developed Distillery District, which will allow Soulpepper to produce a season that runs throughout the year instead of just during the summer months.

Sheila McCarthy in CanStage's *Habeas Corpus*

RANDY HUGHSON, HOLLY LEWIS AND MICHAEL HEALY IN TARRAGON THEATRE'S PRODUCTION OF *THE OPTIMISTS*

MIDSIZE COMPANIES

The home-grown treasures of Canadian theatre are to be found at the city's many midsize houses, the most notable of which date from the Canadian theatre renaissance of the early 1970s. Of these, the Tarragon Theatre is without equal as a presenter of original Canadian scripts, having served as a welcome home to some of the country's finest playwrights, including Judith Thompson, Jason Sherman, John Murrell and Montreal's Michel Tremblay. Another stalwart, the Factory Theatre, is closely associated with the work of playwright George F. Walker, whose scripts have been produced throughout the United States, while Theatre Passe Muraille made its name with experimental, collective

CLEOPATRA AT THE SHAW FESTIVAL

THEATRE AND DANCE

creations but now presents shows scripted more traditionally. Also of note is Buddies in Bad Times Theatre, which produces more gay and lesbian plays than any other theatre on the continent. For family fare, check out the Lorraine Kimsa Theatre for Young People, whose repertoire ranges from adaptations of Dickens and other masters to world premières by Canadian writers whose work mirrors the city's multicultural fabric.

ALTERNATIVE COMPANIES

Then there are the scores of other companies in the city, including Necessary Angel, Theatre Columbus, Nightwood Theatre, Crow's Theatre and Theatre Smith-Gilmour, which produce one or two shows a season in rental spaces around the city. You can find everything from political theatre to performance art, avant-garde presentation to clown-based troupes.

COMEDY CLUBS

During the past decade Toronto has also become a comedy town, with dozens of venues offering standup, sketch, improv, open mic and all sorts of variations on these performance styles. The local Second City troupe always draws a big crowd, as do the downtown and uptown branches of Yuk Yuk's. There's often something happening at Bad Dog Theatre, newly planted in the city's east end. Also worth checking out are the weekly comedy evenings at the Rivoli, the Oasis, the Drake Hotel, the Laugh Resort, the Poor Alex and other venues.

HIGHER BY THE DANNY GROSSMAN DANCE COMPANY

RAY ROMANO AT THE LAUGH RESORT

▲ Toronto's Top Attractions

CANSTAGE'S *PICASSO AT THE LAPIN AGILE*

FESTIVALS

Two summer attractions, the Toronto Fringe and SummerWorks festivals, are browsers' delights. Most shows are an hour long, and although line-ups are common for word-of-mouth hits, prices are low (usually $10 or less). Venues are spread out over an area roughly bounded by Bloor and Queen, to the north and south, and St. George and Bathurst, to the east and west.

Harbourfront Centre, which operates three theatres and a variety of other performance facilities on the shores of Lake Ontario, is festival central. Harbourfront facilitates the World Stage in April, Toronto's main window on the international theatre scene. May's annual Milk International Children's Festival offers scores of performances and free outdoor events. Various summer events are devoted to a celebration of various ethnic communities and usually include a theatre and dance component.

The Stratford Festival and Shaw Festival, which run from April through November, are among North America's leading classical repertory companies. They're both less than two hour's drive from Toronto. The Stratford Festival, a jog off Highway 401 en route to Windsor and Detroit, is the continent's leading Shakespearean interpreter. Since its inaugural season in 1953, when Alec Guinness kicked things off in the role of Richard III, Stratford has presented an expanding program of Shakespeare and other giants of the theatre, from the Greeks to Tennessee Williams. The Shaw Festival, off the Q.E.W. in Niagara-on-the-Lake and close to Buffalo, was founded in 1962. It specializes in the work of Bernard Shaw, with nods toward other modernist visionaries, from Henrik Ibsen to Luigi Pirandello, and has

CHAPLIN AT THE SHAW FESTIVAL

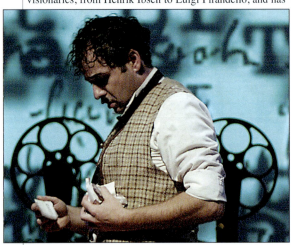

THEATRE AND DANCE

THE NATIONAL BALLET'S *NUTCRACKER*

recently begun staging newer plays as well. Both festivals balance their emphasis on the dramatic classics with lighter fare, including musicals.

DANCE

Harbourfront is a hive of dance activity, much of it on the cutting edge, with the Premiere Dance Theatre serving as host to both visiting and resident productions. Among the Canadian companies to watch for are the Danny Grossman Dance Company, Kaeja d'Dance and Toronto Dance Theatre. DanceWorks presents some fine independent companies during the winter season, while the 8:08 series offers dance works in progress.

Toronto is also home to several talented dance troupes that reflect Toronto's diverse cultural mix. Among the first-rate performers and choreographers working in town are Menaka Thakkar, Rina Singha, Nova Bhattacharya, Vivine Scarlett and Patrick Parson. Dance audiences eagerly await a number of summertime events, including the outdoor Dusk Dances, held in local parks, and fFIDA, the Fringe Festival of Independent Dance Artists.

NATIONAL BALLET SCHOOL

For classical dance, you can't do better than the world-renowned National Ballet of Canada, which in 2006 moves – along with the Canadian Opera Company (see the Symphony, Classical Music and Opera section of *Colourguide Toronto*) – to its new performing home, at the downtown Four Seasons Centre. Traditionalist in orientation but also with a history of creating new and more avant-garde pieces, the company has produced several leading lights of the international dance scene since it was founded in 1951, including such graceful luminaries as Karen Kain, currently the National Ballet's artistic director. Its annual production of *The Nutcracker* is a seasonal favourite.

SYMPHONY, CHAMBER MUSIC AND OPERA

JON KAPLAN

TAFELMUSIK BAROQUE ORCHESTRA

ROY THOMSON REVAMPED

Toronto classical music groups score big with their audiences, since concertgoers can hear anything from A (Tomaso Albinoni) to Z (Alexander Zemlinsky) — including pieces by Bach, Mozart, Schubert and Tchaikovsky. With dozens of companies large and small in town, music buffs can choose among several events nearly every night of the year.

ORCHESTRA

The big kid on the block is the Toronto Symphony Orchestra, which has toured the world. Its home base, in one of Toronto's theatre districts, is Roy Thomson Hall, which resembles nothing so much as a glass-faced volcanic dome. Renovated in 2002, the venue now boasts superior acoustics for all sorts of performances. The symphony's extensive series of concerts begins in September and runs through June, featuring the standard repertoire as well as pieces by lesser-known composers such as Adams, Ligeti and Pärt. The company — which has been led by such luminaries as Seiji Ozawa, Andrew Davis and Jukka-Pekka Saraste and is now headed by

Symphony, Chamber Music and Opera

ROY THOMPSON HALL EXTERIOR

personable music director Peter Oundjian — also prides itself on regularly programming world-première commissions by Canadian composers, including Brian Cherney's *La Princesse lointaine* and Jacques Hétu's *Variations concertantes*. World-renowned soloists such as clarinetist Sabine Meyer, pianists Evgeny Kissin and Emanuel Ax and cellist Yo-Yo Ma are regular guest performers. The Toronto Symphony also offers concerts at the George Weston Recital Hall, located uptown in the Toronto Centre for the Arts; several other groups listed below also perform in the sonically fine hall.

One of the little joys provided by the TSO is its pre-show Evening Overture series, which precedes several

▲ Toronto's Top Attractions

CEILING IN ROY THOMPSON HALL

concerts. Ticket-holders for the series have a chance to listen to musicians discuss the upcoming concert or hear chamber music by composers whose symphonic works will be played later. It's an instructive introduction to the music as well as a fascinating way to compare how artists create on both a small and a large scale.

The TSO also holds a number of special events during the season, featuring performances of Handel's perennial Christmas favourite *Messiah*, solo shows by such guest artists as violinist Itzhak Perlman and pianist Lang Lang, a series of pops concerts for the family and several concerts aimed at youngsters from five to twelve years old.

Another classical group with an international reputation is Tafelmusik, a baroque orchestra led by concert master and first violinist Jeanne Lamon. Playing on period instruments, the group offers a season of music that focuses on the works of Vivaldi, Handel, Bach, Mozart and Purcell. No scratchy, out-of-tune academic recreations here — Tafelmusik plays with a warmth and a skill that sweeps listeners along. Performing in the acoustically superb Trinity-St. Paul's Church, the orchestra offers thematic programs (an evening in Venice, for instance, featuring music by Cavalli, Gabrieli and Vivaldi) or full-scale choral works (Bach's *Mass in B Minor* or its annual *Messiah*, including a singalong performance with its own chamber choir led by Ivars Taurins as Mr. Handel himself).

For modern classical sounds, check out Alex Pauk's Esprit Orchestra, devoted exclusively to contemporary music.

TORONTO MENDELSSOHN CHOIR

CHOIRS

The most venerable of local singing groups is the Toronto Mendelssohn Choir, founded in 1894 and numbering over

Symphony, Chamber Music and Opera

Tafelmusik Chamber Choir

150 singers. Led by Noel Edison, the group performs frequently with orchestras around the country and also offers its own concert series, ranging from carol works and the inevitable *Messiah* at Christmastime to pieces by Bach, Mendelssohn and Stravinsky. Hearing the full-voiced choir in the Hallelujah Chorus makes for a stirring evening. The group has its junior associates, the Toronto Mendelssohn Youth Choir, which provides a fine training and performance opportunity for young singers.

Also worth checking out are concerts by the Amadeus Choir, the Elmer Iseler Singers, the Jubilate Singers, the Tallis Choir and the Canadian Childrens' Opera Chorus, all of which have been performing for more than two decades, and the newer Orpheus Choir, which focuses on some of the more unusual choral repertoire.

Chamber Ensembles and Recitals

Toronto has dozens of smaller groups that make beautiful music throughout the year. The Aradia Ensemble under Kevin Mallon began as a baroque group but has since branched out in its repertoire. The Toronto Consort, led by David Fallis, offers an unusual series of medieval and Renaissance music. The group has performed such rarities as Monteverdi's *The Coronation of Poppea* and an evening devoted to the love story of Tristan and Isolde. Music Toronto mounts a chamber-music series devoted largely to recitals by string quartets and pianists, with the occasional vocalist included as well. The Aldeburgh Connection, run by Stephen Ralls and Bruce Ubukata, highlights Canadian singers in performances that range from Schumann and Schubert — there's an annual Schubertiad evening — to Britten and Grieg. The Off Centre Music series, founded by Inna Perkis and Boris Zarankin, recreates a nineteenth-century musical salon evening, complete with soloists and the occasional bit of poetry. The Amici Chamber Ensemble offers soloists and small ensembles in programs that cover music from the classical period to the twentieth century. New Music Concerts is Canada's oldest presenter of contemporary music.

Several venues offer their own classical music performances, usually as one-time events. Roy Thomson Hall has brought in Amsterdam's Royal Concertgebouw Orchestra, violinist Midori and pianist Evgeny Kissin and sponsors an international vocal series with such guests as

baritone Bryn Terfel, soprano Renee Fleming and mezzo Cecilia Bartoli. The Glenn Gould Studio, a recital and recording hall that's part of the Canadian Broadcasting Corporation, is home to chamber music and vocal recitals by performers such as Canadian pianist Angela Hewitt and tenor Michael Schade.

OPERA

The two main players here are the Canadian Opera Company and Opera Atelier, each with its loyal followers. The COC stages six English-subtitled productions a year, everything from the standard Puccini, Verdi and Rossini to more exotic works by Janacek, Britten and Monteverdi. In September, 2006, the company exits from the Hummingbird Centre, where it's performed for decades, and takes up residence in the new Four Seasons Centre, at the downtown intersection of Queen and University. It will share the space with the National Ballet of Canada (see the Theatre and Dance section of *Colourguide Toronto*). The company's new space is a 2,000-seat theatre with a flexible orchestra pit, allowing the COC to present everything from the chamber works of Handel and Mozart to the large works of the nineteenth and twentieth centuries, pieces by Richard Strauss and Richard Wagner. Speaking of Wagner, the company began presenting segments of his mammoth *Ring*

OPERA ATELIER

Symphony, Chamber Music and Opera

CANADIAN OPERA COMPANY'S PRODUCTION OF WAGNERS *RING CYCLE* OPERA, *DIE WALKÜRE*

Cycle several years ago and opens the new opera house with four performances of the entire cycle, nearly 20 hours of opera-making. General director Richard Bradshaw has a canny way of giving even well-known pieces a new twist, such as a staging of Wagner's *The Flying Dutchman* that draws on German expressionist films of the twenties. He also has a keen eye for fast-rising European singers, often providing them with a North American debut, and he regularly draws on artists from other disciplines — stage directors Robert Lepage and Robin Phillips, film directors Atom Egoyan and Francois Girard — to guide productions. Bradshaw, who conducts half of the season's presentations, also commissions new Canadian operas, such as *The Golden Ass*, with music by Randolph Peters and a libretto by celebrated Canadian author Robertson Davies.

Opera Atelier, founded by Marshall Pynkoski and Jeannette Zingg, has travelled the world with its presentations, many from the baroque period. Beautifully costumed and drawing on dance as much as on singing, works such as Purcell's *Dido and Aeneas* and Rameau's *Pygmalion* are a delight to the eye and the ear. In recent years, the company has included compositions by Mozart, Lully and Gluck.

You'll find lusher and lighter vocal fare in the presentations of the Toronto Operetta Theatre, which draws on the works of Gilbert and Sullivan and Johann Strauss and also offers rare North American productions of Spanish zarzuelas. Its sister company, Opera in Concert, presents just what its title suggests; the piano-accompanied productions are usually little-known or infrequently staged works featuring up-and-coming Canadian singers.

Current classical music performances are listed in the Thursday What's On section of the *Toronto Star* and in *NOW* Magazine. The most complete information is in the monthly publication *WholeNote*. Its articles cover everything from choral music and jazz to opera and new music, while the extensive calendar section includes everything from a solo flute concert in a small church to an orchestral gala at Roy Thomson Hall.

GLENN GOULD

JOHN MILLER

GLENN GOULD AT THE PIANO

Glenn Gould is this city's most famous citizen — a fact that will surely puzzle Torontonians and likely lead to an argument if you say it. But remind your friends that more books are written in more languages about Mr. Gould than about any other Canadian. Tell them that interest in his unique (some would say eccentric) life and artistry grows stronger year after year around the globe. If you doubt this, check with The Glenn Gould Foundation whose website, www.glenngould.ca, is a great place to prepare yourself for your G.G. excursion around the city; their phone number is 416 962-6200.

You might also consider that Gould's music is not just of interest to humans. Extraterrestrials have a chance to hear Gould in a performance of Bach's *The Well-Tempered Clavier* (book 2), *Prelude* and *Fugue in C. No. 1* on board NASA's two Voyager craft launched in 1989 and aimed well beyond our own solar system. Only after 40,000 years have passed will the golden-plated copper discs with the music of Gould, plus 189 other sounds of our earth, approach any other planetary systems!

But you are in an earthly dimension in Toronto, the city which Gould loved above all others, so your tour must either begin or end at the corner of Front Street West and John Street, where you almost meet the man himself and can have your picture taken on his sidewalk bench. This life-sized, bronze sculpture by Ontario artist Ruth Abernethy recreates a famous photo snapped just north of the city by Gould's favourite photographer, Don Hunstein.

The sculpture, unveiled during an international Gould festival in 1999, is a gift to the people of Canada from Toronto philanthropist Clarice Chalmers to honour her husband Wallace Gordon Chalmers, a member of this city's distinguished family of cultural donors.

Nearby is the Canadian Broadcasting Centre's Glenn

Gould Studio, so named because it is a state-of-the-art broadcast facility and not just a performance venue. Gould was strongly against live performances, but his estate consented to sharing his name with this CBC facility because sound emanates from here to Canada and the world via broadcasting, which Gould loved.

YO-YO MA AND FRIENDS WITH GOULD STATUE AT THE CBC

Check out the photographs and album covers in the Studio lobby and take a moment to see his boyhood instrument, the Chickering piano against whose sensitivity the pianist was said to measure every other instrument he owned or played. Here also are the photographs of the Laureates of the Glenn Gould Prize, awarded triennially to renowned figures whose musical genius, like Gould's, has been disseminated through communication technologies.

Another famous Gould piano — the Yamaha instrument on which he recorded his 1981 interpretation of the Goldberg Variations, a year before his death — is on display in the lobby of Roy Thomson Hall. Occasionally, visiting amateur pianists are allowed to play this keyboard.

Glenn Gould was buried in Mount Pleasant Cemetery in October 1982. To find the site it is best to stop by the office in the eastern section of the cemetery, off Mount Pleasant Boulevard. Gould's grave, with its simple but famous marker carved with the opening bars of the Goldbergs, is at Section 38, Plot 1050, Row 1088. Close by are a large stone marker unveiled during another Gould gathering and an Alaskan Sitka spruce tree planted by Glenn's father, Herbert, in 1992. This tree is the only one of its species in the entire cemetery; what makes it appropriate to mark the Gould family plot is that its wood is used to make the sounding boards of pianos.

You might also want to see the two buildings which Glenn Gould called home — 32 Southwood Drive, his boyhood residence in the Beaches, and 110 St. Clair Avenue West, the apartment building he lived in as an adult. Both dwellings have historical plaques on their front lawns saying that Glenn Gould lived there.

Toronto also has Glenn Gould Park on the northwest corner of Avenue Road and St. Clair, not far from the apartment building and the nearby Fran's Restaurant, where the pianist ate many of his late-night meals and delighted in rice pudding with raisins.

Finally, if you want Glenn Gould books or records, you should visit L'Atelier Grigorian, a record store on Yorkville Avenue just west of Bay Street which Gould devotees regard as the world headquarters of Gould memorabilia. The amazing Gould specialists on staff ship packages around the globe and take payment in Canadian dollars — two points which international collectors and travellers especially appreciate.

NIGHTLIFE

DENISE BALKISSOON

For those seeking after-dark entertainment, Toronto is a town with much to offer, from well-shaken martinis to sweaty dance floors to local guitar pickers strumming their stuff. Queen West and Little Italy remain the centres of nightlife action, but other neighbourhoods have much to offer, too.

QUEEN WEST
This is Toronto's cutting edge — though admittedly that edge was sliced twenty years ago. Back in the 1980s, artists and musicians gathered at clubs like the Rivoli, the Horseshoe Tavern, and the Cameron House, all of which are still great places to grab a pint and discuss the latest novel over a soundtrack of local bands. The Rex is a casual spot to hear great jazz from local and visiting players. The Bovine Sex Club has iron pipes and creepy dolls bolted to the ceiling and punk rock blaring from the speakers. The Queenshead is a new pub made to look old, where hipsters play Scrabble on Wednesdays and pack the tiny dance floor on weekends. Around the corner on Bathurst Street is the Paddock, where some of Toronto's tastiest drinks are mixed with faultless precision. The Ultra Supper Club is a sign of how the strip has changed. For two decades, the building housed the Bamboo, ground zero for the city's reggae heads, but it was gutted a few years ago and re-emerged as a sparkling space for pretty people, where the lounge sounds are inoffensive and bottle service denotes a VIP.

Still, the Queen has a lot of grunge left in her. Just to the west lies Toronto's most happening 'hood, bubbling with new art galleries, shops, and, of course, nightspots. Czehoski is a classy three-floor resto-bar with soaring ceilings, cheeky art, and warm wooden tables and chairs; there are two menus, one for impressing a date, the other

NIGHTLIFE

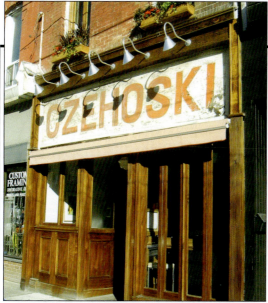

for grabbing a snack with friends. At the intersection with Ossington, there's Sweaty Betty's, a tiny watering hole displaying works from local artists on the walls. Next stop is the Social: housed at 1100 Queen Street West alongside the avant-garde Spin Gallery and vintage haven 69, it's a neon-lit paradise for the painfully cool; Friday night classic-rock parties draw a nattily scruffy crowd. A bit down from there is the Gladstone Hotel, its old bones beautifully restored. Here, upcoming local artists are expressing themselves by choosing a room to decorate as they see fit, and the intimate downstairs bar holds a popular weekly karaoke night. But gathering the biggest buzz on Queen is still the Drake Hotel. Once a falling-down wreck, it reopened in 2004 after a massive overhaul and now sports an intimate concert venue, a sexy dining-cum-drinking salon, and a sprawling rooftop patio. Across the street is the Beaconsfield, itself reborn out of the shell of an old bank

THE SOCIAL

▲ Toronto's Top Attractions

TORONTO SKYLINE AT NIGHT

as a dramatic, black-walled lounge with chandeliers and tasty comfort food. Finally, further west there's Queen from Dufferin Street to Roncesvalles Avenue, where you can find Not My Dog and the Wroxeter. Both are new: the first is a tiny space with a pub vibe, the second features live jazz and graffiti-inspired canvasses. Also in this area is Stone's Place, home to Rolling Stones paraphernalia and weekend dance floor revelry, as well as the Cadillac Lounge, where autos adorn the walls and live music is the norm. The Rhino is a good place to watch the game, and Mitzi's Sister beckons ladies who love ladies and anyone looking to enjoy an order of nachos with friends.

COLLEGE STREET

A more refined experience can be found in Little Italy, otherwise known as College Street between Ossington Avenue and Bathurst Street. Places here tend to be of the dinner-and-cocktails variety, attracting a somewhat older crowd that still dresses to impress. Bar Italia is the grandparent of the strip, still serving Italianate fare downstairs and cocktails to a good-looking thirty-something bunch upstairs. The romance-minded might try sultry Souz Dal, a wee place with dim lighting, a sweet back patio, and an extensive list of libations; its sister, Sutra, offers champagne based cocktails and a slim tropical-wannabe patio, complete with sand and umbrellas in the drinks. Tempo is another good noshing and canoodling choice: here, enjoy inventive sushi while sipping sake cocktails in a very modern environment.

For dancing, there are again many choices. The Revival has soaring ceilings and flickering candles; rotating DJs and bands provide the music. Across the street is the Mod Club Theatre, where pop-art posters gaze down on revellers getting busy to Brit hits on Friday nights (the space has also hosted concerts by everyone from Dizzee Rascal to the Fiery Furnaces). The basement dance floor at Alto Basso is packed with bodies on the weekends, but Shallow Groove, like its regulars, has been doing the same old thing for far too long. King of the College strip is Andy Poolhall, which hosts tuned-in DJs and a more raucous scene: Tuesday night Footwork parties are for hip-hop heads, while the monthly Savour draws girls who like girls who like to dance to electro.

KENSINGTON MARKET

College Street is just steps away from Kensington Market, another Toronto neighbourhood with charm. During

the day, it swarms with the dreadlocked, tattooed, and pierced, plus everyone else who likes to buy organic produce from local vendors. Supermarket, which opened in winter 2004, serves Japanese izakaya snacks at the dinner hour before making way for DJs and bands come nighttime. Programming here tends to be of the groovy, percussive, Afrobeat variety. Down the street is The Embassy, which is a nice spot for an evening of chat and creative cocktails such as the "Leftyon the Rocks," a delectable cassis and bison-grass vodka concoction. Kensington is known for dive bars that mysteriously appear and disappear with zero notice: on the grungy side, there's basement-spot Neutral, bizarre Greek-Jamaican hybrid Thymeless, or the Boat, done up in a trippy nautical theme.

THE ANNEX

Bloor Street West from St. George Street to Bathurst Street is largely the haunt of University of Toronto students — those over twenty-five may feel ancient amidst this crowd. The Madison is a multi-floored sports bar with a huge patio and a frat-house vibe; tucked in a back alley, the rather grungy Green Room shelters those who would rather discuss philosophy than last night's game. Another popular pub is the Victory Café, which has open-mic poetry nights from time to time. Home to all ages is Lee's Palace, one of the best live music clubs in the city. Upstairs is the Dance Cave, which plays mostly retro and Brit pop on the weekends.

RICHMOND AND ADELAIDE

This is the area people call "the club district," a mecca for those whose Saturday night involves skimpy outfits and the crush of hundreds of bodies. Openings and closings are rapid on this strip, as the appetite for the new and the shiny among this crowd is ravenous. Spots that have stayed open long enough to be reliable are: System Soundbar, two rooms that host international DJs from all

▲ Top Attractions

DANCING AT THIS IS LONDON

genres of beat-happy music; Money, which boasts a glass dance floor; the Joker, which plays everything from adult contemporary to brand new thug sounds depending on the night; Fez Batik, which purports to attract a more Bohemian following; and This is London, which keeps out the riff-raff with a high cover charge and a strict dress code. A new contender is Republik, with 14,000 square feet of space-age lighting and eye-candy bar staff.

Off the Richmond Street strip, but offering a similar vibe are two very large clubs that keep on drawing capacity crowds. The Docks features a pool, bungee jumping, and a massive lakeside patio, while Guvernment is a concrete-floored three-room complex with funhouse accents. The bass throbs well into the morning at both.

CHURCH STREET

This area is known as Boystown, the reason for which is immediately obvious. For travellers heading to Toronto for Gay Pride week, this will be the centre of it all. Fans of *Queer As Folk* will recognize Woody's as, well, Woody's, but the stalwart dance club and meat market was a staple on the strip long before Toronto pretended to be Pittsburgh. Another infamous spot here is the Barn, known for weekend underwear parties that see revellers getting down in tighty whities. Younger bodies tend to work it at Five, Lüb and Fly. Karaoke fans can scream out all their favourite songs on Tuesdays and Thursdays at Crews and Tango; lesbians take over the upstairs dance floor on Friday nights. Those who would rather talk than grind prefer Byzantium, which is known for its fine dinners and cocktails; Babylon, where the length of the drink list borders on excessive; and Wish, over on Yonge Street, a snug and pretty space with white walls, candles on dark wood tables and silver accents—the cocktails here are delicious. For those seeking pure camp, there's Zelda's, where zebra prints and blue eyeshadow never went out of style.

DUNDAS STREET WEST

If Queen and College seem saturated with roaming hedonists, this little junction just might be the ticket. One of the city's emerging neighbourhoods, Dundas Street west of Bathurst is popping with new boutiques and nightspots. One of the first to venture out here was the Chelsea Room, a wee space with dim lighting and long banquettes. The bartenders enjoy creating bizarre but tasty drinks incorporating rare international liquors and using everything from sour key candies to Cheez Whiz as

NIGHTLIFE

garnishes. Across the street is Cocktail Molotov. Underlit in gaseous green, it's a convivial place to gather with a group to sip bottles of beer as the conversation gets louder and louder. Down the street, the Communist's Daughter is a tiny place (look hard, it's on the south side with a chalkboard for a sign) that's immediately endearing. On Saturday afternoons, there's often a jazz trio in the window and, in between mixing drinks, the bartender joins them with a trumpet or his voice. Two new spots are the Press Club, heralded by the vintage typewriter in the window, and Magpie, set to open in September, serving only local brews.

If the above is not enough, there are many destination drinking spots worth searching out. Yorkville draws a fancy-pants crowd — the all-white Lobby is a favourite at film festival time. Nearby, the Roof bar at the Park Hyatt is long beloved for providing both a perfect gin martini and a perfect view of the city. Similar grown-up spots can be found along King Street West. Here, old brick banks and warehouses have been renovated into a number of gorgeous resto-bars, ideal for nibbling at small dishes while enjoying heady cocktails; good choices are the massive patio at Brassaii or the nouveau sushi and chandeliers at Blowfish. At Broadview and Danforth is Allen's, where there are eighty-five bottled beers to enjoy with arguably Toronto's best hamburger, made daily from ground sirloin beef. East of here lies Greektown, which draws a crowd ready to eat, drink and be very merry. At the very eastern end of the strip is The Only, a hidden gem of a local pub with a huge beer fridge, chilled-out regulars, kindly-surly bar staff, and good music, from dub reggae to the Doors, on the stereo.

After a day at the AGO, L'Idiot du Village pub is a decent place to rest one's feet with a pint alongside bizarrely coiffed students from the nearby Ontario College of Art and Design. Fans of Art Deco will want to find the Laurentian Room; though hidden on a Cabbagetown side street, its refurbished interior is a gorgeous setting for a bistro dinner or a glass of wine. The Library Bar at the Royal York hotel is a draw for scotch lovers, who might want to start here before heading to the Montreal Bistro for a night of dinner and live jazz.

Local weeklies *eye* and *NOW* are found free all around the city, and are worth skimming to find out what's happening with a particular type of music or scene; www.martiniboys.com is a good web site to find out the very newest place to be, while www.tribe.ca is a worthwhile source if house music is tonight's must-hear.

THE ROOF AT THE PARK HYATT

DINING

CHRISTINE BOOCOCK

FINE DINING AT SCARAMOUCHE

Toronto was once a city of steakhouses, where pasta was considered ethnic and culinary diversity meant drowning otherwise bland dishes in torrents of heavy sauce. What started out as a mecca for meat lovers has become a city known for its authentic, international cuisine, its single-moniker celebrity chefs, and its focus on locally sourced, top quality ingredients and recipes.

BUDGET BITES

Toronto may be Canada's financial centre, but it is also a city of 2.5 million people looking to eat well without going broke. For the budget conscious, then, breakfast begins with hot-from-the-oven croissants and French pastries at Bonjour Brioche, or with eggs and Canadian bacon at one of the city's popular diners. Fran's Restaurant, a twenty-four-hour Toronto institution since the 1940s, and Aunties & Uncles, with its sunlit patio, are two destinations where line-ups confirm solid popularity with the locals. Tasty homemade brunches and greasy-spoon indulgences served cheaply and efficiently have translated into scores of satisfied customers. Located in BCE place, in the heart of the financial district, the sprawling, market-styled Richtree Market Restaurant is good for eating, drinking or relaxing at any time of day. Freshly made muffins, muesli and waffles tempt early-morning patrons while later in the day, themed cooking stations dole out everything from oven-baked pizzas and charbroiled steaks to hand-rolled sushi and crisped rosti potatoes with sour cream.

DINING

SCARAMOUCHE

On Front Street, a short walk from BCE Place, the St. Lawrence Market is a paradise of fresh ingredients and fuss-free meals. Fruits and vegetables, local cheeses and St. Urbain bagels make for easy, spur-of-the-moment picnics, while barbecued chicken at Churrasco of St. Lawrence or substantial veal and eggplant sandwiches at Mustacio's are ready for those wanting lunch with no assembly required.

Kensington Market is another of the city's most famous locations, known for its hippyish vibe, vintage clothing stores and authentically spiced (and priced), ethnic food. Strolling among the many boutiques and vendors, shoppers can stop in at Perola's Supermarket for Hispanic grocery staples and handmade pupusas. A Chilean spot with an appropriate name, Jumbo Empanadas specializes in expertly spiced meat or vegetarian turnovers with or without fiery salsa. Supermarket, where one can eat as much as one likes, is another of the area's hidden gems, offering oriental-inspired tapas. Drink-friendly snacks range from sweet potato chips spiced with chipotle to toothsome shrimp dumplings and addictive fried calamari.

MID-PRICED MUNCHIES

Toronto is one of the world's most multicultural cities and its large Asian population means a true taste of the Orient is never far away. Asian Legend, a stylish, modern space, offers reasonably priced, Northern Chinese dishes to a discerning clientele. Locals rave about the authentic preparations, which avoid the gluey sweetness so common in Chinese food cooked in North America. For the view of Lake Ontario as well as for the food, Pearl Harbourfront Chinese Cuisine is another worthwhile spot. Elegant presentations of familiar dishes such as fried rice mounded into a pineapple shell, demonstrate the kitchen's attention to detail and artistry. Exotic flavours and aromatic sauces, on the other hand, show that Pearl Harbourfront is also in the business of delivering delectable food.

Monsoon, another of Toronto's well-known Asian restaurants, is popular both for its deliberate departure from traditional recipes and for its fusion cuisine. Wood panelling, plush banquettes and artful lighting create an elegant atmosphere that is heightened by the kitchen's inventive cooking. Rare ingredients and the singular creations offered may translate into steeper prices, but

JAMIE KENNEDY WINE BAR

RACK OF LAMB AT CANOE

Monsoon's patrons seem happy to pay for the experience. New Generation Sushi, on Bloor Street West, is one of an abundant crop of sushi joints in the city. Here, low prices are merely a bonus to an extensive menu and generous portions made with the freshest ingredients. All this and a handful of friendly, attentive waiters make it easy to see what distinguishes New Generation from its competitors. Thai food is another Toronto favourite and Green Mango, a local chain, offers some of the best curries, noodles and sticky rice around. Established in 1980, Green Mango now has four locations, each one boasting a serene, well-appointed interior and a menu of Thailand's best-known cuisine. A meal of fragrant lemongrass soup and stimulating curried mussels can be topped off with jackfruit fritters, a less ubiquitous treat than common coconut rice.

But Toronto isn't only about Asian. The city also boasts authenticity when it comes to many other types of cuisine. Dipamo's offers slow-smoked, slow-cooked Southern food that demands a ferocious appetite, a stack of napkins and fearlessness in the face of barbecue sauce–smothered fare. Pulled pork, brisket, ribs and cornbread are just some of the menu items sure to inspire thoughts of warmer climes and southern drawls. A taste of European excellence is also easy to find in Toronto. The restaurant group known as Oliver Bonacini forms the creative and culinary team behind some of the city's most popular dining spots. One of their most successful ventures is Biff's, a Front Street bistro that looks as though it has been plucked from the centre of Paris. Impeccably decked-out waiters serve such bistro favourites as steak tartare and boudin blanc in a room whose warm yellow walls are plastered with French posters. One of the city's best cheeseboards, with European as well as star Canadian offerings, solidifies Biff's Parisian feel. Uptown, on Avenue Road, Trattoria Sotto Sotto is a romantic Italian hideaway known for its hearty dishes and its popularity with visiting celebrities. Luckily, famous faces haven't translated into exorbitant prices for such homey Italian comforts as Risotto Amalfi, bursting with fresh seafood and Bolognese Mamma Laura, where pasta arrives under a meat sauce infused with the kind of old-world flavour only a true Italian "mamma" can provide.

While old-world influences are widespread, new-world flavours are perhaps one of Toronto's specialties. The city may not have easily definable local

dishes, but a cuisine based on the region's abundant produce meshed with techniques and traditions from other cultures, has created a uniquely Canadian style of eating. Jamie Kennedy is one of Toronto's, if not Canada's, most renowned chefs, and with the Jamie Kennedy Wine Bar, he has made his carefully crafted recipes available to a much wider audience. The wine bar's menu of appetizer-sized selections, each with suggested wine pairings, changes to reflect the seasonal availability of local ingredients, as well as the chef's mood. Ever present, however, is one of Kennedy's popular versions of poutine, a Quebec fast-food favourite that consists of french fries doused in gravy and capped off with cheddar cheese curds. Here, the poutine is slightly more elegant thanks to the addition of lamb or foie gras, much tastier due to slow-simmered jus and infinitely more addictive because of Kennedy's legendary Yukon potato frites.

STEEP SUPPERS

Epicures eager to try some of the world's top restaurants might start at the fifty-fourth floor of the financial district's Toronto Dominion Bank Tower. Here one finds Canoe, a restaurant where regional cuisine and Canadian heritage are both brought to centre stage. Lunch hours find it teeming with executives, while the night-time view appeals to romantics eager to sample the best of Canada's bounty. Among other dishes on the inventive menu, caribou from Nunavut, pickerel from Pine Falls, Manitoba, and a dish that incorporates "Newfie Screech," all stand as fitting tributes to the true north. Mark McEwan's North 44°, named after the city's latitude, also relies heavily on Canadian ingredients, but imbues them with continental touches. Flawless service, the restaurant's neutral-hued radiance and the kitchen's stunningly presented offerings, create a silken atmosphere worthy of the hefty price tag. Banana cream pie sounds banal but becomes beguiling in

PERIGEE INTERIOR

▲ TORONTO'S TOP ATTRACTIONS

CHIADO INTERIOR

the hands of the gifted culinary team. Along with warm chocolate torte and caramelized pear mille feuille, the kitchen is known to offer some of the city's best desserts.

Over the last decade, Avalon has quietly built a reputation based on its commitment to freshness, menus that are written daily and for its creativity. Obscure ingredients are used in alluringly outlandish ways. Chef Chris McDonald's Friday night "Adventure Menu" combines a series of dishes, each one based on a different cooking technique. Avalon's elegantly minimalist decor is the perfect backdrop for the inspired, eclectic and ultimately transcendent food. At the other end of the dramatic spectrum, in the heart of Toronto's historic Distillery District, ex-Avalon sous-chef Pat Riley heads Perigee, a thirty-five-seat theatrical space where diners circle a sunken, open kitchen. Perigee's menus are based on the Japanese dining concept "omikase," or "trust me," and diners here are thrilled to put their fate in the kitchen's capable hands. From churning butter and curing meats in-house, Perigee's culinary team pays startling attention to detail. Here, French techniques are applied to Mediterranean ingredients in the noble pursuit of novel dishes like fennel bavarois and crème brûlée topped with sweet glazed squash.

Tradition rather than novelty is the raison-d'être of Marc Thuet's newest venture, Thuet Cuisine. Born in Alsace, France, and introduced to Toronto's culinary scene at Centro Grill and Wine Bar, this chef's reputation made Thuet Cuisine instantly intriguing. From the medallion of pork tenderloin accompanied by a pig's trotter, ragout of potato and autumn vegetables, to the monkfish pot-au-feu and the Alsatian-style Riesling sauerkraut, Thuet's menu is made up of hearty offerings that pay delicious tribute to his roots. Chiado is another Toronto restaurant rooted in tradition and dedicated to preserving the flavours of the homeland. Here, high-end Portuguese takes the form of dishes like slowly roasted salted cod and roasted beef tenderloin finished in old Tawny Port wine sauce. A pioneer that introduced Toronto to the riches of Portuguese cuisine, Chiado's fame is based on its expert treatment of pure ingredients in order to bring out the deepest of flavours. Chiado's wine list also appeals, offering over 300 labels, including some of Portugal's best and rarest tipples. The newly renamed Centro Restaurant and Lounge, Thuet's old home, can also thank a unique approach to dining for its continued success. Suede banquettes, the glow of candlelight and soaring ceilings evoke a luxurious feel, while dishes like miso-glazed foie gras with gooseberry chutney and spiced venison rack in port and balsamic sauce with fresh berries showcase the kitchen's distinctively indulgent approach to cooking.

SCARAMOUCHE

Many of Toronto's hotels are known not only for their architecture and history, but also for the extraordinary restaurants they house. Truffles at the Four Seasons in Yorkville, Hemispheres and Lai Wah Heen at the Metropolitan, and Epic at the venerable Royal York are known for their regal rooms, their ambitious menus and their ability to make diners feel pampered. Fine French cuisine at Truffles translates into a signature dish of spaghettini with Perigord Black Gold and truffle sauce. At Hemispheres, tuna sashimi appears alongside pot-au-feu on a menu that travels the world. Also at the Metropolitan, Lai Wah Heen brings all the traditions of superior Chinese cooking to the heart of Toronto. Reputed to serve Toronto's best dim sum, Lai Wah Heen also prepares dishes from a lengthy à la carte menu imbued with the essence of Hong Kong. At Epic, a stylishly modern yet comfortable room becomes the perfect setting for afternoon tea, lounging over martinis or settling into a dinner of classic fare accentuated with French touches.

Tasting menus have become one of the restaurant world's most enjoyable methods of making high-priced dining truly worthwhile. Sitting down to a procession of exquisitely executed mini-portions not only prolongs an evening's entertainment, but showcases a chef's talents in a way a three-course meal never can. At Susur, internationally known über-chef Susur Lee invites guests to sample a seven-course menu that changes daily. Peppered with oriental influences, the menu might include such astonishing assemblies as soy-marinated rock bass served with lily bulb purée and squid ink tuille, drizzled in dashi and black truffle vinaigrette.

Scaramouche, Splendido, and Rain are other Toronto

CHEFS IN THE KITCHEN OF SPLENDIDO

hot spots where tempting tasting menus vie with sumptuous à la carte offerings. There are many reasons why *Gourmet* magazine has twice chosen veteran Scaramouche as "Toronto's Top Restaurant," and a tasting menu prepared by Executive chef Keith Froggett is just one. With twenty-four hours' notice, Froggett prepares seven-course progressions of carefully connected dishes. The resulting menus are known as much for the simplicity of their design as for the depth of flavour Froggett coaxes out of seemingly ordinary ingredients. Splendido's tasting menu tends, like so many others, to follow the seasonal route; one summer's carte inspired by the freshness of farmer's markets. But Splendido has also toyed around with the idea of pure decadence, as last year's Moet & Chandon tasting menu suggests. At Splendido, which often draws top reviews from restaurant critics, food becomes nourishment, entertainment and the stuff memories are made of. A slight departure from the norm, Rain has a modern, edgy design where waterfalls, bamboo and frosted glass play important roles in setting the scene. Owned by Guy and Michael Rubino, the brothers behind Luce, another local favourite, Rain's menu dips into oriental territory but emerges with only the most innovative of recipes.

This brings us to the end of a whirlwind tour of a city saturated in gastronomy. But to wrap up, one last look at where it all began seems appropriate. Carman's and Barberian's are two of the city's landmark steakhouses, where the menus have never followed fads and dill pickles, garlic bread and more are included with every meal. In the dead of winter, nothing is more appropriate than a sizzling sirloin nuzzling up to a steaming potato heavy with butter and sour cream.

SPLENDIDO

SHOPPING

JOYCE GUNHOUSE AND JUDY CORNISH

Toronto's shopping matches that of any major international city, but what makes it special are the many outlets for Canadian products. Canadians are well known for their clean, well-made designs in everything from children's wear to furniture.

WILLIAM ASHLEY'S

THE EATON CENTRE

The Eaton Centre, located downtown on Yonge Street and running from Queen Street to Dundas, is the most obvious place to shop in Toronto. The largest downtown shopping mall in North America offers a vast array of mid-priced to high-end stores on four levels, making it an easy one-stop shopping area for the entire family. The lowest level features shops with moderately priced clothing, books, music, and kitchenware. Here you will find chains such as HMV, Old Navy, and H&M, as well as some smaller stores and the food courts. The middle level features mid-priced clothing stores like Fairweather, Jacob and Esprit. The upper levels have a number of more expensive clothing and shoe stores for both men and women, including Harry Rosen, Mirabelli, Sephora, Mango and Brown's; jewellery stores like the long-standing Canadian company Birks; and children's clothing and toy stores GapKids and the Disney Store.

BLOOR STREET

BLOOR STREET

Bloor Street, between Yonge and Avenue Road (see also Bloor Street, p. 180), is the heart of Toronto's high-end shopping district. Fashion designers from around the world are represented — international names like Chanel, Versace, Prada, Gucci and Plaza Escada. Holt Renfrew, Canada's most fashionable department store, carries everything from international designers to Canada's own darling, Lida Baday. Baday's attention to detail, fit, and quality has established her as an international and homegrown success. Holt's promotes other Canadian up-and-comers such as Arthur Mendoca, Pink Tartan and Malanrino. While many of the shops on Bloor are expensive, not all price tags are in the thousands. More moderately priced international clothing chains are located here as well, such as Talbot's, Eddie Bauer, Benetton and Club Monaco. For high-quality menswear try Harry Rosen.

Bloor Street boasts top notch beauty and health boutiques such as The Body Shop, MAC cosmetics and the Aveda boutique. This strip is also the place to go for shoes. There is Brown's in Holt Renfrew, as well as Davids and Corbo. Capezio and Nine West offer more mid-range prices. The famous Tiffany and Co. is just one store of many for jewellery, and Ashley's is excellent for fine china and crystal. The Roots flagship store is in a lovely new building beside the Pottery Barn and Williams-Sonoma. If you are not one for shopping, relax and read at Indigo just south of Bloor on Bay Street.

YORKVILLE

Slightly north of Bloor is another exclusive shopping area known as Yorkville. This area offers a mix of expensive restaurants and fashionable shops, featuring clothing, gifts, books and antiques. Here you will find the boutiques of Canadian designers Phillipe Dubuc (at Anti-Hero), Marilyn Brooks, Linda Lundstrom and Nancy Moore for Motion Clothing Co. Other stores include Betsey Johnson and Over the Rainbow (for denim). Delight in the finery and whimsy of The Cashmere Shop, the National Ballet's Paper Things for stationery, the Toy Shop for kids and Muti for hand-painted ceramicware. Nearby Hazelton Lanes provides indoor shopping with several chain stores and many exclusive boutiques. Among its shops are Aquascutum, Hugo Nicholson, Petra Karthaus, TNT and its younger concept store TNT Blu.

CRYSTAL AT ASHLEY'S

Travel north of Hazelton Lanes to discover a clutch of flower shops and antique stores. The little area north of Avenue Road and Davenport (known to Torontonians as "Av-Dav") includes several stores worth visiting.

QUEEN STREET

The lively Queen Street strip between McCaul Street and Spadina Avenue is perfect for the young and hip who don't particularly like malls (see also Queen Street West, p. 150). This strip is home to many trendy restaurants and unique stores selling clothing, shoes, gifts and home furnishings ranging from highbrow to retro cool. Start at Price Roman, the exclusive outlet for a collection of women's clothing. Further west, you will hit the very hip Fluevog Shoe store. John Fluevog's radically innovative shoe designs are an international success. Another highlight is Pam Chorley's Fashion Crimes and, across the street, Misdemeanours, her children's store, inspired by her daughter Jasmine. Here one discovers little fantasies made out of velvet, lace and chiffon in adult and kiddie sizes now located side-by-side.

YORKVILLE

For those willing to go further in young, urban fashion, there is Daily Fraiche by Alex and Maria Michiot, a couple whose design team is based in Paris. Their clothes are innovative, clean-cut and hip with a European flavour. On the other side of the street are two Get Out Side stores, where you will discover some of the funkiest shoes around at affordable prices and also clothing reminiscent of the styles worn by edgy Japanese youth. And check out Groovy for a large selection of runners. Nearby, B2, the younger version of Brown's, carries Prada-esque knock-offs for a fraction of the price. Then there is Caban, which offers hip home furnishings, along with the Gap, Club Monaco and Roots.

WEST QUEEN WEST

If you continue west along Queen, past Spadina, you will encounter a Bohemian neighbourhood of independent shops. Among the tattoo parlors, textile outlets and coffee houses are high-quality second-hand and designer clothing stores. No shortage of amazing furniture and home accessory stores exist here: Red Indian, Morba and Quasi Modo are great for vintage furniture and collectibles, while other stores like Style Garage mix the contemporary with the antique. Be sure to visit Comrags, a boutique carrying the widest available selection from this Canadian clothing collection — everything from bathing suits to winter coats in a whimsical setting. And Annie Thompson offers her very unique fashion designs. Lululemon offers a wonderful selection of workout gear, Nearly Naked for lingerie and Fleurtje for bags and accessories.

THE PAPER PLACE

Toronto's Top Attractions

THE BEACHES, QUEEN STREET

Girl Friday and Fresh Collective help to make the strip complete for unique clothes.

This section of Queen Street is also home to independent music and record stores. New and used CDs and vinyl can be found at such outlets as Rotate This. Songbird and Capsule offer beautiful guitars and other musical instruments. Further along, the Japanese Paper Place carries various types of paper, from origami to large handcrafted pieces for creative souls who want to experiment. Then there is the charming bath and beauty store, Iodine, staffed by its creator, Nurse Julie. Nurse Julie dresses in a red RN uniform and dispenses friendly advice for all your beauty concerns.

THE BEACHES

The Beaches, in Toronto's east end, is also a hot shopping area. Beginning at Woodbine Avenue, the strip of Queen Street running from Woodbine to Neville Park Boulevard has several popular chain stores mixed with children's clothing, toy, book and gift shops. Here you will find Posh for women's clothing, Beadworks for their large selection of beads, Aroma Shoppe for aromatherapy, and Pier 1 for bright and appealing dinnerware, glassware, gifts and linens. This is an excellent area in which the family can spend a day shopping, eating and playing.

ALONG YONGE STREET

Yonge Street from Eglinton Avenue to Lawrence Avenue is another upscale shopping area. Here, once again, are international clothing chains such as the Gap and Club Monaco, as well as Canadian stores such as Kaliyana, Mendocino and the Casual Way. There is also Sporting Life, a large emporium featuring sports equipment, accessories and a wide range of clothing (both active and casual) for men, women and children. This strip also has stores like Future Shop, which sells computers and computer software, La Cache for charming cotton clothing and Restoration Hardware. If you are hungry, the delicious Dufflet Pastries shop is a gastronomic pleasure.

COLLEGE STREET AND KENSINGTON MARKET

College Street, between Markham and Grace, with its little pocket of independent stores, has become a hot spot for Toronto's up-and-comers. Modern clothing can be found at Girl Friday, Mink, Set Me Free, Lilliput Hats, Ewanika and music at Soundscapes. Magnolia and Mercantile are where you'll find gourmet and fine-food items. The young and hip hang out in Toronto's Kensington Market. Tucked in between butcher shops, fish markets, cheese shops, ice

SHOPPING

cream and spice stores are a handful of second-hand boutiques. Many of these carry new clothes from young designers. The best chances for making the ultimate find are Dancing Days and Courage My Love. For high-quality men's clothing at discount prices, Tom's Place can't be beat.

THE DISTILLERY DISTRICT

Toronto's new centre for arts, culture and entertainment is also great for shopping. Several art galleries and retail outlets of some of Toronto's most talented artisans are located in this pedestrian-only area, including Wildhagen, a boutique hosting a variety of unique hats designed by the owner herself, Sheri Wildhagen. The Sandra Ainsley Gallery is another must-see, housing some of Toronto's most beautiful glass sculptures. Shoppers will find a variety of furniture and home decor stores such as FOS and Fluid Living. As far as fashion goes, there are one-of-a-kind boutiques as well as Lileo, which sells an array of upscale-casual clothes, boasting brand names for both men and women such as James Perse, Penguin and Jet.

QUEEN'S QUAY AND FRONT STREET

Queen's Quay and Harbourfront, near Toronto's waterfront, provide an urban oasis that offers great shopping in a park-like setting. In the Queen's Quay terminal building, there are a wide range of specialty shops like Chocolate and Creams, The Canadian Naturalist, First Hand Canadian Crafts and Oh Yes! Toronto. Further west, at the foot of Spadina Avenue, is a permanent antique market and the site of summertime outdoor antique and flea markets. The stretch of Front Street from Jarvis to Yonge is home to many of the city's live theatres, and to a variety of stores as well. High-Tech carries advanced items for the cool and functional kitchen. Europe Bound outfits those who seek the great outdoors. Also on Front is Nicholas Hoare, a large and soothing bookstore, and Timbuktu, a large, colourful craft and clothing store. The St. Lawrence Market, a landmark since 1803, has an excellent farmer's market on Saturdays and an antique market on Sundays. Local craftspeople also sell their goods here.

KEY SHOPPING INFORMATION

Check the listings in this guide for addresses and telephone numbers.

ANTIQUES AND COLLECTIBLES

Stores that sell antiques and collectibles are scattered all over the city. There is a permanent antique market on Queen's Quay near Spadina. Some of the grander stores, such as R.A O'Neil Antiques and Stanley Wagman and Sons, are located in Yorkville. On Yonge near

FRONT STREET

SILK CHIFFON SCARF AND FRAMES FROM THE AGO GIFT SHOP

Furnishings at Urban Mode

Summerhill Avenue, visit the Prince of Serendip and Perkins Antiques. Queen Street East has a pocket of more modest shops between Carlaw Avenue and Jones Avenue. Some other good stores to check out are Zig Zag and Eye Spy. Also try Red Indian and Quasi Modo.

BOOKSTORES

The World's Biggest Bookstore on Edward Street, or Indigo on Yonge north of Eglinton, or on Bay south of Bloor are among the city's biggest bookstores. For smaller stores, try Nicholas Hoare on Front, Pages Books and Magazines on Queen West or This Ain't the Rosedale Library on Church. For children's books, visit Mabel's Fables on Mount Pleasant Road.

CHAIN STORES

Here are some Canadian and international chains that you will find in Toronto: the Gap, GapKids, Banana Republic, Benetton, the Body Shop, the Bay, Club Monaco, Holt Renfrew, Talbots, Williams-Sonoma, the Pottery Barn and H&M.

CANADIAN CLOTHING DESIGNERS

Discover what Canadian fashion has to offer. Look for these labels: Comrags, Lida Baday, Ross Mayer, Wayne Clark, Loucas, Mimi Bizjak, Brian Bailey, Crystal Siemens, Misura, Olena Zylak, Linda Lundstrom, Marilyn Brooks and Motion Clothing Co. You will find them at Finishing Touches, Holt Renfrew, Blue Angel, Sporting Life and Erietta's, as well as in the designers' own boutiques.

CHILDREN'S STORES

Great kids' clothes can be found at Roots, Club Monaco or GapKids. For toys, visit the Toy Shop in Yorkville and Kolkids on Queen West.

CHINA AND CRYSTAL

For china and crystal, shop at Ashley's on Bloor Street or at Birks in the Eaton Centre.

DESIGNER BOUTIQUES

For Canadian labels, visit Price Roman, Psyche and Fashion Crimes on Queen West. Marilyn Brooks in Yorkville, Comrags, Lowen Pope, Annie Thompson on West Queen West and Susan Harris Design on Tecumseh south of Queen. On Dundas Street between College and Queen you'll find Georgie Bolesworth and Skirt, both of which carry Canadian designers.

International design labels can be

Shopping

found at Holt Renfrew and Chanel boutiques, both on Bloor Street.

Gift Shops
Unique and unusual gifts reside at the shops in the Royal Ontario Museum and the Art Gallery of Ontario.

Home Furnishings
Shoppers will find a range of home furnishing stores, from the Swedish giant Ikea to stores such as the Art Shoppe, Ridpath's Urban Mode, Du Verre, High-Tech, Up Country, Fluid Living, Constantine Antiques and Home Furnishings. Homefront, Morba and Pavilion offer unusual and one-of-a-kind home furnishings.

Jewellery
If money is no object, try Fabrice in Hazelton Lanes or Tiffany on Bloor Street. Birks has locations on Bloor and in the Eaton Centre. European Jewellery also has several locations throughout the city. Canadian designers include Anne Sportun of Experimetal, which is located on Queen Street West.

Leather
Roots, Roger Edwards and Perfect Leather all feature leather clothing, shoes or handbags, as does Danier, which has several locations throughout the city.

Malls
Stalwart mall shoppers should try the Eaton Centre, Hazelton Lanes downtown, or Yorkdale, Square One, Sherway Gardens or Bayview Village in the suburbs.

Music
HMV outlets or Canada's own Sam the Record Man stores are located around the city. A good bet on vinyl: Rotate This or Neurotica, located within the same block on West Queen West.

Men's Clothing
Arguably the best-known clothing store for men in the city is Harry Rosen, with locations on Bloor Street and in the Eaton Centre. Tom's Place in Kensington Market features high-quality men's business suits and casual clothing at discount prices. For casual wear, there are all the usual chains: the Gap, Banana Republic, and Eddie Bauer. Canadian-designed menswear can be found at Hoax Couture and Boomer. On West Queen West, go to Grreat Stuff.

Second-hand Clothing
Gently used and vintage clothing abounds at Preloved, Dancing Days, Courage My Love, Circa Forty and Cabaret.

Appliances from Urban Mode

Bloor Street merchandise

SPORTS

DEREK CHEZZI

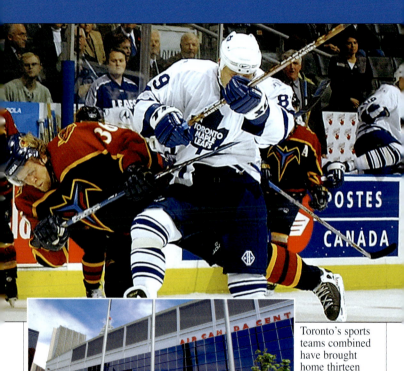

TORONTO MAPLE LEAFS (TOP)
THE AIR CANADA CENTRE (INSET)

Toronto's sports teams combined have brought home thirteen Stanley Cups, two World Series Championships, more Grey Cups than any other franchise in the Canadian Football League and so many Lacrosse championship titles that even the most avid fans have lost count. And the top-notch sporting facilities ensure no team feels unloved. To the delight of visitors, and also those who live here and rely on public transportation every day, the arenas and stadiums are conveniently located in the downtown core.

HOCKEY

Torontonians can't live without their hockey. From October to April each year, blue and white pumps through the city's veins. On important game days, bars and restaurants burst with hardcore and fair-weather fans. And for diehard fans of the sport, it's a great city to set as a destination.

The Toronto Maple Leafs are an integral part of hockey history in North America. The team was founded in 1917 as the Toronto Arenas, one of the first four teams in the new

SPORTS

National Hockey League. Despite winning the Stanley Cup in the league's first year, the struggling club became the Toronto St. Patricks two years later. In 1927, the team was purchased by a group led by one of the city's more colourful historical characters, businessman Conn Smythe, who renamed the team the Leafs and built Maple Leaf Gardens, the sports arena that would serve as the team's home the next 72 years. On February 20, 1999, the Leafs moved to the conveniently located and well-designed Air Canada Centre (even in the nosebleed section, this 18,800 seat arena offers a good view of the action). The venue also houses the Toronto Raptors basketball club and the Toronto Rock lacrosse team.

MAPLE LEAF GARDENS

Since Smythe's renaming of the team, the Leafs have made numerous playoff appearances, winning the Stanley Cup eleven times. The last time the team brought home the coveted prize was in the 1966-67 season—quite a ways back, though that does not prevent the city from cheering it on. Nearly every game is sold out regardless of the team's standing in any given season. It's best to buy tickets early.

THE TORONTO RAPTORS

Professional league hockey isn't the only game in town. For fast action at an affordable price, there's the Toronto Marlies, an American Hockey League franchise and farm club for the Leafs. This team has undergone numerous identity changes. From Newmarket Saints to St. John's Maple Leafs to the Toronto Roadrunners, in 2005 the team was once again renamed. The Marlies play at the Ricoh Coliseum arena on the Canadian National Exhibition (CNE) grounds.

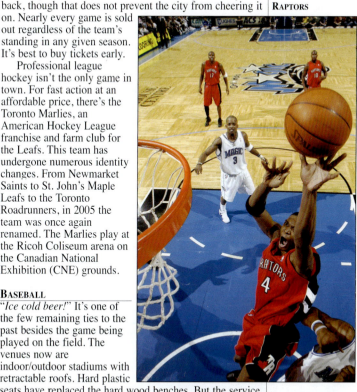

BASEBALL

"*Ice cold beer!*" It's one of the few remaining ties to the past besides the game being played on the field. The venues now are indoor/outdoor stadiums with retractable roofs. Hard plastic seats have replaced the hard wood benches. But the service is always the same: reliable. "*Ice cold beer!*"

The Toronto Blue Jays play in the summer. And in Toronto, summer is the best season to visit. The days are hot, sweaty, lazy and happy. The nights are alive. On perfect days the Rogers Centre (still known by its original

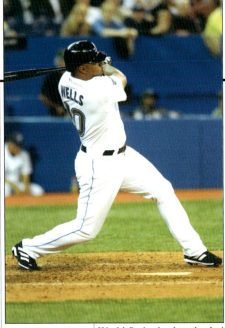

THE TORONTO BLUE JAYS

TORONTO ARGONAUTS FANS

name, the SkyDome) displays its most charming self. With the roof open, a refreshing breeze blows off Lake Ontario, fans with radios in hand tune them to the game, the scent of sun block wafts through the crowd and in hand, a sweating plastic cup of "*Ice cold beer!*" quenches the thirst.

The Toronto Blue Jays have left a moderate mark on the world of pro baseball. The club got its start in 1976, the year the American League voted to start up a franchise in Toronto. They've won five Eastern Division championships and taken the World Series back-to-back, in 1992 and 1993 — their first two seasons at the dome. And sports trivia fans will know that Toronto was the first and only Canadian franchise to appear at the World Series.

The club's original owners consisted of a bank, Labatt Breweries and a holding company for businessman R. Howard Webster. In 2000 Canadian telecommunications company Rogers Communication Inc. purchased eighty percent of the franchise. In 2004 Rogers took ownership of the Skydome — hence the name change.

BASKETBALL

The Toronto Raptors may be in rebuild mode — okay, so the team lost superstar shooting guard Vince Carter — but the games are still action-packed. In fact, the Raps are starting to work more like, well, a team since his departure. Plus, it's a new franchise. The Raptors joined the National Basketball Association in 1995.

FOOTBALL

In 2004 the Toronto Argonauts returned to the Canadian Football League spotlight. They won the Grey Cup for the first time in nearly a decade. Former Argos player Mike "Pinball" Clemons engineered their return to form for the team continues to lead the league in most Cup wins.

The team's roots date to 1873, making the Argos the oldest professional sports team in the city. The team was formed from the Argonauts Rowing Club and was among the first to join the newly created Canadian Football League, which formed two years before its better-known American rival, the National Football League. More than one hundred years later, the Argos

SPORTS

TORONTO ROCK LACROSSE

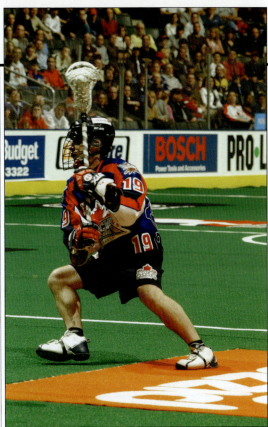

share their current home base, the Rogers Centre, with the Blue Jays. The stadium boasts such amenities as a hotel and private restaurant, a far cry from the rickety Exhibition Stadium where the Grey Cup was once held.

There is a price point for every budget at the Rogers Centre and the game is still very much the same. The differences between the NFL and the CFL are subtle — the Canadians play on a larger field allowing for more creative plays, and the three downs (instead of the NFL's four) move the game along at a quicker pace.

The season runs from July to November with a couple of pre-season games in June. Single game tickets can be purchased through the Rogers Centre box office.

LACROSSE

The city's newest sports franchise has brought fresh life to a piece of Toronto history. The Toronto Rock, the city's first professional lacrosse team, began calling Maple Leaf Gardens home in 1998, after moving to the city from nearby Hamilton. The quick rise in the sport's popularity saw the team's move, a few years later, to the Air Canada Centre.

The Rock brings home so many championships in the National Lacrosse League that it's hard to keep track. The season runs from January to April, with 18 games during regular season. Prices aren't quite as low as they used to be, but it's still an affordable night out with the family.

MOLSON GRAND PRIX

MOLSON GRAND PRIX CAR RACING

In what has become one of the most popular sport draws of the city, the Molson Grand Prix (formerly the Molson Indy) is held in the area around the Canadian National Exhibition for one weekend every July. From miles away, you can hear the roar of Formula One cars peeling around the Exhibition Place at speeds of up to 380 km/h. The more than 160,000 fans fend off the summer sun with sunglasses and baseball caps to watch their favourite drivers wind their way past the CNE grounds in cars that weigh little more than 600 kilograms. But the spectacle around the race is just as much fun. There is a trip on a ride simulator and a variety of exhibits at the consumer and trade show. The Molson Grand Prix hits the streets in mid-July.

OTHER SPORTS/PARTICIPATORY SPORTS

In August, York University hosts the Tennis Canada Rogers Cup, a men's and women's event that rotates between Toronto and Montreal, at the newly built stadium courts. The weekend event attracts the world's top-rank players and many celebrity fans. For information visit www.tenniscanada.com.

DON VALLEY GOLF COURSE

If golf is your game, the city also hosts the Bell Canadian Open, the third-oldest national championship in the world, every second year or so. The Glen Abbey golf course, located in the suburb of Oakville, was designed by Jack Nicklaus and is considered one of the finest in the world.

For fitness buffs, Toronto also offers many opportunities for visitors. In winter months, public ice rinks can be found all over the city — for visitors in the month of December, there's the option of an evening skate at Nathan Philips Square when city hall is decked out in holiday decorations. It's also possible to make day trips to numerous ski and snowboarding destinations only a short drive away.

Cyclists can find many decent off-road trails within or near the city limits. There are also paved paths along some of the most picturesque green spaces the city has to offer, including incredible rides along the lakefront as well as the Don River. Toronto Island's paved pedestrian paths make for some of the city's best inline skating.

Toronto Parks and Recreation Trails

Christine Beevis

Toronto is known as a city with great green spaces, a large urban forest and excellent cycling. The city's tree-lined streets account for much of this greenery, but the most significant contributors are the wooded ravines that line the its major rivers, the creeks and tributaries that feed them, the string of islands just to the south of Toronto harbour and the long shore-based spit on the eastern lakeshore.

You'll discover an entirely different side of Toronto by exploring its parks and recreation trails. Many of them owe their existence to the destruction of Hurricane Hazel in 1954 (one of Ontario's worst natural disasters). Following the hurricane's devastation, the city developed a plan to restrict residential development along its floodplains, thereby protecting many of the city's ravines and the Don Valley.

Today, most of the ravines adjacent to Toronto's three rivers (the Humber, Don and Rouge) and three largest creeks (Etobicoke, Mimico and Highland) are parks, accounting for some 12 percent of the whole city area and covering over eighty square kilometers. Portions of these parks are still undeveloped and are home not only to squirrels, chipmunks, raccoons and skunks, but also to groundhogs, opossums, porcupines, cottontail rabbits, red foxes, eastern coyotes and hundreds of species of birds and waterfowl.

The parks along these routes contain numerous recreational opportunities, from riding stables, golf

Toronto Skyscrapers from atop the Don Valley

▲ Toronto's Top Attractions

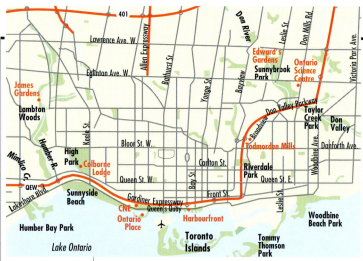

CENTREVILLE TRAIN AT TORONTO ISLANDS PARK

HUMBER VALLEY PARK

courses and quiet formal gardens to a nineteenth-century town, farm and former brickworks. Throughout many trails (often marked by the distinctive Discovery Walks symbol), the city has erected signs with maps and information on the history of each area, as well as the local flora and fauna. Brochures are available at City Hall, the City of Toronto Web site and all library branches for many walks.

Most parks are easily accessible by public transit and feature washroom facilities and picnic areas, as well as trails suitable for walking, biking or in-line skating. They're a great way to get away from the hustle and bustle of urban life. If you've only got a few hours, the best way to explore these parks and trails is to focus on either the Toronto Island, the Waterfront Trail or the Don Valley Trail.

TORONTO ISLANDS PARK
The Toronto Islands are actually a collection of sand bars interrupted by lagoons and rivulets rather than truly separate entities. Originally a peninsula, the area was

PARKLANDS

Toronto Islands

severed from the mainland by a series of storms in the 1850s. By the beginning of the twentieth century the Islands had been enlarged with landfill to three times their original size, and included summer resorts, fancy homes and makeshift cottages.

Today the Islands house an airport, a small community of permanent homes (on Ward's and Algonquin Islands) and Centreville, a small summertime amusement park designed to resemble a nineteenth-century village with a petting zoo. Arriving on Centre Island, a wide floral esplanade—the Avenue of the Islands, along which once were located all the commercial outlets of the long-gone resort community—will lead you to the amusement park. There are some 24 rides suitable for children from toddler age up—bumper cars, boats, a railroad that tours the periphery of the park, a Ferris wheel, paddle boats, pony rides and a beautiful antique carousel that will appeal to all ages.

There are also a number of beaches, several yacht clubs and a school on the Islands. Ward's Island is home to one of the two remaining clusters of modestly built permanent homes on the Islands (the other is on Algonquin Island). A stroll around these bucolic communities is sure to delight, as they show that it is possible even today to live without stores or cars. Islanders bring everything over from the mainland and truck it home in wagons.

The Islands are dotted with clean washrooms, drinking fountains, food vendors and playgrounds. You don't even need to bring a bike from the mainland; you can rent one at Toronto Island Bicycle Rentals. With the fresh lake breezes and the silence that comes from the absence of traffic, you'll feel that you have left the city far behind. As for the city's bright lights, the Islands provide the best view possible of Toronto's twinkling lights across the harbour.

Many other spectacular views of the city are to be had from other points and on the trip coming or going. To reach the Islands, catch one of the ferries located at Bay Street and Queen's Quay, behind the Westin Harbour Castle Hotel.

FERRY ARRIVING AT CENTRE ISLAND

TORONTO'S TOP ATTRACTIONS

SAILING IN TORONTO'S HARBOUR

MARTIN GOODMAN TRAIL

The Martin Goodman Trail, which runs the length of Toronto's waterfront, is a segment of the award-winning Waterfront Trail — an uninterrupted trail that stretches 325 kilometres from Stoney Creek near Hamilton in the west, all the way to Trenton in the east. The trail is also a convenient access point to many of the other areas outlined below.

From the foot of Yonge, the trail heading west meanders past some of Toronto's most renowned landmarks—the CN Tower, Rogers Centre and Harbourfront. Immediately west of Harbourfront is the stunning Toronto Music Garden, inspired by Bach's First Suite for Unaccompanied Cello, with each section in the garden corresponding to a different movement in the suite. At Bathurst Street, the trail passes Little Norway Park, which commemorates the Norwegian aviators who trained at the nearby City Centre Airport during World War Two. Next comes Coronation Park, named in memory of the crowning of King George VI in 1937. Not long afterwards, the trail is flanked by the impressive archways of Exhibition Place to the north (the site of North America's first urban wind turbine) and Ontario Place to the south. The trail then heads on towards Marilyn Bell Park, named for the 16-year-old girl who was the first to swim across Lake Ontario in 1954.

The area from this point to the Humber River is known as the "Western Beaches." Central to this area is Sunnyside Park, whose 1922 Bathing Pavilion remains intact. To the north, and easily accessible, is High Park (see below). Just before crossing the suspension bridge spanning the Humber River (see below), the trail passes the Lion Monument — a majestic limestone sculpture marking King George VI's visit to Canada in 1939.

IMPROMPTU PARADE ON CENTRE ISLAND

Of special interest in this area are the Humber Bay Butterfly Habitat, a series of ponds used to filter storm water runoff, the meditative Sheldon Lookout, the mouth of

PARKLANDS

Mimico Creek and, just a kilometre past the suspension bridge, a delightful footbridge designed by Santiago Calatrara, the architect of BCE Place. The Waterfront Trail continues farther into the former City of Etobicoke, sometimes as a dedicated off-street path, at times an on-street but clearly marked route.

Travelling east from Yonge, the trail leads eastward along Queen's Quay past the Redpath Sugar Refinery Museum, which celebrates one of Canada's first factories (founded in 1854), and on through the Port Lands area.

Approximately seven kilometres east of Yonge, the trail moves through the neighbourhood known as the Beaches. Here the path runs beside a lovely tree-shaded boardwalk, numerous playgrounds, snack bars and washroom facilities, and is only a block from the Beaches' fine restaurants, boutiques and shops. Approximately one kilometre farther east, you will pass the R.C. Harris Filtration Plant. Built in the 1930s, the building is a good example of the Art Deco style of that period. Once it reaches the former City of Scarborough, the trail is almost entirely on city streets and eventually leads to the picturesque Scarborough Bluffs and Bluffers Park — a series of spectacular cliffs primarily formed by the erosion of packed clay soil, which in some places are shaped into interesting sculpture-like formations.

HIGH PARK

High Park, situated in Toronto's west end, is one of the city's largest recreation areas and welcomes over one million visitors annually. The 164-hectare park was formerly the estate of architect and city surveyor John Howard, whose home, Colborne Lodge, sits on a height of land overlooking the lake. Ecologically, the park is unique for its rare savannah habitat treed with black oak, and has been called one of the city's most significant natural areas. In addition to the several kilometres of paved bike and hiking trails (the roads are closed to vehicles during weekends in the summer), the park contains the full-service Grenadier Restaurant, several snack bars, a small zoo, the Jamie Bell Adventure

THE HUMBER VALLEY

103

▲ Toronto's Top Attractions

High Park

Playground (designed by local children, parents and teachers), numerous ponds and streams, a motorized tram, an outdoor skating rink in the winter and baseball diamonds, bocce ball and other sport fields in the summer.

High Park is accessible by subway (at High Park station) or by car (enter via Bloor Street just west of Keele Street). In the summer, there are concerts on Sundays and walking tours on Sundays and Tuesdays. As well, throughout the summer the Canadian Stage Company presents Dream in High Park, its annual Shakespearean season opener, in an outdoor amphitheatre. The production is excellent, the setting magical.

HUMBER RIVER TRAIL (18 KM)

The Humber River was an important transportation route for the area's First Nations inhabitants and for subsequent explorers and missionaries. Although heavily developed throughout the first half of the twentieth century, the Humber now has much of the pastoral feel it must have had in earlier times, thanks largely to the impact of Hurricane Hazel in 1954. Since then, the shore has been reforested and naturalized to prevent future flooding.

The Humber Trail provides a pleasant 13-kilometre ride or walk from the Lakeshore to Scarlett Mills Park at

PARKLANDS

THE HUMBER TRAIL (LEFT AND BELOW)

Eglinton, or if you wish, an additional five kilometres or so all the way to Dixon Road. The route travels in a gently winding northerly direction past the Old Mill (at Bloor Street) and on through Etienne Brûlé Park. It then passes through Home Smith Park and Lambton Woods to James Gardens, a former family estate with spring-fed pools and rare trees. Also nearby are Black Creek Pioneer Garden and Lambton Woods, site of a large wildflower preserve.

To reach the Humber from the Martin Goodman Trail, head north at Windermere Avenue, pass beneath the Gardiner Expressway, around the back of the Humber Treatment Plant and through South Humber Park. From here, a short on-street jog up Stephen Drive is required before rejoining the off-street path opposite the Humber Marshes.

DON VALLEY

The lower reaches of the Don River once meandered gently through a large wetland before draining into Ashbridges Marsh at the edge of Lake Ontario. Gradually, as development in the area increased, the wetland was filled in and the river forced to flow between concrete walls to create more land for industry and the Don Valley Parkway in the 1950s. Today the 38-kilometre river is one of the most urbanized watersheds in Canada and enters Lake Ontario through the Keating Channel at the western end of the Port Lands.

The Don River Trail is ideal for cyclists, hikers, joggers and in-line skaters. The main route can be reached by taking the Martin Goodman Trail east along Queen's

VIEWS OF THE DON VALLEY

Quay and turning north at Cherry Street. The trail itself is a two-lane paved path that winds alongside the Don River and is the access point to a number of points of interest. Bordered by beautiful fields of tall grasses and wildflowers, the trail creates the illusion of being far away from the nearby Bayview Extension and Don Valley Parkway.

The Don River and Valley were seriously degraded in the nineteenth and much of the twentieth century. Concerned citizens working over the last decade, however, have planted over 40,000 trees and uncounted numbers of wildflowers in the Valley. Several wetlands have been created and many degraded sites have been restored to health.

Located just south of the (Bloor Street) Prince Edward Viaduct, the Chester Springs Marsh is a restored wetland that covers 3 hectares (about the size of 7 football fields). Built on the site of an early 1900s landfill, the marsh was

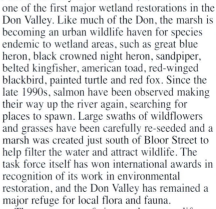

one of the first major wetland restorations in the Don Valley. Like much of the Don, the marsh is becoming an urban wildlife haven for species endemic to wetland areas, such as great blue heron, black crowned night heron, sandpiper, belted kingfisher, american toad, red-winged blackbird, painted turtle and red fox. Since the late 1990s, salmon have been observed making their way up the river again, searching for places to spawn. Large swaths of wildflowers and grasses have been carefully re-seeded and a marsh was created just south of Bloor Street to help filter the water and attract wildlife. The task force itself has won international awards in recognition of its work in environmental restoration, and the Don Valley has remained a major refuge for local flora and fauna.

Three remnants of nineteenth-century life are of particular interest on the Don Trail: Riverdale Farm, Todmorden Mills and the Don Valley Brick Works. Riverdale Farm, the site of

PARKLANDS

RIVERDALE FARM

Toronto's former zoo, is a good example of an early twentieth century farm. Many of its animals and plants are rare examples of nineteenth-century species that might now be extinct were it not for the farm and a number of farmers across Ontario. Located in the Old Cabbagetown area at 201 Winchester Street, it is also accessible directly from the Valley via a footbridge.

Farther north along the valley is the Brick Works, the last of Toronto's brickyards to close 100 years after it opened its doors in 1889. Now part of the park system, its 16.5 hectares have been restored into a magical setting of wetlands, marshes, meadows and forest. The former quarry face clearly displays successive waves of prehistoric glaciation and is internationally acclaimed by geologists.

Todmorden Mills and Art Centre houses the Eastwood-Skinner paper mill — reputed to have been continuously occupied longer than any other building in Toronto. Also on the site are a rustic cottage built in 1797 and a mid-nineteenth-century house. Nearby, a wildflower preserve has been created. Todmorden offers a range of arts and craft activities and is accessible from the Don Trail or Pottery Road (off Broadview or Bayview).

Continuing north from Pottery Road, the Don Trail becomes hillier and leads to E.T. Seton Park, named after the nineteenth-century naturalist and chronicler of the Don Valley. Here, at "the Forks of the Don," the trail splits. The westerly Wilket Creek route leads to Edwards Gardens. A pleasant place to walk, the garden has both formal and natural areas, including a large rose garden and an immense collection of rhododendrons. The on-site Civic Garden Centre is the headquarters for gardeners throughout the city, and houses an

SUNNYBROOK PARK

AERIAL VIEW OF THE SPIT

excellent gift shop, annual sales of plants, bulbs and seeds and numerous lectures and tours.

Taking the easterly route at the Forks will take you to Taylor Creek Park. Nearby stand what looks like giant molars, but is actually an art installation consisting of a series of elevated wetlands that filter water from the Don River. Farther north, in the Central Don region, are Sunnybrook Park's sports fields, a Vita Parcours exercise trail, and the Central Don Stables near Eglinton Avenue and the Leslie Street, with two indoor arenas and some fifteen kilometres of trails.

LESLIE STREET SPIT

Officially called Tommy Thompson Park, the Spit is entirely man-made but may be the world's only Important Bird Area in a major city. Since the 1950s, millions of tons of hard-packed clay, shale, construction debris and concrete have been deposited to create an irregularly-shaped series of peninsulas and coves with names like Rubble Beach.

Often referred to as an urban wilderness, the area has now become a refuge for more than 290 species of shore and water birds and about 300 plant species. The ponds, forests and wetlands are home to a variety of turtles, toads, frogs and snakes, and more than 40 species of fish in the surrounding waters.

The spit is another excellent vantage point from which to see the city, as well as an ideal spot for biking and in-line skating on its 10-kilometre two-lane paved surface ideal for novice cyclists or skaters. Note that aside from the ice cream truck and hot dog vendor usually parked at the entrance, there isn't a single amenity. The area is windy on a summer day and blustery the rest of the time.

No private cars are allowed in the park, but a free shuttle van runs hourly from the main gate at the corner of Leslie and Commissioners Streets, from about May to October. Dog owners are asked to leave their pets outside the park.

LESLIE STREET SPIT

ANNUAL EVENTS

Hardly a day passes in Toronto without a public celebration of some sort, be it a street fair, a parade, a performance or a picnic. Add to this numerous neighbourhood festivals, international music, theatre, dance and literary or culinary events, and it's clear that staid old Toronto loves to party.

In addition, there are annual trade and specialty shows, usually held at Exhibition Place, downtown at the Toronto Convention Centre, or near Pearson Airport at the International Centre, all of which have become major attractions for Torontonians and visitors alike. Many of them appeal to the entire family; these include the Boat, Auto, Dog, Cat, Bicycle, Hobby and Craft, Sportsmen's, Home and Garden Shows. Described here are just a few of the more colourful happenings that occur throughout the year; additional events are listed at the back of the guide, and in daily newspapers, *NOW* magazine, *eye weekly* and *Toronto Life*.

SCENE FROM CARIBANA

SCENE FROM THE NATIONAL BALLET'S *NUTCRACKER*

WINTER

The holiday season truly gets under way with the annual arrival of the National Ballet's *Nutcracker*. In 1995 this highly acclaimed work received a complete overhaul and remains a must-see.

A taste of Victorian or Edwardian Christmas is featured

▲ Toronto's Top Attractions

throughout the holiday season at all the city's historic homes (Colborne Lodge, Spadina House, the Grange, Mackenzie House and Casa Loma are some examples), where the décor and the scents of mulled cider and freshly baked goodies will envelope you and yours in good cheer (see listings under Museums for telephone numbers and locations).

As winter grimly grinds along, people are wont to get a bit silly. The Toronto Storytelling Festival is held late each winter at Harbourfront. If you're suffering from cabin fever, you may be ready to head for the hills by early March when maple sugaring is underway at all Toronto's conservation areas.

CANADA BLOOMS

SPRING

Whatever the calendar may say, Toronto's winter has traditionally ended with the opening of the Home and Garden Show at the International Centre. But now a more recent and wildly popular gardening show at the Convention Centre in mid-March — Canada Blooms — has become the harbinger of warmer weather.

Another sure sign of spring in the city is Cabbagetown's Forsythia Festival, which offers a parade along Parliament Street and craft kiosks in adjacent Riverdale Park, for which organizers always guarantee the real thing will be in bloom. For those visitors who prefer to stay indoors, HOT DOCS International Documentary Festival offers more than 100 documentaries from Canada and around the globe. This ten-day event in late April is North America's largest documentary festival. Home

SKATING AT NATHAN PHILLIPS SQUARE

gardening in Toronto kicks off on Victoria Day weekend and so does the Milk International Children's Festival down at Harbourfront. A single low-price pass permits entry to dozens of performances. The last weekend in May provides a real treat for native Torontonians and visitors alike when some 125 building owners invite the public to free tours of their historically and/or architecturally significant buildings at the appropriately named Doors Open Toronto.

By June festivals are in full bloom. There is the Toronto Worldwide Short Film Festival, during which dozens of films are screened in five days in June. Also in June there is North by Northeast, a three-day extravaganza featuring up to 400 bands playing at roughly 30 clubs.

Caravan is held in June and you can purchase a "passport" to any of thirty or more pavilions featuring the cuisine, entertainment and crafts of the different countries represented in the city's cultural mosaic.

DRAGON BOAT FESTIVAL

A newer tradition is Bloom on the Beaches, a leisurely literary experience held on and around June 16 that includes brunch, music, songs and readings. The event is a celebration of James Joyce's *Ulysses*. Its motto, naturally, is ReJoyce!

As the weather warms up, the waterfront plays an increasingly large role in festivities, of which the Toronto International Dragon Boat Race at Centre Island in mid-to-late June is one of the most colourful. And then, to herald summer, on the last Saturday in June at Woodbine Racetrack there is the running of the Queen's Plate, the oldest stakes race in North America and the one at which people dress as though for Ascot. Royalty often makes an appearance — certainly on the track if not always in the stands.

SUMMER

The air heats up considerably as the notes of the Downtown Jazz Festival waft from some sixty locations throughout the week following the summer solstice. Free daytime concerts, including some especially for youngsters, and a farmer's market, are a Wednesday fixture at Nathan Phillips Square, City Hall, from early June through

▲ TORONTO'S TOP ATTRACTIONS

FIREWORKS AT ONTARIO PLACE

September, where free evening concerts are also held weekly. Other summer-long specials include Kidsummer, a day-by-day schedule of events for children, such as visits to factories and firehalls, craft-making opportunities, concerts and clowns, and free indoor and outdoor films courtesy of the Sprockets International Film Festival for Children for times and locations.

Vying for fame and sparks of a different sort is the Pride Day Parade, held on the last Sunday in June to culminate Gay Pride Week. For colour and flair, it's hard to beat. Canada Day, July 1st, provides an excuse for the year's largest outdoor public celebrations when almost every park in the city hosts performances and grand picnics. One of the largest of these is held at Exhibition Place, hosted by CIIN radio. Theatregoers get a smorgasbord to choose from during The Fringe: Toronto's Theatre Festival, held for ten days in early July and featuring hundreds of performances — none longer than ninety minutes — playing mainly in the Annex area (near Bloor and Spadina). Other standbys include the mid-July weekend Toronto Outdoor Art Exhibition at Nathan Phillips Square.

On the noisier side, there is the Molson Grand Prix in July, with its three solid days of car racing along the lakeshore and around the CNE grounds. More acoustically pleasing is the largely open-air Beaches Jazz Festival in late July, at which more than 40 bands perform on the street and in area parks and clubs.

The theatre fringe festival having proved so popular, there is now also a mid-August, ten-day Fringe Festival of Independent Dance Artists, featuring over 300 artists. As well, in mid-August, Toronto's main alternative theatres host SummerWorks, a ten-day extravaganza with some fifty

BICYCLE RACE SPONSORED BY CHIN

Annual Events

SCENES FROM CARIBANA

performances on a half-dozen stages.

Caribana, the biggest, brightest, happiest festival by far, gets under way in late July to August, depending on the year. This midsummer Mardi Gras-type event includes over thirty competing bands, competitions for the King and Queen of the Bands, numerous performances throughout the city and a major arts festival on Olympic Island. Its pièce de résistance, the attraction that draws up to half a million people, is the parade held on the final Saturday of this two-week jump-up. Check for Toronto Carnival events at www.caribana.com.

After Caribana, the summer starts to wind down. The ever-popular Ex, which runs for the last two weeks in August and over Labour Day weekend, has signalled the start of a new school year for over a century. Along with its midway, amusement park rides and agricultural exhibits, there are dozens of performances daily and, on the Labour Day weekend, a stunning air show.

Fall

The calendar says it's still summer, but the arrival of the Toronto International Film Festival, an important stop on the circuit that includes Cannes and New York, is a clear sign that fall is here. For ten days, the city is filled with glitterati; there are gala parties

WORD ON THE STREET

nightly and all sorts of special shows — as well as, of course, more than 250 new films.

The Canadian Open Golf Championship, regularly held on the Glen Abbey course, the only Canadian stop on the Professional Golfers Association tour, closes the outdoor sporting season, much as the Queen's Plate opens it. And then the literary season starts. On the last Sunday in September Queen's Park Crescent, from Wellesley to Bloor Streets is closed to traffic and opens as Word on the Street, a bookmart with stalls, readings and entertainment for all ages. See the *Toronto Star* the day before for a complete listing.

WORD ON THE STREET

Late September also sees Artsweek, an offering of performances, workshops and specialty tours covering the performing and visual arts at various locations throughout the city.

Next on the calendar is another international biggie down at Harbourfront: the International Festival of Authors, with close to 100 public events (and thousands of private ones) and almost as many authors. Harbourfront also offers weekly readings throughout the year.

THE SANTA CLAUS PARADE

Debate persists over whether winter begins with the early-November Royal Agricultural Winter Fair, the mid-month Santa Claus Parade or the Cavalcade of Lights, held on the last Friday in November.

DAY TRIPS

BETTY ZYVATKAUSKAS

NIAGARA FALLS AND NIAGARA-ON-THE-LAKE

Without a doubt, Niagara Falls is the single most popular day trip for Toronto visitors. There are several bus tours available, or you can reach the falls in about two hours by car. For many decades, the thundering cataract was a honeymoon favourite, and that legacy still remains in many area motels boasting heart-shaped beds and whirlpool baths built for two. The tourism trade has brought with it a hefty dose of kitsch classics from wax-museum monsters to daredevil displays and amusement parks. A new casino towers on the hillside overlooking the falls.

To enjoy the falls up close, nothing beats the "Maid of the Mist" boat rides. Since the mid-1800s, this tiny flotilla of tour boats has ferried passengers to the foot of the falls. Each boat takes several hundred raincoat-clad passengers on a twenty-minute trip to pause at the foot of the magnificent Horseshoe Falls, where everyone gets a good soaking in the spray while listening to the commentary, which chronicles some of the daredevils who went over the falls in assorted contraptions.

The falls are only one highlight in this lovely area of scenic parkland. If you head north from Niagara Falls on the Niagara Parkway, and you will enjoy one of the prettiest drives in North America. The Niagara School of Horticulture's botanical gardens, the wonderful Niagara Parks Butterfly Conservatory and an outstanding arboretum are well worth a visit. Another outstanding tropical attraction is the Niagara Falls Aviary, which recreates a Javanese jungle and is populated by 400 tropical birds.

HORSESHOE FALLS

ARTILLERY PARK, FORT GEORGE (BELOW)
SHAW FESTIVAL (BOTTOM)

The Niagara Parkway winds through some of Canada's most hospitable farmlands. Each spring, thousands of fruit trees bloom in the roadside orchards. Come summer, peaches and cherries are sold at roadside fruit stands. Picnic venues abound, along with bicycle paths and hiking trails that explore the dramatic limestone cliffs of the Niagara Gorge. This is also wine country and amid the vineyards are wineries (including Reif Estate and Inniskillin) where visitors are invited to tour and taste.

The parkway ends at the historic town of Niagara-on-the-Lake, known for its gracious old homes and its popular theatre festival. Each summer, the Shaw Festival mounts critically acclaimed productions of

Day Trips

the works of George Bernard Shaw and his contemporaries.

Visitors looking for drama of a different sort can visit Fort George, the British garrison that was burned to the ground by invading Americans during the War of 1812. Here, red-coated soldiers will tell you about nineteenth-century military discipline and the hardships of life on the frontier.

Explorations of history continue on a walk through town. Among the self-consciously quaint "olde shoppes" that line the main street stands the Niagara Apothecary, a pharmacy whose interior has changed little since the store

opened in 1819. Now operated as a museum, it features shelves stocked with an assortment of patent medicines, salves and potions.

Niagara Winery Tours

Some of Ontario's prettiest scenery can be found in the wine producing and fruit growing regions of the Niagara peninsula, a region known for great wines (many of which can be purchased only at the wineries) and fine dining at winery restaurants. At last count, the region boasted more than fifty wineries along the official Wine Route that starts in Winona and continues to Niagara Falls, with blue signs

FESTIVAL THEATRE AT STRATFORD

STRATFORD

marking the way. Closest to Toronto is the wine-making area known as the Bench, part of the Niagara escarpment that parallels Lake Ontario, creating a microclimate for grape growing and some stunning vistas. At Vineland Estates one can enjoy a tour followed by lunch on an outdoor patio restaurant that overlooks acres of grapevines. Cave Springs Cellars in the pretty village of Jordan welcomes visitors to their tasting bar. The adjoining On the Twenty restaurant is renowned for its pairing of food and local wines.

Wine Route road signs lead from the Bench to Niagara-on-the-Lake, where two major wineries have garnered kudos for both their wine and their very different styles. Jackson-Triggs' sleek, contemporary limestone building houses the latest in wine making technology and a chic Tasting Gallery where visitors sample a flight of three different wines with assorted cheeses on a vineyard patio. In contrast, Peller Estates resembles a European chateau with peaked slate roofs and traditional architectural style. Here cellar tours focus on the art of aging premium reds. The restaurant's six-course tasting menu changes weekly.

Day Trips

Many wineries feature special events (Hillebrand in Niagara-on-the-Lake is famed for its summer jazz series), but the biggest is the Niagara Grape and Wine Festival in September. January brings icewine celebrations, as frozen grapes are harvested and then crushed in the making of Ontario's most famous and precious wine.

Stratford

Summer theatre abounds in southern Ontario. While Niagara-on-the-Lake has its Shaw Festival, Shakespeare can be found in the magnificent Stratford Festival of Canada, just two hours west of Toronto in the town of Stratford, aptly situated on the Avon River. From its

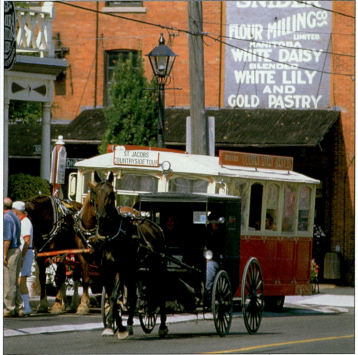

St. Jacobs

humble beginnings under a tent in 1952, the Stratford Festival has grown to encompass four excellent theatres at which both established actors (Maggie Smith and the late Peter Ustinov) and talented up-and-comers are seen in many artfully staged productions. The Festival Theatre uses the Elizabethan theatres as its model, with a jutting stage that puts the action seemingly in the middle of the audience. The festival runs from early May through early November.

Custom has it that a picnic on the grassy banks of the Avon River precedes attendance at either matinee or evening performances. Weather permitting, the setting is picture perfect. Willows overhang the river, where swans silently glide past the landscaped grounds of the Festival Theatre. In addition to the great performances onstage,

Toronto's Top Attractions

ELORA MILL ON THE GRAND RIVER

visitors can enjoy a brilliant behind-the-scenes show on Sunday mornings, when there are backstage tours through the tunnels and technical spaces of the Festival Theatre. Tours of the costume warehouse, which at 28,000 square feet is one of the largest in North America, reveal some of the magic of theatre props, from plastic armour to lifelike corpses.

WATERLOO COUNTY

To the east of Stratford lies the lush farmland of Waterloo County, an area known for its German and Mennonite heritage. As you travel the rural backroads that connect towns with names such as New Hamburg, Baden and Heidelberg, it is not uncommon to find yourself sharing the road with the horse-drawn buggies favoured by Old Order Mennonites, who shun many modern conveniences. At St. Jacobs you can learn more about their way of life at the Visitor Centre, formerly known as the Meeting Place, a museum run by both Old Order Mennonites and more liberal practitioners of the faith.

The area is famed for traditions such as quilting and in St. Jacobs you can still watch straw

FARMERS' MARKET

brooms being made by hand. Waterloo County is known for its hearty German cooking, which can be sampled at several country pubs, including the Olde Heidelberg Restaurant, where a plate of pigtails cooked in brown sugar can be washed down with a pint of house lager.

ELORA

Famed for its quaint stone architecture and its dramatic gorge, the town of Elora, about two hours northwest of Toronto, makes a delightful rural outing, especially during midsummer when the town hosts a music festival with performances in such unusual and acoustically superb venues as the local quarry. Elora's dramatic twenty-one-metre-deep gorge was carved by retreating glacial melt waters. Today the dark and fast-flowing waters of the Grand River are favoured by fly fishing fans in pursuit of trout. Elora's Mill Street boasts many attractively renovated stone buildings, including an old mill that has been turned into a country inn. The selection of gifts, crafts and jewellery make the street a favourite for shopping.

SHOPS ON MILL STREET IN ELORA

WINGS OF PARADISE

In Cambridge, Ontario, thousands of butterflies fly free in a tropical conservatory complete with lush plant life, waterfalls and gurgling streams. Iridescent blue morphos, bright orange Julia butterflies, yellow swallowtails, six-inch Atlas moths and black and red postmen are the more than fifty species that flit through the conservatory, looking for a free meal of rotting bananas and orange segments. In addition, the conservatory's lush vegetation — jasmine, lantana and passion vines — is chosen for both its beauty and nectar. Visitors who wear bright colours or sweetly scented perfume will find butterflies landing on them. On a winter day, this humid conservatory feels like a tropical escape. In summer it is enhanced by 1.5 hectares of outdoor gardens planted with nectar-rich flowers that attract wild butterflies. Monarch butterflies are tagged here

during their early September migration.

BRUCE TRAIL

When the need for a good, long hike sets in, many Torontonians head for the trail — the Bruce Trail, that is — a 770-kilometre hiking path that winds its way along the Niagara Escarpment from Queenston north to Tobermory. Roughly one hour northwest of Toronto, the trail passes through the Caledon Hills, where citified hikers can explore the scenery within easy reach of some fine country inns. At Caledon Hills, several clearly marked footpaths follow the Credit River and meander across cedar-covered hills, eventually connecting with the Bruce Trail.

After working up an appetite on a vigorous country walk, hungry hikers head for the historic Cataract Inn for a satisfying lunch.

Another fascinating spot along the Bruce Trail is the Crawford Lake Conservation Area near Milton, roughly forty minutes west of Toronto via Highway 401. Here, the hiking trails meet at a reconstructed fifteenth-century Iroquoian village. Visitors walk into the smoky longhouses to see fur-covered sleeping benches and corn-grinding tools. Many special programs allow visitors to participate in traditional native occupations, from making maple syrup in a hollowed log heated with rocks to celebrating the corn harvest. The hiking trails are wonderful and one is even wheelchair accessible, with all-terrain wheelchairs on loan at the visitor centre.

BRUCE TRAIL

SANDBANKS PROVINCIAL PARK

One of the world's most impressive freshwater sand dune systems lures beach-loving visitors 2.5 hours east of Toronto to Sandbanks Provincial Park. Situated in the lush farmlands of Prince Edward County, surrounded by Lake Ontario, this popular park is known for its towering sand dunes and exceptional beaches. Learn about dune ecology

DAY TRIPS ▲

on the self-guided Cedar Sands nature trail, then swim at one of the park's two major sandy beaches or just relax in the sun. The Outlet Beach offers easy access from the parking lot and the often-powerful Lake Ontario surf is popular with windsurfers and wave lovers. The West Lake sector (also known as Sandbanks Beach) is famous for its towering dunes that separate Lake Ontario and the warmer waters of West Lake. Nature lovers who walk along these dunes find solitude among marram grass, cottonwood poplars and wild grape vines. For those tiring of the beach, there's the bucolic scenery along Prince Edward County's Taste Trail, a network of roads that connect the region's wineries, farms and restaurants.

Presqu'ile, Tottenham and Kleinburg

Birds, beaches and butterflies make Presqu'ile Provincial Park a favourite of nature lovers. Located east of Toronto,

Visitors at Crawford Lake

Longhouses, Crawford Lake

SOUTH SIMCOE RAILWAY

NIAGARA GRAPES

Presqu'ile juts south into Lake Ontario. Almost an island, this peninsula is situated on a flyway that provides birds a place to rest and feed before and after crossing Lake Ontario in their transcontinental journeys. Great rafts of migrating ducks and geese gather along the shore in early spring as they head north to their nesting grounds. By summer, the gulls and sandpipers are joined by beach-loving humans. Butterflies mark the end of summer as thousands of migrating monarchs travel south through the park.

For a family outing with universal appeal, the South Simcoe Railway offers a steam train ride to "nowhere." This forty-five-minute excursion departs from the village of Tottenham, just north of Toronto, with much huffing and puffing from Steam Locomotive 136, built in 1883 for the Canadian Pacific Railway. Passengers ride in an assortment of old cars, including the last surviving 1926 model from the Toronto, Hamilton and Buffalo Railway. The eerie sound of the steam whistle drifts across farm fields as the train heads north, past a lazy creek where herons and turtles are sometimes sighted, to the town of Beeton, roughly eight kilometres north.

One of Canada's most impressive art galleries lies just a few minutes to the northwest of Toronto, in the pretty village of Kleinburg. The McMichael Canadian Collection is home to a remarkable collection of works painted by the Group of Seven, among the first painters to depict the landscape in truly rugged Canadian style. That style is echoed in the dramatic stone and wood of the gallery's architecture. The gallery enjoys a setting as powerful as the art works it houses — hundreds of acres of Humber Valley forests all visible from the building's dramatic picture windows.

Roughly a ten-minute drive from McMichael is the Kortright Conservation Area, where you can enjoy more of that Humber Valley scenery as you walk the hiking trails or take part in one of the interpretive nature programs, many of which are geared to youngsters.

GAY TORONTO

SKY GILBERT

SAILORS AT WOODY'S

Toronto has one of the largest gay populations per capita of any city in North America. There is a thriving gay scene which offers many opportunities for socializing, entertainment and education. With a gay and lesbian theatre, annual gay and lesbian film festival and the recent legalization of gay marriage in Canada, Toronto is Canada's gay and lesbian mecca. Tourists flock to the town partly because the people are so polite (if sometimes reserved), partly because Toronto the Good is the most fun when it's being a little bit "bad," and partly because it is one of the first cities in North America where you can march down to City Hall and legally get hitched to your same-sex partner.

FESTIVALS AND CULTURE

Toronto's Gay Pride Day is one of the largest in North America and takes place on the last Sunday of June every year. The Pride Parade has become a little more sedate over the years, but tourists come from all over the world and get a little crazy long before and long after the parade itself at the massive circuit parties. On the day itself, there are a number of

THE RAINBOW FLAG

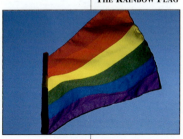

TORONTO'S TOP ATTRACTIONS

THE STEPS

entertainment stages, hundreds of booths selling the gamut of CDs to sex toys, as well as the requisite (and well attended) beer gardens.

If you're visiting in late May, you might want to catch The Inside Out Lesbian and Gay Film and Video Festival, held in several of the main downtown cinemas. Toronto is experimental filmmaker Bruce LaBruce's hometown, as well as the stomping ground for John Greyson (Lilies), so the queer movie fare is bound to be stimulating. The festival shows gay, lesbian, bisexual and transsexual films from around the world and usually features some major premieres.

Buddies in Bad Times Theatre, Toronto's Lesbian and Gay Theatre, recently celebrated its twenty-fifth anniversary in its new 350-seat home at 12 Alexander Street. Favourites every year at Buddies include Rhubarb! (a festival of new works held in February which always features some challenging dyke and lesbian fare), Strange Sisters (a lesbian cabaret which happens two nights a year in fall and spring), and a June Pride lineup of cabarets, drag shows and queer playlets. Buddies' mainspace is a springboard for new Canadian playwrights and the smaller cabaret often features comedy (and a yearly queer comedy festival). The theatre also houses the trendiest mixed-yet-still-queer bar nights in Toronto.

CHURCH STREET

Culture of a slightly different kind is just around the corner. Church Street, between Bloor and Dundas, is Toronto's gay and lesbian village, comparable to San Francisco's Castro Street. Most of the gay bars (and one lesbian bar) and the bathhouses are located on, or very near, this vibrant street. Many of the businesses are gay owned and all are gay

CHURCH AND WELLESLEY

positive. You'll find everything from gay tanning salons to gay video shops to gay veterinarians. It's a lively and upscale street where gay and lesbian couples can feel comfortable walking hand in hand or even smooching. If you want to get the lay of the land, so to speak, you might start at Timothy's Coffee Shop at the corner of Church and Maitland.

GAY TORONTO

THE GLADSTONE HOTEL

Locals love this hangout because of the steps outside the coffee shop, which serve as impromptu seating. The newly erected statute of nineteenth century gay magistrate Alexander Wood (replete with period walking stick and impressive bulge in his pants) is one of the world's only gay monuments — you may want to take time to pay homage to Alexander's memory at this historic spot. Timothy's Coffee Shop is favoured by bears — if you want to have coffee with a preppier crowd, you might go across the street to Starbucks. Twinks hang out at Second Cup at the corner of Church and Wellesley.

If you want a little more than a coffee, there are tons of restaurants to serve you. The most upscale greasy spoon is The Village Rainbow Restaurant (at the corner of Church and Maitland) offering burgers and fries, and all-day breakfasts in a sunny California environment with big windows and a patio on the street. If it's summertime and patios are your style, try O'Grady's, just across the street from Village Rainbow, which boasts a huge deck and the cutest waiters in town. Up the street closer to Church and Wellesley you'll find Zelda's, a restaurant that features drag waiters and drag shows entertaining you while you munch. If you long for Italian food, try Trattoria Al Forno. And Byzantium and Lüb offer extensive martini menus

The Black Eagle (top); Entrance to Woody's (above)

The Toolbox

with your meal. Byzantium, with its long bar and trendy surroundings, is famous as a holding pen for "A" gays (elegant post-white-collar attire only). These are not the only restaurants, or even the best, but might give you an idea of the variety you'll find on Church Street.

If you want to eat off Church — but still in gay positive surroundings (it's always nice to sneak a kiss over dinner) — you might hit Living Well is the Best Revenge, on Yonge Street, or The Rivoli on Queen. The Gladstone and The Drake Hotels on Queen West (just past Dovercourt) are culture savvy in a very queer way, fashionable and newly renovated, featuring queer nights and art parties and trendy bars and restaurants next to their shimmering lobbies.

The Bar Scene

The bar scene on Church is varied and lively. The most popular by far is Woody's and its companion, Sailor (they have different names but are connected at the back). Woody's facade was made famous as the setting for the bar called Babylon in the TV series Queer as Folk — in fact you'll recognize Church Street from that series (most of the episodes were shot there) Woody's/Sailor is Toronto's Cheers, featuring all the cutest boys and studiest men in beautiful surroundings: wood and brass with fireplaces, skylights, exposed brick and witty photos of all kinds of queens — including Elizabeth herself! On weekends the bar is packed. Thursday is "the Best Chest Contest", which always draws a crowd (competing out-of-towners are always welcome!).

Sunday night is drag night on Church Street. You can start at The 501 — right at the corner of Church and Wellesley — at 6:30 p.m. and then move to Woody's and Crews later. Crews offers the raunchiest drag shows in town and has a youthful clientele. Tango — attached to Crews — is a popular lesbian hangout, especially for the younger lesbian crowd or try Pope Joan. The hip-hop and raver fiends will find satisfaction at Five on St. Joseph Street and Fly on Gloucester (both just a couple of blocks north of Church and Wellesley). For leather guys, The Eagle on Church features very dirty videos and a dark atmosphere. There are underwear nights and fetish nights at The Eagle (at all times there is a dress code, no sandals or khaki pants — dark jeans and boots only). Or you may want to try The Toolbox, not for the faint of heart. Please note that most gay bars in Toronto welcome women, but women are especially welcome at Woody's, Crews/Tango and The 501. The rentboys hang out at Sneakers on Yonge Street and at Alexander at George's Play, a bar on Church with a Latino flair.

POPE JOAN

BEYOND BARS

The fun goes on late into the night after the bars close. For those with more on their mind than smooching and holding hands, Toronto offers six bathhouses. On or near Church Street, you'll find Steamworks, The Cellar and The Bijou. Steamworks is quite glitzy with a big gym and The Cellar is dark and gritty for the older leather crowd. The Bijou offers showers (no steam room), glory holes, and lots of dirty movies. G.I. Joe (a bathhouse) offers a mixed crowd on Yonge Street. But the place where all the beauty boys display their gym bodies nightly is the Spa Excess at Jarvis and Carlton — a truly sexy bathhouse in the grand tradition, complete with a bar, glory holes, a pool table and a motorcycle. Toronto has no true lesbian bathhouse yet. But dykes can pamper themselves at

THE DRAKE

▲ Toronto's Top Attractions

Shops along Church

Good For Her at 175 Harbord Street, a store that "celebrates woman's sexuality." On Queen Street, Come As You Are provides a varied collection of dildos and flavourful lubricants.

Other Amenities

If daytime fun is more your style, visit Glad Day Bookstore on Yonge or The Women's Bookstore on Harbord. Both have a wide variety of queer titles and provide information about the gay and lesbian community. Queer shoppers won't want to miss Priape (men's fashions, leather, sex toys and magazines) on Church Street.

For more detailed information about shops, services and organizations, pick up *Xtra* magazine at Timothy's. *Xtra* is a biweekly rag filled with political scuttlebut and gossip on local gay organizations. *FAB* is *Xtra's* slick competition catering to a more middle-class (less political) crowd. Alternatively, have a look at the bulletin board at the 519 Church Street Community Centre — many community activities there are gay lesbian, bisexual or transsexual.

519 Church Street Community Centre

No vacation would be complete without mention of where to get the best and latest safe-sex information. You can reach the Aids Committee of Toronto (ACT) at 416 340-2437. But Toronto is also home to more radical organizations like HEAL (Health, Education and Aids Liaison) at 416 406-4325.

Finally, there are lots of bed-and-breakfasts to make your stay comfortable, some right in the heart of the gay village, including the Cawthra Square Bed and Breakfast, Amazing Space (formerly Catnaps), The House on McGill and the particularly cozy and comfortable Banting House (on Homewood Ave.). Church Street is surrounded by hotels, including Sutton Place and The Primrose. Toronto's charm is that it has all the advantages of a big city like New York, with all the safety and intimacy of a small town.

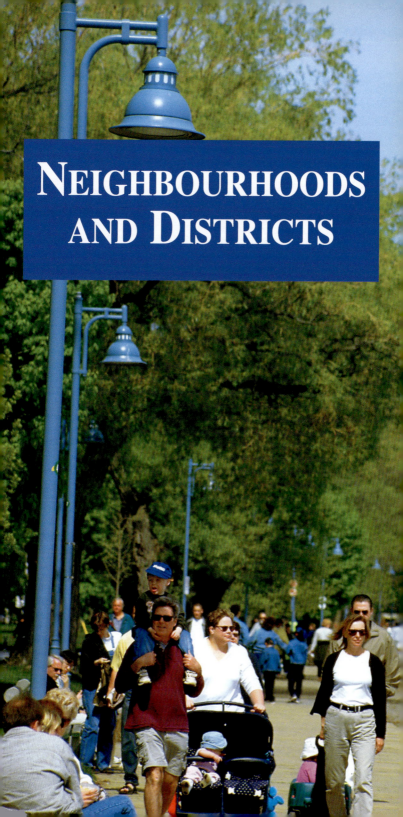
Neighbourhoods and Districts

ST. LAWRENCE NEIGHBOURHOOD

OUTSIDE THE FARMERS' MARKET

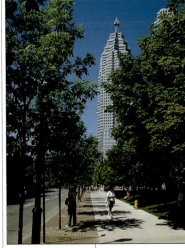

The St. Lawrence neighbourhood, formerly the heart of old Toronto's commercial district, offers lots to see and do. You will want to visit the bustling St. Lawrence Market to enjoy a tasty snack or lunch at one of the many stalls, stop by the Market Gallery or shop for crafts. You can stroll along Front Street, browsing for books, gifts or clothing, or relax on the sunny patios of one of the many restaurants on the Esplanade. For architecture buffs, the neighbourhood offers a cornucopia of interesting sights, from the fanciful nineteenth-century buildings on Front to the imposing St. James Cathedral on King Street.

The pulse of the district can best be taken at Front and Jarvis Streets, at the St. Lawrence Market. Located here are butchers, bakers, fishmongers and greengrocers, many of whom have been serving the same customers, virtually at the same location, for fifty years or more. As well as basic foodstuffs, there are stalls specializing in cheeses, pastas, rice, lentils, coffees, herbs, pies — even caviar! Prepared foods to take on a picnic or eat on the spot are also available, a favourite being sandwiches overflowing with what

St. Lawrence Neighbourhood

Americans call Canadian bacon and Canadians call peameal or back bacon. Although the market is most crowded on Saturdays (you would have to arrive before 6 a.m. to find it less than jammed), it's busy on weekdays, too, especially as office workers hurry to do their shopping while grabbing a bite of lunch (except on Mondays, when the market is closed.) In addition to food, the market offers a sampling of crafts from at the south end of the lower level.

The St. Lawrence Market sits like a large nesting goose atop an egg that actually is a remnant of the city's second city hall, built in 1845. When in the late 1890s the seat of

ST. LAWRENCE MARKET

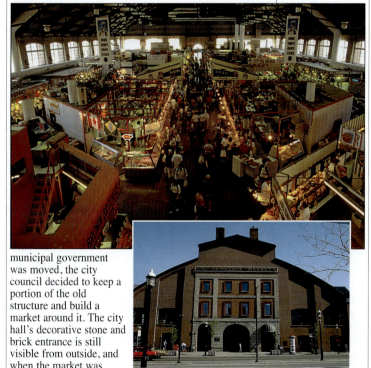

municipal government was moved, the city council decided to keep a portion of the old structure and build a market around it. The city hall's decorative stone and brick entrance is still visible from outside, and when the market was

OUTSIDE THE FARMERS' MARKET

INSIDE THE FARMERS' MARKET

renovated and enlarged in the 1970s its classical rear façade was uncovered, becoming visible from inside the newer structure. At that time, too, the former council chamber was renovated to serve as the Market Gallery. The gallery, which is free, is operated by the City of Toronto and houses well-curated exhibits of paintings, artefacts, photographs, maps and documents pertaining to various aspects of the city's past. To reach the gallery, enter via the Front Street entrance and take the elevator to the second floor.

Across the street from the market is a brightly painted bunker-like building that houses a farmers' market every Saturday featuring fresh produce, Ontario-made cheeses and preserves, homemade pies and sausages, the best yogurt on this side of the ocean and fragrant flowers and herbs. On Sundays it houses a flea market.

One can exit the St. Lawrence Market's lower level onto Market Street and turn left, then right along the Esplanade, one of the most inappropriately monikered streets in Toronto. Even when it was named, the Esplanade was far from the graceful promenade promised by the railway barons in response to widespread complaints about the obstruction of the lake view by railway construction on the intervening landfill. Gradually, however, its name is becoming more apt. To the west, the former warehouses lining the street's north side have been renovated to accommodate numerous publishing houses and architecture and design firms on upper floors, while the ground floors are devoted almost exclusively to oversized bars and restaurants. The area's pioneer was the local franchise of The Old Spaghetti Factory chain, while its neighbours include Scotland Yard, the popular Esplanade Bier Markt serving 150 beers and staples like

St. Lawrence Neighbourhood

steak and frites from Belgium, and Fionn MacCool's Irish Pub. Around the corner on Church are The Keg Steakhouse, as well the Jamie Kennedy Wine Bar, the new home of one of Toronto's best known chefs.

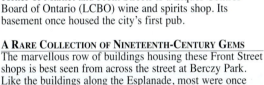

At the farmers' market

The next door up on Church Street is Le Papillon, which specializes in crêpes; its oversized skylight permits many of the delights of eating outdoors, indoors. Along the south side of Front Street, between St. Lawrence Market and Scott Street, are a hodge-podge of shops including Nicholas Hoare, one of Toronto's most venerable book shops, a variety of clothing and shoe stores, the inevitable Starbucks café, a few restaurants of moderate calibre and a very Victorian bath, bedding and gift shop, Wonderful and Whites. At the corner of Market and Front Streets is a Liquor Control Board of Ontario (LCBO) wine and spirits shop. Its basement once housed the city's first pub.

A Rare Collection of Nineteenth-Century Gems

The marvellous row of buildings housing these Front Street shops is best seen from across the street at Berczy Park. Like the buildings along the Esplanade, most were once warehouses; these, however, fronted on a prestigious

Shops along Front Street

FRONT STREET SHOPS

DEREK BESANT'S *FLAT-IRON MURAL* **ON THE GOODERHAM BUILDING**

commercial street. This difference is amply reflected in their fanciful façades. The one at 45–49 is particularly notable for being the last in the city made totally of cast iron.

Berczy Park, an urban oasis, takes up the western half of the triangular block created by the intersection of Front Street, which once followed Lake Ontario's shoreline, with the north-south grid of the city. Seemingly tacked to the wall adjacent to the park is Derek Besant's humorous *trompe-l'oeil*; the Flat-Iron Mural uses as its canvas the neighbouring flat-iron-shaped Gooderham Building, built in 1892 and once the flagship of the distillery-owning Gooderhams. An instant success when it appeared in 1980, the mural has inspired the creative use of many other walls throughout the city. A very modest example lies across the street on Front at Church, helping the stuccoed wall of a newish box blend in with its elegant neighbours.

ST. LAWRENCE NEIGHBOURHOOD

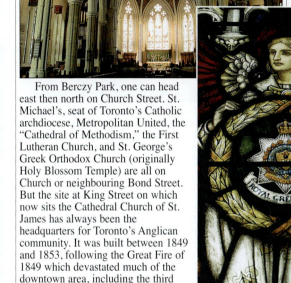

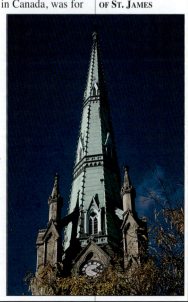

CATHEDRAL CHURCH OF ST. JAMES

From Berczy Park, one can head east then north on Church Street. St. Michael's, seat of Toronto's Catholic archdiocese, Metropolitan United, the "Cathedral of Methodism," the First Lutheran Church, and St. George's Greek Orthodox Church (originally Holy Blossom Temple) are all on Church or neighbouring Bond Street. But the site at King Street on which now sits the Cathedral Church of St. James has always been the headquarters for Toronto's Anglican community. It was built between 1849 and 1853, following the Great Fire of 1849 which devastated much of the downtown area, including the third wooden version of the church at that location. As a result of the fire, brick and stone supplanted wood throughout most of the area. The cathedral is a near-perfect reproduction of a fourteenth-century English gothic cathedral. Its 306-foot spire, the tallest in Canada, was for many years officially used to guide ships into the harbour. On one of the headstones decorating the cathedral's front porch is a memorial to one John Ridout, citing his consignment "to an early grave when a blight came..." The "blight" was a bullet fired by Samuel Peters Jarvis in Toronto's last duel, fought in 1817. Had he lived, Ridout might have met his relative, Thomas Ridout, one of the cathedral's architects.

In 1997 St. James became the only church of some forty in North America with change-ringing bells to boast a "full ring" of twelve bells. On Sundays, they chime out patterns developed in the sixteenth-century (call 416 364-7865 for times and tour information). On the remainder of the block is St. James Park, a charming garden tenderly restored to nineteenth-century horticultural dictates.

LITTLE TRINITY CHURCH

One block to the west is Toronto Street. From here it is possible to get a view of the last gasp, so to speak, of the St. Lawrence district's role as the commercial centre of Toronto. At the close of the century, George Gooderham, a prominent businessman, built the elegant, luxurious and thoroughly Edwardian King Edward Hotel in an effort to forestall the area's decline, a consequence of the city's westward and northward expansion. The hotel succeeded initially as a luxury establishment but failed utterly to stop the area's deterioration. Eventually, even the King Edward fell on hard times, but in the 1980s it was thoroughly modernized and restored to stand again as the epitome of a deluxe hotel of international stature. Along King to the east, you will come to the Toronto Sculpture Garden. This unique space displays new work by Canadians in six-month runs all year.

KING EDWARD HOTEL

To the east, at Jarvis and King, stands St. Lawrence Hall. A graceful building, artfully endowed with a highly visible dome, a splendid display of carved stone, cast-iron balconies, as well as a lavish public hall, it fell on hard times after the First World War but was lovingly restored and returned to its original purpose in 1967, Canada's centennial year. In its heyday — the second half of the nineteenth century — it was the centre of Toronto's social and cultural life. Soprano Jenny Lind sang here, Sir John A. Macdonald campaigned in its great hall, abolitionists spoke and P.T. Barnum presented Tom Thumb. St. Lawrence Hall also

ENOCH TURNER SCHOOLHOUSE

houses Biagio (155 King East), an Italian restaurant with a pleasing patio.

A more leisurely pace is struck at two sites that bracket the St. Lawrence district. Near its northwest corner, at Adelaide and George Streets (260 Adelaide St. E.) is Toronto's First Post Office. This was actually Toronto's fourth post office, but it was officially deemed "the first" when Toronto incorporated as a city in 1834. It has a small display of old philatelic material and an excellent model of the original Town of York. It is also a working post office.

If you are convinced the 3 Rs ain't what they used to be, pay a visit to the Enoch Turner Schoolhouse, located at the easterly end of the district at 106 Trinity Street. Built in 1848 beside Toronto's oldest surviving church, Little Trinity, the school was paid for by subscription from the wealthy congregants of St. James to serve the deserving children of poorer brethren who could not afford an education in the days before public education. It is notable not only for being the first public school in the province, but the first co-educational one, too. Its classroom has been restored to closely resemble the 1849 original.

KING STREET SHOPPING

From St. Lawrence Hall, stroll east along King. With so many of the area's older buildings having been converted to offices and studios for architects and other design professionals, it is not surprising that a significant number of the shops along the area's main shopping street cater to these industries. From the American twentieth-century classic Knoll to modern Canadian Nienkamper, you can find interior furnishings, lighting, framing, arts, crafts and antiques at shops like Up Country and Italinteriors. Other fine shops include Arts on King, an emporium of useful and not-so-useful items for the home made by dozens of local craftspeople and David E. Lake, with its fine old and rare books, maps and prints. By Parliament Street the stores begin to thin and one can return by taking a King streetcar westbound.

ST. LAWRENCE HALL

FINANCIAL AND THEATRE DISTRICT

| City Hall | A bird's-eye view of Toronto at the close of the nineteenth-century would have revealed the spires of dozens upon dozens of churches poking high above the rest of the city |

— the spire of St. James Church was even used as a beacon to guide ships. By the 1920s Toronto aspired more to progress than to godliness, and the skyline's spires had begun to give way to skyscrapers. This process continued through the booming 1960s, 1970s and 1980s, by the end of which the once prominent church spires and even the older skyscrapers were completely overshadowed by the sleek, mostly glass towers of banks.

Today, these towers appear at first to be the essence of Toronto's financial, business and civic core — the area bounded roughly by Yonge, Front, Dundas and John Streets. But despite the fact that Bay Street, the spine of downtown

FINANCIAL AND THEATRE DISTRICT ▲

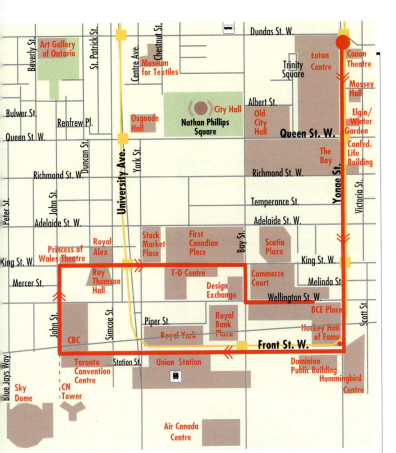

Toronto, is lined with the glass behemoths and, as the nation's financial centre, is frequently compared with New York's Wall Street, Toronto has maintained its vitality as a city precisely because this first impression is not entirely accurate. For it is also a fact that much of the older city remains, both in form and function. Despite being its commercial centre, Toronto's core continues to support a vast array of other activities.

Here lies the city's civic heart: the Old and New City Halls, and the provincial and municipal courts. Also playing a big role are theatres and concert halls: the Hummingbird, the St. Lawrence Centre, the Royal Alex, the Princess of Wales, Roy Thomson Hall, Massey Hall, the Canon and the Elgin and Winter Garden Theatres. Sports are well represented by the Rogers Centre, the Hockey Hall of Fame and since February 1999, the newest facility, the Air Canada Centre, which houses both the Raptors' basketball team and the hockey playing Maple Leafs. These leisure pursuits have spawned a slew of

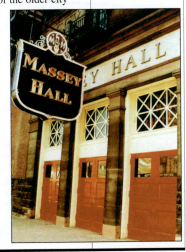

**ABOVE: OLD CANADIAN IMPERIAL BANK OF COMMERCE
BELOW: BANK OF NOVA SCOTIA, OLD & NEW**

restaurants that cater to business people by day, and pre- and post-theatre goers and sports fans by night. Small but interesting art galleries in the core include the Toronto Dominion Gallery of Inuit Art and the Hudson Bay Company Gallery. All these activities, when combined with the miles of shops that line much of the underground PATH network, and the increasing number of office buildings that are being converted to residential lofts, make downtown Toronto lively day or night.

But as visible as the glass towers are from afar, they become difficult to differentiate up close. From the ground, many of the older buildings come into their own. They are generally interesting, built to the street, displaying the skill of stone and brick masons, of ironworkers. They often step back as they rise, ziggurat-like, with windows of varying sizes and columns and cornices that mimic those employed at street level added to the top floors. Originally designed to be visible from afar, many of these buildings were the biggest or tallest in their time: the Royal York Hotel was the largest hotel in the Commonwealth when it opened in 1927, and the old Canadian Imperial Bank of Commerce was the tallest building in the city for 35 years. Their interiors are not to be missed, especially their ground floors, which are filled with carved wood, wrought iron, cast brass, intricately laid marble, gilt-covered ceilings bedecked with chandeliers and a host of other fine details.

With the plethora of things to see and do, it is difficult to imagine "covering" the whole downtown in one attempt. There are bus and trolley tours that provide a good overview and can help you decide where to concentrate your energies. As well, a number of the major attractions, such as the Rogers Centre, the headquarters of the Canadian Broadcasting Corporation (CBC), City Hall, and many of the theatres, offer tours of their own facilities.

FINANCIAL AND THEATRE DISTRICT ▲

A CIRCLE OF PLAY AND DISPLAY

Yonge Street between Dundas and Queen is home to many of Toronto's best-known performance spaces, while several sites right on the Dundas-Yonge intersection are being redeveloped to house new theatres and cinemas. The Canon at 263 Yonge is across from the Eaton Centre and just south of the new facilities. Built originally as a vaudeville house in 1920, it was converted to a grand movie house when talkies supplanted live performances as the main form of popular entertainment. When movie houses began to lose their appeal to television, it was converted again, this time to a six-plex. In 1988 it was restored and reopened as a legitimate theatre yet again, this time to house the wildly successful *Phantom of the Opera*.

ELGIN AND WINTER GARDEN THEATRES ENTRANCE (ABOVE AND BELOW)

South of the Canon, on Shuter just off Yonge, is Massey Hall, Toronto's Carnegie Hall–era concert hall. Noted industrialist and farm-machinery magnate Hart Massey built it as a gift to the city. Like its New York counterpart, it has marvelous acoustics.

The Elgin and the Winter Garden, the only double-decker theatres still operating in the world, are located to the south, at 189 Yonge. The larger 1,563-seat Elgin is decorated in Italian Renaissance-style plasterwork. It is quite magnificent. But the smaller, 991-seat Winter Garden above it is even better. Silk foliage hangs from plaster bowers, while thousands of tiny lights twinkle gaily in a completely fantastic pastoral setting. Built for vaudeville in 1913, the two theatres were easily converted to picture palaces, but the smaller upper theatre was closed for decades as no one was willing to invest the amount needed to meet fire codes for such a modest space. In the 1980s, however, the Ontario Heritage Foundation bought both theatres and restored them to their original glory. Productions such as *Cats*, *Joseph and the Amazing Technicolor Dreamcoat*, and performance troupes such as Stomp have been playing to full houses ever since.

Restaurants and other nightspots are not so plentiful in this area as they are near the King Street theatres, but there are some exceptions. On Victoria Street there's Terroni for

▲ Neighbourhoods and Districts

Stained glass at Hockey Hall of Fame

Hockey Hall of Fame and TD Canada Trust Towers

rustic Italian fare, while on Yonge, the eclectic Superior features a smart sandblasted brick interior, and Baton Rouge in the Eaton Centre's façade, serves some of Toronto's finest ribs.

On the southwest corner of Yonge at Queen is The Bay, the entrepreneurial descendant of Canada's oldest trading company (the Hudson's Bay Company), and one of the country's largest department store chains. Its wide bays, made possible with the introduction of steel frame construction in the late nineteenth century, proved perfect for displaying all the goods carried in the newly fashionable "departmental" stores of the day. Across Yonge and slightly south is the striking Confederation Life building. When it was built in the 1890s, its towers were topped by sharply peaked roofs. Without the peaks, it now looks a bit more like a fortress. Either way, it was an eccentric choice for a staid insurance company.

Continuing south on Yonge, you will pass several fine low-rise buildings constructed just after the 1904 fire that wiped out much of this area, and at number 67 the city's first skyscraper, a fifteen-storey structure built in 1905 by the New York firm of Carrere and Hastings for the now defunct Traders Bank of Canada. Just east of the corner at Adelaide, at number 10, is a posh little beaux-arts gem. Built in 1907 for the Birbeck Investment Company, it was restored in the 1980s by the Ontario Heritage Foundation, which is one of its tenants along with a number of other cultural organizations. The fine restoration job, including one of the few "personned" elevators still operating in the city, has won the building numerous period movie roles.

Returning to Yonge, and still heading south, you will pass BCE Place (see below) before reaching the northwest corner of Yonge and Front. Here stands an ornately rococo former Bank of Montreal. From the sculpted characters hanging around outside, you will have guessed that this is the Hockey Hall of Fame. For over thirty years, the museum was located in a far smaller venue at the exhibition grounds. As part of the BCE Place development, space was created for the museum in the renovated rococo Bank of Montreal building, an odd contrast with a sport that's sleek and fast. For hockey fans, it is a small paradise, containing everything from the original Stanley Cup to video displays of memorable plays. Gretzky groupies eager to see still more of his memorabilia will find it at his restaurant at 99 Blue Jays Way.

Just to the east, on the south side of Front, is the second cluster of Toronto's live theatres. First, there is The Hummingbird Centre for the Performing Arts. When it was completed in 1960, this 3,200-seat house was the first large

FINANCIAL AND THEATRE DISTRICT

hall to have been built in the city since the turn of the century. It serves as home to the National Ballet and the Canadian Opera Company, as well as to visiting troupes representing various performing arts. The Hummingbird has been well used and undoubtedly has a place in the hearts of many. It is here that the National Ballet performed its annual rite of Christmas, *The Nutcracker*, for many years, and to where Mikhail Baryshnikov defected after a performance of the Bolshoi in June 1973. Both the National Ballet and the Canadian Opera Company move into the new Four Seasons Centre for the Performing Arts as of fall 2006. This new facility offers patrons a superior experience.

Just east of the Hummingbird is the St. Lawrence Centre for the Arts, which contains two theatres, the Jane Mallett and the Bluma Appel. A number of companies make the centre their home; chief among them the Canadian Stage Company, which was created in 1988 from the merger of the Toronto Free Theatre and CentreStage, both long-time players on Toronto's theatrical front. Also housed here is Opera in Concert and, under the same director, Toronto Operetta Theatre. Although brutishly bunker-like outside, the St. Lawrence boasts an interior that makes it equal to the arts it hosts.

Head west on Front Street, walking past the grand colonnaded Dominion Public Building to reach the next string of entertainment clusters that ring Toronto's financial district. Along the way, you will pass some significant representatives of this district, of which the first initially will catch your attention as a cheery glow emanating from the vicinity of the Bay and Front intersection. The source is the Royal Bank Plaza, the most eye-catching of the postwar generation of bank complexes. While the others are smooth, box-shaped structures, this one consists of two odd-shaped, almost triangular towers set at an angle to the street and sheathed in serrated curtain walls. To these glass walls were added some 2,600 ounces of gold, about $1.3-million worth at today's prices. The precious metal has proved to be more than worth its weight and a truly happy choice: it casts shimmering water-like reflections on nearby buildings, lighting up lower Bay Street on even the grayest of days and turning a fiery yellow at sunset.

PORTICO UNION STATION

GREAT HALL

The main beneficiary of the Royal Bank's golden glow is Union Station and its front plaza. Most visitors to Toronto today arrive by air, but in the days when virtually everyone came by train, ship or carriage, this area served as the portal to the city. To welcome and impress all comers, a number of grand buildings were constructed

▲ Neighbourhoods and Districts

ROYAL YORK HOTEL

in the 1920s. Union Station was chief among these. Opened in 1927 by the Prince of Wales, it is a colossal edifice stretching 750 feet along Front. It is also monumental in style with its awesome colonnade. Even more impressive is the great hall within. At 260 feet, it remains the largest "room" in Canada (not counting sports facilities), but nonetheless feels comfortable enough to calm even the most harried traveller. Train travel has diminished since its heyday, but because Union Station now functions as the terminal for Toronto's suburban commuter system as well as being a station on the subway system, it is even busier today than when it was built.

Also from the era of mail trains, but in a thoroughly deco rather than classical style, was the old postal station, south of Union Station on Bay. Gutted in 1997 to make way for the new home of the NHL Maple Leafs and the NBA Raptors, major portions of its impressive carved façade remain visible. Inside the Air Canada Centre is a state-of-the-art sports facility that serves players and fans equally well. The seats are wide and comfy, the sightlines excellent.

On the north side of Front Street, across from Union Station and connected to it by the oldest of Toronto's underground passages is the Royal York Hotel, which also opened in 1927. It is one of the many fine château-style hotels built across Canada by the country's two main railroads, Canadian National (CN) and Canadian Pacific (CP). For years it was the largest hotel in the British Commonwealth and thanks to constant renovation and repair, it remains deservedly popular.

TORONTO
CONVENTION
CENTRE (BELOW)
AIR CANADA
CENTRE (BOTTOM)

Continue west on Front Street, across University Avenue. To your left (south) is the Toronto Convention Centre, most notable for its lack of an obvious front door. A huge facility — a major recent addition spans the railroad tracks still further south — it provides tonnes of space in which to host the ever-growing number of conventions held in the city. It is also the site for a number of trade and craft shows and specialty exhibitions.

Opposite the Convention Centre you will pass a silver cube wrapped in red bands that is the CBC Broadcast Centre. Probably no other building in Toronto has raised so much ire across the country. Canadians tend either to love or hate the CBC; few are neutral. Both the money spent on the centre and its design have been vigorously criticized. Programs, both for radio and TV,

FINANCIAL AND THEATRE DISTRICT ▲

are often taped in the main lobby for all to see and hear. Also on the ground floor are the CBC Museum and the Graham Spry Theatre, which programs CBC shows. Both are free. Best of all, there is the Glenn Gould Studio, in which a wide range of programs, from new music to chamber groups, is taped. Admission to this small, comfortable, and acoustically superb space is quite reasonable.

MAMMA MIA! AT THE ROYAL ALEX

You are now at Front and John, within steps of two of the city's most popular tourist attractions: the Rogers Centre, home of the Toronto Blue Jays, and the CN Tower, the world's tallest free-standing structure. You are also on the edge of the city's third live-theatre district. Along King, Peter and John Streets primarily, but also on smaller streets such as Duncan, Mercer and Pearl, are many eateries catering to a wide variety of tastes to serve both the lunch and theatre crowds. The main performance spaces served by all these restaurants are Roy Thomson Hall, and the Royal Alex and the Princess of Wales Theatres.

Roy Thomson Hall, on the south side of King at Simcoe, is home to the Toronto Symphony as well as to such classic groups as the Toronto Mendelssohn Choir. It was designed by West Coast Canadian architect Arthur Erickson and looks a bit like a glass volcano. By some unfathomable trick, it manages to look far smaller from outside than from within. After many complaints about the original acoustics, local architects KPMB with New York acousticians Artec rebuilt the interior in time for the fall 2002 season. Subsequent reviews of the sound have been raves. Across the street from Roy Thomson is the Royal Alexandra Theatre, a classic Edwardian jewel box. It is owned by Toronto businessman Ed Mirvish, who also purchased and restored the Old Vic in London and has been home to such Broadway hits as *Les Miserables* and *Mama Mia!* The Princess of Wales Theatre, located west along King at John Street, was built by son David Mirvish for Broadway extravaganzas and other large-scale

ROYAL ALEXANDRA THEATRE

147

▲ NEIGHBOURHOODS AND DISTRICTS

COMMERCE COURT

SCULPTURE AT THE TD CENTRE

productions such as *Beauty and the Beast*, *The Lion King* and the world premiere of the musical *The Lord of the Rings*. Mirvish kept a tight rein on construction costs, but nonetheless managed to achieve a refined, lovely and extremely comfortable interior. Particularly noteworthy are the highly imaginative washrooms.

In taking a gander at Toronto at play, you have skirted the city's financial core. Now it is time to plunge in.

THE MODERN BUSINESS DISTRICT

Head back east toward King and Bay crossing University Avenue. On this corner — or just off it — are the headquarters of four of Canada's largest banks (the fifth, the Royal Bank, was described earlier). Occupying much of the block on the northwest corner of King and Bay is First Canadian Place, headquarters of the Bank of Montreal, and its mate, the Exchange Tower, which houses the Toronto Stock Exchange. Appropriately, the consulting architect for these towers was the American Edward Durell Stone, for the whole of both buildings is clad in stone, white marble to be precise.

Across the street, on the northeast corner, is the reddish Scotia Plaza, the newer home of the Bank of Nova Scotia, and its more modest, older limestone home. The latter deco-style building was designed in the late 1920s by John Lyle, a noted Canadian architect of that period. At the southeast corner, is the Canadian Imperial Bank of Commerce's complex, the stainless-steel Commerce Court, designed by I.M. Pei, and the very solid, stone, old Bank of Commerce building. Inside Commerce Court is Jump, the supremely trendy (for the business-lunch set) and excellent restaurant featuring international fare.

On the southwest corner is the dark Toronto Dominion (TD) Centre, the first to raise its standard on Toronto's skyline. The architect engaged here was Mies van der Rohe, patriarch of international modernism. Mies designed

FINANCIAL AND THEATRE DISTRICT ▲

two towers and the impenetrable-looking banking pavilion that stands right on the southwest corner. Unfortunately, the TD seems to have been unwilling to leave well enough alone, and in the mid-1980s, added, to the south on Wellington Street, a fourth black tower, which makes a mockery of the careful placement of the first three buildings. Canoe, a fine restaurant with a Muskoka cottage-country theme, is on the fifty-fourth floor and offers a spectacular view to accompany the equally spectacular food.

TD's fifth and last tower squats menacingly on Bay Street atop the original hazy pink and beige Toronto Stock Exchange, the building that now houses the Design Exchange. The marriage is an odd one. Nonetheless, it did save the older building, which is an art-deco delight. The Design Exchange (or DX) is a non-profit organization devoted to good taste as expressed through commercial, industrial and architectural design. In addition to its excellent library, the DX hosts exhibits and lecture series on subjects ranging from interiors and urban design to furniture, clothing and gadgets (416 363-6121). It also contains a small gift shop.

BCE PLACE

While many of the financial district's modern buildings, such as the four banks, were set amidst wide open, windy plazas that landscapers have had to work hard at making more comfortable for mere pedestrians, the trend over the past decade has been to exchange these spaces for inviting, tall, well-lit interior plazas. BCE Place, at Bay and Wellington, is a case in point. Its block-long Galleria contains the façade of an older building that was demolished to make way for the project, shops with street-like fronts, and cafés that overflow into a wide and cheerful atrium. In fact, BCE Place has succeeded in attracting a number of good restaurants. Among them are Acqua, which offers Italian food in a water-theme setting; Masquerade Caffe and Bar, also Italian but more in the carnival than in the power-scene vein.

DESIGN EXCHANGE

QUEEN STREET WEST

NANCY WON

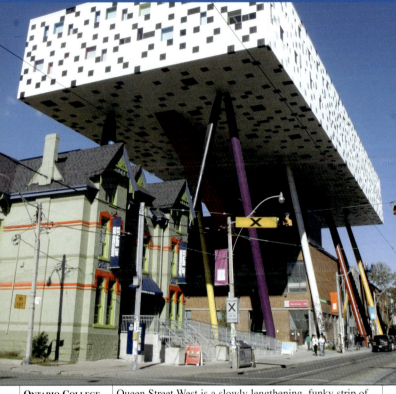

ONTARIO COLLEGE OF ART & DESIGN	Queen Street West is a slowly lengthening, funky strip of shops, galleries, bistros and bars. Near the University of Toronto and the Ontario College of Art and Design and close to downtown, Queen West became the address of choice for many students, artists and other young people in the 1970s. They liked the local shops which, catering mainly to eastern Europeans, offered delicacies not commonly found in Toronto at the time: homemade sausages, dumplings and desserts and pumpernickel and rye breads. Many of the stores and apartments were vacant and the rents were low. By the end of the decade, the street had radically changed. New shops opened selling macramé, candles, offbeat clothes and old furniture passed off as antiques. Booksellers, chased from their digs on Gerrard Street by redevelopment, moved here. Queen West had long had a vibrant nightlife: country and western at the Horseshoe Tavern, jazz at the now defunct Bourbon Street Café and chatter and music wafting from the Portuguese Social Club. But now the street itself had become a major source of entertainment.

In the 1980s, the clothes got funkier, the music raunchier. New clubs and theatres opened. The crafts were better crafted. New cafés, bistros, and restaurants opened. The Salvation Army Thrift Store became Le Château. The rents went up. Funky gave way to trendy, but the fun has stayed.

For the past decade, there has been a wholesale conversion of the district's nearby manufacturing buildings into residential lofts. This, combined with new buildings designed to look like manufacturing buildings converted into lofts, is pushing Queen Street's makeover further and further west. A few years ago, it reached Ossington

STREET LIFE

Avenue, where a former candy factory has been redesigned as home sweet home. It paused here for a while, as though baffled about how to get past the old Queen Street Mental Health Centre, a west-end landmark so frequently referred to simply as "999 Queen" that its street address has been changed to 1001.

It overcame its hesitation, however, and now stretches so far west that it now connects to the district known as Parkdale, and its most westerly end is adopting the moniker, "West Queen West."

YONGE TO SPADINA

Queen Street East and West are separated by Yonge Street, right in the heart of downtown. On the west side of Queen's intersection with Yonge stand Toronto's two best-known downtown shopping centres — the massive Eaton Centre and, across the street, the Hudson's Bay Company's flagship store.

A stone's throw further west on Queen stands a collection of key civic structures, including Toronto's old and new city halls and the neo-classical Osgoode Hall, which houses provincial law courts and administrative offices. An impressive

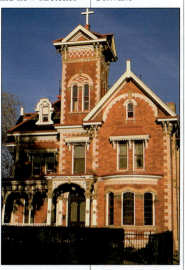

FELICIAN SISTERS CONVENT

151

▲ Neighbourhoods and Districts

Downward Dog Yoga Spa

recent addition to the area is Toronto's new opera house. The elegant glass-and-steel structure is scheduled to open in 2006.

Past University Avenue, the character of the street abruptly changes, with monumental civic edifices giving way to trendy shops and cafés. At the threshold of the two areas, although completely anachronistic in relation to either, stands Campbell House. The Georgian home of Upper Canada's first chief justice, it was shifted from its original moorings next to Toronto's First Post Office (at George and Adelaide) in 1972 and refurbished to serve as the home of the Law Society of Upper Canada, the trade union of Ontario's legal profession.

At the corner of Queen Street and John Street stands a stately office building clad in white terra cotta and decorated with small casts symbolizing various aspects of publishing, reading and writing. Originally built for the Methodist Book and Publishing Company (later Ryerson Press), it is now the home of CHUM Television — a Canadian media empire that includes MuchMusic (the Canadian version of MTV), as well as various other specialty channels and Citytv, a popular local station.

Also at CHUM, for one dollar, you can enter a small booth and speak your mind on any subject to a TV camera (and possibly catch yourself later on the station's program, *Speaker's Corner*). CHUM also has its own museum — MZTV — lodged above the ChumCity store at 299 Queen Street West. Tours are offered at noon, 2 and 4 p.m. on weekdays or by appointment.

Eateries such as Le Sélect bistro (328), Peter Pan (373) and the Queen Mother Café (208) are neighbourhood

stalwarts, practically approaching middle age. Slightly younger is The Rivoli (332) and Babur (273) which offers above-average Indian food and the even-younger Tiger Lily's (257), a noodle house owned by one of Toronto's best-known caterers and purveyors of fine foods. There are also dozens of mainstream shops and boutiques in the area — from Club Monaco's Caban interiors flagship store to Lush, the Canadian handmade cosmetics retailer.

SPADINA TO BATHURST: FASHION AND TEXTILE DISTRICT

Queen West shoppers peering into the grungy-looking regions west of Spadina Avenue would at first see little to draw them over to the other side. The high-gloss shops, boutiques and restaurants that overwhelmed only a few steps back appear to stop abruptly at this major junction. But despite first impressions, the westerly reaches of Queen Street — spanning from Spadina Avenue to the CN railway underpass at Dufferin Street — are in reality home to some of the most interesting boutiques, galleries and people in the city.

Walking westward from Spadina, you will first find yourself in the area known as the Fashion District. A textile lover's dream come true, this particular stretch of Queen is dominated on both sides by fabric and upholstery wholesalers. At the time of the Queen West exodus across Spadina, this area was the centre of the Goth revival in Toronto. Subscribers to the Goth lifestyle took advantage of the cheap textiles here to make their own distinct style. Though the Goth scene has since given way to a more

▲ Neighbourhoods and Districts

CITYTV'S *SPEAKER'S CORNER*

artistic, urbanite sensibility, remnants of this period can be seen in a smattering of mid-1990s nightclubs, including Savage Garden (550) and The Bovine Sex Club (542). Long-standing textile retailers like Worldsew Centre (511) and Downtown Fabrics (436) continue to do a brisk business thanks to the exploding trend of DIY fashion and interiors. In keeping with the area's needle-and-thread philosophy, bead and craft shops also abound. Arton Beads and Findings (523) is a long-time favourite and is perpetually busy. Newcomer The Beadery (446), across the street, stocks all manner of chunky stringables.

If you're not the type to fashion a frock of your own, this strip also plays host to many boutiques specializing in both vintage and reworked vintage. The obvious exception being no-logo giant American Apparel, its sleek white storefront is a sharp contrast to the unkempt charm of its surroundings. Nearby, sneaker emporium Da Zone (468) brings in the occasional gem, but for a veritable gold mine of limited-edition kicks, walk a few paces off Queen to Richmond Street sneaker boutique Goodfoot (431), just one block south near Spadina. While on Richmond, stop by Goodfoot's sister store, Nomad (431), which brings in exclusive high-end street labels previously unavailable in Toronto. For vintage, head back to Queen and check out Brava Vintage Clothing (483), next to American Apparel, or continue a few paces westward to House of Vintage (571), one of the larger, more organized vintage shops in the city. If a coffee break is in order, cross the street and put your feet up at Tequila Bookworm (490). This cozy café encourages lingering; patrons are free to peruse the substantial magazine shelf (heavy on art and design titles) and the library of used books at the back.

QUEEN STREET WEST

Continuing west on Queen, Preloved (613), on the south side, offers unique pieces made in-house from vintage finds. Next door, local DJs and music lovers swear by Cosmos (607) for rare and collectible records. Approaching Bathurst, Shanghai Cowgirl (538) is the first of a number of hip eateries on the strip, offering Asian fusion in a sleek, urban cowboy setting. For a decidedly more low-key meal, popular take-out joint Gandhi Indian Cuisine (554) has the best roti in Toronto.

BATHURST TO TRINITY BELLWOODS PARK: SHOPPING DISTRICT

Things begin to pick up west of Bathurst Street as "West Queen West" shakes off the slightly unkempt aura of the Fashion District. Home-decor stores dominate this stretch and trendy restaurant options abound. Coming up on the south side is Morba (665), filled to the brim with affordable vintage furnishings and other home paraphernalia. A few doors down, Barfly (673) specializes in cool bar accessories, including customized retro beer fridges. French decor boutique Chatalet (717) is ripe with charm and caters to Torontonians who can appreciate *la vie en rose*. Other noteworthy decor shops along this stretch include Pavilion (739) for urban furnishings; Quasi Modo (789) for the design savvy; Commute Home (819) for contemporary wood pieces; and Remnants (685) for awesome vintage accent pieces.

Boutiques are practically door-to-door in this area. Across from Pavilion, on the north side of Queen, Comrags (525) is great for geek-chic frocks and, down the street, recent addition Pho Pa

CAMPBELL HOUSE

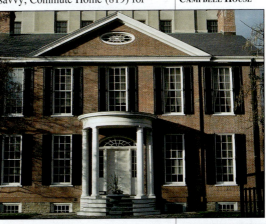

▲ Neighbourhoods & districts

THE DRAKE HOTEL	(968) features trendy pieces with a sexy flare. Stylish moms will adore Kol Kid (670), which carries classic toys and adorable bedroom accessories for babies and toddlers. A few doors down, Magic Pony (694), part gallery and part toy boutique, features playthings for the kid at heart, including limited-edition figures, plush toys and artwork. Next door, Red Tea Box (696) is an odd but delightful combination of tea shop, patisserie and home decor shop. Other confectioners within the next two blocks include The Nutty Chocolatier (700), Dufflet Pastries (787) and J.S. Bonbons (811). Down the street from The Nutty Chocolatier is style mecca Delphic (705), which carries sophisticated casual wear that is consistently ahead of the trend. Their sister store Klaxon Howl (881) is located just down the street, across from Trinity Bellwoods Park. Brimming with character, Klaxon Howl boasts the same trendy sensibility in a more rugged military and vintage shop. For late-night cocktails, backtrack to the restored 1940s era Paddock (178 Bathurst), Habitat Lounge (735) or check out recently renovated Polish butcher shop turned "it spot" Czehoski (678). Queen Street mainstay Gypsy Co-op (815), a cozy combination of restaurant, bar, lounge and candy shop, is perfect for younger visitors looking for a casual night out. Dinner options in this area include Irie Food Joint (745) for top-notch Caribbean fare, San (676) for authentic Korean in a hip, New York setting, Terroni (720) for thin-crust pizza or Noce (875), one of the best authentic Italian restaurants in Toronto. **TRINITY BELLWOODS TO DUFFERIN: THE GALLERY DISTRICT** The stomping grounds of local artists and collectors, this stretch of Queen Street has been known as the Gallery District since 2000. Home to the Museum of Contemporary Canadian Art (952), which is open to the public Tuesday to Sunday (free admission), and to numerous independent galleries, including the Angell Gallery (890), Clint

QUEEN STREET WEST ▲

Roenisch Gallery (944), DeLeon White Gallery (1096) and Engine Gallery (1112), this area thins out quite a bit in terms of shops and boutiques, but there are a few gems worth checking out.

TRINITY BELLWOODS PARK (ABOVE AND BELOW)

Rapid development in recent years, spearheaded by the renovation of the Drake Hotel, has upped this area's hipster cache. Rents have dramatically increased and a number of galleries have left as a result. Eager to snatch up prime territory, new restaurants and bars have jumped in on the action, hoping to hitch their wagons to the Drake's rising star.

Once you pass Trinity Bellwoods Park, stop by Oyster Boy (872) for a midday hit of luscious bivalves, or have a meal at nearby Swan (892), an upscale diner featuring art deco booths and an old Coca Cola cooler. For an energy boost, Fresh by Juice for Life (894) serves up refreshing fruit juices with an herbal kick.

Past Ossington Avenue, Camera Bar (1028) has a sleek coffee bar at the front and a movie theatre screening foreign and independent films at the back. Down the street, Studio Brilliantine (1082) features everyday objects with an artistic twist. At 69 Vintage (1100) discerning staff take the work out of vintage shopping, offering only stylish picks that are practical today. Stop at the renovated Drake Hotel (1150) for lunch at the corner café or for a cool cocktail on the Moroccan-themed rooftop patio. The hard-to-miss visual boundary of the CN railway underpass up ahead marks the end of "West Queen West," but before heading back, drop by the Gladstone Hotel (1214), Toronto's oldest continuously operating hotel. Taking a cue from the Drake, the Gladstone has recently begun major renovations to restore it to its original glory, and this will only add to this exciting Toronto district's appeal.

157

CHINATOWN AND KENSINGTON MARKET

Chinatown, one of Toronto's most vibrant downtown neighbourhoods, radiates out from the intersection of Dundas and Spadina. Always crowded and bustling, the area offers great opportunities for dining and browsing. Some of North America's best Chinese and Vietnamese restaurants are located here. Enjoy hot and sour soup or barbecued duck before you visit the tiny shops selling everything from fresh produce to porcelain vases. Just to the north and west is funky Kensington Market, another entertaining destination for browsing. Here you can enjoy a cup of espresso and a fresh croissant before shopping for a variety of goods. On the eastern edge of this area stands the Art Gallery of Ontario (AGO). Art aficionados will want to visit the gallery for its fine collection of Canadian work as well as its significant holding of sculpture by Henry Moore.

NEW YEAR'S IN CHINATOWN

CHINATOWN

If you did this tour with your eyes closed, Chinatown would be recognizable immediately through your sense of smell: the rich, sweet scents of soy and sesame oil wafting through the air. With your eyes open, the source of the delightful aroma is made visible: dozens of shops festooned with glazed ducks, ribs and suckling pigs, a glimpse of butchers deftly carving portions for a seemingly endless stream of customers and an even greater number of cheerful, unpretentious restaurants, which are open until all hours and constantly full.

At night the streets are brightly lit — mostly in yellows and reds — setting off Toronto's old brick buildings in alternating warm and eerie hues. The pavement is jammed: singles, couples and family groups out for a stroll, shopping, chatting and hurrying to a favourite dining spot. Within the shops, often called "Trading Companies," masses of crisp green vegetables are piled high; the shelves are stocked with tins of abalone, turnips, bamboo shoots, water chestnuts and baby corn ears, as well as herbs and spices and dried foods ranging from jellyfish, squid and shrimp to mushrooms, beans and lotus seeds. These stores

SHOPPING IN CHINATOWN

▲ Neighbourhoods and Districts

Shopping and chopping in Chinatown

Chinatown at night

also carry everything necessary for preparing and serving these exotic delights: woks and whisks, bamboo bowls for steaming rice, floral-patterned dishes, dragon-embellished platters and chopsticks of ivory, ebony, wood lacquered to an Imperial red and even plastic. But your shopping will not be limited to food and kitchenware. Shops are also full to overflowing with items ranging from inexpensive fans, embroidered slippers, hand-carved animals and sandalwood boxes to pricey gifts such as silk dresses, jade and cloisonné jewellery and porcelain vases. The herbalists, with their natural cures for everything from stress and indigestion to baldness and infertility, are also worth a visit.

Toronto's Chinese community first grew up around Elizabeth Street, where new City Hall now stands, in the 1880s. It was a relatively poor community, eking out a living in service industries such as laundering and food. Then, during the late 1950s and 1960s, its character and population began to change dramatically. It grew in size, scope and variety as a result of changes in immigration policy, substantial investment that flowed as a consequence of uncertainty about Hong Kong's future, the arrival of Vietnamese "boat people" (many of Chinese descent) and the demolition required to build the new City Hall, which forced the community westward. Today, the Dundas-Spadina intersection (and surrounding blocks) remains the shopping, political and cultural hub for the thousands of Torontonians of Chinese descent.

With these changes in the Chinese community, in combination with the larger Toronto community's developing a more adventuresome and sophisticated palate, came changes in the restaurant cuisine. Most of the old "chop suey" houses, products of an attempt to cater to Western tastes, are long gone. Today's Chinese restaurants usually specialize in the dishes of one or more regions: Hunan, Beijing, Szechuan or Kwangtung (Canton) are among the areas represented. In recent years, fancy restaurants offering the haute cuisine of each of these areas have opened all around town. For the most part, Chinatown's restaurants continue to exemplify the flaky-paint-and-Formica school of design,

CHINATOWN AND KENSINGTON MARKET ▲

ON SPADINA

although many are excellent and inexpensive.

Favourites among Torontonians are numerous and include Lee Garden (331 Spadina), Wah Sing (47 Baldwin), Xam Yu (339 Spadina) or Eating Garden (43 Baldwin); Chung King (428 Spadina) and Peter's Chung King (281 College at Spadina), both for their hot, zesty Szechuan or Singapore noodles; Lucky Dragon (418 Spadina) for dumplings or Swatow (309 Spadina), which also does a delicate eggplant with shrimps; Kowloon (5 Baldwin) for seafood or dim sum; or Happy Seven (358 Spadina) for mostly Cantonese.

Spadina Avenue, although mostly Chinese today — with a fair representation of Vietnamese — continues at its southern end to be the centre of Toronto's diminished rag, fur and needle trades. Early owners and workers in these sweatshops (for that is what they were and still are) usually were Jews who lived, worshipped and shopped along Spadina and in Kensington Market, which lies just to the west. In those days, Spadina was graced with two rows of trees on each side; it was a real avenue. Later, it became merely an inordinately wide street. Finally the street has been revamped: streetcars again trundle north and south heading all the way to Harbourfront.

SPADINA/QUEEN STREET DRAGON

KENSINGTON MARKET

KENSINGTON MARKET

If you walk west on Baldwin Street from Spadina, you will reach Kensington Market, a neighbourhood that was once almost exclusively Jewish but is now predominantly Portuguese, Latino and West Indian. Kensington's houses are small, often in disrepair and frequently painted chartreuse, aquamarine, forest green, orange, turquoise, lavender, mauve or blue, as well as the more traditional red or white. Along its commercial streets — Nassau, Augusta, Baldwin and Kensington — these small houses serve as shops, their wares spilling out onto the sidewalk and sometimes into the street itself. The market is not for the hyper-hygienic. For almost 100 years, entrepreneurial immigrants who could not afford separate commercial space (or to whom others would not rent space) have made it a place of bustle, disorder and chaos. Not long ago, in addition to the sounds of blaring music and people haggling and tossing about a never-ending stream of fresh deliveries, the area's streets were filled with the sounds of chickens,

161

▲ NEIGHBOURHOODS AND DISTRICTS

KENSINGTON MARKET

pigeons, geese and ducks. Live specimens have been banned, but the market remains boisterous and busy, offering just about everything for sale. Food is central: fresh fish, poultry, game, bread, eggs, vegetables, ingredients for everyday dishes and the rare delicacies of Asian, Jamaican, West Indian, Portuguese and North African cuisine are all on hand. But shops are not restricted to selling food — far from it. You'll find dry goods and clothes, buckets and bicycles, furniture and bedding, electronics, paintings on velvet, tapestries in acrylic, everything including the kitchen sink — several, if you'd like.

Within Kensington Market, there are several places to eat, including the Boat (158 Augusta), a fairly expensive Portuguese restaurant, and Amadeus (184 Augusta), also Portuguese and noted for its seafood, and a delightful French boite, La Palette (256 Augusta).

If all this walking seems overwhelming but you really want a taste of the neighbourhood (in more ways than one), you could simply head back east on Baldwin Street. In its most easterly block, between St. George and McCaul Streets, two blocks north of the AGO, is an amazing collection of inexpensive to mid-priced restaurants, amazing not only because it is perhaps the only quiet, narrow, tree-lined side street in Toronto to have become home to so many eateries — twenty-one at last count — but because of the cultural variety they represent. Where else could you find five Chinese restaurants specializing in seafood (Baldwin Palace, Kowloon, Hua Sung, Wah Sing and Eating Garden), three eateries featuring delicacies of the Indian Subcontinent at Gateways of India, the Jodhpore club and Indian Choice, two in the subtle flavours of Japan (Fujiyama and Kon-nichi-wa are the best, the latter modeled in a modest way on London's wildly popular Wagamama chain), two offering a taste of France (Café La Gaffe and La Bodega, two of the earliest tenants on the street), as well as the Malaysian and Thai Mata Hari, the Mexican of Margaritas First Cantina and Tapas, the Korean Hana, as well as Italian fine dining at Porta Pane and Italian desserts and coffees at John's, and an assortment of "international" spots such as Creations and Sensation Café as well?

Having run out of space, there are some more choices just around the corner on McCaul itself, including the lovely Cassis. For a sedate contrast to the modern eclecticism of immigrant capitalism, you can visit the Grange, located just south of the Art Gallery of Ontario. Built in 1817, the Grange was the very Anglo, Georgian

home of D'Arcy Boulton, Jr., an early Toronto worthy. The oldest extant brick home in Toronto, the Grange housed the Art Gallery of Toronto (as the AGO was then called) from 1900 until 1918. As the gallery expanded, the gallery's curators and administrators used the Grange for office space. Following the 1960s expansion of the gallery, the house was fully restored. Admission to the home's interior is through the AGO only, but its front façade can be seen from the park directly south of the gallery. In the Boulton era, this was but a small portion of the Grange's private park, which stretched from Queen Street all the way to Bloor. Torontonians of the time were shocked at how far out of town Boulton's new residence was: for many years few roofs other than that of the Church of St. George the Martyr would have been visible from The Grange.

Today the treed skyline has been replaced by apartments, offices and the CN Tower, but the church remains, although its tower burnt to the ground in the 1950s. It is now home to a chamber group, Baroque Music Beside the Grange, who perform using period instruments about twice a month, except in the summer (call 416 588-4301). The park remains, too. Still called Grange Park, it is now a city park rather than a private property and sits amidst an area that since the turn-of-the-century has been the centre of one of Toronto's biggest immigrant catchment areas.

STREET LIFE IN KENSINGTON MARKET (ABOVE AND BELOW)

QUEEN'S PARK AND THE UNIVERSITY OF TORONTO

ROYAL ONTARIO MUSEUM

It seems a bit of poetic justice that the Ontario Legislative Assembly, the seat of the provincial government, which perches at the top of University Avenue, replaced a building that once served as a mental institution. In the early days, University Avenue was beautifully treed and stretched from this building clear to the lake. Today, the inmates have a view of one of the city's widest, virtually treeless streets, graced at its southern end mostly by standard-issue office buildings, many of them insurance companies, and at its northern end by a cluster of medically outstanding, but only occasionally distinguished-looking, hospitals — Mount Sinai, the Hospital for Sick Children, Toronto General and Princess Margaret. Queen's Park, the great green oval in which the legislature building is situated, is almost entirely surrounded by the St. George Campus of the University of Toronto (U of T), which consists of over 200 buildings spread out over 2.8 square kilometres (one square mile). With over 55,000 students attending its 16 faculties and nine colleges, this university is the largest in Canada.

QUEEN'S PARK AND THE UNIVERSITY OF TORONTO ▲

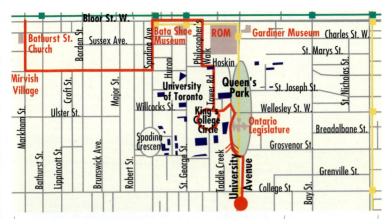

On University Avenue just north of Queen's Park is the Royal Ontario Museum (ROM). Once part of the university, it is now independent, although still publicly owned. The university's influence is particularly strong in the residential and shopping areas to the west of the campus, from Spadina Avenue to at least Bathurst, between College and Bloor Streets. Many of the shops and eateries along these main streets are bohemian, laid back and inexpensive, although there are an increasing number of chain restaurants and coffee shops. Nearby are a number of cultural icons, from the swank Bata Shoe Museum to the bargain basement, "world-famous" Honest Ed's department store. There is Toronto's deservedly world-famous Baroque ensemble, Tafelmusik, which plays in Trinity-St. Paul's United Church (427 Bloor Street West), as well as the Annex Street Theatre (730 Bathurst), and the Poor Alex Theatre (296 Brunswick), three of Toronto's numerous independent medium-sized and small houses.

THE ONTARIO PROVINCIAL LEGISLATURE AT QUEEN'S PARK

ONTARIO LEGISLATURE

The legislature building, best glimpsed from the south at about Dundas Street, is an isolated fortress surrounded by a moat of traffic. Like Toronto's Old City Hall, it caps a long vista, and was designed in the Richardsonian Romanesque style that was popular in the late nineteenth century not only for large public buildings, but also for the homes of the wealthy. Its designer was one Richard A. Waite, a British-born, Buffalo-based architect who was a poker-playing crony of several members of the provincial parliament (MPPs). Unsure of which of two detailed proposals submitted by local architects to pick for the construction of the building, the MPPs turned to their friend Waite. He modestly concluded that only he could undertake such an important commission, and offered his services for a mere $700,000, a figure about $150,000 more than the sum indicated by the locals. Local

▲ NEIGHBOURHOODS AND DISTRICTS

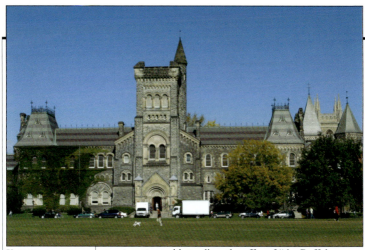

UNIVERSITY COLLEGE

resentment notwithstanding, the offer of "the Buffalo individual" (as the press referred to him) was accepted. And for a mere $1.3-million, the "unspeakable" Waite provided them with their dream house.

Memories of the scandal were slow to fade, but there can be little doubt today that the legislators got their money's worth. The building is rich in detail, both inside and out; ornate carvings, trim, metalwork and windows grace it throughout. Its rooms and halls are both gracious and generous. It has the feel of a fine old men's club, which of course is what it largely has been. Those familiar primarily with modern surroundings of steel, marble, glass and stark white will fall comfortably into the building's embrace. When the House is sitting, all are welcome in the visitors' gallery.

Tours are available throughout the week during the summer months and on weekdays the rest of the year. Call 416 325-7500 for schedule information or take a self-guided walking tour. In its basement cafeteria, you can

CONVOCATION HALL

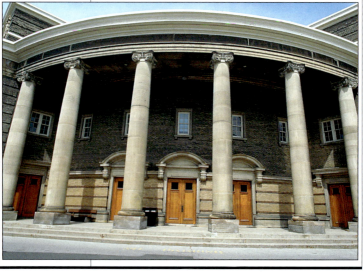

Queen's Park and the University of Toronto

grab fairly good grub for exceptionally low prices. Better yet, if you know an MPP, you might be able to wangle an invitation to the fine restaurant.

University of Toronto

From Queen's Park, you can cross over to King's College Circle and step into the gothic-looking parts of the University of Toronto. Since the 1850s, when University College was completed, the campus has been steadily changing with the addition of new colleges and faculties and the absorption of older ones such as St. Michael's.

The buildings that receive the most attention from modern visitors are University College, Hart House, Knox College, Trinity College and Chapel, and St. Michael's College, where Marshall McLuhan proclaimed, "the medium is the message."

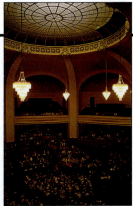

CONVOCATION HALL INTERIOR

Although of course not genuinely medieval, these structures strongly evoke their precursors (with modern plumbing), thereby providing the atmosphere of intellectual depth one expects of a serious university. Being among the older campus buildings, they also come replete with tales and myths. For example, the murder of stonemason Reznikov by his colleague and rival in love, the aptly named Diablos, is part of the lore of University College (UC). Also now at UC is the recently refurbished University Art Centre, while in neighbouring Hart House more art can be found at the Barnicke Gallery. Knox College, meanwhile, which so completely fits the image of the hallowed hall of higher learning, has become a movie star, winning feature roles in *The Paper Chase*, *Class of 44*, *Moonstruck*, *Dead Ringers* and Jell-O commercials.

MEMORIAL TOWER

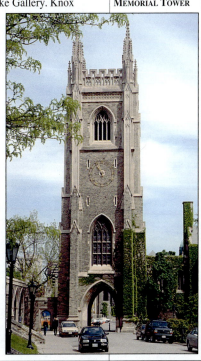

Tours of the campus (offered three times a day throughout the summer) focus mainly on these Oxbridge-like Gothic and Neo-Classical buildings, such as Convocation Hall and the campus administrative centre, Simcoe Hall. The latter houses a complete model of the entire campus, which is good for an overview. Even if you are not taking a tour, you will want to poke around Hart House. This building was a gift to the university from the Massey Foundation and was named for Hart Massey, founder of the Varity Corporation farm-implement empire. It was designed as an undergraduate men's student centre, but now serves the entire community. It encircles a quadrangle used for outdoor summer concerts and contains a

▲ Neighbourhoods and Districts

ST. GEORGE STREET

gym, a pool, lecture rooms, assorted activities rooms (for music, billiards and so on), a chapel, a fine small theatre, the Barnicke Gallery and an excellent, moderately priced restaurant, the Gallery Grill, which is open to the public for lunch.

Finally, there are a host of wonderful modern buildings, such as Massey College, made famous by its long-time principal, author Robertson Davies; New College, which contains a quadrangle to rival those of the Victorians; Innis College, a comfortable, casual place that bespeaks a culture free from the grim formality of the older buildings; the well-designed, power-dressed Rotman School of Management; and the new, very odd looking campus residence imaginatively called Graduate House, with its crane-like superstructure overhanging Harbord Street.

To enable you to really savour the campus flavour, most of the residences offer accommodation from early May to late August. Unfortunately, there is no central booking system; each residence must be contacted separately. The numbers can be obtained from the campus housing service (416 978-8045). (For information about tours, call 416 978-5000.)

If a casual visit is more your style, you can head west from the north side of Queen's Park to Hart House Circle, south a bit to King's College Circle and west from there to take a northward stroll along the revamped St. George Street. For years, St. George sliced awkwardly through the campus, an unfriendly river of traffic. In the mid-90s, however, a $1-million private gift from Judy Matthews was put to use creating a well-planted, narrower street with more space for bicycles and pedestrians. At the Roberts Library, with its grim concrete exterior and periscope-like

ROBARTS LIBRARY

tower which houses its rare books collection, turn west to wander along Harbord Street (see below), or east along Hoskin Avenue, and just before getting back to Queen's Park, turn north onto Philosopher's Walk, a pleasant path through a leafy vale that leads to the Royal Ontario Museum and to Bloor Street.

HONEST ED'S

BLOOR WEST, MIRVISH VILLAGE AND HARBORD STREET

UNIVERSITY COLLEGE

Harbord Street itself is pretty nondescript, but between Spadina and Bathurst, there are at least half a dozen shops of note (and no less than five exceptional restaurants). Visit the Clay Design Studio/Gallery (at Brunswick), a potters' co-op; WonderWorks (79A) for New Age books, crystals, music, herbs, jewellery and other paraphernalia or Things Japanese (159), slightly farther west. In addition, you'll find specialty stores offering new and used books, and the beloved Harbord Bakery, whose bagels, challah, cookies and other goodies draw customers from across the city.

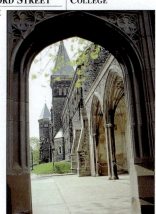

If you continue walking west along Harbord to Markham Street, just one block past Bathurst, and head north, you will soon come to a short stretch, which runs between Lennox and Bloor. David and Ed Mirvish, the Canadian entrepreneurs who own Toronto's Royal Alexandra and Princess of Wales Theatres, also own these shops and restaurants. The buildings here have been tarted up a bit, making them almost too precious or quaint, but nonetheless this block houses numerous shops that are fun to poke through. Among these are David Mirvish Books (596), which offers a wide selection of art books, and Ballenford Books (600A), which specializes in architecture. You'll discover glassworks downstairs at Core (588). Comics are rampant at The Beguiling (601). Journey's End Antiques (612) offers a variety of estate antiques and, for dog lovers, the city's largest collection of French bulldogs! Of the restaurants, Southern Accent (595), Toronto's oldest Cajun spot, provides blackened everything; and the Victory Cafe (581), a watering hole of the neighbourhood's many writers and artists, plays host to numerous literary and music events.

Bloor Street is of course one of Toronto's major thoroughfares, taking on the character of abutting residential communities as it wends its way through the city. Starting just west of Spadina is the university community, which has a wide selection of reasonably good, always comfortable, moderately priced dining spots.

YORKVILLE AND BLOOR STREET

YORKVILLE AND BLOOR STREET

An elegantly attired woman, her hair carefully tinted and styled in the latest mode, steps smartly up the street. Heads turn. But only momentarily. Attention soon is focused on a similarly in-vogue couple. He is tall, tanned and Ralph Lauren-ed; she is Chanel-ed to perfection. But even they can't hold the eyes of those who cruise by in Mercedes, Porsches and SUVs, or sashay along, the street their runway.

The place is Yorkville, centre of the Bloor Street-Annex axis. Fairly oozing with elegance and luxury, this area is the place to see and be seen. Bloor Street is lined with well-known international retailers: Tiffany, Davids, Cole Haan, Vuitton, Chanel, Hermes, Jaeger, Benetton and Giorgio, among others. The Annex consists of blocks and blocks of comfortably large, thoroughly renovated, tastefully landscaped Victorian homes. Avenue Road, the boundary between the residential Annex and the commercial Yorkville, is home to international hotels, posh

TIFFANY ON BLOOR STREET

YORKVILLE AND BLOOR STREET

galleries and antique stores. Davenport Road, the northern boundary of the area, has become Toronto's main drag for interior designers to the carriage trade. And then there is Yorkville itself, with its narrow streets and hidden laneways stuffed with galleries (more than 25 at last count), boutiques and numerous restaurants.

A Little History

The area began life near what is today the busy Bloor-Yonge intersection. There, in the early 1800s, a far-sighted hotelier built the Red Lion Inn, the last stop on the main highway (Yonge Street) before a toll had to be paid to enter Toronto. The inn was a booming success. Residential development began in the mid-1830s, when Sheriff William Botsford Jarvis and brewer Joseph Bloor purchased land in the area and began laying out lots for what became the Village of Yorkville in 1853.

Built as a suburb of Toronto, Yorkville was home to professionals and the burgeoning middle classes: self-employed craftspeople, shopkeepers, clerks and the like. The air was good, the scene was rustic and starting in 1849 a horse-drawn omnibus ran between the Red Lion and the St. Lawrence Market on Front Street. In the 1870s, large lots were created west of Yorkville proper, specifically to attract the wealthy. Among those who built there was the Gooderham brewing family, whose 1890 Romanesque mansion at Bloor and St. George streets is now the fashionable York Club.

CHURCH OF THE REDEEMER AT BLOOR AND AVENUE ROAD

Yorkville became part of Toronto in 1883. The area to the west of it (roughly to Walmer Road) was annexed to the city in 1887 and is called, appropriately enough, the Annex. Continually well-served by public transit and adjacent to the University of Toronto, Yorkville maintained its upper class and upwardly mobile status to a large extent until the mid-twentieth century. Some of the larger homes were by then broken up into rooming houses, or served as shared accommodation for groups of students. But while there were scattered pockets of shabbiness, the area never became down and out.

In the 1960s, Yorkville became Toronto's hippie haven, filled with flower children, peaceniks and acid freaks, a drop-in centre for those who didn't trust anyone over 30. Here Joni Mitchell, Gordon Lightfoot, Ian and Sylvia

▲ Neighbourhoods and Districts

Toronto Reference Library

Tyson and others got their start, and so did the Coffee Mill, which still serves an excellent cup of brew as well as tasty pastries and light snacks, albeit at a slightly different location.

Since those heady days, many of the area's buildings have undergone renovation, while others have been virtually reconstructed. There also has been a substantial amount of new construction. In Yorkville itself, this generally has taken the form of low-rise developments bearing the stamp of the former village's motifs of brick, back lanes, greenery, high art and oodles of sophisticated shops. Along Bloor Street and Avenue Road, there are new high-rise hotels and offices converted to luxury condos.

A Yorkville Tour

Start your walk at the Bloor-Yonge intersection, taking a short two-block stroll north on Yonge before plunging into Yorkville. On Yonge, you'll find Thompson's Homeopathic Supplies (844), a pristine example of an old-type herbal apothecary that could be a museum were it not a shop; the Cookbook Store (850) and the Toronto Reference Library (789). The last, built in the early 1970s, has proved enormously popular with residents and tourists alike. With its plant-filled atrium and sound-dampening waterfall, it is a welcoming, accessible kind of place.

At Yorkville Avenue, turn west and look at two of the area's older civic institutions. The Fire Hall (22) was built in 1876 when Yorkville was still an independent village. The building deteriorated after annexation and all but the tower was rebuilt in 1889. The entire building was refurbished in 1975 and Yorkville's official coat of arms, saved when the town hall was demolished, was placed over the doorway. Next door is the Yorkville branch of the Toronto Public Library (34), built in 1907. It was one of four Toronto libraries built with a 1903 endowment from American philanthropist Andrew Carnegie. It was restored and expanded in 1978. From here, continue west past Bay Street into the heart of Yorkville's shopping district, which stretches along Cumberland Street and Yorkville Avenue to Avenue Road, with significant bits on Scollard Street and north up Hazelton Avenue.

As you stroll west along Yorkville, you will pass a wide variety of good restaurants and interesting shops. For Japanese food, try the very tiny Zerosun (69) or for Italian, Bellini (101). Further west, near Hazelton, pause to visit the Arctic Bear (125), which specializes in Inuit sculpture, prints and other native works.

If you turn north on Hazelton, you will come to a number of galleries that have made their mark on the Canadian art scene over the past two decades: Nancy Poole's Studio (16), Mira Godard (22) and Sable-Castelli (33), each of which has introduced Canadian artists of international calibre, as well as staged international shows of interest and importance. Two additional landmarks here are of note, each of which in turn served as the Olivet Congregational Church. The older, at 35 Hazelton, was built in 1876 and is one of only two surviving board and batten churches in Toronto. Since 1923, it has been owned by the Toronto Heliconian Club, a unique institution that was established in 1909 to bring together women engaged in the arts — writing, painting, music — which flourishes to this day. The second Olivet church was built in 1890 and is a classic example of Richardsonian architecture. The original interior was octagonal, with the pews radiating around the pulpit and organ chamber, putting every congregant directly under the preacher's eye. Since 1973 it has served commercial and office uses and is now home to three fine galleries.

HAZELTON LANES

INSET: YORKVILLE FIRE HALL

When you've seen enough fine art, wander into Hazelton Lanes, a uniquely upscale shopping mall filled with boutiques offering fashions, specialty gifts, jewellery and one-of-a-kind furnishings. Around the corner from Hazelton, on Scollard Street, are still more galleries, two of which, Gallery One (121) and The Drabinsky Gallery (122), specialize in contemporary works.

Retrace your steps to Yorkville to cut through Old York Lane to Cumberland. Here you will find the Guild Shop (118) for exquisite Canadian crafts. While you are here, be sure to have a look at the Village of Yorkville Park, which runs west from Bellair Street along Cumberland. The result of an international design competition, the park became the focus of much controversy, little of which has abated despite its having been the recipient of international awards. It is intended to provide a sense of the varying topography found in Ontario, ranging from an upland conifer garden to a wetland, to a birch grove, a wildflower meadow and a massive granite outcrop moved here from northern Ontario and weighing 650 tonnes. It also features water falling from a steel frame that looks a bit like a harp that can play only one note, a stream and (at night) dramatic lighting.

HELICONIAN CLUB

Neighbourhoods and Districts

A Stroll on Bloor Street

From the Village of Yorkville Park, walk west to Avenue Road and then south to Bloor. On the northwest corner stands the Park Hyatt. Originally called Queen's Park Plaza Hotel, it was built between 1926 and 1929 as an apartment hotel. Atop it sits the Roof Restaurant, a romantic spot where the excellent view is sometimes matched by the food. Opposite, on the northeast corner, is the Church of the Redeemer, which redeemed itself by selling air rights to the rather ghastly Renaissance Centre that frames it. Here you can dine on Cal-Ital at Prego Della Piazza, literally in the bosom of the church.

On the southeast corner sits a very distinguished example of neoclassical revival with a colossal portico, the L.M. Treble Building. Built as a donation from Lillian Massey Treble of the farm machinery family, the facility was intended "to educate young women in the scientific running of a household." Today, it has been renovated to serve as the flagship store for Club Monaco.

In addition to the Park Hyatt, the area's other hotels, the Intercontinental and the Four Seasons, provide several restaurants of note. Signatures, at the Intercontinental, offers global cuisine in an art-deco setting, while at the Four Seasons there are the stylish Studio Cafe, the French and highly rated Truffles and the Avenue, a lounge that offers good lunches and brunches.

Head east along Bloor, and in addition to the aforementioned shops of international fame, you will find dozens of others such as the Gap, Banana Republic and Eddie Bauer. Recent additions include Roots —Canada's new

YORKVILLE STREET SCENES

YORKVILLE AND BLOOR STREET

flagship store — H&M, Winners, Williams-Sonoma, the related Pottery Barn Kids and a renovated Talbot's. Holt Renfrew (50 Bloor St. W.), Canada's swankiest department store with fraternal ties to Niemann Marcus and Bergdorf Goodman, has its flagship store near Yonge.

Other Canadian favourites include William Ashley (55), Birks (55), Stollery's (1) and Harry Rosen (82). In addition to the ever-present Body Shop (86), MAC (89) and Aveda (95) offer designer cosmetics. Specialty shops include the Irish Shop (150), with its lovely wools, Mont Blanc (151) for the fountain pen of your heart's desire and Amarynth (131), which sells Lalique and other fine, hand-blown glassware and Indigo at the Manulife Centre (55), the flagship store of Canada's largest book retailer. If you are into the more traditional forms of smoking, there are several tobacconists in the area, but the most humorous, no doubt, is Groucho and Co. (150) on Bloor, near Avenue Road.

Also on Bloor is the Colonnade (131). Built in the early 1960s, it was the first large-scale project in Canada to combine residences, offices, retail outlets and a theatre. In fact, it was among the first in North America to do so, and it succeeds with an elegant design that provides a comfortable spot to stop and chat in the street while providing an excellent view of its many storefronts — to say nothing of the excellent views available from its large, well-designed apartments.

Among the many favourite dining spots on or near Bloor are Scaccia for straightforward Sicilian fare at the Manulife Centre, Sultan's Tent for Moroccan atmosphere rather than ultrafine cuisine (now 49 Front St. E.), Pangaea for well-prepared fresh foods in a friendly atmosphere (1221 Bay) or Host for an innovative northern Indian menu in a plush setting (14 Prince Arthur).

HARRY ROSEN ON BLOOR

YONGE STREET

Yonge is Toronto's legendary main north-south street, bisecting the city into east and west sides. Its first fifty-three kilometres (forty miles) were laid out in 1796, when the city itself was barely more than a figment of Lieutenant-Governor John Graves Simcoe's imagination. When Toronto's first subway line opened along Yonge in 1954 its continuing role as main street was ensured.

From its starting point at Queen's Quay, where Captain John Letnik presides over his eponymous floating seafood restaurant, through the city's financial district, alongside

the Eaton Centre's ship of commerce, past "the Strip," on to Bloor and northward past Davisville, Eglinton and other subway stops that once were village crossroads, the street offers entertainment ranging from soft-core porn to the international glamour of Broadway shows, and wares from discount electronics and fly-by-night footwear to the broad middle range of the Eaton Centre's hundreds of shops, to carriage trade antiquarians and clothiers.

The crowd and the attractions change from day to night, from year to year, from neighbourhood to neighbourhood, but Yonge always remains a safe street to walk and shop along. An amiable tackiness pervades much of the street's length while recent redevelopment shows signs of a rebirth. But no single activity — reputable or otherwise — has ever managed to gain ascendancy. Toronto's main drag is eclectic, safe and sometimes seedy, but always vibrant.

Yonge Street south of Queen Street is discussed in the chapter Financial and Theatre District. This tour starts on foot at the Eaton Centre, which stretches all the way from Queen Street to Dundas Street, and continues north to Bloor. It is a manageable walk from Bloor as far north as St. Clair Avenue, but it is easier still to take the subway or bus to St. Clair and walk back to Bloor since it is all downhill. North of St. Clair, shops and restaurants start to get further apart, and you may wish to take a bus, subway, car or taxi to a destination and then walk around that area before moving on to the next one.

Although there are a number of excellent restaurants between Lawrence Avenue and the North York City Centre, there is little else worth stopping for. The main attraction in what was, until amalgamation in 1998, the civic centre of North York, is the Toronto Centre for the Arts, adjacent to what was North York's city hall, public square (Mel Lastman Square), main library and art gallery. The Centre's larger theatre has hosted major productions such as *Showboat*, *Sunset Boulevard* and *Ragtime*, while a smaller space, the George Weston Recital Hall, a true gem of a hall, provides acoustics that enable it to attract the world's most distinguished soloists and chamber groups.

Neighbourhoods and Districts

COLLEGE PARK IN FORMER EATON'S

EATON CENTRE
From the 1880s until his death, a stern, teetotaling Timothy Eaton presided over the affairs of the street from the corner of Queen and Yonge. There, he and a Scot named Robert Simpson first established their competing dry goods stores. These men were to become the rulers of two of Canada's greatest department store dynasties and the self-styled arbiters of the street's good taste. Not counting the Bay (now housed in Simpson's former flagship store), which can be reached by an enclosed walkway above Queen Street, the Eaton Centre is one-quarter mile long, its arched glass gallery 127 feet high. Its 300-plus shops are on three levels: food courts, "convenience" merchandise (drug stores, appliance repairs, records) and popularly priced fashions on the lowest; mid-priced clothing, jewellery and some specialty stores on the middle level; and on the most pleasant, uppermost level, fashion and accessories at stores such as Talbot's and Banana Republic. Restaurants are scattered throughout. Although surpassed in size by the mammoth West Edmonton Mall, Eaton Centre remains the largest downtown shopping complex in North America, and since its construction in the late 1970s has almost always topped tourists' must-do list. A lot of Torontonians visit it regularly, too — over 42 million people a year in total.

The centre's new Yonge Street façade is an unloved postmodern mishmash meant to look like a line of separate buildings, enlivened by backlit billboard spaces. Its interior, however, with its fountains, fancy paving and soaring sky lit arch, was meant by architect Eb Zeidler to be reminiscent of Milan's airy Galleria, albeit with an exposed-duct-work industrial twist. The centre was accused of killing life on Yonge Street, so a new extension brought the walls out closer to the street, to allow for new stores and restaurants with access to the street at several points. While a few of the tackier areas along Yonge

YONGE STREET

DUNDAS SQUARE

Street have changed little despite the centre, some of the best old buildings opposite the centre, in particular the Elgin, Winter Garden and Canon Theatres, along with the Ryrie Building, have all been restored to at least their former glory. In addition, many rundown buildings near Dundas were demolished to make way for Dundas Square and a vast new entertainment and retail complex under construction at the northeast corner.

Some thought that shopping in a mall would suburbanize or sterilize the downtown core. While there is no denying that the vast majority of the centre's retailers are chain stores, the sheer variety of goods, prices and people using the centre has ensured that urban vibrancy prevails. The vitality is augmented by artwork, most notably Michael Snow's flock of non-migrating geese; by some of the centre's surroundings, especially the sophisticated Trinity Square, which flanks the west side of the centre and which features a café, fountains, and a labyrinth for walking. Frequent performances occur, both scheduled (inside the mall, or at the new Dundas Square) and non-scheduled (at the corner of Dundas and Yonge). One block north of the centre (on Edward Street) is the similarly gargantuan World's Biggest Bookstore; it's actually not the largest in the world, but with about 100,000 titles, it comes close.

DUNDAS TO BLOOR

Starting at Dundas and running north past Gerrard Street is the infamous "Strip." Its centre piece is the recently opened Dundas Square – a large open space at Yonge and Dundas reserved for concerts and events.

Running west off Yonge two blocks north of Dundas is Elm Street. For some reason, it was the site of some of Toronto's earliest fine restaurants, a tradition that continues to this day with Barberian's (7), one of the city's first steak-houses, Oro (45) and Bangkok Garden (18), which has long offered Thai food in an elegant atmosphere.

From Gerrard north to College, there's a momentary interruption of the otherwise nineteenth-century character of the street. In the 1920s, it was thought that College Street soon would overtake Queen and King Streets as the

▲ NEIGHBOURHOODS AND DISTRICTS

TOWER OF FORMER FIRE HALL NO. 3

centre of retailing. Construction of new buildings began on a vast scale, both along Yonge and eastward along Carlton Street. Kresge's, Toronto Hydro, Warner Brothers and most ambitious of all, what was to have been Eaton's flagship store, all bear the undeniable stamp of art-deco. The stockmarket crash of 1929 interrupted plans for the area when less than a quarter of the Eaton's project, which was to have included a forty-storey office tower, had been completed. Nevertheless, Eaton's opened its grand store with an opulent deco interior. It closed, along with Eaton's original Queen Street store, in 1977 when the first phase of the Eaton Centre opened. Much of the original deco interior still is visible, however, incorporated into the reworked College Park mall now within the walls. The seventh-floor Eaton Auditorium, a concert hall and restaurant that has been closed for decades, has been restored and reopened as an event space named The Carlu, after its French architect, Jacques Carlu.

Yonge serves as the boundary dividing the east side of Toronto from the west, and many of the smaller streets end at Yonge. The small, offset blocks created by all these dead ends have helped preserve Yonge Street's nineteenth-century scale along this stretch: it is difficult to assemble large blocks of land for megaprojects when there are so many little streets. This pattern also has created surprisingly quiet neighbourhood enclaves just around the corner from bustling Yonge Street, and nowhere is this more evident than between College and Bloor Streets. On Yonge itself, clear up to Bloor, except for a few government offices, you will find mainly shops offering fast food and its equivalent in clothing, cameras and electronics. The buildings here are less camouflaged than to the south, however, revealing more of the street's busy past. The tower jutting from the St. Charles is all that remains of Firehall No. 3, which was built in the 1870s. Around the corner on Grosvenor Street is the Metro YMCA, a sleek and muscular building appropriate for its purpose. On the other side of Yonge, at 26 Alexander Street, is another of Toronto's ever-popular early steakhouses, Carman's Club.

FORMER MASONIC TEMPLE

In the pleasantly sainted little area near Bloor (St. Nicholas and St. Mary's Streets, St. Joseph Avenue) are two pleasant restaurants: Segovia, at 5 St. Nicholas, offers a taste of Spain and Le Matignon serves up French fare in a cozy setting at number 51. At Gloucester Street stands Gloucester Mews, originally the Masonic Hall, which was among the earliest renovation projects undertaken in Toronto. Just to the north at 675 is Postal Station F. It too was renovated early on, now serving as a Starbuck's, a McDonald's and a fitness club.

YONGE STREET

Something about this stretch of Yonge seems always to have put it just on the edge of success without ever quite making it.

BLOOR TO ST. CLAIR

That feeling changes as soon as Yonge reaches Bloor. From there, north to Hogg's Hollow and with only the occasional break (for the Mount Pleasant Cemetery between Davisville and St. Clair, for instance), Yonge Street reflects the class and cachet of the neighbourhoods through which it runs. To its west lies Yorkville (see p. 170). To the east lies Rosedale, originally a wealthy suburb, and now one of Canada's wealthiest inner-city neighbourhoods. These are followed by such other areas as Moore Park, Lawrence Park and North Toronto, all comfortably upper-middle class.

Just past Yorkville's end at Davenport Road is the large Masonic Temple, which replaced the one at Gloucester Mews and was renovated in the mid-1900s to serve as a venue for concerts. Opposite is the original flagship Canadian Tire store (839), looking pretty modest by today's standards, despite having been spruced up recently. Here, too, are Ridpath's (906), for *Architectural Digest*-class furnishings, and Petit Pied and Bon Lieu (890) for kids shoes and clothes straight from the pages of Paris *Vogue*. Having passed these, you are already at the Rosedale subway stop, which seems more like the suburban commuter train stations of the early twentieth century than the busy urban Bloor-Yonge maelstrom that lies practically within spitting distance.

The tone continues. North of the Rosedale stop, clusters of mid- to high-end antique stores proliferate. The quality in all these shops is high. Prices vary from real bargains to the astronomical. So have fun, but beware! You are practically at the Summerhill stop now and just passing one of the area's best eateries, the Rosedale Diner (1164), which is not at all a diner, but more relaxed than most of Rosedale. Nearby is the old CPR North Toronto train station. Nearby is a host of precious food shops, which locals call "The Five Thieves." Here, for a price, you can find such rarities as fresh gooseberries, red and black currents, figs, raspberries and blackberries year-round. There are bakeries and butchers and, opposite the Thieves, two kitchen suppliers, Embros (1170) and Word of Mouth (1134), whose wares will enable all these delicacies to be properly prepared and presented. And if cooking isn't what you have in mind, but eating is, there are more restaurants still, before you reach St. Clair.

THE ROSEDALE DINER

CABBAGETOWN

CARLTON STREET

ALLAN GARDENS

Cabbagetown most likely acquired its name in the late nineteenth century because residents in the area often planted cabbages in their front gardens. Today, it is an affluent mid-town neighbourhood chockablock with almost every style of Victorian house imaginable. The area is worth a visit just for a look at its well-tended streets and gardens. But it has other attractions as well. On a fine day, you can picnic in Riverdale Park or take youngsters for a visit to the nearby Riverdale Farm. The quiet, well-treed St. James Cemetery, the charming St. James-the-Less Chapel, and the picturesque buildings of the Necropolis also offer interesting sights to explore. Finally, the Palm House at Allan Gardens, a glittering greenhouse on the edge of Cabbagetown, is worth a visit, especially if the day is grey, for its lush array of ferns, palms and blooms.

A VICTORIAN NEIGHBOURHOOD

Start your tour at Sherbourne and Carlton at the edge

of Cabbagetown. Set amidst a thirteen-acre park known as Allan Gardens, half of which was an 1858 gift from local politician George Allan, is a fanciful glass dome, the Palm House, connected to six small greenhouses. Contained within are an array of horticultural exhibits gleaned from the far-flung empire of Victorian times and beyond: a little swamp composed of Egyptian papyrus, Japanese sweet flag and Ontario pond weed, or a thick jungle with silver thatch palm from Trinidad, screw pine from Madagascar and poinsettias from Mexico. In short, a lovely glassed-in cabinet full of assorted collections and curiosities. Serious but extravagantly eclectic, this is a good place to get in the mood for a stroll through the rest of the neighbourhood.

ALLAN GARDENS GREENHOUSE

THE HEART OF CABBAGETOWN

Head east on Carlton until you reach Parliament and then walk south to Spruce Street. The suggested walking route winds through the residential heart of Cabbagetown, providing a good sampling of the area's varied Victorian character. On the south side of Spruce Street just west of Sackville Street stands Trinity Mews, which incorporates the large, red-and-yellow brick, rehabilitated Trinity College Medical School, a remnant of the days when Toronto's General Hospital was located in the area. The former Ontario Medical College for Women stands a block south at 289 Sumach Street, now serving as a condo. East of Sackville on the north side are the Spruce Court Apartments, Toronto's first government-sponsored housing project, which

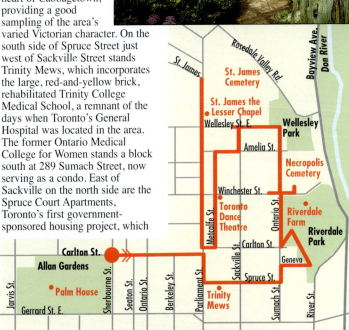

▲ Neighbourhoods and Districts

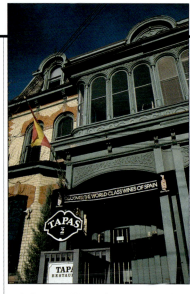

was built in the Garden City fashion advocated by urban planners of the day and which is now a nonprofit co-op.

Turn north on Sumach and head east along Geneva Street. For its entire length, this admittedly short street is lined with totally intact working-class cottages in what is known as the "Alpha-style." You will now have reached Riverdale Park. The park spans the Don Valley, and this vantage offers a sweeping view of Riverdale, the community edging its eastern side.

Turn north alongside the park for a short walk to Riverdale Farm (p. 107), or head back to Sumach either by taking Carlton Street or by cutting diagonally across the park. This portion of Riverdale Park (which has a wading pool, by the way) is the site of high-quality spring and fall craft fairs. At the corner of Winchester Street and Sumach is a sometime tea shop of ye olde variety where you may wish to pause for refreshments. Take a brief detour down to 156 Winchester, parts of which were built in 1830, making it one of the oldest homes in the area. It was originally the residence of Alderman Daniel Lamb, remembered today primarily as the founder of the Riverdale Zoo (now Farm). North of

GENEVA COTTAGES (BELOW); 37 METCALFE STREET (BOTTOM)

CHAPEL OF THE NECROPOLIS CEMETERY

NECROPOLIS CEMETARY GATE

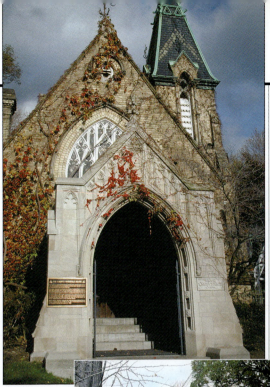

the park are the highly picturesque chapel, gate and gatehouse of the Necropolis Cemetery. This nonsectarian "city of the dead" is the final resting place of many of Toronto's early pioneers. Among them are the city's first mayor, William Lyon Mackenzie; Samuel Lount and Peter Matthews, both hanged for their part in Mackenzie's 1837 rebellion; George Brown, a father of Confederation and the founder of the *Globe and Mail*; John Ross Robertson, founder of the rival *Toronto Telegram*; and Ned Hanlan, world-famous sculler.

MODEST COTTAGES AND GRAND HOUSES

Continuing up Sumach and east on Amelia Street, along the edge of the Necropolis, will take you to Wellesley Park, which serves as the front yard for a number of homes. Walk north through the park, then turn west on Wellesley Street. Just past Sackville is a street sign for the Wellesley Cottages. Now a rarity, cheap housing of wood lath and stucco was once common. These cottages, all extensively and expensively renovated, retain their simple, almost rural look.

NEIGHBOURHOODS AND DISTRICTS

WELLESLEY COTTAGES

Zigzag your way south, taking in portions of Sackville, Amelia, Metcalfe, Winchester and Carlton Streets. At Winchester and Metcalfe stands the Toronto Dance Theatre, originally a Romanesque church and one of the few nonresidential buildings in the area. Winchester was once a major thoroughfare, leading to a bridge across the Don River. Further down at 37 Metcalfe is another of the area's few really large homes, this one a rambling Italianate villa that once stood on substantial grounds but now is hemmed in tightly by its neighbours.

Once back on Parliament head north. Opposite the high-rise enclave of St. Jamestown stand St. James Cemetery and St. James-the-Less Chapel. Suggestive of a

THE SHIELDS HOUSE

thirteenth-century English parish church, the chapel is widely considered to be one of the most beautiful church buildings in Canada. Like the Necropolis, St. James is the resting place of many leading founders of Toronto and their families, among them the Gooderhams, Jarvises, Howlands and Mannings. Also of note here are the abundant funereal statuary and large mausoleums.

186

LITTLE ITALY AND GREEKTOWN ON THE DANFORTH

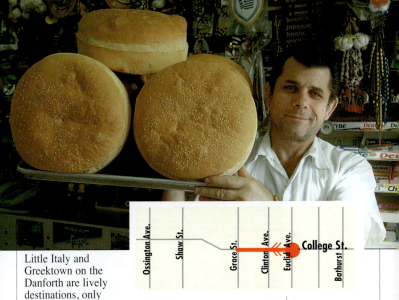

Little Italy and Greektown on the Danforth are lively destinations, only slightly off the beaten track. While you won't find the top tourist attractions in either of them, these neighbourhoods are nonetheless interesting places to explore, especially when you want to combine a good meal with a bit of browsing or shopping.

LITTLE ITALY

Little Italy, which is about fifteen minutes west of Yonge Street on the College streetcar (506), stretches along College Street from just west of Bathurst almost to Ossington. Its heart, however, lies between Euclid and Shaw. Here the streetlights are festooned with lights in the shape of the boot of Italy, and the air is perfumed with garlic, basil and a hint of espresso. Once the heart of Toronto's 415,000-plus Italian community, it is now the southernmost shopping and residential district of that community, which has moved north.

It never has been the Italy of the Via Venuto or the Pontevecchio, but rather the slightly provincial street of a nondescript Mediterranean city, a mélange of Italian with a generous dollop of Portuguese. Until very recently, stores like Rimini Family Clothing nudged Napoli Family Clothing, which jostled Firenze Clothing; these contained not the clothing of Milan's runways and *Vogue*, but the little black boots of working-class Europeans' children, the black garb of widows, the frilly dresses of young girls.

NEIGHBOURHOODS AND DISTRICTS

In just a few short years, this has largely changed. Gone or pushed further west are most of the old clothiers — replaced by a smattering of their Generation X and Y counterparts — and many of the groceries that made the street bright with bell peppers, aubergines and oranges. Today the area seems devoted predominantly to ready-to-eat gastronomy and, increasingly, is lined with restaurants, bars, bistros and clubs including the current "it spot" Revival (783), with its cathedral ceilings, plush sofas and spacious dance floor. While few are four-star eateries, most serve high-quality food in a comfortable setting at moderate to the low end of high prices ($90 to $160 for a complete dinner for two including a glass of wine each).

Although dining is the main object, there are a few shops worth a look. Lilliput Hats (462 College) is a custom millenary, Ewanika (490) carries custom clothes for professional women and Mink (550) custom jewellery ranging from subtle to delightfully gaudy. Peering into Motoretta (554), with its scooters "authentic and true," takes you straight to the Italy of "Three Coins in a Fountain." And while on the subject of water, have a look at Splish Splash (590), a combination convenience store and Laundromat. If words are your thing, you can browse for hours at the very fine, secondhand Balfour Books (601). Word lovers also will get a kick out of Fratelli

LITTLE ITALY AND GREEKTOWN ON THE DANFORTH

Porco, an excellent, very Italian grocery and butcher, bountifully stocked with fresh and dried pastas great rounds of cheeses and — a special treat for Americans — prosciutto, which is owned by the aptly named "Pork Brothers."

In evidence, too, are a smattering of old men's clubs, filled with smoke, talk and caffeine and the fabulous baked goods of the long popular Riviera Bakery (576). Also still here is CHIN, the world's first non-government multi-cultural radio station, which broadcasts in over 30 languages (and now boasts a TV signal, too). And finally, when you turn a corner, the houses are small, often brightly coloured, their wooden porches replaced with curlicued wrought iron, their yards bright with the colours of the old country.

In the dining department it is hard to go radically wrong. For fairly traditional Italian fare in a comfy setting, there is Gamelle (468), Trattoria Giancarlo (around the corner at 41 Clinton), Grappa (797) and, with the added advantage of being surprisingly inexpensive as well as excellent, Tavola Caldo (671). Also excellent, a bit more pricey and almost at Ossington is Café Societa (796). Less comfy and more limited is the delightful Café Diplomatico (594), which for more than 30 years has drawn customers from across the city to enjoy the great Italian tradition of mating espresso with a quick drink, a small bite, an Italian ice or other dessert. Pizza lovers will enjoy Giovanna (637), which serves other robust fare as well, or for the thin-crust variety, John's Classic Pizza (591).

Another oldtimer, but completely revamped in a minimalist style to attract a younger crowd is Bar Italia (582). The more adventurous might try the Airport

RIVIERA BAKERY

Neighbourhoods & districts

Lounge (492), fusion cooking with a Japanese emphasis in a psychedelic setting or Tempo (783), which offers highly praised sushi and a stylish, modernist interior. Weird but very good. In a similar vein, but with a more Italian slant and down-to-earth setting is Pony (488). Moving even further from Italian fare is the beautiful and ultra-chic Xacutti (503), where the Caribbean tastefully meets southeast Asia, and Brasserie Aix, which became *the* in place the moment it opened in 2001 even though its French fare does not always match its high price or reputation. Purely Caribbean and very cheap jerk can be had at Irie (808).

Portuguese favourites can be had Chiado (864), Sintra (588), which is a better deal at lunch, and further west at Piri-Piri Churrasqueira (928) or Cataplana (938). If your taste runs to the hotter aspects of Latin culture, you could try a Sunday evening tango lesson at Mania Bar and Lounge (722) or the 1:30 a.m. Saturday night drag show at El Convento Rico (750).

Greektown on the Danforth

Toronto's first Greek restaurant opened on Danforth Avenue in 1900. Along this street, and in the surrounding neighbourhood, immigrant Greeks settled in large numbers during the post–World War II era. Some of their early shops, the Athens Meat Market (which dates from 1951), Seven Stars Bakery and Hermes House of Bomboniere among them, continue to flourish. In the late 1960s and 1970s the souvlaki outlets and homey restaurants began to attract non-Greek Torontonians. It was exotic to stand over steam tables, point at unknown dishes and have them brought to your table. They were also cheap, cheap, cheap!

Today, the surrounding neighbourhood has changed, many of the Greeks having moved north and east; it is now a sort of off-beat yuppie enclave, filled with media types,

LITTLE ITALY AND GREEKTOWN ON THE DANFORTH

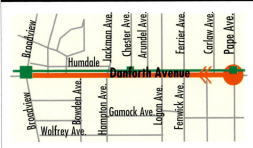

editors, writers, musicians and artists (not your starving variety; these come with mortgages, kids and Volvos). But the Danforth, especially between Chester and Pape Avenues, remains exuberantly Greek. Since about 1988, it has seemed as though a new restaurant has opened every month. In the summer especially, the sidewalks are teeming with diners until all hours (the restaurants are open late and often are not crowded much before 9:30 p.m.), and whenever the weather is warm, doors and windows are flung open, the relaxed but always talkative customers adding to the festive street life.

For one weekend in early August, Taste of the Danforth, a festival of food, allows you to sample restauranteurs' wares before selecting the eatery at which you want to stop. Gone, though, are the steam tables with their admittedly overcooked and greasy offerings. It is evident, even in traditional dishes, these second- and third-generation Greeks have learned all the tricks of light cooking using fresh ingredients. And now that they're vying with each other for exotically designed spaces, the area has become a feast for the eye, as well as the ear and the palate. And if it no longer is cheap, cheap, cheap, most places still are relatively moderate in price ($55 to $75 for a complete meal for two, including wine).

On the long-established side, there is the casual Omonia (426), which has been serving lamb cooked on a spit and such familiar Greek specialties as calamari, tsasiki, moussaka and spanakopita since 1978, Pappas Grill (440), a favourite with families, or the even older Astoria Shish Kebob House (390). Newer, more expensive and far fancier, but still traditional, are Myth (417), Nefeli (407) and Mezes (456). If you desire more innovative cuisine, there is the colourful little Pan on the Danforth (516), where standard dishes like lamb are inventively sauced or spiced. For partying there is Ouzeri (500A), which is a pioneer of the haute-moderne Greek cuisine having opened way back in 1990.

On the quieter side decoratively and acoustically, there is Avli (401) or Soda (425). For dessert there is Demetre (400) or the cafeteria-like Iliada (550). Also, there are a number of very good non-Greek restaurants. Sher-E-Punjab, recently renovated in a sophisticated Indo-European manner, is justifiably considered one of Toronto's top Indian eateries. Mocha Mocha (489) is a neighbourhood favourite for lunch, as are the Auld Spot (347) for fine pub fare, Dora Keogh's (141), mainly for the

▲ NEIGHBOURHOODS & DISTRICTS

many beers, and Allen's (143), a New York-style bar with great burgers, beer, fries and desserts that sports one of Toronto's nicest outdoor patios at the rear.

As well, there are a growing number of shops of interest. Just east of Broadview is a pet emporium Small Wonders, offering unusual treats for you to bring back to your stay-at-home furry friends, and Another Story, a unique outlet for books for all ages on politics and social issues. Further east are Treasure Island for toys, Romancing the Home, Alchemy, Blue Moon, Lily Lee and a growing number of others for both imported and locally designed clothing, jewellery and items for the home.

There are two outlets that provide household necessities for the environmentally conscious. The more clothing-oriented of these is housed in Carrot Common, a mini-mall that also has a health-food supermarket, a Japanese restaurant and a number of the many kids' clothing shops along the Danforth.

Starting in 1996, Greektown on the Danforth became a destination for tour buses done up as fake trolleys. The neighbourhood is also easy to reach via the Bloor subway line, at Broadview, Chester and Pape and Donlands.

Contents

Getting There	**194**
By Air	194
By Road	194
By Rail	194
Travel Essentials	**194**
Money	194
Passports	195
Customs	195
Taxes	195
Guides and Information Services	195
Getting Acquainted	**196**
Time Zone	196
Climate	196
Getting Around	**196**
Travelling in Toronto	196
Tours	197
Boat and Yacht Tours	198
Accommodation	**198**
Hotels: Airport	198
Hotels: Downtown	199
Hotels: Midtown	201
Bed and Breakfasts	201
Hostels and College Residences	202
Top Attractions	**202**
Museums	**203**
Galleries	**204**
Theatre and Dance	**205**
Live Theatre	205
Cinemas	206
Comedy	206
Symphony, Chamber Music, Opera	**206**
Nightlife	**207**
Queen St. West	207
College St./Little Italy	207
Kensington Market	207
Richmond and Adelaide/Entertainment District	207
Dundas St. West	208
Bloor-Yorkville	208
Gay Toronto	208
The Annex	208
Other Neighbourhoods	208
Dining	**208**
Shopping	**211**
Antiques and Collectibles	211
Beauty and Health	211
Books	211
Canadiana	212
China and Crystal	212
Clothing: Canadian Designers	212
Clothing: Children's	212
Clothing: Men's	213
Clothing: Second-hand	213
Clothing: Women's	213
Crafts and Hobbies	214
Electronics	214
Gourmet	214
Hats and Accessories	215
Home Furnishings	215
Jewellery and Watches	215
Leather	216
Malls and Department Stores	216
Museum Shops and Galleries	216
Music	216
Outfitters and Sports	217
Outlets	217
Shoes	217
Sports	**217**
Spectator Sports	217
Golf	218
Festivals and Events	**218**
Day Trips	**220**
Gay Toronto	**221**
Festivals and Theatres	221
Bars and Restaurants	221
Shops	221
Accommodation	222

GETTING THERE

Set on the northwestern shore of Lake Ontario, and located farther south than Minnesota and much of Michigan, Metropolitan Toronto is one of the most accessible cities in North America by highway, air, rail and water.

BY AIR
- Lester B. Pearson International Airport: Located in the northwestern corner of Metro Toronto, the airport is accessible from highways 401, 427 and 409. Trillium Terminal (Terminal 3) serves Air France, Air Transat, American Airlines, British Airways, BWIA International, Canjet, Cathay Pacific Airways, Cubana, Delta, EL AL, KLM, Korean Airlines, Northwest, Olympic, Pem-Air, QANTAS, Royal Airlines, US Air and others. For information call 416 776-5100, www.gtaa.com. Terminal 2 serves Air Canada (domestic and U.S. flights), United Airlines, Westjet and others. Terminal 1 serves Air Canada (international flights), Air Ontario, Alitalia, All Nippon Airways, American Trans Air and others. Some thirty-five major airlines offer regularly scheduled flights. For information on Terminals 1 and 2 call 416 247-7678, www.gtaa.com
- Toronto City Centre Airport: Located on the western tip of a series of islands in Toronto Harbour, this island airport handles scheduled, private and corporate flights. The airport serves Air Ontario. For information call 416 203-6942.

BY ROAD
Whether approaching by car or by bus, the traveller will reach Toronto by one of several major routes paralleling the shore of Lake Ontario. Highways 401 and 2, and the Queen Elizabeth Way, enter Toronto from the west. Highways 401 and 2 also enter Toronto from the east. Hwy. 400 runs from the north and connects with Hwy. 401. Major bus routes converge in Toronto. Out-of-town buses arrive and depart from the Toronto Coach Terminal, located at 610 Bay St. Service to points all over Ontario and Canada is frequent and fast. National and regional bus lines serve Metro Toronto. Call 416 393-7911 for bus company fares and schedules.

BY RAIL
Toronto is served by the VIA Rail Canada System, the network that provides all rail service throughout Canada (with connections to the Amtrak system through Niagara Falls, New York). Union Station is located on Front Street, between Bay and University (across the street from the Royal York Hotel). The station is right on Toronto's subway line, and is within walking distance of SkyDome, the CN Tower, the financial district and many downtown hotels, shops and restaurants. For information call 416 366-7788.

TRAVEL ESSENTIALS

MONEY
Currency can be exchanged at any Toronto bank at the prevailing rate. If you use a small local branch, it's best to call ahead to confirm its capacity to exchange, on the spot, any currency other than American funds. There are currency exchange booths at the airport, and at many of Ontario's Travel Information Centres near the U.S./Canada border. Ontario Travel Information Centres can exchange Canadian dollars for most major international currencies, and vice versa. If you wish to exchange a large amount, or to exchange a less common currency, telephone ahead to ensure the centre can serve you. Units of currency are similar to those of the United States, except for the Canadian one-dollar (loonie) and two-dollar (toonie) coins.

Most major North American credit cards and traveller's cheques are welcome in Toronto, including American Express, Carte Blanche, Diners Club, EnRoute, MasterCard and Visa. Many stores and services will accept U.S. currency, but the exchange rate they offer may vary greatly. Since there are no laws enforcing foreign currency rates of exchange, we strongly recommend that you convert to Canadian funds before you make your purchases.

TRAVEL ESSENTIALS

American visitors may also use bank or credit cards to make cash withdrawals from automated teller machines that are tied into international networks such as Cirrus and Plus. Before you leave home, check with your bank to find out what range of banking services its cards will allow you to use.

PASSPORTS

American visitors may be asked to verify their citizenship with a document such as a passport or a birth or baptismal certificate. Naturalized U.S. citizens should carry a naturalization certificate. Permanent U.S. residents who are not citizens are advised to bring their Alien Registration Receipt Card. Citizens of all other countries, except Greenland and residents of St.-Pierre et Miquelon, must bring a valid passport. Some may be required to obtain a visitor's visa. For details, please consult the Canadian embassy or consulate serving your home country.

CUSTOMS

ARRIVING

As a nonresident of Canada, you may bring in any reasonable amount of personal effects and food, and a full tank of gas. Special restrictions or quotas apply to certain specialty goods, and especially to plant-, agricultural- and animal-related materials. All items must be declared to Customs upon arrival and may include up to 200 cigarettes, 50 cigars, 200 grams of manufactured tobacco, and 200 tobacco sticks. Visitors are also permitted 1.14 litres (40 oz) of liquor, 1.5 litres (50 oz) of wine, or 8.5 litres (24 x 12-oz cans or bottles) of beer.

You may bring in gifts for Canadian residents duty-free, up to a value of $60.00 (Canadian) each, provided they do not consist of alcohol, tobacco or advertising material. For more detailed information, see the federal Customs (Revenue Canada) website (www.cbsa-asfc.gc.ca), the Customs information booklet "I DECLARE" or contact Revenue Canada, Customs/Border Services Office, #303, 6725 Airport Rd., PO Box 6000, Mississauga ON L4V 1V2; 1 800 461-9999, 905 308-8613, www.cbsa-asfc.gc.ca. In Toronto, call 416 952-5555 or 416 954-6700.

DEPARTING

For detailed customs rules for entering or re-entering the United States, contact a U.S. Customs office before you visit Toronto. Copies of the U.S. Customs information brochure "Know Before You Go" are available from U.S. Customs offices or by mail. You can also call the U.S. Customs office in Toronto at 905 676-2606. Travellers from other countries should also check on customs regulations before leaving home.

TAXES

GOODS AND SERVICES TAX (GST)

The federal Goods and Services Tax is 7%. This is a value-added consumption tax that applies to most goods, purchased gifts, food/beverages and services, including most hotel and motel accommodation.

PROVINCIAL SALES TAX (PST)

The Ontario provincial sales tax is 8% on any goods you buy, but not on services or accommodation.

ROOM TAX

A 5% provincial tax (in place of PST) is added to most tourist accommodation charges, as well as the 7% GST.

FOOD SERVICE

In restaurants, 7% GST and 8% PST will be added to the food portion of your final bill, as well as a 10% provincial tax on alcoholic beverages (in addition to the 7% GST).

GUIDES AND INFORMATION SERVICES

Toronto offers docking facilities and complete services for boaters. For information on harbour facilities, call the Toronto Port Authority at 416 863-2000.
- Transport Canada Airport Information: Located in Terminals 1 and 2 of Pearson. Multilingual information available on the airport, flights and tourist attractions. Call 905 676-3506.
- The City of Toronto: Toronto City Hall, 100 Queen St. W., Toronto ON

M5H 2N2; 416 338-0338, www.toronto.ca
- Tourism Toronto: Queen's Quay Terminal at Harbourfront, Suite 590, 207 Queens Quay W., Toronto ON M5J 1A7; 416 203-2600, 1 800 499-2514, www.torontotourism.com
- Visitor Information Ontario: For comprehensive travel information about the Province of Ontario (including Toronto), visit the Ontario Ministry of Tourism's Travel Centre in The Eaton Centre; or call 1 800 ONTARIO (English), 1 800 268-3736 (French), www.ontariotravel.net

GETTING ACQUAINTED

TIME ZONE
Toronto falls within the Eastern Standard Time Zone.

CLIMATE
Here are average Toronto temperatures, highs and lows; fluctuations from the norm are common:

Month	°F	°C
Jan.	30.1°F to 18.1°F	-1.1°C to -7.7°C
Feb.	31.5°F to 18.9°F	-0.3°C to -7.3°C
March	39.5°F to 26.7°F	-0.3°C to −2.9°C
April	53.4°F to 37.8°F	11.9°C to 3.2°C
May	64.3°F to 47.2°F	17.9°C to 8.4°C
June	75.6°F to 57.4°F	24.2°C to 14.1°C
July	80.3°F to 62.3°F	26.8°C to 16.1°C
August	78.7°F to 61.2°F	25.9°C to 16.2°C
Sept.	70.8°F to 54.2°F	21.6°C to 12.3°C
Oct.	59.6°F to 44.8°F	15.3°C to 7.1°C
Nov.	46.1°F to 35.3°F	7.8°C to 1.8°C
Dec.	34.2°F to 23.4°F	1.2°C to -4.8°C

AVERAGE ANNUAL RAINFALL: 27.25 inches/68.9 cm.

AVERAGE ANNUAL SNOWFALL: 53.2 inches/135 cm.

AVERAGE TEMPERATURES:
+7.4°C (45.3°F) in spring,
+20.7°C (69.3°F) in summer,
+10.8°C (51.4°F) in autumn,
-3.3°C (26.1°F) in winter.

GETTING AROUND

TRAVELLING IN TORONTO
Metro Toronto is laid out in a grid pattern of major north-south and east-west arteries. Streets not on the grid follow natural features such as ravines and escarpments. The following expressways provide access to the city from the major highways: the Don Valley Parkway, the Gardiner Expressway and the Allen Expressway. If you're a member of any recognized auto club affiliates (AAA, CAA, etc.), the CAA Toronto at 461 Yonge St.; 416 221-4300, will provide all club services. Head Office 905 771-3111, www.caa.ca

PUBLIC TRANSPORTATION
Toronto's clean, safe and efficient public transit is operated by the TTC (Toronto Transit Commission), and consists of over 4,000 kilometres of subway, bus, RT and streetcar routes. Many of the principal downtown bus and streetcar routes, including those that run along Queen, College, St. Clair and Eglinton, operate 24 hours a day. Night bus service is also available along Yonge and Bloor streets and Danforth Avenue. Exact fares are required and day passes are available. For information on subway, streetcar and bus routes, schedules and fares, call Customer Information at 416 393-4636 (7 am-10 pm), www.toronto.ca/ttc

GO TRANSIT
Regular GO Bus and Train service is provided to Oshawa, Hamilton, Georgetown, Brampton, Milton, Newmarket and Richmond Hill, as well as limited service to Barrie, Guelph, Sutton and Uxbridge. Call 416 869-3200 for more information, or go to www.gotransit.com

Ferry boats to the Toronto Islands are operated by the City of Toronto

GETTING AROUND

Parks and Recreation Dept., Island and Ferry division. They leave from the foot of Bay Street on a regular basis. Call 416 392-8193 or go to www.toronto.ca/parks/island for schedules and rates.

BY CAR

A valid driver's license from any country is good in Ontario for three months. Evidence of a car's registration is required (a car-rental contract will also serve). If you are driving into Ontario or importing a vehicle, bring with you its registration documents, and either a Canadian Non-Resident Motor Vehicle Liability Insurance Card (obtained from your insurance agent), or else the insurance policy itself. If you're driving a rented car, bring a copy of the rental contract. Speed limits are measured in kilometres per hour and vary depending on the type of road, with 400-level controlled-access highways having the highest limit. Speed limits on most highways are 80 to 90 kph, and 100 kph on freeways. On city streets the normal speed is 50 kph unless otherwise posted. Seat belt use by passengers and drivers is mandatory in Toronto. One kilometre equals about 5/8 of a mile. To convert from kilometres to miles, multiply kilometres by 0.6. To convert from miles to kilometres, multiply miles by 1.6. Metric measurements are used for motor fuel. One litre equals about one-quarter of an American gallon, or about one-fifth of an Imperial gallon.

CAR RENTALS

- Avis, 1 800 TRY-AVIS, downtown 416 777-AVIS, www.avis.com
- Discount Car Rentals, Yonge and Bloor, Charles Promenade, 730 Yonge St. 416 921-1212, www.discountcar.com
- Dollar Rent-a-Car, downtown 416 515-8800, airport 905 673-8811, www.dollar.com
- National Car Rental, 1 800 227-7368, www.nationalcar.com
- Thrifty Car Rental, Royal York Hotel 416 947-1385, www.thrifty.com

Consult the Yellow Pages for more agencies.

TOURS

- A Taste of the World — Neighbourhood Bicycle Tours and Walks. Unearth off-beat nooks and crannies of Toronto's ethnic neighbourhoods: Chinatown, Kensington Market, etc. 416 923-6813, www.torontowalksbikes.com
- All About Toronto. Step-on guide service, very professional, yet fun and exciting. 27 Clovercrest Rd., 416 495-8687, www.allabouttoronto.com
- CU Tours Incorporated. Daily tours year-round of Niagara Falls. 53 Langtry Pl., Thornhill ON L3T 1A1; 905 660-6255.
- Haunted Toronto. Ghost walks throughout Toronto. 416 487-9017, www.muddyyorktours.com/haunted.html
- Helicopter Company. A bird's-eye view of Toronto. 416 203-3280, www.thehelicoptercompany.com
- Hop-On Hop-Off City Tour offered by Gray Line. Scheduled sightseeing of Toronto and Niagara Falls. 184 Front St. E., #601; 416 594-3310, www.grayline.ca
- Lost World Tours. Their eco-friendly, personable approach gives you a unique view of Toronto. Here's your chance to visit the out-of-the-way places that other tourists never get to see! Your tour will be customized to your interests. 259 Sumach St.; 416 947-0778, otto_reid@yahoo.com
- National Helicopters Inc. Spectacular sightseeing rides featuring the Toronto Islands, CN Tower, SkyDome and Casa Loma. Operates May to September. 11339 Albion-Vaughan Rd., Kleinburg ON; 905 893-2727 or 1 888 361-1100, www.nationalhelicopters.com
- Summer Walking Tours. The Heritage Toronto summer walking tour series offers a wide variety of walks exploring many areas and topics of Toronto. 416 338-0684, www.heritagetoronto.org
- Tripmate Travel and Tour Guide Company. Experienced multilingual guides highlight the beauty, history and culture of Toronto and Niagara. 177 Spadina Ave.; 416 599-8892, www.itripmate.com
- Toronto Footsteps. Become a Torontonian for a day; smaller groups and families welcome. 25 Lascelles Boulevard, #609; 416 483-5483.
- Unique Views. Dynamic, interactive and interesting tours of Toronto. 171 Parkside Drive, Unit 1; 416 531-7770.

BOAT AND YACHT TOURS

- Empress of Canada. Toronto's luxury yacht cruises around the Toronto Islands. 260 Queen's Quay W., Suite 1408; 416 260-8901, Fax: 416 260-5547, www.empressofcanada.com
- Great Lakes Schooner Company. See Toronto's skyline from the open deck of a tall ship. April to October. 249 Queens Quay W., Suite 111; 416 260-6355, 1 800 267-3866, Fax: 416 260-6377, www.greatlakesschooner.com
- Jubilee Queen Cruises. Tour Toronto's harbour aboard a luxury 120-foot river showboat. April to October. 207 Queens Quay W.; 416 203-7245, Fax: 416 203-7177, www.jubileequeencruises.ca
- Klancy's Yacht Charters Incorporated. Cruise Lake Ontario aboard the *Klancy II*, a 100-passenger custom-designed yacht. Suite 1001 - 480 Queen's Quay W.; 416 866-8489, www.klancycharters.com
- Mariposa Cruise Line Limited. One-hour narrated harbour tours, private charters, lunch cruises and dinner cruises. 207 Queen's Quay W., Suite 415; 416 203-0178, 1 866 627-7672, www.mariposacruises.com
- Miss Toronto Yacht Charters and Tours. Unique 70-foot Florida-style yacht suitable for all occasions. 264 Queens Quay W., Suite 506; 416 861-0437, www.chartermisstoronto.com
- Nautical Adventures. Two unique ships for corporate functions, receptions, parties, special events and public cruises. 600 Queen's Quay W., Suite 103; 416 364-3244, Fax: 416 593-4078, www.nauticaladventure.com
- Toronto Harbour Tours. An entertaining, one-hour, fully narrated cruise of the Toronto Harbour. April to November. 145 Queen's Quay W.; 416 203-6994.

ACCOMMODATION

Tourism Toronto operates a central reservation service representing 123 member properties throughout the Greater Metropolitan Toronto Area. Contact them at Queen's Quay Terminal at Harbourfront Centre, PO Box 126, 207 Queens Quay W., Toronto ON M5J 1A7; 416 203-2600, 1 800-499-2514 (North America), Fax: 416 203-6753, www.tourismtoronto.com. The services of the Travellers' Aid Society include providing tourist information, maps and suggestions on what to see and do in Toronto, and acting as a link between stranded travellers and social services agencies. Contact them at Room B23, Union Station, Toronto ON M5J 1E6; 416 366-7788, Fax: 416 366-0829, www.travellersaid.ca Approximate prices are indicated, based on the average cost at time of publishing, for two persons staying in a double room (excluding taxes): $ = $50-$90; $$ = $90-$180; $$$ = $180-$300; $$$$=above $300.

For the locations of downtown and midtown hotels, see the map on page 8.

HOTELS: AIRPORT

- Days Hotel and Conference Centre, 6257 Airport Rd., Mississauga ON L4V 1E4; 905 678-1400, 1 800 329-7466, 1 800 387-6891 (ON, QC), Fax: 905 678-9130, daysres@royalequator.com, www.daysinn.com. Indoor pool and health club. Airport shuttle service. $$
- Doubletree International Plaza Hotel and Conference Centre, 655 Dixon Rd., Toronto ON M9W 1J3; 416 244-1711, 1 800 222-8733 (Canada and USA), Fax: 416 244-8031, yyzip_doubletree@hilton.com, www.internationalplaza.com. Indoor waterslide park, nightclub, swimming pool/fitness centre. $$$
- Holiday Inn Express Toronto — North York, 30 Norfinch Dr., North York ON M3N 1X1; 416 665-3500, Fax: 416 665-0807, whg4106@whg.com, www.ichotelsgroup.com. Complimentary continental breakfast. $$
- Holiday Inn Select Toronto Airport, 970 Dixon Rd., Etobicoke ON M9W 1J9; 416 675-7611, 1 888 465-4329, Fax: 416 675-9162, historonto-aprt@ichotelsgroup.com, www.ichotelsgroup.com. Complimentary airport shuttle service. Indoor/outdoor pools, sauna and whirlpool. $$$
- Renaissance Toronto Airport Hotel, 801 Dixon Rd., Etobicoke ON

ACCOMMODATION

M9W 1J5; 416 675-6100, 1 800 668-1444, Fax: 416 675-4022, www.mariott.com. Eighteen-hole golf course. Continuous airport shuttle. Swimming pool and spa/fitness centre. $$$
- Sheraton Gateway Hotel, Terminal 3, Departure Level, PO Box 3000, Mississauga ON L5P 1C4; 905 672-7000, Fax: 905 672-7100, reservations.00692@sheraton.com, www.starwoodhotels.com/sheraton. Attached to Terminal 3 of Pearson International Airport; saunas and a restaurant. $$-$$$
- Toronto Airport Marriott Hotel, 901 Dixon Rd., Etobicoke ON M9W 1J5; 416 674-9400, 1 800 905-2811, Fax: 416 674-8292, www.marriott.com. Volleyball and basketball court on property, golf and tennis nearby. Swimming pool and spa/fitness centre. Secretarial services and business centre. $$$
- Travelodge Toronto Airport, 925 Dixon Rd., Etobicoke ON M9W 1J8; 416 674-2222, 1 888 483-6887, Fax: 416 674-5757, reservations@travelodgedixon.com, www.travelodgedixon.com. Swimming pool, health club and sauna. $$
- The Wyndham Bristol Place Hotel, 950 Dixon Rd., Toronto ON M9W 5N4; 416 675-9444, 1 800 996-3426, Fax: 416 675-4426, www.wyndham.com. Five-star property with business centre and Women Travellers business select rooms. Swimming pool and spa/fitness centre. $$$

HOTELS: DOWNTOWN

See the map on page 8 for the map references.
- Best Western Primrose Hotel — Toronto-Downtown, 111 Carlton St., Toronto ON M5B 2G3; 416 977-8000, 1 800 268-8082, Fax: 416 977-6323, www.bestwestern.com. Saunas/exercise room and an outdoor swimming pool. $$ **Map 12**
- Bond Place Hotel, 65 Dundas St. E., Toronto ON M5B 2G8; 416 362-6061, 1 800 268-9390, Fax: 416 360-6406, bondres6@bellnet.ca, www. bondplacehoteltoronto.com. Walking distance to all top tourist attractions. $$ **Map 17**
- Cambridge Suites Hotel, 15 Richmond St. E., Toronto ON M5C 1N2; 416 368-1990, 1 800 463-1990, Fax: 416 601-3751, asktoronto@cambridgesuites.com, www.cambridgesuitestoronto.com. Complimentary continental breakfast, spa/fitness centre. $$$ **Map 22**
- Comfort Hotel Downtown, 15 Charles St. E., Toronto ON M4Y 1S1; 416 924-1222, 1 800 228-5150, Fax: 416 927-1369, comfortdowntown.sites.toronto.com. Newly renovated rooms, business facilities. $$ **Map 8**
- Comfort Suites City Centre, 200 Dundas St. E., Toronto ON M5A 4R6; 416 362-7700, 1 877 316-9951, Fax: 416 362-7706, info@comfortsuitestoronto.ca, www.toronto.com/comfortsuites. New suite-style accommodation, close to the Eaton Centre and the financial district.
- Days Inn Toronto Downtown, 30 Carlton St., Toronto ON M5B 2E9; 416 977-6655, 1 800 329-7466, Fax: 416 977-0502, www.daysinn.com. Heated indoor pool, sauna and fitness centre. $$ **Map 11**
- Delta Chelsea Inn, 33 Gerrard St. W., Toronto ON M5G 1Z4; 416 595-1975, 1 800 243-5732, Fax: 416 585-4375, reservations@deltachelsea.com, www.deltahotels.com. Swimming pool and spa/fitness centre. Business centre. $$ **Map 14**
- Grand Hotel and Suites Toronto, 225 Jarvis St., Toronto ON M5B 2C1; 416 863-9000, 1 877 324-7263, Fax: 416 863-1100, reservations@grandhoteltoronto.com, www.grandhoteltoronto.com. Spa/fitness centre. $$ **Map 16**
- Hilton Toronto, 145 Richmond St. W., Toronto ON M5H 2L2; 416 869-3456, 1 800 445-8667, Fax: 416 869-3187, info_toronto@hilton.com, www.hilton.com. Heated indoor/outdoor pool with health club. $$$ **Map 21**
- Holiday Inn Express Downtown, 111 Lombard St., Toronto ON M5C 2T9; 416 367-5555, 1 888 465-4329, Fax: 416 367-3470, whg4104agm@whg.com, www.hiexpress.com. Centrally located, continental breakfast buffet included. $$ **Map 23**
- Holiday Inn on King, 370 King St. W., Toronto ON M5V 1J9; 416 599-4000, 1 800 263-6364, Reservation Fax: 416 599-7394,

ACCOMMODATION

info@hiok.com, www.hiok.com. Swimming pool and spa/fitness centre. $$ **Map 31**
- Hotel Le Germain Toronto, 30 Mercer St., Toronto ON M5V 1H3; 416 345-9500, 1 866 345-9501, Fax: 416 345-9501, reservations@germaintoronto.com, www.germaintoronto.com. New boutique hotel. A small, luxurious cross between a bed and breakfast and a large luxury hotel. In the entertainment district. $$$-$$$$ **Map 30**
- Hotel Victoria, 56 Yonge St., Toronto ON M5E 1G5; 416 363-1666, 1 800 363-8228, Fax: 416 363-7327, reception@hotelvictoria.on.ca, www.hotelvictoria-toronto.com. A small historic property located in the heart of Toronto's theatre and financial district. $$ **Map 26**
- InterContinental Toronto Centre, 225 Front St. W., Toronto ON M5V 2X3; 416 597-1400, 1 800 227-6963 (Canada), Fax: 416 597-8128, torontocentre@interconti.com, www.torontocentre.intercontinental.com. Swimming pool and spa/fitness centre. $$$ **Map 28**
- Le Royal Meridien King Edward Hotel, 37 King St. E., Toronto ON M5C 1E9; 416 863-9700, 1 866 559-3821, Fax: 416 367-5515, www.toronto.lemeridien.com. An elegant hotel, renowned for its Edwardian splendour. Spa/fitness centre. Business centre. $$$ **Map 24**
- Madison Manor Boutique Hotel, 20 Madison Avenue, Toronto ON M5R 2S1; 416 922-5579, 1 877 561-7048, Fax: 416 963-4325, info@madisonavenuepub.com, www.madisonavenuepub.com/madisonmanor. Four floors in a Victorian manor. No elevator. Non-smoking. Complimentary continental breakfast. $$$ **Map 15**
- Marriott Eaton Centre, 525 Bay St., Toronto ON M5G 2L2; 416 597-9200, 1 800 905-0667, Fax: 416 597-9211, www.marriott.com. Swimming pool and spa/fitness centre. Business centre. $$$ **Map 18**
- Metropolitan Hotel, 108 Chestnut St., Toronto ON M5G 1R3; 416 977-5000, 1 800 668-6600, Fax: 416 977-6351, reservations@tor.metropolitan.com, www.metropolitan.com. Swimming pool and spa/fitness centre. $$ **Map 19**
- Novotel Toronto Centre, 45 The Esplanade, Toronto ON M5E 1W2; 416 367-8900, 1 800 668-6835, Fax: 416 360-8285, H0931@accor.com, www.novotel.com. Swimming pool and spa/fitness centre. $$$ **Map 37**
- Radisson Plaza Hotel Admiral, 249 Queens Quay W., Toronto ON M5J 2N5; 416 203-3333, 1 800 333-3333, Fax: 416 203-3100. Business centre. Swimming pool. $$ **Map 35**
- Ramada Hotel and Suites Downtown, 300 Jarvis St., Toronto ON M5B 2C5; 416 977-4823, 1 800 567-2233 (Canada and U.S.A.), Fax: 416 977-4830, reservations@ramadahotelsandsuites.com, www.ramadahotelsandsuites.com. Indoor swimming pool and spa/fitness centre. $$-$$$ **Map 13**
- Renaissance Toronto Hotel Downtown, at the Rogers Centre, 1 Blue Jays Way, Toronto ON M5V 1J4; 416 341-7100, 1 800 237-1512, Fax: 416 341-5091, www.marriott.com. One quarter of the rooms have floor-to-ceiling windows which offer an exclusive view of the stadium. Business centre. Swimming pool and spa/fitness centre. $$$ **Map 34**
- Royal York Hotel, 100 Front St. W., Toronto ON M5J 1E3; 416 368-2511, 1 800 441-1414, Fax: 416 368-9040, royalyorkhotel@fairmont.com, www.fairmont.com. Business centre. Swimming pool and spa/fitness centre. $$$-$$$$ **Map 27**
- Sheraton Centre Toronto Hotel and Towers, 123 Queen St. W., Toronto ON M5H 2M9; 416 361-1000, 1 800 325-3535, Fax: 416 947-4854, guestservice.00271@sheraton.com, www.sheratontoronto.com. Olympic-sized pool, sauna, hot tub, sundeck, spa/fitness centre and children's playroom. $$$ **Map 20**
- The SoHo Metropolitan Boutique Hotel, 318 Wellington St. W., Toronto ON M5V 3T3; 416 599-8800, 1 866 764-6638, Fax: 416 599-8801, reservations@soho.metropolitan.com, www.metropolitan.com/soho. New luxury boutique hotel in the entertainment district with all the amenities. $$$-$$$$ **Map 32**
- The Suites at 1 King West, 1 King Street W., Toronto, ON M5H 1A1; 416 548-8100, 1 866 470 5464,

ACCOMMODATION

- Fax: 416 548-8101, www.onekingwest.com. Deluxe hotel with fully equipped suites, some with special features such as fireplaces or private balconies. $$$
- Strathcona Hotel, 60 York St., Toronto ON M5J 1S8; 416 363-3321, 1 800 268-8304, Fax: 416 363-4679, info@thestrathconahotel.com, www.thestrathconahotel.com. $$ **Map 29**
- The Town Inn Suites, 620 Church Street, Toronto ON M4Y 2G2; 416 964-3311, 1 800 387-2755, Fax: 416 924-9466, www.towninn.com. Apartment suites with kitchen facilities. $$ **Map 9**
- Travelodge Toronto, 621 King St. W., Toronto ON M5V 1M5; 416 504-7441, Fax: 416 504-4722. Free continental breakfast, morning and evening coffee, tea and donuts. $$ **Map 33**
- Westin Harbour Castle, 1 Harbour Sq., Toronto ON M5J 1A6; 416 869-1600, 1 800 228-3000, Fax: 416 869-0573, harca@westin.com, www.westin.com. Swimming pool and spa/fitness centre. $$-$$$ **Map 36**
- The Windsor Arms, 18 St. Thomas St., Toronto ON M5S 3E7; 416 971-9666, Fax: 416 921-9121, reserve@windsorarmshotel.com, www.windsorarmshotel.com. Small, centrally located luxury hotel with spa and 24-hour butler service. Small pets allowed. $$$$ **Map 6**

HOTELS: MIDTOWN

See the map on page 8 for the map references.

- Comfort Hotel Downtown, 15 Charles St. E., Toronto ON M4Y 1S1; 416 924-1222, 1 800 424-6423, Fax: 416 927-1369, www.choicehotels.ca. $-$$ **Map 8**
- Four Seasons Hotel, 21 Avenue Rd., Toronto ON M5R 2G1; 416 964-0411, 1 800 268-6282, Fax: 416 964-2301, www.fourseasons.com/toronto. CAA/AAA Five Diamond hotel. Swimming pool and spa/fitness centre. $$$$ **Map 2**
- Holiday Inn Toronto Midtown, 280 Bloor St. W., Toronto ON M5S 1V8; 416 968-0010, 1 800 465-4329, Fax: 416 968-7765, cn312res@whg.com, www.holiday-inn.com. Located in fashionable Yorkville. Includes free access to Miles Nadal JCC fitness facility and pool. $$ **Map 5**
- Hotel InterContinental Toronto, 220 Bloor St. W., Toronto ON M5S 1T8; 416 960-5200, 1 800 267-0010, Fax: 416 960-8269, toronto@interconti.com, www.toronto.intercontinental.com. Swimming pool and spa/fitness centre. $$$ **Map 4**
- Howard Johnson Inn Yorkville, 89 Avenue Rd., Toronto ON M2R 2G3; 416 964-1220, 1 800 446-4656, Fax: 416 964-8692. $$ **Map 1**
- Park Hyatt Toronto, 4 Avenue Rd., Toronto ON M5R 2E8; 416 925-1234, 1 800 233-1234, Fax: 416 924-4933, www.parktoronto.hyatt.com. Spa/fitness centre. $$$ **Map 3**
- Sutton Place Hotel, 955 Bay St., Toronto ON M5S 2A2; 416 924-9221, 1 866 378-8866, Fax: 416 924-1778, res_toronto@suttonplace.com, www.toronto.suttonplace.com. Indoor swimming pool and spa/fitness centre. $$$ **Map 10**
- Toronto Marriott Bloor-Yorkville Hotel, 90 Bloor St. E., Toronto ON M4W 1A7; 416 961-8000, Fax: 416 961-4635, www.marriott.com. Spa/fitness centre. $$-$$$ **Map 7**

BED AND BREAKFASTS

Toronto has more than 200 bed and breakfast establishments, operating either independently or grouped together in association. The following represents a selection of these associations.

- Abodes of Choice Bed and Breakfast Association of Toronto, 102 Burnside Dr., Toronto ON M6G 2M8; 416 537-7629. Co-op group of homes in desirable neighbourhoods with affiliates across Canada. Various locations.
- The Downtown Toronto Association of Bed and Breakfast Guest Houses, PO Box 190, Station B, Toronto ON M5T 2W1; 416 410-3938, Fax: 416 483-8822, info@torontobedandbreakfast.com, www.bnbinfo.com. Toronto's largest selection of fully inspected Victorian homes in downtown Toronto. Non-smoking.
- Bed and Breakfast Homes of Toronto, 416 363-6362, www.bbht.ca
- Toronto Bed and Breakfast Inc., Box 269, 253 College St., Toronto ON M5T 1R5; 705 738-9449, 1 877

ACCOMMODATION

922-6522, Fax: 705-738-0155, beds@torontobandb.com, www.torontobandb.com. Toronto's oldest B & B reservation service.

HOSTELS AND COLLEGE RESIDENCES

Almost all of the residences listed below are available in summer only, but they provide a safe, economical alternative to hotels. Make sure you book in advance.

- Hospitality York, York University, 4700 Keele St., North York ON M3J 1P3; 416 736-5020, Fax: 416 736-5648, hospyork@yorku.ca, www.yorku.ca/hospyork. Swimming pool and spa/fitness centre. May to September. $
- Hostelling International Toronto, 76 Church St., Toronto ON M5C 2G1; 416 971-4440, 1 877 848-8737, Fax: 416 971-4088, toronto@hihostels.ca, www.hihostels.ca/hostels/Ontario. Central location. Rooms have vanity ensuite and air conditioning. Kitchen and laundry. $
- Massey College—University of Toronto, 4 Devonshire Place, Toronto ON M5S 2E1; 416 946-7843, Fax: 416 978-1759, massey.summer@gmail.com. Downtown Toronto. May to August. $
- Neill-Wycik College-Hotel, 96 Gerrard St. E., Toronto ON M5B 1G7; 416 977-2320, 1 800 268-4358, Fax: 416 977-2809, hotel@neill-wycik.com, www.neill-wycik.com. Shared kitchens and washrooms. Sauna. May to August. $
- The Residence, 90 Gerrard St. W., 22nd floor, Toronto ON M5G 1J6; 416 351-1010, Fax: 416 351-8583, www.theresidence.net. Central downtown location. Shared kitchen, bathroom and laundry facilities. $
- Ryerson Polytechnic University, 350 Victoria Street, Toronto, ON, M5B 2K3; 416 979-5000. Mid-May to August. $
- University of Toronto at Scarborough, 1265 Military Trail, Scarborough ON M1C 1A4; 416 287-7369, Fax: 416 287-7323, conferences@utsc.utoronto.ca, www.utsc.utoronto.ca /~facilities. East Metro location. Mid-May to August. $
- University of Toronto—St. George Campus, 45 Willcocks St., Toronto ON M5S 1C7; 416 978-8735, 1 888 834-7778, Fax: 416 978-1081, www.fs.utoronto.ca/English/Campus-Conferences.html. Central location. Rooms with ensuite bathrooms. Mid-May to August. Swimming pool and spa/fitness centre. $
- Victoria University, 140 Charles St. W., Toronto ON M5S 1K9; 416 585-4524, Fax: 416 585-4530, www.vicu.utoronto.ca. May to August. $-$$

TOP ATTRACTIONS

Toronto is replete with attractions. Here we have chosen to provide a selective listing of many of the points of interest. Check local newspapers, *Toronto Life* magazine, *eye weekly*, *Now* magazine, www.torontolife.com, www.torontotourism.com and www.toronto.com for more information.

- Allan Gardens. Huge greenhouses. Carlton and Sherbourne Sts.; 416 392-7288.
- Black Creek Pioneer Village. A recreated nineteenth-century village. Open year-round. 1000 Murray Ross Pkwy., Downsview ON M3J 2P3; 416 736-1733, www.blackcreek.ca
- Campbell House. Toronto's only Georgian historic house. Restored 1822 residence of Sir William Campbell. Open year-round. 160 Queen St. W., Toronto ON M5H 3H3; 416 597-0227, Fax: 416 597-0750, www.campbellhousemuseum.ca
- Canadian Broadcasting Centre (CBC). See behind the scenes at a world-class radio and television production facility. Open year-round, weekdays. 250 Front St. W., Room 3C409, PO Box 500, Station A, Toronto ON M5W 1E6; 416 205-3147, www.cbc.ca
- Canadian National Exhibition. Exhibition Place, Lakeshore Blvd., between Strachan and Dufferin; 416 393-6300 or 416 263-3800, www.theex.com
- Casa Loma. Toronto's majestic castle estate. Open year-round. 1 Austin Terrace, Toronto ON M5R 1X8; 416 923-1171, Fax: 416 923-5734, www.casaloma.org
- Centreville Amusement Park. A turn-of-the-century theme amusement park located on the

TOP ATTRACTIONS

- Toronto Islands, a short ferry ride away. Open Victoria Day to Labour Day and weekends only in September. Toronto Islands, 84 Advance Rd., Toronto ON M8Z 2T7; 416 203-0405, www.centreisland.ca
- City Hall. 100 Queen St. W. Book a tour of Toronto City Hall. 416 338-1200, accesstoronto@toronto.ca, www.toronto.ca/city_hall
- CN Tower Limited. The world's tallest free-standing structure. Open year-round. 301 Front St. W., Toronto ON M5V 2T6; 416 360-8500 or 416 868-6937, www.cntower.ca
- David Dunlap Observatory. Site of the largest optical telescope in Canada. 123 Hillsview Dr., Richmond Hill; 416 978-2016, www.astro.utoronto.ca/DDO
- Distillery District. Cafes, restaurants, galleries and live entertainment at 55 Mill St., Toronto ON M5A 3C4; 416 364-1177, Fax: 416 364-4793, www.thedistillerydistrict.com
- Enoch Turner Schoolhouse. Toronto's first school. Call ahead to book a visit. 106 Trinity St.; 416 863-0010, www.enochturnerschoolhouse.ca
- Fantasy Fair. This indoor amusement park features a Victorian town with eight rides, games, restaurants and a children's play area. Woodbine Shopping Centre, 500 Rexdale Blvd.; 416 674-5437.
- Gibson House. Restored 1851 farmhouse of rebel, politician and surveyor, David Gibson, his wife Eliza and their family. Open year-round, closed Mondays. Special weekend events. 5172 Yonge St.; 416 395-7432.
- Harbourfront Centre. Year-round centre features cultural and recreational activities. 235 Queens Quay W., Toronto, ON M5J 2G8; 416 973-4000, www.harbourfrontcentre.com
- Medieval Times Dinner and Tournament. Re-enactment of an eleventh-century medieval banquet. CNE near Dufferin Gate, Exhibition Place, Toronto ON M6K 3C3; 1 888 935-6878, www.medievaltimes.com/ 2006/tohomepage.htm
- Old City Hall. 60 Queen St. W.; www.toronto.ca/old_cityhall
- Ontario Place. Unique entertainment complex on Toronto's waterfront. Open mid-May to Labour Day. 955 Lake Shore Blvd. W., Toronto ON M6K 3B9; 416 314-9900 or 416 314-9811, 1 866 663-4386, www.ontarioplace.com
- Ontario Science Centre. Over 800 interactive exhibits emphasizing fun with science. Open year-round. 770 Don Mills Rd., Don Mills ON M3C 1T3; 416 429-4100 or 416 696-1000, www.ontariosciencecentre.ca
- Osgoode Hall, 100-130 Queen St. W., Toronto ON M5H 2N6; 416 947-3300, www.osgoodehall.com
- Queen's Quay Terminal. A specialty retail centre with unique shopping and dining on Toronto's waterfront. 207 Queens Quay W., www.queens-quay-terminal.com
- Rogers Centre (formerly The Skydome). Downtown stadium, home to the Toronto Blue Jays and the Toronto Argonauts. 1 Blue Jays Way; 416 341-1000, www.rogerscentre.com
- Toronto Zoo. World-class zoological park featuring over four thousand animals. Open year-round. 361A Old Finch Ave., Hwy. 401 and Meadowvale Rd., Scarborough ON M1B 5K7; 416 392-5900, www.torontozoo.com
- Waterfront Regeneration Trust. The Trust coordinates the 325-kilometre Waterfront Trail that stretches along the shore of Lake Ontario. 372 Richmond St. W., Suite 308, Toronto ON M5J 1A7; 416 943-8080, Fax: 416 943-8068, www.waterfronttrail.org

MUSEUMS

- Bata Shoe Museum, 327 Bloor St. W.; Tues., Wed., Fri. and Sat. 10-5, Thurs. 10-8, Sun. 12-5; 416 979-7799, Fax: 416 979-0078, www.batashoemuseum.ca
- First Post Office. 260 Adelaide St. E.; 416 865-1833, www.townofyork.com. Free admission.
- Gardiner Museum of Ceramic Art. 111 Queen's Park (temporary location of the school and shop while renovations are underway is at 60 McCaul Street); Mon., Wed., Fri. 10-

Museums and Galleries

- 6, Tues. and Thurs. 10-8, Sat. 10-5; 416 586-8080, Fax: 416 586-8085, www.gardinermuseum.on.ca
- Heritage Toronto. Visit one of four historic sites: Colborne Lodge, home of John George Howard (at High Park), 416 392-6916, www.toronto.ca/culture/colborne.htm; Fort York, the nineteenth-century fort that recreates the drama of the war of 1812 (off Fleet St., east of Strachan), 416 392-6907, www.fortyork.ca; Mackenzie House, home of William Lyon MacKenzie, Toronto's first mayor (82 Bond St.), 416 392-6915, www.toronto.ca/culture/mackenzie_house.htm; and Spadina House, a magnificent 1866 estate with fine art and elegant furnishings (285 Spadina Rd.), 416 392-6910, www.toronto.ca/culture/spadina.htm. Contact Toronto Convention & Visitors Association, PO Box 126, 207 Queens Quay W. Toronto ON M5J 1A7; 416 203-2600, Fax: 416 203- 6753, toronto@torcvb.com, www.torontotourism.com
- Hockey Hall of Fame, BCE Place, 30 Yonge St.; hours vary by season; Open seven days a week; 416 360-7765, www.hhof.com
- Textile Museum of Canada, 55 Centre Ave; Daily (except Wed.) 11-5, Wed. 11-8; 416 599-5321, www.textilemuseum.ca
- Todmorden Mills Heritage Museum and Arts Centre, Pottery Rd. between Broadview Ave. and Bayview Ave.; Tues. to Fri. 10-5, Sat. and Sun. 12-5; 416 396-2819, www.toronto.ca/todmorden
- Riverdale Farm, 201 Winchester St.; Daily 9-5; 416 392-6794, www.toronto.ca/parks/riverdalefarm.htm
- Royal Ontario Museum, 100 Queen's Park; Mon. to Thurs. 10-6, Fri. 10-9:30, Sat. 10-6, Sun. 10-6; 416 586-5549 or 416 586-8000, www.rom.on.ca

GALLERIES

This list of public galleries is a select one. Consult the latest edition of *Slate*, available at most galleries, for listings of current shows.

- A Space, 401 Richmond St. W., #110; Tues. to Fri. 11-6, Sat. 12-5; 416 979-9633, Fax: 416 979-9683, www.aspacegallery.org
- Art Gallery of Ontario, 317 Dundas St. W.; Tues. to Fri. 11-6, Wed. 11-8:30, Sat. and Sun. 10-5:30, closed all Mondays (including holidays); 416 979-6648, Fax: 416 979-6646, everyone@ago.net, www.ago.net
- Art Metropole, 788 King St. W.; Tues. to Fri. 11-6, Sat. 12-5; 416 703-4400, Fax: 416 703-4404, info@artmetropole.com, www.artmetropole.org
- Christopher Cutts Gallery, 21 Morrow Ave., #204; Tues. to Sat. 11-6; 416 532-5566, Fax: 416 532-7272, info@cuttsgallery.com, www.cuttsgallery.com
- Deleon White Gallery, 1096 Queen St. W.; Tues. to Sat. 12-5, or by appt.; 416 964-7838, Fax: 416 964-9377, White@eco-art.com, www.eco-art.com,
- Corkin Shopland Gallery, 55 Mill St., Bldg. 61; Tues. to Fri. 9:30-5:30, Sat. 10-5; 416 979-1980, Fax: 416 979-7018, info@corkinshopland.com, www.janecorkin.com
- Katharine Mulherin, 1080 and 1086 Queen St. W.; 416 537-8827, info@kmartprojects.com, www.kmartprojects.com
- Mira Godard Gallery, 22 Hazelton Ave.; Tues. to Sat. 10-5:30; 416 964-8197, www.godardgallery.com
- Olga Korper Gallery, 17 Morrow Ave.; Tues. to Sat. 10-6; 416 538-8220, Fax: 416 538-8772, www.olgakorpergallery.com
- Paul Petro Contemporary Art, 980 Queen St. W.; 416 979-7874, Fax: 416 979-3390, info@paulpetro.com, www.paulpetro.com
- Peak Gallery, 23 Morrow Ave.; 416 537-8108, Fax: 416 537-9518, zack@peakgallery.com, www.peakgallery.com
- The Power Plant, Harbourfront Centre, 231 Queens Quay W.; Tues. to Sun. 12-6, Wed. 12-8, Holiday Mondays 12-6; 416 973-4949, www.thepowerplant.org
- Sandra Ainsley Gallery, 55 Mill St. Bldg. 32; 416 214-9490, 1 877 362-2929, Fax: 416 214-9503, contact@sandraainsleygallery.com, www.sandraainsleygallery.com
- Wynick/Tuck Gallery, 401 Richmond St. #128; 416 504-8716, Fax: 416 504-8699, www.wynicktuckgallery.ca
- Ydessa Hendeles Art Foundation,

THEATRE AND DANCE

778 King St. W., PO Box 757, Station F, Toronto ON M4Y 2N6; Sat. 12-5 and by appt. (please fax or mail requests); 416 413-9400, ydessa@yhaf.org

For tickets to most theatres, contact Ticketmaster, 1 Blue Jays Way; 416 870-8000. For same-day tickets, contact T.O. Tix, Toronto's Half-Price Ticket Centre, for a wide variety of theatre, dance and musical events. Half-price tickets are available only on the day of the performance and must be purchased in person at Yonge-Dundas Square. Call 416 536-6468 for recorded information, or go to www.totix.ca

LIVE THEATRE

- Buddies in Bad Times, 12 Alexander St.; 416 975-8555, Fax: 416 975-9293, www.buddiesinbadtimestheatre.com
- Canadian Stage Company, at Bluma Appel Theatre in the St. Lawrence Centre, 27 Front St. E.; 416 366-1656; and at the Berkeley Street Theatre, 26 Berkeley St.; 416 368-3110, www.canstage.com
- Canon Theatre, 244 Victoria St.; 416 364-4100.
- Crow's Theatre, 54 Wolseley St. 2nd Floor; 416 504-5962, Fax: 416 504-4003, www.crowstheatre.com
- DanceWorks, 55 Mill St., Case Goods Building Suite #304; 416 204-1082, Fax: 416 204-1085, www.danceworks.ca
- Danny Grossman Dance Company, 157 Carlton Street, Suite 202; 416 408-4543, Fax: 416 408-2518, www.dannygrossman.com
- Elgin and Winter Garden Theatres, 189 Yonge St.; 416 314-2901, Fax: 416 314-3583, www.heritagefdn.on.ca
- The Factory Theatre, 125 Bathurst St.; 416 504-9971, Fax: 416 504-4060, www.factorytheatre.ca
- Four Seasons Centre for the Performing Arts. New home of the Canadian Opera Company and the National Ballet of Canada. Queen St. and University Ave.; 416 642-5679, www.fourseasonscentre.ca
- Harbourfront Centre, 235 Queens Quay W.; 416 973-4000, www.harbourfrontcentre.com
- Kaeja d'Dance, 734 Euclid Ave.; 416 516-6030, Fax: 416 537 5205, www.kaeja.org
- Lorraine Kimsa Theatre for Young People (formerly Young People's Theatre), 165 Front St. E.; 416 862-2222, www.lktyp.ca
- National Ballet of Canada, King's Landing, 470 Queens Quay W.; 416 345-9686, www.national.ballet.ca
- Necessary Angel, 55 Mill St., Case Goods Building Suite 303; 416 703-0406, Fax: 416 703-4006, www.necessaryangel.com
- Nightwood Theatre, 55 Mill Street, Case Goods Building Suite 301; 416 944-1740 ex. 4, Fax: 416 944-1739, www.nightwoodtheatre.net
- Premiere Dance Theatre, at Harbourfront Centre, 207 Queens Quay W.; 416 973-4000, www.harbourfrontcentre.com
- Princess of Wales Theatre, 300 King St. W.; 416 872-1212, 1 800 461-3333, Fax: 416 593-7759, www.mirvish.com/OurTheatres/Princess.html
- Roy Thomson Hall, Home of the Toronto Symphony Orchestra, 60 Simcoe St.; 416 872-4255.
- Royal Alexandra Theatre, 260 King St. W.; 416 872-1212, 1 800 461-3333, Fax: 416 593-7759, www.mirvish.com/OurTheatres/Royal.html
- Series 8:08, c/o Dance Umbrella of Ontario, 490 Adelaide St. W. #201; 416 504-6429 ex. 40, www.series808.ca
- Shaw Festival, 10 Queens Parade, Niagara-on-the-Lake; 1 800 511-7429, www.shawfest.com
- Soulpepper Theatre, Young Centre for the Performing Arts, 55 Mill St. Bldg. 49; 416 203-6264, Fax: 416 203-1531, Box Office: 416 866-8666, www.soulpepper.ca
- St. Lawrence Centre for the Arts. Houses the Bluma Appel Theatre and the Jane Mallet Theatre, 27 Front St. E.; 416 366-7723, 1 800 708-6754, www.stlc.com
- Stratford Festival, Stratford; 519 271-4040, 1 800 567-1600, Fax: 519 271-1126, orders@stratfordfestival.ca, www.stratfordfestival.ca
- Tarragon Theatre, 30 Bridgman Ave.; 416 536-5018, Fax: 416 531-1827, www.tarrontheatre.com
- Theatre Columbus, 174 Spadina Ave., Suite 403; 416 504-0019, Fax: 416 504-6001, www.theatrecolumbus.ca

SYMPHONY, CHAMBER MUSIC, OPERA

- Theatre Passe Muraille, 16 Ryerson Ave.; 416 504-7529, www.passemuraille.on.ca
- Theatre Smith-Gilmour, 720 Bathurst St., Suite 413; Ph/Fax: 416 504-1277, www.theatresmithgilmour.com
- Toronto Dance Theatre, 80 Winchester St.; 416 967-1365, Fax: 416 967-4379, www.tdt.org

CINEMAS

For current movies, showtimes and venues, check the entertainment pages of the *Toronto Star*, *Now* magazine or *eye weekly*.

COMEDY

- Bad Dog Theatre. 138 Danforth Ave.; 416 491-3115, www.baddogtheatre.com
- Drake Hotel. 1150 Queen St. W.; 416 531-5042, 1 866 372-5386, www.thedrakehotel.ca
- The Laugh Resort. Independent club featuring stand-up comedy and variety artists. 370 King St. W.; 416 364-5233, www.laughresort.com
- Oasis Restaurant & Bar. 294 College St.; 416 975-0845, www.oasisoncollege.com
- The Poor Alex. 416 324-9863, www.pooralextheatre.com
- The Rivoli. 334 Queen St. W.; 416 596-1908, www.rivoli.ca
- Second City. The well-known comedy troupe guarantees laughs. 51 Mercer St.; 416 343-0011, 1 800 263-4485, www.secondcity.com
- Yuk Yuk's Comedy Club. Canada's original home of stand-up comedy. 224 Richmond St. W.; 416 967-6425, www.yukyuks.com

SYMPHONY, CHAMBER MUSIC, OPERA

- Aldeburgh Connection, 74 Follis Ave.; www.aldeburghconnection.org
- Amadeus Choir, 75 The Donway W. Suite 410; 416 446-0188, Fax: 416 446-0187, www.amadeuschoir.com
- Amici Chamber Ensemble, 173B Front St. E.; 416 368-8743, Fax: 416 368-4345, www.amiciensemble.com
- Aradia Ensemble, Baroque Orchestra, 78 25th St.; 416 461-3471, www.aradia.ca
- Canadian Children's Opera Chorus, 416 366-0467, www.canadianchildrensopera.com
- Canadian Opera Company, Hummingbird Centre for the Performing Arts, 1 Front St. E.; 416 393-7469.
- Elmer Iseler Singers, chamber choir music, 2180 Bayview Ave.; 416 217-0537, www.elmeriselersingers.com
- Esprit Orchestra, 603 - 174 Spadina Ave.; 416 815-7887, 1 800 708-6754, Fax 416 815-7337, www.espritorchestra.com
- Glenn Gould Studio, Canadian Broadcasting Centre, 250 Front St. W.; 416 205-5555, Fax: 416 205-5551, www.glenngouldstudio.cbc.ca
- Jubilate Singers, 905 857-2152, www.jubilatesingers.ca
- New Music Concerts, 157 Carlton St., Suite 203; 416 961-9594, Fax 416 961-9508, www.newmusicconcerts.com
- Off Centre Music Series, 968 Logan Ave.; 416 466-1870, Fax: 416 466-0610, www.offcentremusic.com
- Opera Atelier, St. Lawrence Hall, 157 King St. E., 4th Fl.; 416 703-3767, Fax: 416 703-4895, www.operaatelier.com
- Orpheus Choir, PO Box 662, Station F, Toronto; 416 530-4428, www.orpheus.on.ca
- Tafelmusik, performing at Trinity-St. Paul's Church, 427 Bloor St. W.; 416 964-9562, Fax: 416 964-2782, www.tafelmusik.org
- Tallis Choir, 416 533-6179, www.tallischoir.com
- Toronto Centre for the Arts, 5040 Yonge St.; 416 733-9388, Fax: 416 733-9478, www.tocentre.com
- Toronto Consort, performing at Trinity-St. Paul's Church, 427 Bloor St. W.; 416 964-6337, Fax: 416 966-1759, www.torontoconsort.org
- Toronto Mendelssohn Choir, 60 Simcoe St.; 416 598-0422, www.tmchoir.com
- Toronto Symphony Orchestra, Roy Thomson Hall, 60 Simcoe St.; 416 598-3375, www.tso.ca

NIGHTLIFE

This list will help guide you through Toronto after dark. Refer to the Nightlife section (page 74) for more details and the map at the beginning of the book. Be sure to check local newspapers; there is something for everyone in Toronto. For up-to-date listings, try the most recent edition of *Now* magazine, or *eye weekly*, both available free of charge in bars and restaurants throughout Toronto.

QUEEN ST. WEST

- The Beaconsfield, 1154 Queen St. W.; 416 516-2550.
- The Bovine Sex Club, 542 Queen St. W.; 416 504-4239, www.bovinesexclub.com
- Cadillac Lounge, 1296 Queen St. W.; 416 536-7717, www.cadillaclounge.com
- Cameron House, 408 Queen St. W.; 416 703-0811. Soul, R and B, alternative or acid-jazz. www.thecameron.com
- Czehoski, 678 Queen St. W.; 416 366-6787.
- Drake Hotel, 1150 Queen St. W.; 416 531-5042, 1 866 372-5386, www.thedrakehotel.ca
- Gladstone Hotel, 1214 Queen St. W.; 416 531-4635, www.gladstonehotel.com
- Horseshoe Tavern, 370 Queen St. W.; 416 598-4753. Features great local bands. A jeans-and-draught pub. www.horseshoetavern.com
- Mitzi's Sister, 1554 Queen St. W.; 416 532-2570.
- Not My Dog, 1510 Queen St. W.; 416 532-2397, www.notmydog.ca
- The Paddock, 178 Bathurst St.; 416 504-9997.
- Queenshead, 659 Queen St. W.; 416 368-9405.
- The Rex, 194 Queen St. W.; 416 598-2475. Don't be fooled by the run-down appearance. www.therex.ca
- The Rhino, 1249 Queen St. W.; 416 535-8089.
- The Rivoli, 334 Queen St. W.; 416 596-1908. Dinner or drinks. The best place for live bands. www.rivoli.ca
- The Social, 1100 Queen St. W.; 416 532-4474.
- Stone's Place, 1255 Queen St. W.; 416 536-4242.
- Sweaty Betty's, 13 Ossington Ave.; 416 535-6861 www.sweatybettysbar.com
- Ultra Supper Club, 314 Queen St. W.; 416 263-0330, www.ultrasupperclub.com
- Wroxeter, 1564 Queen St. W.; 416 850-9245, www.wroxeter.ca

COLLEGE STREET/LITTLE ITALY

- Alto Basso, 718 College St.; 416 534-9522.
- Andy Poolhall, 489 College St.; 416 923-5300.
- Bar Italia, 582 College St.; 416 535-3621. Attracts all types of people, including families. Billiards, football and live jazz upstairs. www.bar-italia.ca
- The Mod Club Theatre, 722 College St.; 416 588-4663.
- Revival, 783 College St.; 416 535-7888.
- Shallow Groove Lounge, 559 College St.; 416 944-8998, www.shallowgroove.com
- Souz Dal, 636 College St.; 416 537-1883. Cozy and dark. Listen to the eclectic mix of music over a few martinis or margaritas (the best in town).
- Sutra, 612 College St.; 416 537-8755.
- Tempo, 596 College St.; 416 531-2822, www.tempotoronto.com

KENSINGTON MARKET

- The Boat, 158 Augusta Ave.; 416 593-9218.
- The Embassy, 223 Augusta Ave.; 416 591-1132.
- Neutral Lounge, 349a College St.; 416 926-1212, www.neutralzone.ca
- Supermarket, 268 Augusta Ave.; 416 840-0501, www.supermarkettoronto.com
- Thymeless, 355 College St.; 416 928-0556.

RICHMOND AND ADELAIDE/ENTERTAINMENT DISTRICT

- The Docks, 11 Polson St.; 416 469-5655, www.thedocks.com
- Fez Batik, 129 Peter St.; 416 204-9660.
- Guvernment, 132 Queens Quay E.; 416 869-0045. A huge central dance space gives way to other unique rooms. www.theguvernment.com

NIGHTLIFE

- Joker, 318 Richmond St. W.; 416 598-1313. Explore all three floors to find your niche, www.jokernightclub.ca
- Money, 199 Richmond St. W.; 416 591-9000, www.moneynightclub.ca
- Republik, 261 Richmond St. W.; 416 598-1632.
- System Soundbar, 117 Peter St.; 416 408 3996. Star DJs spin for crowds on two dance floors, www.systemsoundbar.com
- This is London, 364 Richmond St. W.; 416 351-1100.

DUNDAS STREET WEST
- Chelsea Room, 923 Dundas St. W.; 416 364-0553.
- Cocktail Molotov, 928 Dundas St. W.; 416 603-6691.
- Communist's Daughter, 1149 Dundas St. W.; 647 435-0103.
- Press Club, 850 Dundas St. W.; 416 364-7183.
- Magpie, 831 Dundas St. W.; 416 916-6499.

BLOOR-YORKVILLE
- Lobby, 193 Bloor St. W.; 416 929-7169.
- The Roof, Park Hyatt Hotel, 4 Avenue Rd.; 416 924-5471. Beautiful outdoor patio in summer.

GAY TORONTO
See page 221

THE ANNEX
- Dance Cave, 529 Bloor St. W.; 416 532-1598, www.leespalace.com/dancecave.html
- The Green Room, 296 Brunswick Ave.; 416 929-3253.
- Lee's Palace, 529 Bloor St. W.; 416 532-1598, www.leespalace.com
- The Madison Avenue Pub, 14 Madison Ave.; 416 927-1722.
- Victory Café, 581 Markham St.; 416 516-5787, www.victorycafe.ca

OTHER NEIGHBOURHOODS
- Allen's, 143 Danforth Ave.; 416 463-3086, www.allens.to
- Blowfish Restaurant and Sake Bar, 668 King St. W.; 416 860-0606, www.blowfishrestaurant.com
- Brassaii, 461 King St. W.; 416 598-4730.
- L'Idiot du Village/The Village Idiot, 126 McCaul St.; 416 597-1175.
- Laurentian Room, 51A Winchester St.; 416 925-8680, www.thelaurentianroom.com
- The Library Bar, 100 Front St. W., Royal York Hotel; 416 368-2511.
- Montreal Bistro and Jazz Club, 65 Sherbourne St.; 416 363-0179. Best local and visiting talent, www.montrealbistro.com
- The Only Café, 972 Danforth Ave.; 416 463-7843.

DINING

Toronto boasts some of the finest restaurants in North America. With a huge cultural diversity, there is something for everyone. The following is a select list of the restaurants available. Restaurants are listed alphabetically. The numerous restaurants mentioned in the Chinatown section of the book have not been included in the listings.

The map on page 9 shows the restaurants included in this selective listing that are located in central Toronto. The listings and brief descriptions that follow give you the numbers you can use to find central-city restaurants on the map.

Approximate prices are indicated, based on the average cost, at time of publication, of dinner for two including wine (where available), taxes and gratuity: $ = under $45; $$ = $45-$80; $$$ = $80-$120; $$$$ = $120-$180; $$$$$ = over $180. Meals served are indicated as: B = breakfast; L = lunch; D = dinner; Late = open past midnight; G = "grazing"; T-O = take-out. Credit cards accepted are also indicated: AX = American Express; V = Visa; MC = MasterCard.

- Acqua, 10 Front St. W., BCE Place; 416 368-7171. Closed Saturday lunch and Sunday. L/D, $$$$, AX/V/MC **Map 45**
- Asian Legend, 418 Dundas St. W.; 416 977-3909. L/D, $$ **Map 21**
- Aunties and Uncles, 74 Lippincott St.; 416 324-1375. B/L, $, Cash only **Map 58**
- Avalon, 270 Adelaide St. W.; 416 979-9918. Lunch only Thursday. Closed Monday and Sunday. Discover chef Christopher McDonald's sublime Italian-influenced cooking. L/D, $$$$$, AX/V/MC **Map 38**

DINING

- The Avenue Lounge, 21 Avenue Rd., Four Seasons Hotel; 416 928-7330. B/L/D/Late, $$$, AX/V/MC. **Map 10**
- Babur, 273 Queen St. W.; 416 599-7720. Weekend Brunch, L/D, $$$, AX/V/MC.
- Bangkok Garden, 18 Elm St.; 416 977-6748. Closed weekend lunch. Fabulous decor. Polished versions of traditional standards. L/D, $$$, AX/V/MC **Map 24**
- Barberian's, 7 Elm St.; 416 597-0335. Closed for weekend lunches. L/D, $$$$$, AX/V/MC **Map 25**
- Baton Rouge, 216 Yonge St.; Toronto Eaton Centre; 416 593-9667. L/D, $$, AX/V/MC **Map 42**
- Bellini, 101 Yorkville Ave.; 416 929-9111. D, $$$$ **Map 3**
- Biagio, 155 King St. E.; 416 366-4040. Closed Sunday, closed for weekend lunch. Traditional northern Italian fare paired with great Italian wines. L/D, $$$$, AX/V/MC **Map 44**
- Biff's, 4 Front St. E.; 416 860-0086. Closed Sunday, closed for weekend lunches. L/D, $$$$, AX/V/MC **Map 46**
- Bonjour Brioche, 812 Queen St. E.; 416 406-1250. Closed Mondays. B/L, $, Cash only.
- Canoe, Toronto-Dominion Tower, 66 Wellington St. W.; 416 364-0054. Closed Saturday and Sunday. Finest local ingredients cooked with Japanese refinement. L/D, $$$$$, AX/V/MC **Map 43**
- Captain John's, 1 Queens Quay W.; 416 363-6062. L/D, $$$.
- Carman's, 26 Alexander St.; 416 924-8697. Closed Sunday. Glorious beef. Olives and dill pickles pass as vegetables. Hundreds of celebrity photos. New steak house section. D, $$$$$, AX/V/MC **Map 18**
- Centro Restaurant and Lounge, 2472 Yonge St.; 416 483-2211. Closed Sunday. High-end Italian food with contemporary twists. Awe-inspiring wine cellar. L/D/Late, $$$$$, AX/V/MC.
- Chiado, 864 College St.; 416 538-1910. Light, elegant Portuguese cooking in graceful surroundings. D, $$$$$, AX/V/MC.
- Churrasco of St. Lawrence, Upper Level 49, South St. Lawrence Market; 416 862-2867. L/D/T-O, $ **Map 51**
- Dipamo's, 514 Eglinton Ave. W.; 416 483-4227. Closed Monday, closed for weekend lunches. L/D, $$$, AX/V/MC.
- Epic, 100 Front St. W., Fairmont Royal York Hotel; 416 860-6949. B/L/D, $$$$$, AX/V/MC **Map 54**
- Esplanade Bier Markt, 58 The Esplanade; 416 862-7575. A huge selection of beers from across the world complements brasserie food. L/D, $$, AX/V/MC **Map 50**
- Fionn MacCool's Irish Pub, 70 The Esplanade; 416 362-2495. L/D/Late, $$, AX/V/MC.
- Fran's Restaurant, 20 College St.; 416 923-9867. B/L/D/Late, $, AX/V/MC **Map 19**
- Gallery Grill, 7 Hart House Circle; 416 978-2445. Closed Saturday. L, $$$, AX/MC/V **Map 16**
- Gamelle, 468 College St.; 416 923-6254. Closed for lunch on weekends and Monday. Closed Sunday. L/D, $$$$, AX/V/MC **Map 20**
- Gandhi Cuisine, 554 Queen St. W.; 416 504-8155. L/D/T-O, $ **Map 34**
- Green Mango, 730 Yonge St.; 416 928-0021. 3006 Bloor St. W.; 416 233-5004. L/D, $$, AX/V/MC **Map 8**
- Hemispheres, 110 Chestnut St.; Metropolitan Hotel, 416 599-8000. Closed Sunday, closed for dinner Monday. B/L/D, $$$$$, AX/V/MC **Map 26**
- The Host, 14 Prince Arthur Ave.; 416 962-4678. No lunch on Sunday. Aristocratic cooking. Magical nut and cream sauces. L/D/G/T-O, $$$, AX/V/MC **Map 10**
- Jamie Kennedy Wine Bar, 9 Church St.; 416 362-1957. L/D, $$$, AX/V/MC **Map 47**
- Jumbo Empanadas, 245 Augusta Ave.; 416 977-0056. L/D/T-O, $, Cash only **Map 22**
- Jump, 16 Wellington St. W.; 416 363-3400. Closed Saturday lunch and Sunday. A Cal-Ital bistro at the city's financial heart. L/D, $$$, AX/V/MC **Map 52**
- The Keg Steakhouse, 12 Church St.; 416 367-0685. D, $$$, AX/V/MC **Map 40**
- Lai Wah Heen, 108 Chestnut St.; Metropolitan Hotel; 416 977-9899. Haute Cantonese and superlative Dim Sum. L/D, $$$$$ **Map 26**
- Le Matignon, 51 St. Nicholas St.; 416 921-9226. Closed for Saturday lunch and Sunday. L/D, $$$, AX/V/MC **Map 9**
- Le Papillon, 16 Church St.; 416 363-0838. Closed Monday, closed for brunch during the week. Crepes

DINING

- are the point here but the onion soup is a hit with Saturday crowds. Brunch/L/D, $$$, AX/V/MC **Map 48**
- Le Select Bistro, 328 Queen St. W.; 416 596-6405. **Map 29**
- Luce, 30 Mercer St.; Hotel Le Germain; 416 599-5823. Closed Sunday. D, $$$$$, AX/V/MC **Map 37**
- Masquerade Caffe & Bar, 181 Bay St., BCE Place; 416 363-8971. **Map 53**
- Messis, 97 Harbord St.; 416 920-2186. Closed for lunch on weekends and Monday. L/D, $$$, AX/V/MC **Map 14**
- Mustacio's, Lower Level B34, South St. Lawrence Market; 416 368-5241. L/D/T-O, $ **Map 49**
- Monsoon, 100 Simcoe St.; 416 979-7172. L/D, $$$$, AX/V/MC **Map 39**
- New Generation Sushi, 493 Bloor St. W.; 416 963-8861. L/D, $$ **Map 13**
- North 44°, 2537 Yonge St.; 416 487-4897. Closed Sunday. D, $$$$$, AX/V/MC.
- The Old Spaghetti Factory, 54 The Esplanade; 416 864-9761, Closed for weekend lunches. L/D, $$, AX/V/MC.
- Oro, 45 Elm St.; 416 597-0155. Closed Sunday and Saturday lunch. Thorough pampering in a lovely dining room. L/D, $$$$, AX/V/MC **Map 23**
- Pangaea, 1221 Bay St.; 416 920-2323. Closed Sunday. Inventive culinary notions backed by technical expertise. Afternoon tea. L/D, $$$$, AX/V/MC **Map 6**
- Pearl Harbourfront Chinese Cuisine, Queen's Quay Terminal, 207 Queens Quay W.; 416 203-1233. L/D, $$$, AX/V/MC **Map 57**
- Perigee, 55 Mill St.; 2nd floor of The Cannery Building, Distillery District; 416 364-1397. Closed Sunday and Monday. D, $$$$$.
- Perola's Supermarket, 247 Augusta Ave. (in Kensington Market); 416 593-9728. T-O, $ **Map 22**
- Peter Pan, 373 Queen St. W.; 416 593-0917. Sunday brunch. Burgers, warm salads and Thai noodles. L/D/Late/G, $$$, AX/V/MC **Map 31**
- Pony, 488 College St.; 416 923-7665. Closed Sunday. D, $$$, AX/V/MC **Map 20**
- Prego Della Piazza, 150 Bloor St. W.; 416 920-9900. Closed Sunday. Spot the celebrities over veal chops and a bottle of Barolo. L/D/G, $$$$, AX/V/MC **Map 11**
- Queen Mother Cafe, 208 Queen St. W.; 416 598-4719. Lots of arty atmosphere. Choice of excellent small dishes. L/D/Late/G/T-O, $$, AX/V/MC **Map 28**
- Rain, 19 Mercer St.; 416 599-7246. Closed Sunday and Monday. Superb fusion food in one of the continent's most beautiful rooms. D, $$$$$, AX/V/MC **Map 55**
- Richtree Market Restaurant, BCE Place, 42 Yonge St.; 416 366-8986. B/L/D/Late, $, AX/V/MC **Map 53**
- Rivoli, 332 Queen St. W.; 416 596-1908. Elegant fare borrows flavours from the Orient. Quirky decor and staff. L/D/Late/G, $$$, AX/V/MC **Map 30**
- Roof Lounge, 4 Avenue Rd., 18th Floor of the Park Hyatt; 416 925-1234. L/D/Late **Map 11**
- Scaccia, 55 Bloor St. W.; 416 963-9864. L/D, $$ **Map 7**
- Scaramouche, 1 Benvenuto Pl.; 416 961-8011. Closed Sunday. A gifted chef, top-drawer service and lavish dining room. D, $$$$$, AX/V/MC.
- Segovia, 5 St. Nicholas St.; 416 960-1010. Dinner Mon.-Sat., lunch Mon.-Fri.; closed Sun. Authentic Spanish flavours in paella; garlicky chicken. Flamenco dancers upstairs. L/D, $$$, AX/V/MC **Map 11**
- Shanghai Cowgirl, 538 Queen St. W.; 416 203-6623. L/D, $$ **Map 33**
- Signatures, 220 Bloor St. W., Hotel Inter-Continental Toronto; 416 324-5885. Closed Sunday evening. B/L/D, $$$$, AX/V/MC **Map 12**
- Southern Accent, 595 Markham St.; 416 536-3211. Blackened chicken livers a must. Festive patio music. Closed Monday. D, $$$, AX/V/MC.
- Splendido, 88 Harbord St.; 416 929-7788. Closed Monday. Meaty green olives to fruit garnishes are chosen and prepared with care. D, $$$$$ **Map 15**
- St. Lawrence Market, 91-95 Front St. E.; 416 392-7219. Closed Mondays. A collection of businesses including specialty food stores and restaurants.
- Studio Café, 21 Avenue Rd., Four Seasons Hotel; 416 928-7330. B/L/D, $$$, AX/V/MC **Map 10**
- Sultan's Tent, 49 Front St. E.; 416 961-0601. Closed for weekend lunches. L/D, $$$, AX/V/MC **Map 5**

SHOPPING

- Superior, 253 Yonge St.; 416 214-0416. Closed Sunday. Pre-show fine dining for nearby Canon, Elgin, Winter Garden theatre crowds. L/D, $$$$ **Map 41**
- Supermarket, 268 Augusta Ave.; 416 840-0501. Closed Sunday. D/G, $$, AX/V/MC **Map 22**
- Susur, 601 King St. W.; 416 603-2205. Closed Sunday. Star chef Susur Lee is the king of Fusion. D, $$$$$ **Map 36**
- Terroni, 106 Victoria St.; 416 955-0258, 720 Queen St. W.; 416 504-0320. Closed Sunday. Upmarket pastas and thin crispy pizzas in a relaxed setting. L/D, $$, V.
- Tequila Bookworm, 490 Queen St. W.; 416 504-7335. $ **Map 32**
- Thuet Cuisine, 609 King St. W.; 416 603-2777. Closed Sunday and Monday. D, $$$$$, AX/V/MC **Map 35**
- Tiger Lily's Noodle House, 257 Queen St. W.; 416 977-5499. Healthy East-Asian soups and noodle dishes with flair. L/D/G/T-O, $$, AX/V/MC **Map 27**
- Trattoria Sotto Sotto, 116A Avenue Rd.; 416 962-0011. Romantic, subterranean setting. Irresistible grilled dishes, especially the radicchio. D, $$$$, AX/V/MC **Map 1**
- Truffles, 21 Avenue Rd., Four Seasons Hotel; 416 964-0411. Closed Sunday. Canadian Heart Association's stamp of approval on haute cuisine selections. Deluxe ingredients. D, $$$$$, AX/V/MC **Map 10**
- Victory Café, 581 Markham St.; 416 516-5787. L/D, $.
- Wayne Gretzky's, 99 Blue Jays Way, 416 979-7825. L/D, $$$ **Map 56**
- Zerosun, 69 Yorkville Ave.; 416 961-8349. **Map 4**

SHOPPING

ANTIQUES AND COLLECTIBLES

Toronto's antique dealers are diverse and far-flung. It's easiest if you pick a neighbourhood and start by visiting all the shops in the vicinity.

- Bayview Village Shopping Centre: Antique Market. Bayview and Sheppard; 416 226-0404. Runs one Sunday each month and spans the entire mall from 10 a.m. to 5 p.m.
- Perkins Antiques, 1198 Yonge St.; 416 925-0973. Fine Canadian pine furniture and primitive ceramics.
- Prince of Serendip, 1402 Queen Street E.; 416 925-3760.
- Quasi-Modo Modern Furniture, 789 Queen St. W.; 416 703-8300. Vintage furniture and collectibles.
- R.A. O'Neil Antiques, 100 Avenue Road; 416 968-2806. Country furniture, primitive ceramics and other decorative accessories.
- Red Indian Art Deco, 536 Queen St. W.; 416 504-7706. Very cool vintage furniture and collectibles. Deco lamps, cocktail shakers, chrome items.
- St. Lawrence Market, 92 Front St. E.; 416 392-7219.
- Stanley Wagman and Sons Antiques Ltd., 224 Davenport Rd.; 416 964-1047.
- Style Garage, 938 Queen St. W.; 416 534-4343. A mix of contemporary and antique furnishings.
- Zig Zag, 1142 Queen St. E.; 416 778-6495.

BEAUTY AND HEALTH

- Aroma Shoppe, 1940 Queen St. E.; 416 698-5850. Aromatherapy.
- Aveda Environmental Lifestyle Store, 95 Bloor St. W.; 416 921-2961, 416 413-1333. Full line of Aveda products, including shampoo, hair care products, and cosmetics.
- The Body Shop, 100 Bloor St. W.; 416 928-1180. Most major malls and assorted other locations; Toronto Eaton Centre, 220 Yonge St.; 416 977-7364. Environmentally-friendly skin care products, cosmetics and toiletries.
- Iodine, 867 Queen St. W.; 416 681-0577.
- Lush, 312 Queen St. W.; 416 599-5874; Toronto Eaton Centre and Toronto International Airport. A blitz of bath bombs from London, England, along with other bubbly concoctions.
- M.A.C., 89 Bloor St. W.; 416 929-7555; Hudson's Bay Centre (at Bloor and Yonge), 416 972-3363; The Bay at Queen and Yonge, 416 861-4508 as well as 12 other locations. A makeup store that contributes to AIDS charities through a wide range of cruelty-free products.

SHOPPING

- Sephora, Toronto Eaton Centre; 416 595-7227; Yorkdale Mall; 416 785-4400. A seemingly endless array of beauty & body products.

BOOKS

- Indigo, 55 Bloor St. W.; 416 925-3536, and other locations of this biggest Canadian bookseller that includes Chapters stores.
- Mabel's Fables Children's Book Stores, 662 Mount Pleasant; 416 322-0438.
- Nicholas Hoare, 45 Front St. E.; 416 777-2665. A publisher's dream and cornucopia of colour: almost all the books face out, framed by fine wood display stands and walls.
- Pages Books and Magazines, 256 Queen St. W.; 416 598-1447. Queen West's most popular newsstand and bookroom.
- This Ain't The Rosedale Library, 483 Church St.; 416 929-9912. A great store for fiction in the heart of the Church Street community.
- World's Biggest Bookstore, 20 Edward St.; 416 977-7009. Before Chapters and Indigo, there was this two-floor giant. It's still a contender.

CANADIANA

- Bowring, 220 Yonge St.; in Toronto Eaton Centre; 416 596-1042. Gifts and Canadiana.
- Canadian Naturalist, 207 Queen's Quay W.; 416 203-0365, Eaton Centre; 416 581-0044.
- First Hand Canadian Crafts, Queen's Quay Terminal; 416 603-7413.
- Oh Yes! Toronto, Queens Quay Terminal; 416 203-0607, two locations in Eaton Centre; 416 593-6749 and 416 596-0443. Clothing for all ages to take home as souvenirs from Toronto.

CHINA AND CRYSTAL

- Bowring, 220 Yonge St. in Toronto Eaton Centre; 416 596-1042. Gifts and Canadiana.
- Du Verre, 186 Strachan Ave.; 416 593-0182. Hand-blown glassware and hand-crafted iron furnishings.
- Muti and Company, 88 Yorkville Ave.; 416 969-0253. An ample selection of imported Italian majolica ceramics.
- William Ashley, 55 Bloor St. W.; 416 964-2900. Toronto's largest selection of fine china, crystal, silver and gifts.

CLOTHING: CANADIAN DESIGNERS

- Anti-Hero Inc., 113 Yorkville Ave.; 416 924-6121.
- Blue Angel, 2237 Bloor St. W.; 416 763-2098.
- Brian Bailey, 878 Queen St. W.; 416 516-7188; Bayview Village Shopping Centre; 416 221-3355.
- Comrags, 654 Queen St. W.; 416 360-7249. Canadian duo Joyce Gunhouse and Judy Cornish offer feminine clothing such as ethereal floral rayon dresses and tight-fitting cotton-Lycra knits.
- Fashion Crimes, 395 Queen St. W.; 416 592-9001. Velvet wear for the goth crowd, Edwardian morning coats, Empire-waisted bodice gowns and glamourous accessories.
- Finishing Touches, 3281 Yonge St.; 416 482-9034.
- Lida Baday Studio, 70 Claremont St.; 416 603-7661. Simple, elegant, high-end women's fashion, using excellent fabrics and knits.
- Linda Lundstrom, 136 Cumberland St.; 416 927-9009; Bayview Village (Bayview and Sheppard); 416 225-7227. Women's outerwear including the four-coats-in-one La-Parka.
- Lowon Pope Design, 779 Queen St. W.; 416 504-8150.
- Marilyn Brooks, 10 Avoca St.; 416 504-5700. A well-known line of fine, sensible women's clothing.
- Price Roman, 267 Queen St. W.; 416 979-7363. Elegant women's suits and dresses, with simple lines and subtle detailing.
- Psyche, 708 Queen St. W.; 416 599-4882.
- Ross Mayer, 74 Bathurst St.; 416 703-4361; 2587 Yonge St.; 416 932-9282.
- Wayne Clark Designs, 49 Spadina Ave.; 416 599-9515.

CLOTHING: CHILDREN'S

- Gap Kids, Toronto Eaton Centre, 220 Yonge St.; 416 348-8800; 80 Bloor St. W.; 416 515-0668; 2574 Yonge St.; 416 440-0187. Well-made clothing for babies and children in natural fabrics; a bit on the preppy side.
- Misdemeanours, 322 1/2 Queen St. W.; 416 351-8758. This wonderful

shop makes you step through the looking-glass: storybook dresses for girls, accented with Victorian frills.
- Old Navy, Toronto Eaton Centre; 416 593-2551; Yorkdale Mall; 416 787-9384 and other locations. Affordable fashion for men, women and children.
- Roots, 100 Bloor St. W.; 416 323-3289; Toronto Eaton Centre; 416 593-9640. 12 other stores, plus 3 factory outlets. Look for the Baby Roots line at each of these locations.

CLOTHING: MEN'S

- Banana Republic, 80 Bloor St. W.; 416 515-0018; Toronto Eaton Centre; 416 595-6336. Trendy chain featuring casual and office wear for young professionals; also carries accessories and shoes.
- Boomer, 309 Queen St. W.; 416 598-0013. A variety of mid-range to upscale men's clothing.
- Eddie Bauer, 50 Bloor St. W.; 416 961-2525; Toronto Eaton Centre; 416 586-0662. Outdoor gear, hiking boots, down vests, flannel shirts and other icons of the comfortable male.
- The Gap, 60 Bloor St. W.; 416 921-2711; First Canadian Place; 416 777-1332; 375 Queen St. W.; 416 591-3517; Toronto Eaton Centre; 416 599-8802. Casual wear for some, workwear for others, and dancewear if you watch too much television.
- Grreat Stuff, 870 Queen St. W.; 416 536-6770.
- H&M, 13-15 Bloor St. W.; 416 920-4029; Toronto Eaton Centre; 416 593-0064; other locations. Cheap faddish finds from this popular European retailer.
- Harry Rosen, 82 Bloor St. W.; 416 972-0556; Toronto Eaton Centre; 416 598-8885; Yorkdale Shopping Centre; 416 787-4231. Upscale men's business and casual wear, including Giorgio Armani, Hugo Boss, Canali, Brioni and Versace, and the V2 collection; also shoes and accessories.
- Hoax Couture, 301-163 Spadina Ave.; 416 597-8924.
- Holt Renfrew, 50 Bloor St. W.; 416 922-2333; Yorkdale Shopping Centre; 416 789-5377. Fine fashions for men: Giorgio Armani, Calvin Klein and Holt Renfrew's own label.
- Hugo Nicholson, Hazelton Lanes; 416 927-7714.
- Old Navy, Toronto Eaton Centre; 416 593-2551; Yorkdale Mall; 416 787-9384 and other locations. Affordable fashion for men, women and children.
- TNT, 388 Eglinton W.; 416 488-8210 as well as Hazelton Lanes.

CLOTHING: SECOND-HAND

- Cabaret Nostalgia, 672 Queen St. W.; 416 504-7126.
- Circa Forty, 456 Queen St. W, 416 504-0880.
- Courage My Love, 14 Kensington Ave.; 416 979-1992. Standby funky vintage clothing with all the trappings (beads, chains, charms); reasonably priced.
- Dancing Days, 17 Kensington Ave.; 416 599-9827.
- Preloved, 613 Queen St. W.; 416 504-8704. Features clothes from the 1970s.

CLOTHING: WOMEN'S

HIGH-END

- Annie Thompson, 674 Queen St. W.; 416 703-3843. Canadian designer boutique.
- Aquascutum, Hazelton Lanes; 416 929-3753. Upscale women's clothing.
- Betsey Johnson, 102 Yorkville Avenue; 416 922-8164. Dresses and more.
- The Cashmere Shop, 24 Bellair St.; 416 925-0831. Sweaters, scarves, throws and blankets; you can have them customized, too.
- Chanel Boutique, 131 Bloor St. W.; 416 925-2577. Fragrances, shoes, clothes and leather bags.
- Gucci, 130 Bloor St. W.; 416 963-5127. Internationally famous fashion retailer.
- Lileo, 55 Mill St. (Distillery District); 416 413-1410.
- Nancy Moore for Motion Clothing Co., 106 Cumberland St.; 416 968-0090. The Canadian designer's exclusive boutique.
- Over the Rainbow, 101 Yorkville Avenue; 416 967-7448. Designer denim.
- Petra Karthaus, Hazelton Lanes; 416 922-5922. Exclusive boutique.
- Plaza Escada, 110 Bloor St. W.; 416 964-2265. Escada designer lines, including Couture, Elements,

SHOPPING

Laurèl and Escada Sport.
- Prada, 131 Bloor St. W.; 416 513-0400. Clothing, shoes and accessories.
- Susan Harris Design, 135 Tecumseth St., Unit 2; 416 703-8537.
- TNT, 388 Eglinton W.; 416 488-8210 as well as Hazelton Lanes.
- Versace, 83 Bloor St. W.; 416 920-8300. Featuring Versace couture as well as mid-range clothing.

MEDIUM RANGE AND CASUAL WEAR
- Georgie Bolesworth, 891 Dundas St. W.; 416 703-7625. Curvy woman's fashions.
- Casual Way, 2541 Yonge St.; 416 481-1074.
- Club Monaco, 157 Bloor St. W.; 416 591-8837; 403 Queen St. W.; 979-5633; Toronto Eaton Centre; 416 593-7299. Canadian company with trendy, fashionable clothing including suits, dresses, club and athletic wear.
- Banana Republic, 80 Bloor St. W.; 416 515-0018; Toronto Eaton Centre; 416 595-6336. Another trendy chain featuring casual and office wear for young professionals; also carries accessories and shoes.
- Benetton, 102 Bloor St. W.; 416 968-1611.
- Daily Fraiche, 348 Queen St. W.; 416 341-8606. Clean, European-styled innovative fashions.
- Eddie Bauer, 50 Bloor St. W.; 416 961-2525. This flagship store offers jackets and corduroy pants, as well as classic career wear.
- Esprit, Toronto Eaton Centre; 416 979-2876. Mid-priced clothing.
- Ewanika, 490 College St.; 416 927-9699. Modern clothing.
- Fairweather, Toronto Eaton Centre; 416 586-7700; First Canadian Place; 416 586-7718; Yorkdale Shopping Centre; 416 781-9105. Reasonably priced work wear for young women who want to preserve a touch of funk; a good source for sweaters and t-shirts.
- Fresh Collective, 692 Queen St. W.; 416 594-1313. Handmade clothes and accessories.
- The Gap, 60 Bloor St. W.; 416 921-2711; First Canadian Place; 416 777-1332; 375 Queen St. W.; 416 591-3517; Toronto Eaton Centre; 416 599-8802. Trendy, well-made clothing in the younger line; t-shirts, khakis and cotton.
- Girl Friday, 740 Queen St. W.; 416 364-2511; 776 College St.; 416 531-1036. Unique clothing for women.
- H&M, 13-15 Bloor St. W.; 416 920-4029; Toronto Eaton Centre; 416 593-0064; other locations. Cheap faddish finds from this popular European retailer.
- Jacob, 55 Bloor St. W.; 416 925-9488; Yorkdale Mall; 416 785-3043 and other locations.
- Kaliyana, 2516 Yonge St.; 416 480-2397.
- La Cache, 120 Yorkville Avenue; 416 961-3053 and other locations. Cotton clothing.
- Lululemon, 734 Queen St. W.; 416 703-1399; 130 Bloor St. W.; 416 964-9544; and other locations. Trendy Canadian workout and yoga wear and accessories.
- Mendocino, 2647 Yonge St.; 416 646-0812; and other locations.
- Mango, Toronto Eaton Centre; 416 595-7130; Yorkdale Mall; 416 787-7957. Spanish clothing chain for young, urban women.
- Mink, 550 College St.; 416 929-9214.
- Mirabelli, 456 Eglinton Avenue W.; 416 322-3130; Yorkdale Mall; and other locations.
- Nearly Naked, 749 Queen St. W.; 416 703-7561. Attractive lingerie.
- Old Navy, Toronto Eaton Centre; 416 593-2551; Yorkdale Mall; 416 787-9384, and other locations. Affordable fashion for men, women and children.
- Posh Boutique, 2016 Queen St. E.; 416 690-5533.
- Set Me Free, 653 College St.; 416 516-6493. Clothing and occasionally bicycles.
- Skirt, 903 Dundas St. W.; 647 436-3357.
- Talbots, 2 Bloor St. W.; 416 927-7194. Conservative women's clothing, reasonably priced.

CRAFTS AND HOBBIES
- Beadworks, 2154 Queen St. E.; 416 693-0780.
- Japanese Paper Place, 887 Queen St. W.; 416 703-0089. Imported origami and handcrafted papers.

ELECTRONICS
- Future Shop, 2400 Yonge St.; 416 489-4726; and other locations.

National electronics superstore.

GOURMET

- Chocolate and Creams, 207 Queens Quay W.; 416 368-6767.
- Dufflet Pastries, 2638 Yonge St.; 416 484-9080; 787 Queen St. W.; 416 504-2870. Cakes and other sweet treats.
- Magnolia, 548 College St.; 416 920-9927. High-quality fresh foods and gourmet items.
- Mercantile, 626 College St.; 416 531-7563. Fine foods, mostly dry goods.
- Timbuktu, 39 Front St. E.; 416 366-3169.

HATS AND ACCESSORIES

- Fleurtje, 764 Queen St. W.; 416 504-5552. Whimsical handmade bags and other local artisan goods.
- Fresh Collective, 692 Queen St. W.; 416 594-1313. Handmade clothes and accessories.
- Lilliput Hats, 462 College St.; 416 536-5933. Wonderful assortment of hand-made hats; fairly pricey, but worth it.
- Prada, 131 Bloor St. W.; 416 513-0400. Clothing, shoes and accessories.
- Wildhagen, 55 Mill St. (Distillery District), Case Goods Warehouse. Fine and fancy hats.

HOME FURNISHINGS

- Art Shoppe, 2131 Yonge St.; 416 487-3211. Upscale home furnishings in a wide range of styles.
- Bowring, 220 Yonge St. in Toronto Eaton Centre; 416 596-1042. Gifts and Canadiana.
- Caban, 262 Queen St. W.; 416 496-0386; and other locations. The sleek home furnishing arm of Club Monaco.
- Constantine Interiors, 1110 Yonge St.; 416 929-1177. Beautiful furnishings, mostly antique, as well as an eclectic assortment of home accessories; great Venetian overhead lamps, some fabrics; friendly service.
- Eye Spy, 1100 Queen St. E.; 416 461-4061.
- Fluid Living, 55 Mill St. (Distillery District); 416 850-4266.
- fos, 55 Mill Street (Distillery District); 416 364-6877.
- High Tech, 106 Front St. E.; 416 861-1069. Modern kitchenware.
- Homefront, 371 Eglinton Ave. W.; 416 488-3189.
- Home Furnishings, 11 William Kitchen Rd.; 416 293-3591; and other locations.
- IKEA, 15 Provost Dr.; 416 222-4532; and other locations. Sturdy, inventive, diverse and at the extreme end of the subway line.
- Morba, 665 Queen St. W.; 416 364-5144.
- Pavilion, 739 Queen St. W.; 416 504-9859.
- Pier 1, 1986 Queen St. E.; 416 698-3426; and other locations. Cheery housewares and dinnerware.
- Pottery Barn, 100 Bloor St. W.; 416 962-2276; Toronto Eaton Centre; 416 597-0880; Yorkdale Shopping Centre; 416 785-1233.
- Restoration Hardware, 2434 Yonge St.; 416 322-9422; and in Bayview Village. Upscale U.S. home furnishings chain.
- Ridpath's, 906 Yonge St.; 416 920-4441. Another long-established Toronto quality furniture shop.
- Style Garage, 938 Queen St. W.; 416 534-4343. A mix of contemporary and antique furnishings.
- Up Country, 214 King St. E.; 416 777-1700. Comfortable couches, lamps, and wooden furniture in a trendy industrial setting; personal items also.
- Urban Mode, 145 Tecumseth St.; 416 591-8834. Hip modern furnishings.
- Williams-Sonoma, Toronto Eaton Centre; 416 260-1255; Yorkdale Shopping Centre; 416 781-3770; 100 Bloor St. W.; 416 962-8248.

JEWELLERY AND WATCHES

- Birks, 55 Bloor St. W.; 416 922-2266; Toronto Eaton Centre; 416 979-9311; and six other locations. Extensive, conservative collection of jewellery, silverware, crystal, watches and china.
- European Jewellery, Toronto Eaton Centre; 416 599-5440.
- Experimetal, 742 Queen St. W.; 416 363-4114. Unique jewellery.
- Fabrice, 55 Avenue Rd.; 416 967-6590.
- Gucci, 130 Bloor St. W.; 416 963-5127. Internationally famous fashion retailer.

SHOPPING

- Tiffany and Co., 85 Bloor St. W.; 416 921-3900. The jewellery here includes collections by Elsa Peretti, Paloma Picasso and Jean Schlumberger; also diamonds, pearls, gold, silver and platinum. Watches, flatware, sterling silver, china, fragrances and even stationery.

LEATHER

- Danier Leather, Toronto Eaton Centre; 416 598-1159; Yorkdale Shopping Centre; 416 783-8304. In-house designs at reasonable prices from this Canadian chain.
- Perfect Leather Goods, 555 King St. W.; 416 205-9775. A great place for leather, located in Toronto's old garment district.
- Roger Edwards, 2811 Dufferin St., North York; 416 366-2501.
- Roots, 100 Bloor Street W.; 416 323-3289; 195 Avenue Rd.; 416 927 8585; Toronto Eaton Centre; 977-0041; and five other locations. In addition to the trademark clothing and shoes, this Canadian company also produces jackets, handbags and luggage, plus a new line of leather furniture.

MALLS AND DEPARTMENT STORES

- The Bay, 44 Bloor St. E.; 416 972-3333.
- Bayview Village Shopping Centre, 2901 Bayview Ave. at Sheppard; 416 226-2003. Almost 100 shops, restaurants and services, including Talbots, Havana Tobacconist, La Vie En Rose, Capezio Shoes and Rodier.
- Hazelton Lanes, 55 Avenue Rd.; 416 968-8600. Over 80 unique boutiques and a few chain stores, with mid- to high-end shops for fashion and the home. Toronto's serious shopping zone.
- Holt Renfrew Centre, 50 Bloor St. W.; 416 922-2333. Over 25 shops, including HMV, Eddie Bauer, Sunglass Hut and Science City, as well as unusual boutiques.
- Manulife Centre, 55 Bloor St. W.; 416 923-9525. 50 upscale shops, including Indigo, William Ashley, Mephisto, and an LCBO; a Thomas Cook Foreign Exchange is upstairs.
- Queens Quay Terminal, 207 Queens Quay W.; 416 203-0510. A magnificent Deco terminal building on the waterfront, renovated to house specialty shops with a Canadian focus. Also features restaurants and special events.
- Sherway Gardens, 25 The West Mall, Etobicoke; 416 621-1070. Over 50 shops, including Holt Renfrew and Co., Eddie Bauer, Harry Rosen, Japan Camera and SmithBooks.
- Square One, 100 City Centre Dr., Mississauga; 905-279-7467. More than 360 stores featuring the Bay, M.A.C., Sears, Blacks Camera and Merle Norman.
- Toronto Eaton Centre, 220 Yonge St.; 416 598-8700. The place visitors to Toronto visit first and most often, with over 320 shops, restaurants and services, under the protective wings of Michael Snow's geese.
- Yorkdale Shopping Centre, Hwy. 401 and Allen Rd.; 416 789-3261. Over 200 shops and services, including Benetton, Club Monaco, Harry Rosen, Holt Renfrew, Nine West, Roots and Tall Girl, La Senza Lingerie and P.J.'s Pet Centre.

MUSEUM SHOPS AND GALLERIES

- Gallery Shop, Art Gallery of Ontario, 317 Dundas St. W.; 416 979-6610. A great shop with an extensive collection of Canadian and international art prints, plus cards, books, toys for children and grownups, and jewellery.
- Royal Ontario Museum, 100 Queen's Park Cres.; 416 586-5549. Three shops, each with its own emphasis. The ROM Shop carries jewellery, objets d'art, distinctive cards and books; the ROM Reproduction Shop offers sculpture and jewellery inspired by the museum's collections; and the Museum Toy Shop, underground, contains a wide variety of inventive and educative toys.
- Sandra Ainsley Gallery, 55 Mill St.; 416 214-9490.

MUSIC

- Capsule, 921 Queen St. W.; 416 203-0202. Beautiful guitars and other instruments.
- HMV, 333 Yonge St.; 416 596-0333; 50 Bloor St. W.; 416 324-9979. The flagship store on Yonge St. is the challenger to Sam's; 4 floors of music, videos and magazines.

SHOPPING/SPORTS

- Neurotica, 642 Queen St. W.; 416 603-7796.
- Rotate This, 620 Queen St. W.; 416 504-8447. New and used CDs and vinyl.
- Sam the Record Man, 347 Yonge St.; 416 977-4650. Canada's homegrown music superstore.
- Songbird, 801 Queen St. W.; 416 504-7664. Unique instruments.
- Soundscapes, 572 College St.; 416 537-1620. Wonderful and diverse selection of CDs.

OUTFITTERS AND SPORTS

- Europe Bound, 47 Front St. E.; 416 601-1990. A worthy challenger to Mountain Equipment Co-op when both were on Front St.
- Sporting Life, 2665 Yonge St.; 416 485-1611; Sherway Mall; 416 620-7750; and Sporting Life Bikes and Boards, 2454 Yonge St.; 416 485-4440. An excellent all-round sports shop, but especially good if you cycle; also a great shoe selection.

OUTLETS

- Roots Canada Factory Store, 120 Orfus Rd.; 416 781-8729. Great bargains year-round from Canada's retailing wunderstore.
- Tom's Place, 190 Baldwin St. (Kensington Market); 416 596-0297. Racks and racks of high-quality business and casual clothing for men and women; don't forget to haggle.

SHOES

- B2, 399 Queen St. W.; 416 595-9281.
- Browns, at Holt Renfrew Centre, 50 Bloor St. W.; 416 960-4925; Sherway Gardens; 416 620-1910. Three in-house lines complement a good selection of fine footwear for men and women.
- Capezio, 70 Bloor St. W.; 416 920-1006; 218 Yonge St.; 416 597-6662. Trendy, cutting-edge women's shoes by Guess, Steve Madden, Nine West, Unisa and others; also stocks belts, handbags and leathergoods.
- Corbo Boutique, 131 Bloor St. W.; 416 928-0954.
- Davids, 66 Bloor St. W.; 416 920-1000. Top designer shoes and accessories for men and women, including David's own line. Large selection of fashionable boots.
- Get Out Side, 437 Queen St. W.; 416 593-5598.
- Groovy, 323 Queen St. W.; 416 595-1059. Hip running shoes.
- Harry Rosen, 82 Bloor St. W.; 416 972-0556. The upscale men's clothier also has a shoe salon upstairs.
- John Fluevog, 242 Queen St. W.; 416 581-0132. Wild platform shoes, go-go boots and more. Not for the tame or weak of sole.
- Nine West, Toronto Eaton Centre; 220 Yonge St.; 416 977-8126; First Canadian Place, King west of Bay; 416 368-0611; 99 Bloor St. W.; 416 920-3519.

TOYS

- Disney Store, Toronto Eaton Centre; 416 591-5132; Yorkdale Mall; 416 782-3061.
- Kolkids, 670 Queen St. W.; 416 681-0368.
- The Toy Shop, 62 Cumberland St.; 416 961-4870. Wonderful selection of children's toys, dolls, books, arts and crafts supplies, as well as other items. Great place to visit; lots of fun.

WEIRD AND WONDERFUL

- Paper Things, 99 Yorkville Avenue; 416 922-3500.

SPORTS

SPECTATOR SPORTS

- Molson Grand Prix. Features the superstars of Indy Car racing at Exhibition Place and Lake Shore Blvd. 175 Bloor St. E., North Tower, 2nd Floor; Tickets: 1 877 865-7223, www.grandprixtoronto.com
- Toronto Argonauts Football, Rogers Centre, 1 Blue Jays Way; Individual tickets: 416 872-5000, www.argonauts.on.ca. See the CFL at its best.
- Toronto Blue Jays Baseball, Rogers Centre, 1 Blue Jays Way; Individual tickets: 416 872-5000, www.bluejays.com. Another season of exciting American League baseball.
- Toronto Maple Leafs Hockey, Air Canada Centre, 40 Lower Bay St.; Individual tickets: 416 872-5000, www.mapleleafs.com. Toronto's National Hockey League team.
- Toronto Marlies Hockey, Ricoh Coliseum, 100 Princes' Blvd., at the

CNE grounds; Individual tickets: 416 872-5000, www.torontomarlies.com. American Hockey League team.
- Toronto Raptors Basketball, Air Canada Centre, 40 Lower Bay St.; Individual tickets: www.nba.com/raptors. See the Toronto Raptors hit the court.
- Toronto Rock Lacrosse Club, Air Canada Centre, 40 Lower Bay St.; Individual tickets: 416 872-5000, www.torontorock.com

GOLF
- Don Valley Golf Course, 4200 Yonge St., south of Hwy. 401; 416 392-2465.
- Glen Abbey Golf Club, 1333 Dorval Dr., Oakville ON L6H 1A1; 905 844-1811. Home of the PGA Tour's Bell Canadian Open and the Canadian Golf Hall of Fame.

FESTIVALS AND EVENTS

ALL WINTER
- Harbourfront Centre's Skating Rink. Outdoor skating, skate rentals, change rooms, rental lockers and skate-sharpening. Open daily, 10am - 10pm. The Rink at Harbourfront, York Quay Centre, 235 Queens Quay W.; 416 973-4866.

DECEMBER
- The Nutcracker. National Ballet of Canada at the Four Seasons Centre for the Performing Arts; 416 345-9595, www.national.ballet.ca

JANUARY
- Toronto International Boat Show. National Trade Centre, Exhibition Place; 905 951-0009, www.torontoboatshow.com

FEBRUARY
- Canadian International Auto Show. Canada's premier automotive showcase. Rogers Centre, 1 Blue Jays Way, and Metro Toronto Convention Centre, 255 Front St. W.; 905 940-2800, www.autoshow.ca

MARCH
- Canada Blooms. Metro Toronto Convention Centre; 416 447-8655, 1 800 730-1020, www.canadablooms.com
- International Home and Garden Show. The International Centre, 6900 Airport Rd.; 416 512-1305, www.home-show.net
- Toronto Festival of Storytelling. Storytelling, workshops, evening concerts and free afternoon storytelling; over 70 storytellers from Canada and beyond. Harbourfront Centre and various other locations; 416 656-2445, www.storytellingtoronto.org/Pages/Festival.html
- Toronto International Bicycle Show. National Trade Centre, Exhibition Place; 416 363-1292, www.telsec.net/bicycleshow

APRIL
- Hot Docs Canadian International Documentary Festival. Showcasing the best in documentary film and television; 416 203-2155, www.hotdocs.ca
- International Spring Bike Show. International Centre, 6900 Airport Rd.; 416 674-4636.
- National Home Show/National Kitchen and Bath Showcase. Exhibition Place; 416 263-3000.
- Spring Classic Car Auction. International Centre, 6900 Airport Rd.; 416 674-4636.
- Spring Family Show. International Centre, 6900 Airport Rd.; 416 674-4636.
- Toronto Toy Show. International Centre, 6900 Airport Rd.; 416 674-4636.

MAY
- Cabbagetown Forsythia Festival. Riverdale Park; 416 410-4259.
- Doors Open Toronto. Various locations; 416 338-0496, www.doorsopen.org
- Milk International Children's Festival. North America's largest performing arts festival for the whole family. Performers from around the world, as well as right here in Canada. For seven days visitors can see the very best the world has to offer in theatre, dance, music, visual arts, storytelling, physical comedy and puppetry for young audiences. Harbourfront Centre; 416 973-4000.

JUNE
- Bloom in the Beaches. A literary festival. Various venues; 416 365-7877, www.pathcom.com/~livia

FESTIVALS AND EVENTS

- Downtown Jazz Festival. Featuring high-profile international and Canadian jazz favourites. Various venues; 416 928-2033, Tickets: 416 870-8000, www.torontojazz.com
- Fireworks. Ontario Place, 955 Lake Shore Blvd. W. Four nights in late June and early July; 416 314-9900, Tickets: 416 870-8000, www.ontarioplace.com
- North By Northeast. Enjoy up-and-coming rock bands over a three-day festival. Various venues in downtown Toronto; 416 863-6963, www.nxne.com
- Pride Week Toronto. The largest Lesbian and Gay Pride event in North America. Church and Wellesley neighbourhood. 65 Wellesley St. E., Suite 501; 416 927-7433, www.pridetoronto.com
- Queen's Plate. The running of this internationally renowned race. Woodbine Racetrack, 555 Rexdale Blvd.; 416 675-7223, 1 888 675-7223, www.woodbineentertainment.com
- Toronto International Dragon Boat Race Festival. Dragon boat racing and multicultural performances on the Toronto Islands; 416 595-1739, www.torontodragonboat.com
- Toronto International Caravan. Visit 50 pavilions located throughout Toronto representing the world's greatest cities. 263 Adelaide St. W., Suite 503; 416 856-6482, www.caravan-org.com
- Toronto Worldwide Short Film Festival; 416 445-1446 ex. 815, www.worldwideshortfilmfest.com

JULY

- Beaches International Jazz Festival. This popular jazz streetfest features over 40 bands performing everything from calypso, to Latin, fusion and steel drum nightly on selected street corners, balconies and parks. Queen St. E., between Woodbine Ave. and Victoria Park Ave.; 416 698-2152, www.beachesjazz.com
- Caribana. A two-week celebration attracting more than one million people, capped with a parade. Various venues; www.caribana.com
- CHIN Picnic. Canada Day weekend festivities. Exhibition Place; 416 531-9991, www.chinradio.com/chinpicnic.asp
- The Fringe of Toronto Theatre Festival. Various venues in the Annex area (near Bloor and Spadina Sts.); 416 966-1062, www.fringetoronto.com
- Kidsummer Festival. Various locations, throughout July and August; 1 866 363-5437, www.kidsummer.com
- Molson Grand Prix. 175 Bloor St. E., North Tower, 2nd Floor. Features the superstars of Indy Car racing. Exhibition Place, Lake Shore Blvd.; Tickets: 416 870-8000, 1 877 865-7223, www.grandprixtoronto.com
- Toronto Outdoor Art Exhibition. This free outdoor exhibit showcases the original paintings, ceramics, jewellery, sculpture and mixed-media creations of talented Canadian and international artists. Nathan Phillips Square, 100 Queen St. W.; 416 408-2754, www.torontooutdoorart.org

AUGUST

- Canadian National Exhibition. The world's largest and longest annual exhibition in Canada. Featuring midway rides, display buildings, top-name concert performers, roving entertainers, live music and much more. Mid-August to Labour Day. Exhibition Place, Lake Shore Blvd. W.; 416 393-6300, www.theex.com
- Fringe Festival of Independent Dance Artists. Various indoor and outdoor sites; 416 214-5854, www.ffida.org
- Rogers Cup. Men compete at the Rexall Centre in Toronto, women in Montreal. Ticket info: 1 800 398-8761, www.tenniscanada.com
- SummerWorks. Ten days of theatre. Various venues; 416 410-1048, www.summerworks.ca

FALL

- Artsweek. Various venues; 416 392-6800, www.artsweek.ca
- Bell Canadian Open. Hamilton Golf & Country Club, Ancaster, Ontario; 1 800 263-0009, www.rcga.org/cdnopen
- International Festival of Authors. The world's largest literary festival. Harbourfront Centre, 235 Queens Quay W.; 416 973-4000, www.readings.org/events.php
- Toronto International Film Festival; 416 968-3456, www.bell.ca/filmfest
- Word on the Street. Open-air book

and magazine festival celebrating literacy and the printed word. Queen's Park, between St. Charles and Wellesley Sts.; 416 504-7241, www.thewordonthestreet.ca/toronto.php

NOVEMBER

- The Cavalcade of Lights. Lighting displays, fireworks and special events, beginning late November and continuing throughout December. Various locations; 416 868-0400, www.toronto.ca/special_events/cavalcade_lights
- The Hobby Show. The International Centre, 6900 Airport Rd.; 905 428-6466, www.thehobbyshow.com
- Royal Agricultural Winter Fair. Featuring the Agricultural Show, the Royal Horse Show and the Winter Garden Show, among other attractions. National Trade Centre, Exhibition Place; 416 263-3400, www.royalfair.org
- Santa Claus Parade. This crowd-pleasing parade takes place the third Sunday in November each year; 416 249-7833, www.thesantaclausparade.com

DAY TRIPS

- Butterfly Conservatory at the Niagara Parks Botanical Gardens. 2405 Niagara River Parkway, Niagara Falls; 905 356-2241, www.niagaraparks.com/nature/butterfly.php
- The Bruce Trail. Contact Bruce Trail Association, PO Box 857, Hamilton ON L8N 3N9; 905 529-6821, 1 800 665-4453, www.brucetrail.org
- Cataract Inn. 1498 Cataract Rd., Alton ON L0N 1A0; 519 927-3033, www.creditriver.ca
- Cave Springs Cellars. 3836 Main St., Jordan ON; 905 562-3581, www.cavespringcellars.com
- Crawford Lake Conservation Area. May through October. At Steeles Ave. and Guelph Line; 905 854-0234, www.conservationhalton.on.ca
- Elora Festival. July/August. PO Box 370, Elora ON N0B 1S0; 519 846-0331, Fax: 519 846-5947, info@elorafestival.com, www.elorafestival.com
- Fort George, Niagara-on-the-Lake. A recreated British garrison. Open April 1 to October 31; 905 468-4257, www.pc.gc.ca/lhn-nhs/on/fortgeorge
- Inniskillin Winery. Located on Line 3 (Service Road 66) off the Niagara Parkway; 905 468-3554, 1 888 466-4754 ex. 311, www.inniskillin.com
- Jackson-Triggs Niagara Estate Winery. 2145 Regional Road 55, Niagara-on-the-Lake ON L0S 1J0; 905 468-4637, 1 866 589-4637, www.jacksontriggswinery.com
- Kortright Centre for Conservation. 9550 Pine Valley Dr., Woodbridge. 10 am-4 pm every day; 905 832-2289, www.trca.on.ca
- Maid of the Mist. Niagara Falls; 905 358-5781, www.maidofthemist.com
- The McMichael Canadian Collection, 10365 Islington Ave., Kleinburg; 905 893-1121, 1 888-213-1121, www.mcmichael.com
- Niagara Apothecary. Open from Mother's Day to Labour Day, 5 Queen St.; Niagara-on-the-Lake; 905 468-3845, 1 800 220-1921 ex. 226, www.niagaraapothecary.ca
- Niagara Falls Aviary, 5651 River Rd., Niagara Falls; 905 356-8888, 1 866 994-0090, www.niagarafallsaviary.com
- Niagara Grape and Wine Festival. A ten-day celebration of the grape harvest, featuring winery tours, concerts and parades. 8 Church St., Suite 100, St. Catharines ON L2R 3B3; 905 688-0212, www.grapeandwine.com
- Niagara Parks Botanical Gardens and School of Horticulture. On the Niagara Parkway 9 km north of Niagara Falls; 905 356-2241 (Niagara Parks) or 905 356-8554, www.niagaraparks.com/nature/botanical.php
- The Olde Heidelberg Restaurant. 3006 Lobsinger Line (R.R.#15), Heidelberg ON; 519 699-4413, www.oldhh.com
- On the Twenty. Restaurant featuring regional cuisine and fine wines. 3845 Main St., Jordan ON L0R 1S0; 905 562-7313, www.innonthetwenty.com
- Peller Estates Winery. 290 John St. E., Niagara-on-the-Lake ON L0S 1J0; 905 468-4678, 1 888 673-5537, www.peller.com
- Presqu'ile Provincial Park. R.R.#4, Brighton ON K0K 1H0 (off the 401,

GAY TORONTO

155 km east of Toronto); 613 475-4324, www.ontarioparks.com
- Reif Estate Winery. 15608 Niagara Parkway, Niagara-on-the-Lake; 905 468-7738, www.reifwinery.com
- Sandbanks Provincial Park. R.R.#1, Picton ON K0K 2T0; 613 393-3319, www.ontarioparks.com
- Shaw Festival. Late March to November. Shaw Festival Theatre, 10 Queens Parade, Niagara-on-the-Lake; 1 800 511-7429, www.shawfest.com
- South Simcoe Railway. PO Box 186, Tottenham ON L0G 1W0; 905 936-5815, www.steamtrain.com
- St. Jacobs Visitor Centre (formerly known as the Meeting Place). 1408 King St. N., St. Jacobs ON N0B 2N0; 519 664-3518, www.stjacobs.com
- Stratford Festival, Stratford; 519 271-4040, 1 800 567-1600, orders@stratford-festival.on.ca, www.stratford-festival.on.ca
- Vineland Estates Winery. 3620 Moyer Rd., Vineland ON L0R 2C0; 905 562-7088, 1 888 846-3526, www.vineland.com
- Wings of Paradise Butterfly Conservatory. 2500 Kossuth Rd., Cambridge ON N3H 4R7; 519 653-1234, www.wingsofparadise.com

GAY TORONTO

- The 519 Church Street Community Centre, 519 Church St.; 416 392-6874, www.the519.org

FESTIVALS AND THEATRES
- Buddies in Bad Times Theatre, 12 Alexander St.; 416 975-8555, Fax: 416 975-9293, www.buddiesinbadtimestheatre.com
- Inside Out Lesbian and Gay Film and Video Festival. End of May, multiple venues; 416 977-6847, www.insideout.on.ca
- Pride Week Toronto. The largest Lesbian and Gay Pride event in North America. Church and Wellesley neighbourhood. 65 Wellesley St. E., Suite 501; 416 927-7433, www.pridetoronto.com

BARS AND RESTAURANTS
- Babylon, 553 Church St.; 416 923-2626, www.technofunk.ca/babylon.html
- The Barn/Stables, 418 Church St.; 416 977-4684.
- The Bijou, 370 Church St.; 416 971-9985.
- Black Eagle, 457 Church St.; 416 413-1219, www.blackeagletoronto.com
- Byzantium, 499 Church St.; 416 922-3859, www.interlog.com/~byz
- The Cellar, 78 Wellesley St. E.; 416 975-1799.
- Channel 501 Video Bar, 501 Church St.; 416 944-3272, bar501.com
- Crews, 508 Church St.; 416 972-1662.
- Five, 5 St. Joseph St.; 416 964-8685, www.5ive.com
- Fly, 8 Gloucester St.; 416 410-5426, www.flynightclub.com
- George's Play, 504 Church St.; 416 963-8251, www.playonchurch.com
- GI Joe, 543 Yonge St.; 416 927-0210.
- Living Well Restaurant and Bar, 692 Yonge St.; 416 922-6770.
- Lub, 487 Church St.; 416 323-1489, www.lub.ca
- O'Grady's, 518 Church St.; 416 323-2822.
- The Rivoli, 332 Queen St. W.; 416 596-1908, www.rivoli.ca
- Second Cup, 548 Church St.; 416 964-2457, www.secondcup.com
- Sneakers, 502 Yonge St.; 416 961-5808, www.gaytoronto.com/sneakers
- Spa Excess, 105 Carlton St.; 416 260-2363, www.spaexcess.com
- Starbucks, 485 Church St.; 416 922-2440, www.starbucks.com
- Steamworks, 540 Church St.; 416 925-1571, www.steamworksonline.com
- Tango, 508 Church St.; 416 972-1662.
- Timothy's World Coffee, 3-500 Church St.; 416 925-8550, www.timothys.ca
- Trattoria Al Forno, 459 Church St.; 416 944-8852.
- Village Rainbow Restaurant, 477 Church St.; 416 961-0616.
- Wish, 3 Charles St. E.; 416 935-0240.
- Woody's/Sailor, 465-67 Church St.; 416 972-0887, www.woodystoronto.com
- Zelda's, 542 Church St.; 416 922-2526, www.zeldas.ca

SHOPS
- Come As You Are, 701 Queen St. W.; 416 504-7934, www.comeasyouare.com
- Glad Day Bookstore, 598A Yonge St.; 416 961-4161, www.gladday.com
- Good For Her, 175 Harbord St.; 416 588-0900, 1 877 588-0900, www.goodforher.com
- Priape, 465 Church St., 2nd Floor; 416 586-9914, www.priape.com
- Toronto Women's Bookstore, 73 Harbord St.; 416 922-8744, 1 800 861-8233, www.womensbookstore.com

ACCOMMODATION
- Amazing Space, 246 Sherbourne St.; Toronto ON M4Y 1K7; www.purpleroofs.com/amazingspace.html
- Banting House Inn Bed & Breakfast, 73 Homewood Ave., Toronto ON M4Y 2K1; 416 924-1458, www.bbcanada.com/1960.html
- Cawthra Square Bed and Breakfast, 10 Cawthra Square, Toronto ON M4Y 1K8; 416 966-3074, 1-800 259-5474, www.cawthrasquare.com
- The House on McGill, 110 McGill St., Toronto ON M5B 1H6; 416 351-1503, 1 877 580-5015 www.home.interlog.com/~mcgillbb
- The Primrose Hotel, 111 Carlton Street, Toronto ON M5B 2G3; 416 977-8000, www.torontoprimrosehotel.com
- Sutton Place, 955 Bay St.; Toronto ON M5S 2A2; 416 924-9221, www.suttonplace.com

INDEX

"Archer, The", 37
360 restaurant, 21
501, The, 128, 129, 221
519 Church Street Community Centre, 130
69 Vintage, 75
A Space, 58, 204
A Taste of the World - Neighbourhood Bicycle Tours and Walks, 197
Abodes of Choice Bed and Breakfast Association, 201
Access Toronto, 14
accommodation
  airport hotels, 198-199
  bed and breakfasts, 201-202
  downtown hotels, 199-201
  midtown hotels, 201
Acqua, 149, 208
Aids Committee of Toronto, 130
Air Canada Centre, 94, 95, 97, 141, 146
Airport Lounge, 189-190
Alchemy, 192
Aldeburgh Connection, 69, 206
Alexander Wood statue, 127
Algonquin Island, 101
All About Toronto, 197
Allan Gardens, 182, 183, 202
Allan, George, 183
Allen's, 79, 192, 208
Alto Basso, 76, 207
Amaci Chamber Ensemble, 69, 206
Amadeus Choir, 69, 206
Amadeus, 162
Amarynth, 175
Amazing Space, 130, 222
American Apparel, 154
Andy Poolhall, 76, 207
Angell Gallery, 156
Ann Tindal Park, 26
Annex Street Theatre, 165
Annex, 77, 170, 171, 208
Annie Thompson, 89, 92, 213
Another Story, 192
Anti-Hero, 88, 212
antique market, Queen's Quay, 91
Aquascutum, 88, 213
Aradia Ensemble, 69, 206
Arctic Bear, 172
Aroma Shoppe, 90, 211
Art Gallery of Ontario (AGO), 41, 50-51, 93, 158, 204, 216
Art Metropole, 58, 204
Art Shoppe, The, 93, 215
artists' gardens, 24
Arton Beads and Findings, 154
Arts on King, 139
Artsweek, 114, 219
Ashley's. See William Ashley
Asian Legend, 81, 208
Astoria Shish Kebob House, 191
Athens Meat Market, 190
Auld Spot, 191
Aunties and Uncles, 80, 208
Austin, James, 33
Auto Show, 109
Avalon, 84, 208
Aveda, 88, 175, 211
Avenue Lounge, 174, 209
Avis, 197
Avli, 191
Avon River, 119
B2, 89, 217
Babur, 153, 209
Babylon, 78, 221
Bad Dog Theatre, 63, 206
Baldwin Palace, 162
Balfour Books, 188
Ballenford Books, 169
Bamboo, 74
Banana Republic, 92, 93, 174, 178, 213, 214
Bangkok Garden, 179, 209
Bank of Montreal, 144, 148
Banting House, 130, 222
Bar Italia, 76, 189, 207
Barberian's, 86, 179, 209
Barfly, 155
Barn, The, 78, 221
Barnicke Gallery, 167, 168
Baroque Music Beside the Grange, 163
Bata Shoe Museum, 41, 52-53, 165, 203
Baton Rouge, 144, 209
Bay, The, 92, 144, 151, 178, 216
Bayview Village, 93, 211, 216
BCE Place, 103, 149
Beaches, the
  attractions, 103
  Beaches International Jazz Festival, 112, 219
  Bloom on the Beaches, 111, 218
  Glenn Gould residence, 73
  shopping, 90
Beaconsfield, The, 75, 207
Beadery, The, 154
Beadworks, 90, 214
Beauty and the Beast, 148
Bed and Breakfast Homes of Toronto, 201
Beguiling, The, 169
Bell Canadian Open Golf Championship, 98, 114, 219
Bellini, 172, 209
Benetton, 88, 92, 170, 214
Berczy Park, 135
Besant, Derek, 136
Best Western Primrose Hotel, 130, 199, 222
Betsey Johnson, 88, 213
Biagio, 139, 209
Biff's, 82, 209
Bijou, The, 129, 221
Birks, 87, 92, 93, 175, 215
Black Creek Pioneer Garden, 105
Black Creek Pioneer Village, 20, 41, 55-56, 202
  Spring Fair, 56
Bloom on the Beaches, 111, 218
Bloor Street shopping, 88
Bloor Street, 174-175
Bloor, Joseph
Blowfish Restaurant and Sake Bar, 79, 208
Blue Angel, 92, 212
Blue Jays Way, 22
Blue Moon, 192
Bluffers Park, 103
Bluma Appel Theatre, 61, 145, 205
Boat Show, 109
Boat, the, 77, 162, 207
Body Shop, The, 88, 92, 175, 211
Bon Lieu, 181
Bond Place Hotel, 199
Bonjour Brioche, 80, 209
Boomer, 93, 213
Boulton, D'Arcy, Jr., 163
Bovine Sex Club, The, 74, 154, 206
Bowring, 212, 215
Brassaii, 79, 208
Brasserie Aix, 190
Brava Vintage Clothing, 154
Brian Bailey, 92, 212
Brickworks. See Don Valley Brickworks
Brown, George, 185
Brown's, 87, 88, 217
Bruce Trail, 122, 220
Buddies In Bad Times Theatre, 63, 126, 205, 221

223

INDEX

Byzantium, 78, 127-128, 221
Caban, 89, 153, 215
Cabaret, 93, 213
Cabbagetown
  attractions, 107, 182-186
  Carlton Street, 183
  cemeteries, 182, 185
  Forsythia Festival, 110, 218
  homes, 185-186
  Spruce Street, 183
Cadillac Lounge, 76, 207
Café Diplomatico, 189
Café La Gaffe, 162
Café Societa, 189
Caledon Hills, 122
Cambridge Suites Hotel, 199
Camera Bar, 157
Cameron House, 74, 207
Campbell House, 152, 202
Canada Blooms, 110, 218
Canada Day, 54, 112, 219
Canadian Broadcasting Corporation (CBC), 20, 70, 72, 73, 142, 146-147, 202
Canadian Childrens' Opera Chorus, 69, 206
Canadian Imperial Bank of Commerce, 148
Canadian International Auto Show, 109, 218
Canadian National Exhibition (CNE), 20, 27-29, 98, 202, 219
Canadian Naturalist, The, 91, 212
Canadian Opera Company (COC), 65, 70, 145, 206
Canadian Stage Company, 61, 104, 145, 205
Canadian Tire, 181
Canoe, 82, 83, 149, 209
Canon Theatre, 61, 141, 179, 205
Capezio, 88, 217
Capsule, 90, 216
Captain John's, 23, 176, 209
car rental, 197
Caravan, 111, 219
Caribana, 109, 113, 219
Carlu, Jaques, 180
Carlu, The, 180
Carman's, 86, 180, 209
Carr, Emily, 49
Carrot Common, 192
Carsen Centre, 24
Casa Loma, 20, 32-33, 34, 55, 110, 202
Cashmere Shop, The, 88, 213
Cassis, 162
Casual Way, The, 90, 214

Cat Show, 109
Cataplana, 190
Cataract Inn, 122, 220
Cathedral Church of St. James, 137
Cavalcade of Lights, 114, 220
Cave Springs Cellars, 118, 220
Cawthra Square Bed and Breakfast, 130, 222
CBC Broadcast Centre, 146, 206
CBC Museum, 147
Cedar Sands nature trail, 123
Cellar, The, 129, 221
Central Don Stables, 108
Centre Island, 101
Centreville Amusement Park, 101, 202
Centro Grill and Wine Bar, 84
Centro Restaurant and Lounge, 85, 209
Chanel Boutique, 93, 170, 213
Chatalet, 155
Chelsea Room, 78, 208
Chester Springs Marsh, 106
Chiado, 84, 190, 209
CHIN Radio, 112, 189
Chinatown
  dining, 160-161
  history, 160-161
  shopping, 158-161
Chinese of the Pearl, 23
Chocolate and Creams, 91, 215
Christopher Cutts Gallery, 59, 204
CHUM Television, 152
ChumCity store, 152
Chung King, 161
Church of the Redeemer, 174
Church Street, 78
Churrasco of St. Lawrence, 81, 209
cinemas, 206
Circa Forty, 93, 213
City Hall (new), 14, 35-36, 37, 140, 141, 142, 203
City of Toronto, 32, 195-196
City Shop, 36
Citytv, 152
Civic Garden Centre, 107
Clay Design Studio/Gallery, 169
climate, 196
Clint Roenisch Gallery, 157
Club Monaco, 88, 89, 90, 92, 174, 214
CN Tower, 14, 20-21, 147, 203

Cocktail Molotov, 79, 208
Coffee Mill, 172
Colborne Lodge, 55, 110, 203
Cole Haan, 170
College Park mall, 180
Colonnade, 175
Colville, Alex, 51
Come As You Are, 130, 222
Comfort Hotel Downtown, 199, 201
Comfort Suites City Centre, 199
Commerce Court, 148
Communist's Daughter, 79, 208
Commute Home, 155
Comrags, 89, 92, 155, 212
Confederation Life building, 144
Constantine Antiques and Home Furnishings, 93, 215
Convocation Hall, 167
Cookbook Store, 172
Corbo, 88, 217
Core, 169
Corkin Shopland Gallery, 40, 59, 204
Coronation Park, 102
Cosmos, 155
Courage My Love, 91, 93, 213
Craft Studio, 25
Craven, David, 58
Crawford Lake Conservation Area, 122-123, 220
Creations, 162
Credit River, 122
Crews, 78, 128, 129, 221
Crow's Theatre, 63, 205
Crystal Siemens, 92
CU Tours Inc., 197
CHUM Television, 152
customs, 195
cycling, 98, 99, 101, 105, 108
Czehoski, 74, 156, 207
Da Zone, 154
Daily Fraiche, 89, 214
Dance Cave, 77, 208
dance, 24, 65, 205-206
DanceWorks, 65, 205
Dancing Days, 91, 93, 213
Danier, 93, 216
Danny Grossman Dance Company, 65, 205
David Dunlop Observatory, 203
David E. Lake, 139
David Mirvish Books, 169
Davids, 88, 170, 217
Days Hotel and Conference Centre, 198
Days Inn Toronto Downtown, 199

224

INDEX

DeLeon White Gallery, 59, 157, 204
Delphic, 156
Delta Chelsea Inn, 199
Demetre, 191
Design Exchange, 149
Dipamo's, 82, 209
Discount Car Rentals, 197
Disney Store, 87, 217
Distillery District, 38-40, 61, 203
   shopping, 91
Docks, The, 78, 207
Dog Show, 109
Dollar Rent-a-Car, 197
Dominion Bank, 33
Don River, 99, 105, 106, 186
Don Valley Brickworks, 54, 106, 107
Don Valley Trail, 100
Don Valley, 20, 54, 99, 105-108, 218
Doors Open Toronto, 111, 218
Dora Keogh's, 191-192
Doubletree International Plaza Hotel and Conference Centre, 198
Downtown Fabrics, 154
Downtown Jazz Festival, 111-112, 219
Downtown Toronto Association of Bed and Breakfast Guest Houses, 201
Drabinsky Gallery, 173
Drake Hotel, 63, 75, 128, 157, 206, 207
Dream in High Park, 61, 104
driver's licences, 197
Du Verre, 93, 212
Dufflet Pastries, 90, 156, 215
Dundas Square, 179
Dundas Street West, 78
Dusk Dances, 65
E.T. Seton Park, 107
Eagle, The, 129, 221
early settlement, 15-17
   Andaste nation, 15
Eastwood-Skinner paper mill, 107
Eating Garden, 161, 162
Eaton Auditorium, 180
Eaton Centre, 87, 93, 151, 177, 178-179, 216
Eaton, Timothy, 178
Eddie Bauer, 88, 93, 174, 213, 214
Edge Arcade, 21
Edison, Noel, 69
Edwards Gardens, 107
El Convento Rico, 190

Elgin Theatre, 141, 143, 179, 205
Elmer Iseler Singers, 69, 206
Elora, 121. 220
Embassy, The, 77, 207
Embros, 181
Empress of Canada, 198
Engine Gallery, 157
Enoch Turner Schoolhouse, 139, 203
Epic, 85, 209
Erickson, Arthur, 147
Erietta's, 92
Esplanade Bier Markt, 134, 209
Esprit Orchestra, 68, 206
Esprit, 87, 214
Etienne Brule Park, 105
Etobicoke Creek, 99
Europe Bound, 91, 217
European Jewellery, 93, 215
Ewanika, 90, 188, 214
Exchange Tower, 148
Exhibition Place, 109, 218
Experimental, 93, 215
Eye Spy, 92, 215
eye weekly, 14, 79, 109, 202, 206
FAB, 130
Fabrice, 93, 215
Factory Theatre, 62, 205
Fairweather, 87, 214
Fantasy Fair, 203
farmers' markets
   Distillery District, 39
   Nathan Phillips Square, 36
   St. Lawrence Market, 91, 134
Fashion Crimes, 89, 92, 212
Felician Sisters Convent, 151
ferry boats, 14, 101, 196
Festival Theatre, 119-120
festivals, 25, 64, 65, 109-114, 119, 218-220
Fez Batik, 78, 207
film festivals
   HOT DOCS International Documentary Festival, 110, 218
   Inside Out Lesbian and Gay Film and Video Festival, 126, 221
   Toronto International Film Festival, 113-114, 219
   Toronto Worldwide Short Film Festival, 111, 219
Financial District, 20, 80, 140-142, 148-149
Finishing Touches, 92, 212
Fionn MacCool's Irish Pub, 135, 209

Firehall No. 3, 180
First Canadian Place, 148
First Hand Canadian Crafts, 91, 212
First Lutheran Church, 137
Five Thieves, The, 181
Five, 78, 129, 221
Flat-Iron Mural, 136
Fleurtje, 89, 215
Fluevog Shoe Store, 89, 217
Fluid Living, 91, 93, 215
Fly, 78, 129, 221
Forsythia Festival, 110, 218
Fort George, 117, 220
Fort Rouille, 16
Fort York, 16, 29, 41, 54, 204
FOS, 91, 215
Four Seasons Centre, 65, 70, 145, 205, 218
Four Seasons Hotel, 85, 174, 201
Fran's Restaurant, 73, 80, 209
Fratelli Porco, 188-189
Fresh by Juice for Life, 157
Fresh Collective, 90, 214, 215
fringe festivals
   Fringe Festival of Independent Dance Artists (fFIDA), 65, 112, 219
   Toronto Fringe Festival, 64, 219
Fujiyama, 162
Future Shop, 90, 214
G.I. Joe, 129, 221
galleries, 57-59, 204-205
Gallery Grill, 168, 209
Gallery One, 173
Gamelle, 189, 209
Gandhi Indian Cuisine, 155, 209
Gap, The, 89, 90, 92, 93, 213, 214
GapKids, 87, 92, 212
Gardiner Museum of Ceramic Art, 41, 51-52, 203-204
Gateways of India, 162
gay and lesbian scene
   accommodation, 130
   Church Street, 126-128
   festivals, 125-126, 219, 221
   nightlife, 78, 128-130
   organizations, 130
Gay Pride Week, 78, 112, 221
Gehry, Frank, 50
George Weston Recital Hall, 67, 177
George's Play, 129, 221

INDEX

Georgie Bolesworth, 92, 214
Get Out Side, 89, 217
Giorgio, 170
Giovanna, 189
Girl Friday, 90, 214
Givens, Phil, 37
Glad Day Bookstore, 130, 222
Gladstone Hotel, 75, 128, 157, 207
Glen Abbey golf course, 98, 114, 218
Glenn Gould Foundation, 72
Glenn Gould Park, 73
Glenn Gould Studio, 70, 72-73, 147, 206
Gloucester Mews, 180
GO Transit, 196
Good For Her, 130, 222
Gooderham and Worts distilling empire, 38-39, 171
Gooderham Building, 136
Gooderham, George, 138
Gooderham, William, 39, 136
Goodfoot, 154
Gould, Glenn, 72-73
Graduate House, 168
Graham Spry Theatre, 147
Grand Hotel and Suites Toronto, 199
Grand River, 121
Grange Park, 163
Grange, The, 50, 55, 110, 162-163
Grappa, 189
Great Lakes Schooner Company, 198
Greektown
  dining, 191-192
  history, 190-191
  shopping, 192
Greektown, 79
Green Mango, 82, 209
Green Room, 77, 208
Grenadier Restaurant, 103
Groovy, 89, 217
Groucho and Co., 175
Group of Seven, 51, 124
Grreat Stuff, 93, 213
Gucci, 213, 215
Guild Shop, 173
Guvernment, 78, 207
Gypsy Co-op, 156
H&M, 87, 92, 175, 213, 214
Habitat Lounge, 156
Hana, 162
Hanlan, Ned, 185
Happy Seven, 161
Harbord Bakery, 169
Harbourfront Centre Theatre, 24, 205
Harbourfront, 14, 20, 22-26, 58, 64, 65, 91, 114, 203, 218

Hard Rock Café, 22
Harry Rosen, 87, 88, 93, 175, 213, 217
Hart House, 167-168
Haunted Toronto, 197
Hazleton Lanes, 88, 93, 173, 216
HEAL, 130
Helicopter Company, 197
Hemispheres, 85, 209
Heritage Toronto Summer Walking Tours, 197
Heritage Toronto, 14, 33, 54, 204
Hermes House of Bomboniere, 190
Hermes, 170
High Park, 102, 103-104
Highland Creek, 99
High-Tech, 91, 93, 215
Hiking. See recreation trails
Hillebrand, 119
Hilton Toronto, 199
historical attractions
  Black Creek Pioneer Village, 20, 41, 55-56
  Campbell House, 152
  Casa Loma, 20, 32-33, 34, 55, 110, 202
  Cathedral Church of St. James, 137
  Colbourne Lodge, 103
  Crawford Lake Conservation Area, 122-123
  Don Valley Brickworks, 54, 106, 107
  Enoch Turner Schoolhouse, 139
  Fort George, 117
  Fort York, 16, 29, 41, 54
  Gibson House, 203
  Gooderham Building, 136
  Grange, The, 50, 55, 110, 162-163
  Mackenzie House, 55, 110
  Necropolis Cemetery, 182, 185
  Redpath Sugar Refinery Museum, 103
  Riverdale Farm, 54, 106-107, 182, 184, 204
  Spadina House, 20, 33-35, 55
  St. Jacobs Visitor Centre, 120
  Todmorden Mills, 55, 106, 107, 204
  Toronto's First Post Office, 54, 139
  Yorkville Fire Hall, 172, 173

HMV, 87, 93, 216
Hoax Couture, 93, 213
Hobby and Craft Show, 109, 220
Hockey Hall of Fame, 141, 144, 204
Holiday Express Downtown, 199
Holiday Inn Express Toronto - North York, 198
Holiday Inn on King, 199-200
Holiday Inn Select Toronto Airport, 198
Holiday Inn Toronto Midtown, 201
Holt Renfrew, 88, 92, 93, 175, 213, 216
Home and Garden Show. See International Home and Garden Show
Home Furnishings, 215
Home Smith Park, 105
Homefront, 93, 215
Honest Ed's, 165
Hop-On Hop-Off City Tour, 197
Horizons café, 21
Horseshoe Falls, 115
Horseshoe Tavern, 74, 150, 207
Hospital for Sick Children, 164
Hospitality York, 202
Host, 175, 209
Hostelling International Toronto, 202
HOT DOCS International Documentary Festival, 110, 218
Hotel Inter-Continental Toronto, 174, 201
Hotel Le Germain Toronto, 200
Hotel Victoria, 200
House of Vintage, 154
House on McGill, The, 130, 222
Howard Johnson Inn Yorkville, 201
Hua Sung, 162
Hudson Bay Company Gallery, 142
Hugo Nicholson, 88, 213
Humber Bay Butterfly Habitat, 102
Humber Marshes, 105
Humber River Trail, 104
Humber River, 99, 102, 104
Humber Valley, 20
Hummingbird Centre, 70, 141, 144-145
Ikea, 93, 215
Iliada, 191

INDEX

IMAX theatre
  Ontario Place, 26
  Ontario Science Centre, 29
immigration, 17-18
Indian Choice, 162
Indigo, 88, 92, 175, 212
Innis College, 168
Inniskillin, 116, 220
Inside Out Lesbian and Gay Film and Video Festival, 126, 221
Intercontinental Hotel, 174
Intercontinental Toronto Centre, 200
International Centre, 109, 218
International Festival of Authors, 114, 219
International Home and Garden Show, 109, 110, 218
Iodine, 90, 211
Irie Food Joint, 156
Irie, 190
Irish Shop, The, 175
Italinteriors, 139
J.S. Bonbons, 156
Jackson-Triggs, 118, 220
Jacob, 87, 214
Jaeger, 170
James Gardens, 105
Jamie Bell Adventure Playground, 104
Jamie Kennedy Wine Bar, 82, 83, 135, 209
Jane Mallett Theatre, 145, 205
Japanese Paper Place, 90, 214
Jarvis, Samuel Peters
Jarvis, Sheriff William Botsford, 171
Jodhpore Club, 162
John, Augustus, 48
John's Classic Pizza, 189
John's, 162
Joker, 78, 208
Journey's End Antiques, 169
Jubilate Singers, 69, 206
Jubilee Queen Cruises, 198
Jumbo Empanadas, 81, 209
Jump, 148, 209
Kaeja d'Dance, 65, 205
Kaliyana, 90, 214
Katharine Mulherin Gallery, 59, 204
Keg Steakhouse, The, 135, 209
Kensington Market
  dining, 81
  neighbourhood, 158, 161-163
  nightlife, 76-77, 207
  shopping, 90

Kidsummer, 112, 219
King Edward Hotel, 138
Kiwanis Club, 33
Klancy's Yacht Charters Inc., 198
Klaxon Howl, 156
Knoll, 139
Knox College, 167
Kolkids, 92, 156, 217
Kon-nichi-wa, 162
Kortright Conservation Area, 124, 220
Kowloon, 161
KPMB architects, 40, 147
Kresge's, 180
L.M. Treble Building, 174
La Bodega, 162
La Cache, 90, 214
La Palette, 162
Lai Wah Heen, 85, 209
Lake Erie, 17
Lake Ontario, 15, 17, 26
Lake Simcoe, 20
Lakeside Eats, 23
Lamb, Alderman David, residence, 184
Lamon, Jeanne, 68
L'Atelier Grigorian, 73
Laugh Resort, The, 63, 206
Laurentian Room, 79, 208
Law Society of Upper Canada, 38, 152
Lawrence Park, 181
Le Chateau, 151
Le Matignon, 180, 209
Le Papillon, 135, 209
Le Royal Meridien King Edward Hotel, 200
Le Select Bistro, 152, 210
Lee Garden, 161
Lee's Palace, 77, 208
Legare, Joseph, 50
Lennox, E.J., 37
Lennox, John, 32
Les Miserables, 61, 147
Leslie Street Spit, 108
Lester B. Pearson International Airport, 13, 194
Libeskind, Daniel, 43
Library Bar, The, 79, 208
Lida Baday, 92, 212
Lilliput Hats, 90, 188, 215
Lily Lee, 192
Linda Lundstrom, 88, 92, 212
Lion King, The, 61, 148
Lion Monument, 102
Liquor Control Board of Ontario (LCBO), 135
literary festivals
  Bloom in the Beaches, 111, 218

International Festival of Authors, 25
  Word on the Street, 113, 114
Little Italy, 74, 76
  dining, 188, 189-190
  history, 187-188
  nightlife, 76, 207
  shopping, 188-189
Little Norway Park, 102
Living Well is the Best Revenge, 128, 221
Lobby, 79, 208
Lord of the Rings, The, 61, 148
Lorraine Kimsa Theatre for Young People, 63, 205
Lost World Tours, 14, 197
Loucas, 92
Lount, Samuel, 185
Lowen Pope, 92, 212
Lub, 78, 127, 221
Luce, 86, 210
Lucky Dragon, 161
Lululemon, 89, 214
Lush, 153, 211
Lyle, John, 148
Ma, Yo-Yo, 24, 67
Mable's Fables, 92, 212
MAC, 88, 175, 211
Mackenzie House, 55, 110, 204
Mackenzie, William, 185, 204
Madison Manor Bouique Hotel, 200
Madison, Avenue Pub, The, 77, 208
Magic Pony, 156
Magnolia, 90, 215
Magpie, 79, 208
Maid of the Mist, 115, 220
Mama Mia, 61, 147
Mango, 87, 214
Mania Bar and Lounge, 190
Manulife Centre, 175, 216
Maple Leaf Gardens, 95, 97, 146
Margaritas First Cantina and tapas, 162
Marilyn Bell Park, 102
Marilyn Brooks, 88, 92, 212
Mariott Eaton Centre, 200
Mariposa Cruise Line Ltd., 198
Market Gallery, 132, 134
Martin Goodman Trail, 102-103, 105
Masonic Hall, 180
Masonic Temple, 180, 181
Masquerade Caffe and Bar, 149, 210
Massey College, 168, 202
Massey Hall, 141, 143
Massey, Hart, 143, 167

INDEX

Mastermind, 30
Mata Hari, 162
Matisse, Henri, 50
Matthews, Peter, 185
McDonald's, 180
McMichael Canadian Collection, 124, 220
Medieval Times dinner theatre, 28, 203
Mel Lastman Square, 177
Mendocino, 90, 214
Mercantile, 90, 215
Messervy, Julie Moir, 24
Messis, 210
Metro YMCA, 180
Metropolitan Hotel, 85, 200
Metropolitan United church, 137
Mezes, 191
Milk International Children's Festival, 25, 64, 111, 218
Mill Street, Elora's, 121
Mimi Bizjak, 92
Mimico Creek, 99, 103
Mink, 90, 188, 214
Mira Godard Gallery, 57, 172, 204
Mirabelli, 87, 214
Mirvish Productions, 60-61
Mirvish, David, 60, 147, 169
Mirvish, Ed, 60, 147, 169
Misdemeanours, 89, 212
Miss Toronto Yacht Charters and Tours, 198
Mississauga (people), 16
Misura, 92
Mitzi's Sister, 76, 207
Mocha Mocha, 191
Mod Club Theatre, 76, 207
Molson Amphitheatre, 26
Molson Grand Prix, 98, 112, 217, 219
Molson Place, 24
money, 195-196
Money, 78, 208
Monsoon, 81-82, 210
Mont Blanc, 175
Monte Clark Gallery, 39
Montreal Bistro and Jazz Bar, 79, 208
Moore Park, 181
Moore, Henry, 37, 48, 49, 51, 158
Morba, 89, 93, 155, 215
Moriyama, Raymond, 29
Motion Clothing Co., 88, 92
Motoretta, 188
Mount Sinai Hospital, 164
Museum of Contemporary Canadian Art, 156
museums, 203-204
  Bata Shoe Museum, 41, 52-53
  Museum of Contemporary Canadian Art, 156
  MZTV museum, 152
  Niagara Apothecary, 117
  Redpath Sugar Refinery Museum, 103
  Royal Ontario Museum, 41, 42-50, 93, 165, 204, 216
music festivals
  Beaches Jazz Festival, 112, 219
  Downtown Jazz Festival, 111-112, 219
  Elora, 121
  North by Northeast, 111, 219
Music Toronto, 69
Mustacio's, 81, 210
Muti, 88, 212
Myth, 191
MZTV Museum, 152
Nancy Moore, 213
Nancy Poole's Studio, 172
Nathan Phillips Square, 36-37, 38, 98
National Ballet of Canada, 24, 65, 70, 145, 205 The Nutcracker, 65, 109, 145
National Ballet School's Sugar Plum Fair, 33
National Car Rental, 197
National Helicopters Inc., 197
National Home Show, 109, 218
National Trade Centre, 29, 218
Nautical Adventures, 198
Nearly Naked, 89, 214
Necessary Angel, 63, 205
Necropolis Cemetery, 182, 185
Nefeli, 191
Neill-Wycik College-Hotel, 202
Neurotica, 93, 217
Neutral Lounge, 77, 207
New College, 168
New Generation Sushi, 82
New Music Concerts, 69, 206
Niagara Apothecary, 117, 220
Niagara Falls Aviary, 115, 220
Niagara Falls Parkway, 115-116
Niagara Falls, 20, 115
Niagara Gorge, 116
Niagara Grape and Wine Festival, 119, 220
Niagara Parks Butterfly Conservatory, 115, 220
Niagara School of Horticulture botanical gardens, 115, 220
Niagara Wine Route, 117-119
Niagara-on-the-Lake, 64, 115-117
Nicholas Hoare, 91, 135, 212
Nienkamper, 139
Nightwood Theatre, 63, 205
Nine West, 88, 217
Noce, 156
Nomad, 154
North 44°, 83, 210
North by Northeast, 111, 219
North Toronto, 181
Not My Dog, 76, 207
Novotel Toronto Centre, 200
NOW magazine, 14, 60, 71, 79, 109, 202, 206
Nutty Chocolatier, The, 156
Oasis Restaurant and Bar, 63, 206
Off Centre Music Series, 69, 206
O'Grady's, 127, 221
Oh Yes! Toronto, 91, 212
Old Canadian Imperial Bank of Commerce, 142
Old City Hall, 32, 35, 36-37, 141, 203
Old Navy, 87, 213, 214
Old Spaghetti Factory, The, 134, 210
Olde Heidelberg Restaurant, 121, 220
Olena Zylak, 92
Olga Korper Gallery, 58, 204
Oliver Bonacini group, 82
Olivet Congregational Church, 173
Omnimax Theatre
Omonia, 191
On the Twenty, 118, 220
Only Café, The, 79, 208
Ontario College of Art and Design, 79, 150
Ontario Court of Appeal, 38
Ontario Heritage Foundation, 143, 144
Ontario Legislative Assembly, 164
Ontario Legislature building, 165-167
Ontario Medical College for Women, former, 183
Ontario Place, 20, 26-27, 203, 219
Ontario Science Centre, 29-30, 203
Ontario Travel Information Centres, 194, 196
Ontario Travel, 12

INDEX

Opera Atelier, 70, 206
Opera in Concert, 71, 145
Oro, 179, 210
Orpheus Choir, 69, 206
Osgoode Hall, 38, 151, 203
Osgoode, William, 38
Oundjian, Peter, 67
Outlet Beach, 123
Ouzeri, 191, 192
Over the Rainbow, 88, 213
Oyster Boy, 157
Paddock, The, 74, 156, 207
Pages Books and Magazines, 92, 212
Palm House, 182, 183
Pan on the Danforth, 191
Pangaea, 175, 210
Paper Things, 88, 217
Pappas Grill, 191
Park Hyatt, 79, 174, 201
parks, 99-108
Partridge, David, 36
passports, 195
PATH underground network, 142
Pauk, Alex, 68
Paul Petro Contemporary Art, 59, 204
Pavey, Mary, 59
Pavilion, 93, 155, 215
Peace Garden, 37
Peak Gallery, 59, 204
Pearl Harbourfront Chinese Cuisine, 81, 210
Pei, I.M., 148
Pellatt, Sir Henry, 32, 33
Peller Estates, 118, 220
Perfect Leather, 93, 216
Perigee, 83, 84, 210
Perkins Antiques, 92, 211
Perola's Supermarket, 81, 210
Peter Pan, 152, 210
Peter's Chung King, 161
Petit Pied, 181
Petra Karthaus, 88, 213
Phillips, Nathan, 37
Philosopher's Walk, 169
Pho Pa, 155-156
Pier 1, 90, 215
Piri-Piri Churrasqueria, 190
Plaza Escada, 213
Pony, 190, 210
Poor Alex Theatre, 63, 165, 206
Pope Joan, 129
population, 17-18
Porta Pane, 162
Portuguese Social Club, 150
Posh, 90, 214
Postal Station F., 180
Pottery Barn Kids, 175
Pottery Barn, 88, 92, 215
Power Plant, The, 25, 58, 204

Prada, 214, 215
Prego della Piazza, 174, 210
Preloved, 93, 155, 213
Premiere Dance Theatre, 24, 65, 205
Presqu'ile Provincial Park, 123-124, 220
Press Club, 79, 208
Priape, 130, 222
Price Roman, 89, 92, 212
Pride Day Parade, 112, 125
Primrose, The. See Best Western Primrose Hotel.
Prince of Serendip, 92, 211
Princess Margaret Hospital, 164
Princess of Wales Theatre, 61, 141, 147, 205
Producers, The, 61
Psyche, 92, 212
Quasi Modo, 89, 92, 155
Queen Mother Café, 152, 210
Queen Street Mental Health Centre, 151
Queen Street West
  Bathurst to Trinity Bellwoods Park, 155-156
  galleries, 59, 156-157
  history, 150-151
  nightlife, 74-76, 207
  shopping, 88-89, 155-156
  Spadina to Bathurst, 153-155
  Trinity Bellwoods to Dufferin, 156-157
  Yonge to Spadina, 151-153
Queen's Park, 164-165
Queen's Plate, 111, 219
Queen's Quay Terminal, 24, 25-26, 91, 203, 216
Queenshead, The, 74, 207
R. A. O'Neil Antiques, 91, 211
R.C. Harris Filtration Plant
Radisson Plaza Hotel Admiral, 200
Rain, 85, 210
Ramada Hotel and Suites Downtown, 200
recreation trails, 99-108, 122-123, 124
Red Indian, 89, 92, 211
Red Tea Box, 156
Redpath Sugar Refinery Museum, 103
Reif Estate, 116, 221
Remnants, 155
Renaissance Toronto Airport Hotel, 198-199
Renaissance Toronto Hotel Downtown, 22, 200

Republik, 78, 208
Residence, The, 202
Restaurant at Osgoode Hall, 38
Restoration Hardware, 90, 215
Revell, Viljo, 35, 37
Revival, 76, 188, 207
Rex, The, 76, 207
Rhino, The, 76, 207
Rhubarb!, 126
Richmond and Adelaide, 77
Richtree Market Restaurant, 80, 210
Ricoh Coliseum, 95
Ridout, John, 137
Ridout, Samuel, 137
Ridpath's, 181, 215
Riverdale Farm, 54, 106-107, 182, 184, 204
Riverdale Park, 182, 184, 218
Riverdale, 184
Riviera Bakery, 189
Rivoli, The, 63, 74, 128, 153, 206, 207, 210, 221
Robarts Library, 168-169
Robertson, John Ross, 185
Roger Edwards, 93, 216
Rogers Centre, 14, 20, 21-22, 95-96, 141, 142, 147, 203, 218
Romancing the Home, 192
Roof Bar/Restaurant, 79, 174, 208, 210
Roots, 88, 89, 92, 93, 174, 213, 217
Rosedale Diner, 181
Rosedale, 181
Ross Mayer, 92, 212
Rotate This, 90, 93, 217
Rotman School of Management, 168
Rouge River, 99
Roy Thomson Hall, 66, 67, 68, 69, 71, 73, 141, 147, 206
Royal Agricultural Winter Fair, 28, 114, 220
Royal Alexandra Theatre, 61, 141, 147, 205
Royal Bank Plaza, 145
Royal Ontario Museum, 41, 42-50, 93, 165, 204, 216
Royal York Hotel, 13, 79, 85, 142, 146, 200
Ryerson University, 202
Ryrie Building, 179
Sable-Castelli, 172
Sailor, 128
Sam the Record Man, 93, 217
San, 156
Sandbanks Provincial Park, 122-123, 221

INDEX

Sandra Ainsley Gallery, 59, 91, 204, 216
Santa Claus Parade, 114, 220
Savage Garden, 154
Scaccia, 175
Scaramouche, 80, 81, 85, 86, 210
Scarborough Bluffs, 103
Scarlett Mills Park, 104
Scotia Plaza, 148
Scotland Yard, 134
Second City theatre troupe, 63, 206
Second Cup, 127, 221
Segovia, 180, 210
Sensation Café, 162
Sephora, 87, 212
Series 8:08, 65, 205
Set Me Free, 90, 214
Seven Stars bakery, 190
Shallow Groove, 76, 207
Shanghai Cowgirl, 155, 210
Shaw Festival, 64, 116, 205, 221
Sheldon Lookout, 102
Sheraton Centre Toronto Hotel and Towers, 200
Sheraton Gateway Hotel, 199
Sher-E-Punjab, 191
Sherway Gardens, 93, 216
Shim Sutcliffe architects, 40
Signatures, 174, 210
Simcoe Day, 54
Simcoe Hall, 167
Simpson, Robert, 178
Sintra, 190
skating, ice, 98, 104
skating, inline, 98, 100, 105, 108
Skirt, 92, 214
SkyDome. See Rogers Centre
Small Wonders, 192
Sneakers, 129, 221
Snow, Michael, 179
Social, The, 75, 207
Soda, 191
SoHo Metropolitan Boutique Hotel, The, 200
Songbird, 90, 217
Soulpepper Theatre Company, 40, 61, 205
Soundscapes, 90, 217
South Simcoe Railway, 124, 221
Southern Accent, 169, 210
Souz Dal, 76, 207
Spa Excess, 129, 221
Spadina House, 20, 33-35, 55, 110, 203
Speaker's Corner, 152, 154
speed limits, 197
Spin Gallery, 75
Splendido, 85, 210

Splish Splash, 188
Sporting Life
Sports Hall of Fame, 28
sports, professional
  baseball, 95-96
  basketball, 96
  car racing, 98
  football, 96-97
  golf, 98
  hockey, 94-95
  lacrosse, 97
  tennis, 98
Spring Classic Car Auction, 218
Spring Family Show, 218
Sprockets International Film Festival for Children, 112
Spruce Court Apartments, 183
Square One, 93, 216
St. George Street, 168
St. George's Greek Orthodox Church, 137
St. Jacobs Visitor Centre, 120, 221
St. Jacobs, 120-121
St. James Cathedral. See Cathedral Church of St. James
St. James Cemetery, 182, 186
St. James Park, 137
St. James-the-Less Chapel, 182, 186
St. Lawrence Centre, 61, 141, 145, 205
St. Lawrence Hall, 138-139
St. Lawrence Market, 81, 91, 132-134, 210, 211
St. Lawrence neighbourhood
  Front Street, 132, 135-136
  King Street, 139
  shopping, 132-135, 139
  St. Lawrence Market, 81, 91, 132-134, 210, 211
  The Esplanade, 132, 134-135
St. Lawrence Seaway, 23
St. Michael's church, 137
St. Michael's College, 167
Stanley Wagman and Sons, 91, 211
Starbucks, 127, 135, 180, 221
Steamworks, 129, 221
Stollery's, 175
Stone, Edward Durell, 148
Stone's Place, 74, 207
Strange Sisters lesbian cabaret, 126
Stratford Festival, 64, 119-120, 205, 221
Stratford, 119-120
Strathcona Hotel, 201

Studio Brilliantine, 157
Studio Café, 174, 210
Style Garage, 89, 211, 215
Suites at 1 King West, The, 200
Sultan's Tent, 175, 210
SummerWorks Festival, 64, 112, 219
Sung, Doris, 59
Sunnybrook Park, 108
Sunnyside Park Bathing Pavilion, 102
Sunnyside Park, 102
Superior, 144, 211
Supermarket, 77, 81, 207, 211
Susan Harris Design, 92, 214
Susur, 85, 211
Sutra, 76, 207
Sutton Place Hotel, 130, 201, 222
Swan, 157
Swatow, 161
Sweaty Betty's, 75, 207
System Soundbar, 77, 208
T.O. Tix, 205
Tafelmusik, 66, 68, 69, 165, 206
Talbots, 88, 92, 175, 178, 214
Tallis Choir, 69, 206
Tango, 78, 128, 129, 221
Tarragon Theatre, 62, 205
Taste of the Danforth, 191
Taste Trail, 123
Tavola Caldo, 189
taxes
  Food Service, 195
  Goods and Services Tax (GST), 195
  Provincial Sales Tax (PST), 195
  Room Tax, 195
Taylor Creek Park, 108
Tempo, 76, 190, 207
Tennis Canada Rogers Cup, 98, 219
Tequila Bookworm, 154, 211
Terroni, 143-144, 156, 211
Textile Museum of Canada, 41, 53-54, 204
The Fringe: Toronto's Theatre Festival, 112
Theatre Columbus, 63, 205
Theatre District
  attractions, 140-148
  dining, 143-144
  theatres, 66, 147-148
Theatre Passe Muraille, 62, 206
Theatre Smith-Gilmour, 63, 206
theatre, 40, 60-65, 143, 205-206
Things Japanese, 169
This Ain't the Rosedale Library, 92, 212
This Is London, 78, 208
Thompson, Tom, 49, 51

INDEX

Thompson's Homeopathic Supplies, 172
Thrifty Car Rental, 197
Thuet Cuisine, 84, 211
Thymeless, 77, 207
Ticketmaster, 205
Tiffany and Co., 88, 93, 170, 216
Tiger Lily's, 153, 211
Timbuktu, 91, 215
time zone, 196
Timothy's Coffee Shop, 126-127, 221
TNT Blu, 88
TNT, 88, 213, 214
Todmorden Mills, 55, 106, 107, 204
Tommy Thompson Park. See Leslie Street Spit
Tom's Place, 91, 93, 217
Toolbox, 129
Toronto Airport Mariott Hotel, 199
Toronto Argonauts, 21, 22, 96-97, 217
Toronto Bed and Breakfast Inc., 201-202
Toronto Blue Jays, 21, 22, 95, 217
Toronto Centre for the Arts, 67, 177, 206
Toronto City Centre Airport, 194
Toronto Consort, 69, 206
Toronto Convention & Visitors Association, 204
Toronto Convention Centre, 109, 146, 218
Toronto Dance Theatre, 65, 186, 206
Toronto Dominion (TD) Centre, 148- 149
Toronto Dominion Galley of Inuit Art, 142
Toronto Festival of Storytelling, 110, 218
Toronto Footsteps, 197
Toronto Fringe Festival, 64, 219
Toronto Garden Club, 33, 34
Toronto General Hospital, 164
Toronto Harbour Tours, 198
Toronto Heliconian Club, 173
Toronto Hydro, 180
Toronto International Bicycle Show, 109, 218
Toronto International Boat Show, 109, 218
Toronto International Dragon Boat Race, 111, 219
Toronto International Film Festival, 113-114, 219
Toronto Island Bicycle Rentals, 101
Toronto Islands, 14, 20, 100, 196

Toronto Life magazine, 14, 109, 202
Toronto Maple Leafs, 94-95, 141, 146, 217
Toronto Marlies, 95, 217
Toronto Marriott Bloor-Yorkville Hotel, 201
Toronto Mendelssohn Choir, 68, 147, 206
Toronto Mendelssohn Youth Choir, 69
Toronto Music Garden, 23-24, 102
Toronto Operetta Theatre, 71, 145
Toronto Outdoor Art Exhibition, 112, 219
Toronto Port Authority, 195
Toronto Public Library, 172
Toronto Purchase, 16
Toronto Raptors, 95, 96, 141, 146, 218
Toronto Reference Library, 172
Toronto Rock, 95, 97-98, 218
Toronto Sculpture Garden, 138
Toronto Star, 60, 71, 114, 206
Toronto Stock Exchange, 148, 149
Toronto Symphony Orchestra, 66-8, 147, 206
Toronto Toy Show, 218
Toronto Transit Commission, 13, 196
Toronto Worldwide Short Film Festival, 111, 219
Toronto Zoo, 13, 20, 30-32, 203
Toronto's First Post Office, 54, 139, 203
Toronto's transit system, 13, 196
Tourism Toronto, 12, 196, 198
tours
   boat and yacht tours, 198
   CHUM museum tour, 152
   guided tours, 14, 142, 197-198
   Lost World Tours, 14, 197
   Ontario Legislature, 166
   Royal Ontario Museum ROMwalks, 14
   Stratford Festival theatre tour, 119-120
   Toronto Harbour Tours, 14, 198
   Toronto Hippo Tours, 14
Town Inn Suites, The, 201
Toy Shop, The, 88, 92, 217
trade shows, 109
   Boat Show, 28
   Home Show, 28
Transport Canada Airport Information, 195

transportation
   air, 194
   bus, 194
   car, 194, 197
   rail, 194
Trattoria al Forno, 127, 221
Trattoria Giancarlo, 189
Trattoria Sotto Sotto, 82, 211
Travellers' Aid Society, 198
Travelodge Toronto Airport, 199
Travelodge Toronto, 201
Treasure Island, 192
Treble, Lillian Massey
Trinity Bellwoods Park, 157
Trinity College and Chapel, 167
Trinity College Medical School, 183
Trinity Mews, 183
Trinity Square, 179
Trinity-St Paul's Church, 68, 165, 206
Tripmate Travel and Tour Guide Company, 197
Truffles, 85, 174, 211
Ultra Supper Club, The, 74, 207
Union Station, 13, 145-146, 194
Unique Views, 197
University Art Centre, 167
University College, 166, 167
University of Toronto at Scarborough, 202
University of Toronto, 150, 164-165, 167-169, 202
Up Country, 93, 139, 215
Urban Mode, 92, 93, 93, 215
van der Rohe, Miles, 148-149
Versace, 214
VIA Rail, 194
Victoria University, 202
Victory Café, 77, 169, 208, 211
Village of Yorkville Park, 173
Village Rainbow Restaurant, 127, 221
Vineland Estates, 118, 221
Visitor Information Ontario, 196
Vuitton, 170
Wah Sing, 161
Waite, Richard A., 165-166
Walking. See recreation trails
Ward's Island, 101
Warner Brothers, 180
Waterfront Regeneration Trust, 203
Waterfront Trail, 100, 102-103, 203
Waterloo County, 120-121
Wayne Clark, 92, 212
Wayne Gretzky's (restaurant), 22, 144, 211

INDEX

Welland canal, 17
Wellesley Cottages, 185, 186
Wellesley Park, 185
West Lake, 123
West Queen West, 59, 151
Western Beaches, 102
Westin Harbour Castle, 201
White, Bishop William Charles, 47
WholeNote, 71
Wildhagen, 91, 215
William Ashley, 88, 92, 175, 212
Williams-Sonoma, 88, 92, 175, 215
Windsor Arms, The, 201
Wine Route. See Niagara Wine Route
wineries, 116, 117-119
Wings of Paradise, 121-122, 221
Winners, 174
Winter Garden Theatre, 61, 141, 143, 179
Wish, 78, 221
Women's Bookstore, The, 130, 222
Wonderful and Whites, 135
WonderWorks, 169
Woodbine Racetrack, 219
Woody's, 78, 128, 129, 221
Word of Mouth, 181
Word on the Street, 113, 114, 219
World Stage, 64
World's Biggest Bookstore, The, 92, 179, 212
Worldsew Centre, 154
Worts, James, 38
Wroxeter, 76, 207
Wyndham Bristol Place Hotel, 199
Wynick/Tuck Gallery, 58, 204
Xacutti, 190
Xam Yu, 161
Xtra magazine, 130
Ydessa Hendeles Art Foundation, 58, 204-205
Yonge Street, 16, 87
  Bloor-St. Clair, 181
  dining, 179, 180, 181
  Dundas-Bloor ("The Strip"), 179-181
  Eaton Centre, 177, 178-179
  shopping, 90, 177-181
York Club, 171
York University, 98
Yorkdale, 93
Yorkville
  Bloor Street, 171, 174-175
  dining, 85, 172, 174, 175
  galleries, 57, 172, 173
  history, 171-172
  nightlife, 79
  shopping, 88, 173-175
Yorkville Fire Hall, 172, 173
Yuk Yuk's Comedy Club, 63, 206
Zeidler, Eb, 178
Zelda's, 78, 127, 221
Zerosun, 172, 211
Zig Zag, 92, 211

PHOTO CREDITS

Legend: Top – T; Centre – C; Bottom – B
Photography by Vincenzo Pietropaolo except for those listed below:
A Space: 59C; Graig Abel: 94T, 97; Art Gallery of Ontario: 48, 49, 50T&B, 51T&B; Bata Shoe Museum: 52B, 53; BDS Studios: 73T&B; Black Creek Pioneer Village: 56T&B; Canada Blooms: 110T; CanStage: 64T, CanStage (Cylla Von Tiedmann), 61B; Comrags: 92T; Dwayne Coon: 116T; David Cooper: 117; The Corporation of Massey Hall and Roy Thomson Hall: 67T, 141B; Danny Grossman Dance Company: 63T;Don Hunstein/Sony Classical: 72; Steven Evans: 118T; Gallery One: 57B, 59T; Mary Gerry: 120T; Heritage Toronto: 15B, 55T&B; Hike Ontario: 122B; Steve Jenkinson: 75T&B; Marc Mantha marcmantha.com: 77T; Joan Marcus: 10, 147T; Mirvish Productions (Joan Marcus): 14B, 60T; Barbara McCracken: 121; Molson Indy: 98T; National Ballet: 65, 109B; National Trade Centre: 27B; Niagara National Historic Sites: 116C; Ontario Place: 26; Ontario Science Centre: 29T, 30T&B;Opera Atelier: 70B; Perigee Restaurant: 83T&B; Power Plant: 57T; Royal Ontario Museum: 42T, 43T,C&B, 44T,C&B, 45T&C46T,C&B, 47; Roy Thomson Hall: 66B, , 68T, Sable-Castelli Gallery: 58T; Sandra Ainsley Gallery: 58C; Scaramouche Restaurant (Richard Johnson interiorimages.ca): 14T, 80, 81T, 85T&B; Splendido Restaurant: 86T&B; Tarragon Theatre (Michael Cooper): 62T; Textile Museum of Canada (Rachel Ashe): 41T; Textile Museum of Canada (Raoul): 41B, 54; Shaw Festival: 62B, 64B, 116B; South Simcoe Railway: 124T; Stratford Festival: 118C; Tafelmusik (Cylla von Tiedmann): 66T, 69; Toronto Blue Jays: 96T; Toronto Mendelssohn Choir: 68B; Toronto Raptors: 95B, 96C; Toronto Zoo: 2B, 31T, C&B, ; Toronto Transit Commission: 7; William Van Veen: Tobias Wang: 78; 120C; William Ashley: 2B, 87T; Scott Wishart: 118T; Willy Waterton: 122T; Woody's: 125T; Word on the Street: 113B, 114T

Library and Archives Canada Cataloguing in Publication

Coopersmith, Penina
    Toronto : a colourguide / Penina Coopersmith ; photography by Vincenzo Pietropaolo. -- 5th ed.

(Colourguide series)
Includes index.
Fourth ed. published under title: Toronto colourguide.
ISBN10: 0-88780-693-7
ISBN13: 978-0-88780-693-3

  1. Toronto (Ont.)--Guidebooks. I. Pietropaolo, Vincenzo II. Title.
III. Series.

FC3097.18.C66 2006   917.13'541044   C2005-907602-X